"I'll leave you ⋯⋯ ing a glance at MacFa⋯⋯ he sight of him standi⋯⋯ her had left her strang⋯

"Wash my bac⋯⋯

She didn't move.

"Are you so afraid of getting a little soap and water on you?" he snapped.

Reluctantly, she went to him and took the cloth.

She dipped the cloth into the water and slowly drew it up his back, trailing a soothing stream across the sun-bronzed skin. Beneath the fabric of the cloth she was acutely aware of the structure of him, the even ridges of his ribs, the rippled chain of his spine, the firm depth of his flesh.

Appalled by the sensations flooding through him, Malcolm jerked away, sloshing water onto the floor.

"That's enough," he commanded brusquely. "Leave me."

Something had changed between them, Ariella realized. Her touch had evolved into a forbidden exploration of his body, which was heavily scarred, but still warm and firm and seething with power.

And although loath to admit it, she had enjoyed touching him.

ONCE A WARRIOR

ONCE A WARRIOR

Karyn Monk

Bantam Books
New York   Toronto
London   Sydney   Auckland

For Mark,
who also loves to tell stories.

ONCE, A
WARRIOR

PROLOGUE

The Highlands of Scotland
Spring 1207

"I am dying."

The words were steeped in bitterness, and perhaps a shade of incredulity, as if he hoped his bleak conclusion might elicit an argument to the contrary.

Instead Alpin regarded him with gentle calm, his ancient face betraying none of the regret clawing at his soul. He had held this man in his arms the night he had gasped his first lusty breath. Alpin had told the boy's father of the magnificent chief his son would grow to be, of the peaceful and prosperous decades that lay before the Clan MacKendrick. And as he had looked down at the pink, squalling babe, and spun golden stories about the brilliance of his future, he had known with painful, hopeless acuity that this dark moment would come. And that he would be here, by his side, to watch over this beloved child grown to man, as he released his last ragged breath from his lungs.

"It is time," Alpin told him simply.

The MacKendrick contemplated this a moment, trying to resign himself to the idea. Screams of fear and grief tore through the corridor just beyond his chamber, suffusing his final moments with torment. Seizing the last vestiges of his strength, he angrily gripped the pulsing wound at his side and forced himself to sit up.

"But he has not come," he protested, trying to show Alpin he must be wrong. "I must continue to lead the battle against Roderic. I will stay alive long enough to see the Black Wolf. I have to be certain he is the one."

"That is not for you to decide," Alpin said quietly. "Only Ariella can determine if he is fit to be laird of the clan. The decision is hers alone."

The MacKendrick's expression hardened. "If he is the one, he should goddamn well be here," he grated out. "Where the hell is he?" The query thundered through the air before dissolving into a pathetic fit of coughing.

"He will come," promised Alpin, guiding the dying laird back against his bed. "I have seen it. The Black Wolf will come."

"You are certain?" he demanded, his voice rough with menace. "You do not seek to ease my final moments by lying?"

"I have seen it," Alpin assured him. "He will come."

The laird regarded him a long moment, desperate with the need to believe him. And then, seeing what he sensed was the truth reflected in Alpin's dark stare, he permitted himself to close his eyes. "You will care for Ariella until he comes," he commanded softly. "Keep her safe, until he comes."

Alpin laid his pale, wizened hand against the laird's

brow and said nothing. It was not within his ability to make empty assurances of things he could neither control nor foresee. He knew MacKendrick understood this. Still, he found he could not deny a dying father a small measure of comfort. "I will watch over her, MacKendrick," he swore. "As if she were my own."

The words flowed over the laird in a soothing ripple. "Very well," he murmured gruffly.

Alpin watched as he drew a few more labored breaths, fighting the onslaught of death, though they both knew it was a battle he could not win. The MacKendrick squeezed Alpin's hand as the final breath stretched his lungs taut, holding fast to this world, until ultimately he could resist no longer. Life trickled out of him in a ragged sigh, and his grip on his friend eased a fraction of a moment later, just as Alpin had known it would.

Loss swept over him, cold and empty, as it always did when one he had loved for so many years succumbed to the frailty of their flesh. He held the laird's hand a while longer, more to comfort himself than the battered body that lay before him, now free of suffering and void of spirit. The sounds of brutality and fear raged around him, but nothing could penetrate the wall of his grief. Finally the acrid scent of smoke permeated his frozen senses, wresting him from his trance and drawing him to the window.

He stared across the courtyard at the scarlet and gold flames licking hungrily at the wooden structure of the tower. Men and women were racing back and forth on the ground below, yelling and screaming as they desperately carried sloshing buckets of water from the well. They heaved small silvery streams up at the blaze, but the fire only laughed at their pitiful attempts to control it. A thick veil of heavy smoke gushed into the crystalline blue of the spring sky, staining it black and gray, clouding it with delicate wisps of cinders that danced on the hot breath of the fire before floating to the ground in a charcoal shower.

"Ariella!" screamed Elizabeth, her heart bursting with anguish as she stared at the inferno. *"Ariella!"*

Fear pierced through Alpin as he struggled to comprehend what was happening. Roderic had locked Ariella in the tower, forcing her to watch as he ransacked her home and brutalized her people. Now the tower was afire.

Ariella was trapped inside.

"No," he said vehemently, shaking his head. "It cannot be. It cannot."

He watched, helplessly transfixed by the brilliant torch of deadly flames as they engulfed the room at the top of the tower. The people below continued to desperately throw water at the blaze, but their efforts could not arrest its insatiable appetite. Still they fought on, until their faces were black with smoke, until their bodies ached and their throats were raw.

Finally their cries for Ariella faded into numb, stricken silence, and they could only stand and watch the tower burn.

CHAPTER 1

Summer 1207

As always, his first sensation was pain.

He frowned and stirred restlessly on his pallet, grasping at the murky waters of sleep, which were swiftly ebbing away. In sleep the pain could be held at bay. Not completely, and not for any great length of time. Just enough that he preferred the hazy, alcohol-saturated respite to the harsh, clear glare of day.

He felt himself losing the battle of slumber to his relentless enemy. Pain streaked down his back. A familiar throbbing pulsed through his left leg. Then, of course, there was his arm. Capable of only a shadow of the strength it had once wielded, the spasm gripping the shrunken muscles was as debilitating as any warrior or weapon he had ever known. He struggled to float into the refuge of sleep once more. In sleep he could be almost whole again.

"Get up, Malcolm," called an irritatingly cheerful voice. "You have guests."

He did not bother to crack open an eye. "Get the hell out of here," he growled. His tongue felt thick within the woolen dryness of his mouth. "Before I knock your head from your shoulders."

Unperturbed, Gavin moved to the window and threw open the rough shutters. Midday light poured into the small hut in a golden stream, spilling across the cluttered dirt floor as it made its way onto Malcolm's face.

"Jesus Christ—" Scowling against the beam, he grasped the empty pitcher lying on the ground beside him and heaved it at Gavin.

Gavin dodged to one side, and the pitcher shattered against the wall. "I realize this is early for you," he said, his tone apologetic, "but there are some men outside who have traveled for over a week to find you. They say it is urgent they speak with you."

Malcolm turned his head from the light and drew his aching arm over his eyes. "Tell them I am indisposed," he drawled wearily.

"I did. I also suggested if they needed help, they should go to Harold. They said they had already been to the MacFane holding, and Harold sent them here."

"Then they have wasted their time." The pronouncement was absolute. "Harold should know better than to send people here."

"They told Harold they were seeking the Black Wolf."

Malcolm hesitated, then snorted in disgust. "The Black Wolf is dead," he stated harshly. He rolled to face the wall, dismissing him. "Tell them that."

"They seem to know otherwise," remarked Gavin. "And they have assured me they will not leave until they have spoken with him. They are from the Clan MacKendrick."

Malcolm frowned, searching his pounding, ale-soaked brain for the name MacKendrick. After a moment it came to him. "Sweet Jesus, MacKendrick is a persistent man," he grumbled sourly. "I already told his messengers I was not interested in his offer. What the hell does he want now?"

"I don't know," replied Gavin, shrugging. "But if you want to get rid of this lot, you will have to come out and speak with them."

"Christ." He slowly pushed himself to a sitting position. The pain was bad, but he supposed it was no worse than it had been yesterday, or last week, or last year. It was becoming difficult to remember ever being without it.

The sun assaulted him with blinding brilliance as he followed Gavin outside. Through squinting eyes he saw his unwelcome visitors. Two of them were tall and sufficiently well built, one with shoulder-length hair of brown, the other with hair of black. Malcolm judged them to be no more than five and twenty. The third was barely more than a lad, with filthy, tangled hair of an indeterminate color, and a face that hadn't been washed for weeks. Not that he was in a position to criticize on matters of appearance, he reflected ironically. As usual, Gavin had laid a meal of ale, bread, and cheese for him on the table in front of the hut. Ignoring his visitors, Malcolm reached for the jug of ale. He took a swig, swished it around in his mouth, and spat it noisily onto the ground. Thus refreshed, he tilted his head back and drank deeply, emptying the jug of its contents. Then he wiped his dripping mouth on his arm and calmly regarded the trio, who were staring at him, their expressions ranging from shock to barely disguised revulsion.

"What do you want?" he demanded brusquely.

The tall one with brown hair seemed to recover first. "I am Duncan MacKendrick," he began, looking uncertain. "And this is Andrew, and that is Rob." He gestured to the boy, who was glaring at Malcolm. "We are here to speak with the warrior known as the Black Wolf," Duncan finished, evidently deciding the man standing before him could not possibly be the mighty warrior they sought.

"You have found him," stated Malcolm curtly.

Sharp dismay flooded the faces of the two men, followed by pity. Malcolm endured their scrutiny, betraying none of his bitter humiliation. Only the boy seemed unmoved. He continued to glare at Malcolm, his expression burning with something more akin to fury than sympathy.

"Forgive us," stammered the dark-haired one known as Andrew. "We went first to MacFane castle and learned you were no longer laird. The new MacFane sent us here, but he did not mention—that is—we were not told—" He broke off uncertainly.

Malcolm cursed silently, wondering why Harold had sent these men to him.

"What happened to the other messengers your laird sent to speak with me?" he demanded.

"They never returned," replied Duncan. "We did not know if they had reached you with the MacKendrick's offer."

"They did," Malcolm said. "And I told them, as I tell you now, I am not interested. Tell MacKendrick I consider the matter closed and do not wish to be disturbed again." He turned and began to retreat slowly toward the quiet darkness of his hut.

"He is dead," announced the boy, his voice flat.

Malcolm stopped. The boy's gray eyes were seething with hatred, as if he believed Malcolm were somehow responsible.

"How?"

Rob opened his mouth to respond, but Duncan interjected. "The clan was attacked by a band of marauding warriors," he explained. "The MacKendrick was cut down by a sword. It happened several weeks after he sent word to you, asking you to come."

"We fought them as best we could," Andrew added, "but we are not trained in the ways of warfare. The MacKendrick hoped you and your army would be able to protect us."

Malcolm controlled the acrid impulse to laugh. He could not fault MacKendrick for his plan. Once he had been laird of the Clan MacFane, with more than a thousand highly trained warriors ready to fight and die for him. For six long years he had fought in the army of King William, and had led his men to victory in countless bloody battles. But that was a lifetime ago. The only man he could call upon today was Gavin. If Malcolm had gone to MacKendrick and said he was accepting his offer of lairdship, the man would have fallen flat on the floor with laughter.

And these three damn well knew it.

"Were many hurt?" he demanded, wishing it did not matter to him.

"Fourteen men were killed," answered Duncan. "Dozens more wounded. The warriors stripped the castle of what valuables they could carry. And then it was set afire."

"I am sorry."

Sorry he hadn't been there to protect what at another time he could easily have defended. In MacKendrick's letter to him the laird had described his clan as small, consisting of only a few hundred people. They had no allies, he had explained, but neither did they have any enemies. MacKendrick hoped the great Black Wolf would honor them by accepting the position of laird. As a token of faith, he offered the hand of his only child, whom he believed would make the mighty Black Wolf a gracious and devoted wife.

Malcolm had burned the letter.

"As you can see, there is little I could have done to help you," he drawled. "My circumstances have changed somewhat since I was laird of the Clan MacFane." He turned away abruptly. The pounding in his head had become unbearable, and he needed to numb it with another pitcher of ale.

"You must come with us, MacFane."

Malcolm turned back and stared at the boy. "Do you think to mock me?" he demanded savagely.

"Of course not," interjected Duncan, lifting his hand to silence Rob. "What the lad meant to say is that we desperately need your help, and we would be honored if you would return to our home with us."

Malcolm studied him a moment, wondering if he was blind or mad. Ultimately he decided he would have to be both to make such a ludicrous suggestion.

"I am no longer MacFane," he said, struggling to control his rearing temper. "And I am no longer the Black Wolf. If you are in need of assistance, go back to Harold and ask him to defend your clan."

Duncan and Andrew glanced uncertainly at the boy. He frowned and shook his head. "It has to be you," he stated, his gray gaze locked on Malcolm. "There is no other who can help us."

Shallow laughter erupted from Malcolm's chest. "How can I help you? I lead no army. My body is little better than that of a cripple. What in the name of God could I do to defend your clan?"

"I do not know," admitted the boy. "But you will come with us."

He regarded Malcolm with grim resignation, as if he wished it were otherwise. Malcolm found himself strangely transfixed by that cool slate stare, which was condemning yet haunted, the look of a child who has witnessed terrible things he will never be able to forget. As they gazed at each other, Malcolm forgot his pain. For one brief moment he felt strong and whole, like the warrior he had once been, who would not have hesitated to rush to the aid of this frightened, brutalized clan. As quickly as it came, the sensation abandoned him, leaving him aching and tired and empty.

And acutely aware that he had nothing left to offer anyone, least of all a helpless clan in need of a chief with a powerful army.

"I can't help you," he snapped. "Now, get the hell out of here and leave me be."

He turned and limped back into the dark cave of his hut, feeling broken and ashamed, and badly in need of a drink.

Ariella stared pensively into the fire, watching the scarlet and gold flames offer beauty and warmth as they mercilessly drew the life out of the wood that sustained them. Alpin had once told her that nothing in the world existed in isolation, that everything was dependent upon something else in order to survive. Ariella had immediately thought of her unconditional love for her father and had understood completely. Without him Ariella knew she could not survive.

On the terrible day he was murdered, she had curled into a tiny ball beside him and willed herself to die as well. To her bitter disappointment, she did not. For weeks after, she awoke each morning to find herself very much alive, despite the fact that her heart was bursting with such grief, she felt certain she could not bear it another moment.

Finally, realizing she had to go on, she learned to temper her grief with hate.

At first she directed her hatred at Roderic. He had lied to her, pretending to be a friend, then betraying her trust by bringing an army to attack her clan, thinking to force her to give him the sword and make him laird. Hating Roderic was easy. But it was not enough. So she included all of his warriors beneath the mantle of her loathing, those evil savages who had derived such vile pleasure from attacking her people and her home, easily slaughtering defenseless men who barely knew how to lift a weapon. But these were faceless, nameless figures, and hating them could not begin to ease the agony coursing through her veins.

And so she had sharpened the dagger of her hatred and thrust it ruthlessly into the heart of the Black Wolf.

Alpin had told her father he would come. He had seen it in a vision, and Alpin's visions, though sometimes hazy, were never wrong. Her father waited, jubilant with the knowledge that the next laird of his clan would be a man with the exceptional bravery and honor of the chief known as the Black Wolf. As his wariness of Roderic increased and the Black Wolf failed to arrive, Ariella's father grew concerned. He sent two clansmen to find this warrior and deliver his message, offering him lairdship of the Clan MacKendrick and Ariella for his wife, if he would come immediately with his great army.

The Black Wolf never came.

For that, Ariella would never forgive him. Although she had not known his reasons, his failure to fulfill Alpin's vision was too awful to be pardoned. She had raged at Alpin that it did not matter if he ever came, for she wanted nothing to do with him.

Unfortunately, Alpin saw things differently.

The Clan MacKendrick was isolated and without a laird, which put it in a dangerously vulnerable position. For one hundred years they had been at peace. Consequently, the ways of warfare had been lost. Instead of building fortifications and training for battle, the clan had cultivated its skills in the arts. This enabled them to amass a splendid collection of rich silverware and carvings, tapestries and jewelry, fine furniture and fabrics. The Mac-Kendricks viewed these objects as a part of everyday life. But Roderic had taught them that others were not so casual in their attitude. To an outsider these objects were worth a fortune. Which meant when Roderic's men spread tales of what they had found there, others would come, seeking to steal from them as well.

And then, of course, there was the sword.

She did not know how Roderic had learned of its existence. She could not bring herself to believe that one of her people would betray the clan. But Roderic had known of it, and he knew she was the only one with the ability to give it to him. No one actually understood the extent of the sword's powers, for it had not been wielded in battle for over a century. But legend said he who was granted the power of the sword could walk without fear into the bloodiest of battles. The weapon could not fell an entire army, but it would protect its master. Unfortunately, after generations of peace, the sword had come to be revered as a sacred, ceremonial object, and her father did not keep it with him, did not even store it within the walls of the castle. That was why it had not been able to protect him that day. Because her father had died without a male heir, it was now Ariella's duty to find the next bearer of the sword, who would become laird of the Clan MacKendrick, taking their name. If she chose well, her clan would continue to prosper in peace. But if she chose unwisely, death and destruction would come to her people and swiftly spread throughout the Highlands. It was an awesome responsibility. When she had refused to give Roderic the sword, he had locked her in the tower, swearing to slaughter her clansmen one by one until she relented. She'd had no doubt he was evil enough to fulfill his promise.

Which was why Ariella MacKendrick had to die.

Once he was convinced she had perished in the

fire, Roderic had angrily decided there was nothing more there for him. He and his men had taken all they could carry and left, bitterly disappointed that he had not procured the one object he lusted for above all else. But Ariella knew it was only a matter of time before Roderic, or another like him, attacked her clan again. Stories would travel of the riches they had found, and the legend of the sword, and the weakness of the Clan MacKendrick. Her people were in danger, and it was her duty to protect them. This was why Alpin had instructed her to find the Black Wolf and grant him the power of the sword. With that solemn charge he had sent her off to seek out this mighty warrior and bring him and his great army home.

As she had faced that foul, drunken, crippled shell of a man today, she had not known whether to rage or weep.

"You must eat something, Ariella," ordered Duncan gently, interrupting her thoughts. He seated himself on the ground and offered her a morsel of roasted rabbit. "Here."

She sank her hand into the filthy, tangled nest of her hair and shook her head. "I am not hungry."

Andrew stopped plucking the strings of his small harp and regarded her with concern. "We have a long journey ahead of us. If you fall ill, Alpin will be displeased."

"He will be more displeased by the fact that we have failed to bring back the mighty Black Wolf," pointed out Ariella bitterly.

"The man we saw today could not have been the one in Alpin's vision," argued Duncan. "Either Alpin's sight is failing, or we tracked down the wrong man. Perhaps some other warrior has acquired the title the Black Wolf," he suggested hopefully.

"Alpin said it was the one known as MacFane," countered Ariella. "That was the man we saw today. Even though he has been cast out by his clan and no longer goes by that name."

"Then Alpin's vision must be flawed," Andrew concluded, his fingers strumming lightly over his instrument. "Because that poor, drunken fellow could never defend himself, never mind lead and defend an entire clan."

"I know," sighed Ariella. "But Alpin was so adamant we bring him back, I had to try, even when I saw how vile and pathetic he was. It was just as well he refused us." She prodded the fire with a slender twig. "When we get home, I will explain to Alpin and the council why MacFane is not the one. Perhaps Alpin will have another vision. Until then we must try to train ourselves, so we can be better prepared against another attack."

"But as long as Roderic believes you are dead, he will not return," insisted Andrew. "Without you there is no sword, and that is what he was after."

"If not Roderic, then another like him," Ariella replied grimly. "His warriors will spread the tale of our supposed riches, and how easy we were to vanquish. And though they may report my death, the legend of the sword could become distorted, so another might think he can force the clan to turn the weapon over."

"Do not torment yourself with such thoughts," soothed Duncan. "You will find the next laird before that happens, and he will ensure we are safe."

"In a few days we will be home and you will be able to wash and put on a gown again," added Andrew, trying to cheer her. "I must say, I have all but forgotten what you look like beneath that filth."

"So have I," she muttered, wiping self-consciously at her grubby cheek. "Although this disguise has been effective in discouraging attention, I find myself longing for a bath and the modesty of a gown."

"After this journey you can put young Rob away for a while," said Duncan. "You will have to become him again only if a stranger comes to the clan. Until we find a new laird, no outsider can know you survived the fire, lest that information find its way to Roderic."

Andrew strummed a chord on his harp and began to sing. "There once was a maiden, slender and fair, who wore plaid for a gown, and ashes in her hair. . . ."

"She darkened her skin, and rode through the trees," continued Duncan, "and struggled to cover her pale little knees!"

"Duncan!" exclaimed Ariella, mortified that they had noticed her knees, or any other part of her legs that her woefully short plaid failed to cover. She leaned over to playfully strike his shoulder.

An arrow split the air where her head had been.

"Don't move!" snarled a voice through the darkness. "Or ye're all dead."

Four figures emerged from the trees around them. Three of them brandished heavy swords, while the fourth held an arrow against the taut string of his bow. As they moved into the soft aura of the fire, Ariella could see they were a filthy, shaggy group, with thick beards and worn, tattered shirts and plaids. Incongruous to their thread-bare attire, each sported an impressive array of gem-studded jewelry. A delicately wrought lady's chain and pendant were draped around the thick, beefy neck of one, while the others had several gleaming silver brooches pinned to the plaids flung on their shoulders. *Thieves,* Ariella realized, her stomach clenching with fear. She quickly scanned the campsite, searching for her bow. It lay with her blanket on the other side of the fire, hopelessly out of reach.

"Up with ye now," ordered the burliest of the group, waving his sword in front of him, "and throw down yer weapons and yer valuables."

Too shocked to argue, Duncan and Andrew instantly removed their brooches and tossed them onto the ground. Then they withdrew their dirks and dropped them as well. Ariella hesitantly began to unfasten her brooch, desperately trying to think of some way to keep her dirk obscured from view.

"Hurry up there, lad," said the heavyset thief impatiently. "Let's have that dirk at yer waist."

Realizing she had no way of keeping it, she reluctantly added her weapon to the pile.

"Get their horses," the thief instructed his cohorts.

Ariella's heart sank as she watched the men move to their horses and begin to untie them. It was a three-day ride back to their castle. She did not know how they would make it home without horses, weapons, or provisions.

"Those are fine-lookin' boots ye're wearin'," observed the thief standing guard over them. "We'll be takin' those as well."

Andrew and Duncan immediately knelt and began to unlace their boots.

"But you are already stealing our horses," protested Ariella, appalled at the thought of being left barefoot. "If you take our boots and our mounts, we will never get home."

The thief lifted his bushy brows in astonishment. It was clear he was unaccustomed to having his victims complain about their treatment. "I'm thinkin' ye're right, lad," he agreed, pensively stroking his beard. "Since ye cannot get home barefoot, and since we're takin' yer food and weapons, I suppose we should be merciful. Duff, Calum, and Giles will be happy to slit yer throats for ye before we go." He broke into a loud, rasping guffaw.

"Here are my boots," offered Duncan hastily. "I am quite sure I can manage without them."

"And mine as well," added Andrew. "Wear them in good health."

"That's right generous of ye," said the thief, chuckling, "but ye won't be needin' them where ye're goin'."

His gaze focused on Ariella. "Hurry now, laddie. I'm not of a mind to be standin' here holdin' this sword over ye all night."

Ariella knelt and began to fumble at her laces. "They're knotted," she declared helplessly. "I need my dirk to cut them."

The thief cast her a knowing smile, revealing a brown row of crooked, rotting teeth. "I have me a better idea, laddie," he announced, amused by her little ruse. "We'll cut them with my sword."

Ariella stood as he moved toward her and lowered himself onto one knee.

"Now, then," he began, bending his head, "which one is it?"

"This one," she hissed, smashing her booted foot with all her might into his face.

He let out a bellow of pain and went flying back against the ground. Momentarily stunned, he gingerly raised his hands to his bleeding nose, enabling Ariella to scramble for his sword.

"Don't move!" she commanded, glaring at Calum, Duff, and Giles as she pressed the tip of the sword into the bushy-browed thief's throat. "Or I'll stake him to the ground through his neck!"

The thieves stared at her dumbfounded. Then the one named Calum raised his bow and arrow and calmly aimed it at Andrew. "I'm thinkin' ye don't have the ballocks to carve open a man's throat with his own sword, laddie," he reflected sardonically. "So give Owen back his sword, before I shoot this arrow clean through yer friend's quiverin' heart."

Ariella hesitated a second, frantically searching her mind for another course of action. Calum raised his weapon slightly higher, and she realized she had no choice. The sword slipped from her grasp and dropped with a thud onto the ground.

"Shoot the wee bastard!" shrieked Owen furiously,

his blood-soaked fingers cradling his nose. "He broke my bloody nose!"

Calum obligingly shifted his aim to Ariella and drew back his arrow.

A faint, whispering sound sliced the air.

Ariella lurched, but the arrow did not find its mark. Confused, she raised her eyes to Calum. He was staring in bewilderment at the handle of a dirk lodged firmly in his chest. Frowning, he looked up at Ariella. A shallow whimper leaked from his throat as he collapsed, still clutching the arrow meant for her.

A terrible roar of fury shattered the stunned silence. Ariella watched in disbelief as two riders thundered into the clearing, their heavy swords glinting silver-orange in the firelight. The Black Wolf bore down on Owen, expertly guiding his horse with his legs as he lifted his sword with both arms. A terrified Owen was easily dispatched in one swift, merciless thrust. Then MacFane wheeled his powerful charger about to meet Giles. The thief slashed in wild fear at his approaching executioner and landed a blow to his arm. A bellow of fury filled the air as MacFane raised and felled his sword, driving it with deadly determination into the man's soft flesh. His friend Gavin, meanwhile, was battling the thief named Duff, who managed a few desperate swings of his weapon before joining his companions on the ground.

Suddenly the clearing was silent except for the snorting and prancing of the horses. Ariella stared blankly at the bodies littering the ground, unable to speak.

"Jesus bloody Christ," swore Malcolm, dropping his sword so he could clamp his hand over the raw wound in his right forearm. His face contorted with pain, he cast his gaze on Gavin. "Come help me down."

Gavin swiftly dismounted and moved to assist his friend as he awkwardly swung off his horse. "How bad is it?"

"Not the worst I've seen," replied Malcolm tautly. "But I don't know how much more this goddamn arm can take."

The realization that the Black Wolf was injured snapped Ariella out of her trance. "Let me look at it, MacFane," she offered. "I can stitch it for you."

The two men regarded her with dubious expressions. "I will take care of it," Gavin assured her. "When we get home."

"But it is bleeding badly," argued Ariella impatiently. "I have medicines in my bag. If it is stitched and bandaged right away, it will stay clean and heal better."

Malcolm cast her a look of irritation mingled with pain. "What can a stripling like you know about tending wounds?"

Ariella almost shot back that she had many years' experience in the art of healing. Then she remembered that MacFane was not looking at a woman, but at a filthy young boy named Rob. "My mother taught me about healing," she replied, scrambling for a plausible explanation. "I was her only child, and she did not want her skills to be lost."

He studied her a moment, his face creased with discomfort as he held fast to his dripping limb. "Then get your needle," he relented finally, "and close this cursed arm of mine. You two," he continued, looking at Duncan and Andrew, "help Gavin move the bodies away from the camp, before the stench of blood attracts wolves."

Duncan's and Andrew's faces went even paler. Glancing nervously around them, they swiftly pulled on their boots and hurried over to Gavin, who was single-handedly hoisting one of the dead thieves onto a horse.

"It is clear you three haven't spent much time sleeping outdoors," observed Malcolm.

Ariella retrieved a pitcher of water, a wooden bowl,

and the leather bag containing her medicines. She seated herself beside him, poured water into the bowl, and began to scrub her filthy hands with a small lump of soap. "Why do you say that?"

"Because only a goddamn fool would build a fire this size in woods where he could not be certain of his safety," he snarled. "You might as well have sent those men an invitation to come and rob you. And why the hell wasn't one of you standing watch?"

"We didn't know it was necessary," she admitted, feeling foolish. He was right. They had not understood the dangers of building a fire in the woods. None of them had ever traveled so far from home, and on MacKendrick lands there was no threat of being attacked.

At least there hadn't been, she amended bitterly, until Roderic had come.

She poured water from the pitcher onto his arm, causing a scarlet fall to splash against the ground. As fast as the blood washed away, new blood pulsed to the surface. Ariella swiftly wrapped a clean cloth around his arm and gripped the wound with gentle pressure. "Hold fast here," she instructed, "so the bleeding will slow while I thread my needle."

His hand looked large and dark as it pressed against the pale cloth. It was a strong hand, bronzed by the sun and sculpted by the weight of wielding a heavy weapon. The pathetic, broken man she had met that afternoon bore little resemblance to the murderous warrior who had thundered into their camp to help them. But now, as he sat there breathing deeply, his jaw clenched and his forehead lined with pain, she recognized that injured man once more. An image of him, guiding his horse with his legs as he used both hands to wield his sword, swept into her mind. She glanced at his wounded right arm and noticed a thick, pale scar snaking across the length of it. It started just above his elbow, disappeared beneath the cloth he was holding firm, and reappeared over the smooth, round bone of his wrist. Something had sliced the hard muscle of his forearm, splitting the tissue open like the soft belly of a fish. The line was slashed with large, uneven stitch marks. The wound had been deep and had probably needed to be closed quickly. Seeing his other arm adjacent to it, it was apparent that his right arm was slightly smaller than his left. The laceration had robbed it of its strength and agility, forcing him to use his left arm, or both, when necessary. Ariella wondered how much more damage this new gash would inflict upon the scarred, atrophied muscles.

"You may take your hand away now, MacFane."

"I am no longer MacFane," he informed her stiffly as he lifted his hand. "Address me as Malcolm." It was a command, not a request.

Ariella considered this as she gently dabbed at the blood coating his wound. The new MacFane, Harold, had told them the Black Wolf had been relieved of his position as laird and cast from the clan in shame. There had been no trace of fury or condemnation as he had relayed this news. Instead, his expression had been veiled with regret, as if he'd wished he could somehow change what had passed. She knew better than to ask what the Black Wolf had done to merit such an appalling punishment. It was the affair of the Clan MacFane, and for an outsider to question the matter would have been an insult. The Black Wolf's physical condition and thirst for alcohol were clearly reason enough to replace him as laird. But to strip a man of his name and banish him from his clan was a sentence inflicted only for the most horrendous crimes. She pressed her needle into his flesh, wondering what unforgivable offense the Black Wolf had committed to be condemned so harshly by his own people.

"You learned your mother's skills well, Rob," commented Malcolm, watching the boy as he carefully stitched the wound closed. The lad's hands were small and soft, a testament to his youth and to a lack of familiarity with heavy chores. "It is obvious you have had some practice."

"There were many wounded after the attack on my clan."

Guilt slashed through Malcolm. He could think of nothing to say, so he remained silent.

"Why did you come to help us?" asked Rob after a moment.

Malcolm shrugged, then winced at the streak of pain that flashed down his neck.

In his letter MacKendrick had described his clan as peaceful, and completely unskilled in the ways of warfare. That and the knowledge that the previous messengers had never made it home had grated incessantly on Malcolm throughout the day. By the time darkness was falling, his unease had been worn raw. He had told Gavin he was in need of a ride—which was ridiculous, of course. Gavin knew Malcolm's battered body ached far too much for him to find pleasure in the sport of riding anymore. Nevertheless, his friend had not questioned him but swiftly saddled their horses and solemnly produced their dirks and swords. It was Gavin's habit to keep the weapons polished and sharpened at all times, ready for battle at a moment's notice. This was the mark of a good warrior, Malcolm had thought ruefully as he accepted his glimmering, heavy blade. Gavin was older than he by over a decade, and his career as a warrior had been that much longer. Evidently his training was more firmly ingrained.

"Gavin convinced me you were likely to find trouble and not know how to defend yourselves," he lied.

"It was fortunate he decided to come after us," commented Rob, tying the last stitch into place. The boy opened a small jar from his bag and smeared a foul-smelling substance on Malcolm's arm. "You are far stronger than you appear."

"I'm not," countered Malcolm. "We were lucky those men were so inept. Arrogance made them careless, and fear made them weak. Had those men possessed even a vague understanding of what it is to be a warrior, the encounter could have ended very differently."

"Are you saying that with proper training those men could have defeated you?" she asked curiously, wrapping a bandage around his arm.

"Proper training," affirmed Malcolm, "and attitude. From the moment we charged into the camp bellowing and swinging our swords, those men believed they were finished. That made them easy to kill."

Ariella frowned as she considered this. There was no denying that the Black Wolf was severely injured. His right arm was all but useless. He walked with a limp. His stiff movements and constant grimaces suggested he suffered from acute back pain. On top of that, he had no army, and he was clearly dependent on alcohol, probably to help deaden his pain. Yet he and his friend had ridden hard for many miles, then charged in and defeated four armed thieves who had been about to kill her, Duncan, and Andrew.

Training and attitude.

"Can any man be trained to be a warrior?" she demanded.

"Perhaps not a warrior," qualified Malcolm, "but any man can be trained to fight better. Training is trial and error and exhaustive repetition. If a man is well trained, he reacts instantly and lethally, without the fatal weakness of hesitation. He learns not only how to wield a weapon, but how to make *himself* a weapon. When he is attacked, he responds not from fear, but from the deeply entrenched methods of his training. This makes him far more dangerous to his enemy."

"And when you were called the Black Wolf and had your great army, were you the one who trained them?"

His expression grew shadowed. "When I was Mac-Fane, I had a thousand men under my command," he stated, his voice resonant with bitter pride. "And I trained every last goddamn one of them."

He looked beyond her, into the darkness, remembering. A pale wash of firelight flickered across his face, which was mostly hidden beneath a dark growth of unkempt beard. His tangled hair was also excessively long and in need of washing—the hair of a man who has withdrawn from society and is uninterested in matters of appearance. But in that hushed, firelit moment, it was his eyes that held her captivated. They were illuminated by the glow of the flames, or perhaps by the memory he was reliving in his mind. As they glittered with the bittersweet reminiscence of his past, Ariella suddenly saw a flash of pain within the depths of blue. It startled her, to recognize such vulnerability in the man who had been so disgustingly drunk and self-absorbed earlier that day, and then so powerful and ruthlessly savage. Before she could study him further, he closed his eyes and shook his head.

"I need a drink," he stated harshly. "Then Gavin and I must be on our way." He awkwardly moved to stand, bracing his hand against his aching back as he rose.

"I have something to ask you, MacFane."

"I am no longer MacFane," he growled. "And if you are thinking you would like to squire, I have no need for one. Besides, I doubt your friends would approve if you told them you wanted to come with me."

"I do not want to go with you," Ariella assured him. "I want you to come with us."

He shook his head. "I already told you, I cannot help your clan."

"MacKendrick hoped you would come with your great army and assume the position of laird," she continued, ignoring his refusal. "Obviously, that isn't possible. But you could still come and train us in the ways of warfare. If what you say is true, any man can be trained to fight, as long as he has the right teacher. Even me," she finished hopefully.

"You could be trained to fight," agreed Malcolm. "But not by me. My days of training and battle are over." He began to limp toward Gavin.

"You have trained a thousand men," she persisted. "You have led armies to countless victories. You could help the Clan MacKendrick learn to defend itself until we find a new laird."

"No."

"Why not?" demanded Ariella. "You have nothing here."

His expression grew dark. "You are right," he agreed brusquely. "And that is how I choose to live my life now. Without responsibilities."

Anger flared within her. Alpin had sent her to find the Black Wolf, despite her hatred of him. At first she'd been convinced there was nothing this drunken, crippled hermit could do for her clan. But after witnessing the brutal efficacy with which he had dispatched those thieves, Ariella was no longer certain this broken warrior had nothing left to offer.

Beyond that, he owed her something for failing her so completely.

"The Clan MacKendrick was assaulted because you were unable and unwilling to come to its aid," she stated, her voice hard. "Now we are dangerously vulnerable. Until we find another laird with an army, we must learn to defend ourselves. We cannot do that without an experienced warrior. You owe it to my people to help us, MacFane."

"If you are trying to appeal to my innate sense of honor, don't bother," he drawled. "As for guilt, I have so much already, I barely notice when more is added to the flames. Gavin," he growled, "it is time we left." He moved toward his horse.

She was losing him. She cast Duncan a desperate look.

"We will pay you," he swiftly offered.

Malcolm hesitated.

"Handsomely," added Andrew, realizing they had captured his attention. "In gold."

His expression hovered tenuously between rejection and intrigue. "How much?"

Ariella opened her mouth to speak, but Duncan lifted his hand, throwing her a warning look.

"Your fee would depend," he began, "on how long you stayed with us, and how satisfactory a job you did. I would think to help us with our fortifications and train our men would require a commitment of no less than six months." He flashed a covert glance at Ariella.

She imperceptibly tilted her head in agreement.

"Too long," replied Malcolm flatly. "I could not possibly stay more than two months. If the MacKendricks manage to learn something in that time, fine. If not, I get paid anyway."

Ariella lifted four fingers and began to casually scratch her face.

"Four months," countered Duncan, "and you get paid according to the performance of the men."

"Three months," returned Malcolm, "and I get paid one hundred gold coins, regardless of their performance. And Gavin gets paid a fee as well," he added. "Equal to mine."

Duncan glanced at Ariella, who barely nodded. "Done."

Malcolm scowled, suddenly irritated that he had permitted himself to be hired. "You," he snapped, pointing to Andrew. "You will begin your training tonight by taking the first watch. If anything moves, shoot it, then come and tell me. Is that clear?"

Andrew nodded blankly and went to retrieve his bow and arrow.

Malcolm eased himself down by the fire, resting his injured arm in his lap as he stared moodily into the flames. "Gavin," he called brusquely, "for Christ's sake, bring me a drink."

Ariella moved to the opposite side of the fire, putting distance between herself and her hired warrior. She arranged her blanket around her shoulders and lay down. After a while Gavin and Duncan also settled on the ground. MacFane remained upright, drinking and contemplating the dying fire as it hissed in greedy protest at the shrinking black embers. For the next hour Ariella watched him sink deeper into drunkenness. Finally he collapsed with a groan and began to snore. She closed her eyes and tried to sleep, but the uncertainty of what she had just done plagued her mind.

She had found the Black Wolf. He looked and acted like a savage, he was badly disabled, he had no army, and he was an appalling drunk. To crown it all, he was not coming out of any desire to help, but only for the greedy desire for gold.

How she would get her people to accept him as their leader, even for a short while, she had no idea.

CHAPTER 2

Pain again.

The fog in his brain had cleared enough for him to realize he should try to remain still and keep his breathing shallow. There. That seemed to help. But the pain in his leg . . . He groaned and shifted his weight. Pain surged over his arm as it touched the ground, and a small sound escaped his throat, part curse and part sob.

"Get up, Malcolm. It's time to go."

He opened his eyes. "Go where?" he mumbled thickly.

He followed Gavin's gaze. The MacKendricks were mounted on their horses, regarding him with impatience.

"Jesus Christ," he groaned, closing his eyes once more.

"It won't seem so bad once we're on our way," Gavin assured him. "But they've been up since sunrise, and by the looks on their faces I'd say they're rather anxious to leave."

Then let them go, Malcolm thought acidly.

He rose, trying to suppress his grimaces as his body protested. He walked stiffly to his horse and heaved himself up, clenching his jaw. He was acutely aware of being watched and had no desire to reveal how difficult even the simplest of movements were for him upon waking. It had been his custom as the Black Wolf to rise well before first light, using the morning stillness to practice with his weapons before his men wakened. He had loved the clarity of morning, the quiet solitude of waking and preparing to face the day. His current lack of discipline was embarrassing. He was supposed to be leading these men, and a leader did not sleep the morning away.

"Let's go," he ordered brusquely, as if it were they who had kept him waiting. He dug his heels into his horse and headed north, leaving them to follow.

Tomorrow he would try to waken earlier.

It was well past midday when Malcolm finally surrendered to his weariness. The MacKendricks immediately went to their saddlebags and began to unpack bread and cheese to lay for their nooning meal.

"Never mind the food. It is time to begin your training."

The trio looked at him in confusion. "Training?"

"Yes, training." He handed his sword and dirk to Gavin. "You first," he said, pointing to Andrew. "Remove your sword and dirk, and attack me."

Andrew appeared dumbfounded. "Attack you?"

"I am not in the habit of repeating commands," Malcolm warned.

"Forgive me," Andrew hastily apologized, "but I have no wish to hurt you."

"I am relieved to hear it," he replied dryly. "I am ordering you to attack me all the same."

"But you are unarmed."

"And you will be as well," he pointed out, "as you all were last night."

Andrew cast Duncan and Rob a questioning glance. Duncan shrugged his shoulders. The boy nodded. With obvious reluctance Andrew removed his weapons and hesitantly moved toward Malcolm, his arms outstretched.

"You move like a lovesick suitor," Malcolm said impatiently. "Are you attacking me or asking me to dance?"

His insult pierced Andrew's caution. With a huff of determination Andrew ran toward him.

Malcolm grabbed Andrew's arm and spun him around, imprisoning him against his body as he hooked his aching right arm under Andrew's neck.

"One strong pull and your neck is broken. You moved too slowly, and your attack lacked surprise. I had decided how to deal with you before you were halfway here." He released his grip, setting Andrew free. "Now you," he said, looking at Duncan.

Duncan quickly shed his weapons and sprinted toward Malcolm. As he approached, Malcolm took one step back, leaving only his leg in place. Duncan tripped and went sprawling onto the ground. Malcolm stood over him and pressed his foot into his back.

"Were I your enemy, this would be a sword carving your ribs. Your attack had speed but was still too obvious." He lifted his foot from Duncan's back. "Now you," he commanded, glancing at Rob.

"No!" exclaimed Duncan, horrified. Realizing his protest might seem strange, he hastily added, "Rob is just a boy. Barely more than thirteen years of age. He cannot be expected to fight."

"Of course he can," countered Malcolm. "Those men last night made no exceptions for his youth, and neither will I. If he is old enough to be in danger, he is old enough to learn how to get out of it. Come on, lad," he said. "Try to attack me."

The boy bit his lip, evidently afraid. "I do not think—"

"Does the Clan MacKendrick wish to learn how to defend itself or not?"

"Yes, but—"

"Then attack me!" Malcolm growled. "Before I give up on all of you and go home!"

The boy's gray eyes grew cold. With a fierce shout he flew toward Malcolm, his hands balled into fists. Malcolm wrapped his good arm around the youth's slight frame and easily plucked him off his kicking feet. His waist was small and soft, betraying his coddled lifestyle. Malcolm deposited him on his backside in disgust.

"Get up and try again. And this time surprise me."

With Duncan and Andrew watching anxiously, Rob slowly got to his feet.

"It is obvious you and your clan are accustomed to a life of little more than eating and resting. That is about to change. Now, attack me."

Rob hesitated.

"Now," commanded Malcolm, growing impatient.

The boy regarded him with huge, pleading eyes. Finally he shook his head. "I cannot," he whimpered. He hung his head in shame.

"God grant me patience," muttered Malcolm darkly. He turned to Gavin. "I suppose that is all I can expect from them today. Give me my weapons and let's eat."

Suddenly something plowed hard into his back, wrapping him in pain as he lurched forward and landed facedown in the dirt.

"There," huffed Rob, triumphant. He stood and brushed off his filthy plaid. "I surprised you."

Malcolm glared at the boy, struggling to control his fury. "If you ever do anything like that again," he warned, his voice dangerously low, "I will make sure you cannot sit for a month." He knocked away Gavin's proferred hand and awkwardly rose on his own. Then he faced his three pupils.

"During the time it will take to reach your lands, you will train twice a day, at noon and at dusk, before eating. Though you will not be warriors when you arrive home, at least you will have some limited understanding of what it is to fight. And if we are attacked again along the way, perhaps you will be of more use than you were last night. Now, go and eat." He moved away from them, seeking solace beneath the shade of an enormous pine tree.

Ariella went to her horse and unpacked some bread and cheese from her saddlebag. She was glad she had knocked him to the ground. He had been trying to humiliate them, and it did her good to see a little of that humiliation on his astounded face.

"What are we going to do?" whispered Duncan, worried. "You cannot be expected to train like a man."

"I will not train like a man," she replied quietly, seating herself beside him. "I will train like a boy."

"But he dropped you on the ground!" protested Andrew, clearly horrified.

"I wasn't hurt," pointed out Ariella, trying to calm them. "Besides, he is right. We have hired him to teach us to fight, and what better time to begin than now? When we get home, we will need everyone who is able to train, and that will include boys of thirteen. Therefore we cannot argue that Rob is too young."

"But if you are hurt—"

"I don't believe he will allow us to actually get hurt," interjected Ariella.

Andrew regarded her curiously. "Why do you say that?"

She shifted her weight on her bruised backside and glanced at Malcolm, who was drinking heavily from a wineskin Gavin had brought to him. Despite his admirable performance during their training session, it was clear his body was protesting the long hours spent in the saddle.

Because, she reflected silently, *he knows too well what it is to feel pain.*

Malcolm stared up at the cool black tent of night.

He was drunk, but not nearly as drunk as he would have liked. Gavin had not realized they would be gone for so long and had packed only enough wine to last him a day. Malcolm had drunk most of it last night and had needed to start drinking again that afternoon to control the discomfort of riding. By evening there had been only one wineskin left, which he had quickly finished. It had blunted the edge of his pain, but it was not sufficient to deaden the throbbing in his back, leg, and arm. His suffering kept him from retreating into sleep, and so he lay awake, his senses only blurred as he fought the despair that rose within him at night when his mind remained chained to his aching body.

He wished Gavin had let him die.

He had never imagined it would be like this. In truth he had not expected to live, so he'd had no concept of what his future would be at all. After that final, brutal battle, as he lay with his leg shattered and his body gashed by sword thrusts, he had simply thought he would die. His initial feeling was more surprise than anger. After six years of service in King William's army, he did not know why the idea of dying should seem so foreign. He had seen scores of men suffer the most appalling ends, and had no reason to think his turn would not come. The ground had grown warm with his blood, and hazy, pleasant reflections of his clan and

Marrian had swirled through his head. There was pain, but it was not intolerable.

Until someone suddenly hauled him up, threw him onto a horse, and took him away from the battlefield. Then there was pain unlike any he had ever known.

And it had never abated.

Gavin had done his best to heal him. He had bound his leg between two strong, straight lengths of wood. He stitched the wounds in his sides and chest, and closed the deep, jagged gash in his right arm. And then he took him home. When they arrived, Malcolm had been overcome with suffering and fever. But he was lucid enough to understand that his father had died, and the clan was anxiously awaiting his return as chief. As was Marrian.

The horror in her eyes when she saw him would haunt him forever.

Uneasiness swept over him, clearing the mists of his reflections. He gazed around the camp, trying to determine what had disturbed him. Gavin, Duncan, and Rob were asleep by the fire. Andrew, who was supposed to be on watch, sat slumped against a tree, snoring. Malcolm strained to listen but heard nothing unusual.

Taking up his sword, he slowly moved into the surrounding woods, searching the darkness. His feet made a rustling sound as they crushed leaves and needles. He attempted to lighten his step, but his limp made this impossible. Other than the occasional chirp of a bird and the uneven drag of his footsteps, the woods were silent. Moving deeper into the shadows, he listened to the quiet. His senses were heavily fogged by wine, and he suspected his uneasiness was likely his imagination. Nevertheless, he continued to explore the darkness, electing to trust his instincts. At one point he was strangely aware of being watched. He whirled about, his sword raised menacingly in front of him. Nothing but trees and blackness.

Cursing, he lowered his throbbing arm, wondering what the hell was the matter with him.

A savage roar split the air. Malcolm whipped about to see an enraged wolf hurtling toward him, its massive jaws locked in a snarl. Before he could lift his sword, the animal howled with pain and dropped to the ground. Malcolm stared at it in astonishment.

Then he turned to see Rob standing behind him, another arrow aimed at the luckless beast in case he stirred again.

"You shouldn't go off in the woods alone," observed the boy, lowering his bow.

"Where the hell did you learn to shoot like that?"

"My father. He insisted I practice often so I could hunt with him."

"But that wolf was racing through blackness," Malcolm pointed out, amazed. "Even my best warriors would have had trouble making a shot like that."

Rob shrugged. "I am quite skilled with a bow."

"Evidently your father taught you something of tracking as well," observed Malcolm, realizing it was Rob who had been following him. He glanced at the lifeless form of the wolf. "I look forward to meeting him when we reach your lands. Perhaps he can assist me in training others."

"He is dead." The boy jammed his arrow into his quiver. "He was killed in the attack." His tone was void of emotion, but it seemed an accusation nonetheless. He turned and began to head back to the camp.

"Rob."

He stopped but did not turn.

"Thank you."

He sensed the boy's surprise. Perhaps Rob thought simple courtesy was beyond the realm of the Black Wolf's conduct. Given Malcolm's behavior thus far, the lad had no reason to think otherwise. There was a moment of awkward silence.

"We are paying you well for your services, MacFane," Rob finally said. "Try not to get killed before you have earned your fee."

With that he continued toward the camp, leaving Malcolm alone with the dead wolf.

"Today we will learn to attack a man's most vulnerable areas. Do you know what those are?"

Duncan, Andrew, and Ariella exchanged uncertain glances.

"The heart?" suggested Andrew.

"The heart is vulnerable if you pierce it with a weapon," agreed Malcolm. "But I mean places you can attack without a weapon, which can effectively disable a man."

"The eyes," said Duncan.

"Right." Malcolm proceeded to demonstrate on Gavin. "Grab your opponent's head, like so, and sink your thumbs deep into his eyes until he screams. While he is blind, smash your forehead into his nose, breaking it, then immediately raise your knee and crush his ballocks, sending him to the ground. The trick is to inflict each injury in rapid succession, before he has a chance to recover. Once he is down, kick him as hard as you can in either the head or ribs. The head is better. Then take his weapon and slit his throat or stab his chest, being sure to kill him, not just wound him. Any questions?"

He raised his eyes to find his pupils staring at him in mute horror.

"What's wrong?"

"It's so—so violent," stammered Andrew.

"That's why it's called fighting."

"But surely one needn't resort to such brutality," protested Duncan. "There must be other ways of dealing with an opponent."

"You could simply ask him to go away," Malcolm drawled aridly. "I have never found that to be particularly effective."

Andrew shook his head. "You can't possibly expect Rob to use such vile methods. He is just a boy."

"It is because of Rob that I am suggesting these methods," Malcolm asserted. "He is short and slight, so he cannot defeat a full-grown man using tactics requiring strength. But he can easily gouge eyes, bite flesh, knee ballocks, and pull hair. These are things that will distract your opponent, giving you the advantage. Now, you two start fighting each other," he ordered, indicating Andrew and Duncan. "Try not to actually kill each other. Rob, you will fight Gavin."

Andrew and Duncan looked at Ariella, their faces taut with apprehension.

She could not blame them for worrying about her. As the cherished daughter of Laird MacKendrick, she had been gently raised to a life of elegance and beauty. Ariella's father had never permitted her to be exposed to harsh words or rough behavior. And he certainly would never have allowed her to wrestle with a man. But that was before Roderic, she reflected grimly. Before her father was killed, her clansmen murdered and terrorized, and her home ransacked.

That was a different Ariella.

"Very well," she said. She straightened her shoulders and walked toward Gavin. "Let us begin."

In the training that followed, Ariella was dropped on her backside more times than she cared to count. Although Gavin never seriously hurt her, he treated her with the same casual roughness one would use when wrestling with a boy of thirteen years. Fortunately her small breasts were firmly bound against her chest, so the odd time she found herself pinned against him, Gavin did not seem to notice any undue softness. They were not supposed to actually hurt each other, but

Ariella's movements were spontaneous and lacking in control, causing her twice to strike Gavin far harder than she intended. He assured her he was fine, but she adjusted her attacks after that, trying to hit him gently. Duncan and Andrew seemed to have the same problem, as they were constantly stopping and apologizing to each other while they rubbed a bruised knee or rib.

"For God's sake, how do you intend to learn to fight if you stop every time you inflict one little bruise?" growled Malcolm impatiently.

"I hit him harder than I should have," explained Andrew, casting Duncan an apologetic glance. "I'm sorry."

"Tell him you're bloody sorry afterward, but get on with it! And you," he continued, scowling at Ariella, "I've seen children of four summers fight with more conviction. Hit Gavin like your life depends on it."

"I don't want to hurt him," objected Ariella.

"You won't hurt me, lad," Gavin assured her cheerfully. "Go ahead. Give me your worst."

Ariella hesitated.

"Do it," commanded Malcolm, "or I'll fight you myself. And I vow I won't be nearly as easy on you as Gavin has been."

She gave him a withering look.

"Imagine Gavin has come to attack your home," Malcolm instructed harshly. "He has already butchered two of your clansmen. Now he is about to cut you in half with his sword. After you're dead, he will ransack your home, brutalize your clan's women and children, and set everything afire. You have no weapon. What are you going—"

Rage was surging through Ariella long before he finished. Overwhelmed with hideous memories, she flew at Gavin. He waved his sword before him, but Ariella already knew how to deal with the weapon. She scooped up a fistful of dirt and hurled it at Gavin's eyes. He blinked and shook his head, his sword lowered, and Ariella rammed her knee into his groin. Gavin gasped in pain and dropped to his knees. Panting, Ariella turned to look at Malcolm.

"Very good," said Malcolm, masking his surprise. "Except you should have taken his sword and run him through."

Gavin groaned. "I think that's enough training for today," he suggested, his voice strained. "The boy can run me through tomorrow."

Malcolm felt the corners of his mouth twitch. "Help your opponent to his feet, Rob. I think poor Gavin has discovered you are a more formidable adversary than your size indicates." He began to limp away.

Ariella went to Gavin and offered her hand. "I am truly sorry, Gavin," she apologized. "I did not mean to hurt you."

"That's all right, lad," he said, rising to his feet. "It was worth it."

Ariella frowned. "Why?"

"That is the closest I've seen him smile in over three years," he replied, looking almost jubilant. "And for that, I'd gladly let you knock me down again."

Warm light grazed his face, rousing him. His familiar enemy was there to greet him, hacking through muscles, stiffening his back and limbs. But his head was oddly clear, allowing the cloak of sleep to be torn away despite his exhaustion. He opened his eyes and frowned at the sunlight drifting through the branches above, wondering why he was not experiencing his customary morning haze. Then he remembered there had been no wine for him last night. That was why he was so tired. He had lain awake for hours on this damp, hard ground, battling his pain as he fought to enter the refuge of sleep.

He needed to find some drink soon.

The camp was empty except for young Rob, who was occupied with laying the morning meal. Malcolm watched as the boy carefully spread a cloth upon the ground, smoothed out the wrinkles, and adjusted the corners. He then neatly arranged a loaf of bread, a chunk of cheese, some dried herring, and a pitcher upon it, and placed some wooden cups around. The lad frowned at the result, cut the loaf, and rearranged it amongst the other food, intent on making the meal look pleasing. Then he produced a kerchief and wiped the inside of each cup. It was clear the MacKendricks were an unusually fastidious clan. Malcolm scowled with impatience. Their time would be better spent turning their young men into warriors.

"Where are the others?" he demanded, rising.

Rob looked up, startled.

"This evening we will be reaching my home," he said, shoving the kerchief into his saddlebag. "They have gone to the river to bathe and prepare themselves for our arrival."

Malcolm stretched, cursed at the pain the action caused him, then belched loudly. Seating himself by the cloth, he grabbed a chunk of bread and began to eat. Gavin, Duncan, and Andrew approached from the river, their faces freshly shaved and their hair wet. Malcolm regarded Gavin's pink cheeks with amusement. It had been a long time since he had seen his friend without the dark growth of a beard.

"Makes you look years younger," Malcolm commented dryly as Gavin sat down. "I'd never guess you to be past forty."

Gavin self-consciously stroked his smooth cheek. "I am curious to see what you look like beneath yours, my friend."

"I have no intention of shaving," Malcolm assured him, reaching for a chunk of cheese.

"But you must!" exclaimed Rob.

Malcolm raised an eyebrow.

"What I mean to say is," the boy hastily amended, "my clan is anxiously awaiting our return with the mighty Black Wolf. They have heard stories of your exceptional courage and strength, and your many glorious feats over the years. They are expecting to welcome the arrival of a magnificent warrior. You cannot possibly ride into their midst looking like a—"

"Like a what?" prodded Malcolm ominously.

"Like a warrior who did not have time to bathe," supplied Duncan. "We MacKendricks are rather particular on matters of cleanliness."

Malcolm cast a sardonic eye at Rob. "You would never know it."

"We are not so particular when it comes to children," qualified Andrew. "Only adults and warriors."

"That's your problem," stated Malcolm with a shrug. "I have no intention of either bathing or shaving."

"How do you expect my clan to respect you if you arrive looking like a filthy, savage wild man?" demanded Rob impatiently. "Do you think they will believe you are the Black Wolf?"

Malcolm felt his irritation deepen. "They can believe whatever they goddamn—"

"It is going to be a warm day," interrupted Gavin pleasantly. "A swim would be good, Malcolm, before we begin our journey."

Malcolm glared at his friend, furious that he was taking their side. No one said anything in the silence that followed, but Malcolm was acutely aware of their disapproving scrutiny.

"Fine," he finally growled. "I'll have a bloody swim."

A short while later Ariella saw Gavin and Malcolm returning from the river. The Black Wolf's ragged beard was gone, revealing a strong, square jaw and well-formed cheekbones. He was naked except for the worn plaid wrapped carelessly around his waist. His chest, shoulders, and stomach were thickly muscled, and although his body bore many scars, it was obvious this was a man of considerable strength. It was only pain, she realized, not weakness, that limited his abilities. His dark-brown hair was dripping wet, causing rivulets of water to trickle down his sun-bronzed chest and shoulders. Ariella watched in fascination as the shimmering streams slid across his body before disappearing into the fabric at his waist.

"Better?" demanded Malcolm sourly.

She nodded.

"You might want to try a bath yourself, lad," he suggested. "A pound of soap and a stiff brush might strip away some of that filth."

"My clan is uninterested in my appearance," she replied tautly. "But they will be very interested in yours. Which is why I must trim your hair. If you will permit me," she swiftly qualified as his newly shaved jaw clenched.

"After you have cut Malcolm's, you may cut mine," said Gavin, before Malcolm had a chance to respond. "Living alone for so long, I fear we have neglected our appearance. We do not want your clan to think we are uncivilized." He gave Malcolm a meaningful look.

"Hurry up and cut it, then," Malcolm snapped. "The morning is wasted with this nonsense."

Ariella fetched her comb and scissors and proceeded to give the Black Wolf a good trim. Once she had combed out the tangles and removed a ragged length, his dark-brown hair began to wave as it spilled over his shoulders. He endured her ministrations in hostile silence. Taking courage from his cooperation, however unwilling, she quickly plaited a small lock on one side. Then she wrapped a fresh bandage around his injured arm and declared herself finished.

"Then do Gavin and let us be off," said Malcolm, reaching for his shirt.

Ariella gazed in disgust at the filthy, worn garment crumpled in his hand. "Don't you have anything better to wear?"

"When we set out to find you, I did not anticipate needing a fine outfit," he drawled.

"But I did." Gavin went to his horse and withdrew some garments and a pair of boots from his saddlebag. "Here."

Malcolm stared at the clothes in astonishment. They were from his own wardrobe when he had been Laird MacFane. After being cast out, he had abandoned his belongings, even though Harold had generously told him to take whatever he needed. Evidently Gavin had been more prudent. But why had he brought this outfit, Malcolm wondered, when they had planned only to make sure the MacKendricks were all right and then return home that same night?

"A pity you didn't think to pack more wine for the journey as well," he commented acidly.

Gavin shrugged. "There wasn't enough room."

Malcolm scowled and dropped his plaid.

Cheeks flaming, Ariella turned away. "If you come over here, Gavin, I will trim your hair for you."

She took her time with the task, wanting to be sure Malcolm was dressed before she looked again. After packing her scissors and comb in her bag, she cautiously turned.

The stranger standing before her bore no resemblance to the filthy, drunken hermit she had met four days earlier. This man was truly splendid in his saffron shirt, leather jerkin, and magnificent plaid of brown, green, and black, which was pinned to his shoulder with an old, battered brooch. A strong belt strapped his sword to his waist, and new deerskin boots were laced up his calves. He regarded her calmly, his blue eyes clear and faintly taunting. Everything about him spoke of power and confidence, the stance of a man who knows he has strength and is ready to wield it. This was the Black Wolf her father and Alpin had spoken of. This was the warrior who led an army of a thousand, who performed deeds of unparalleled bravery, and who emerged unscathed and victorious from virtually every battle.

It was an illusion, she reminded herself bitterly. He was a drunk, and under those clothes he was slashed with scars, and if he took a few steps, he would betray the weakness of his back and leg. But in this moment, with the sun shining warmly upon him, she found herself captivated by the glorious figure he presented.

"Well? Do I finally meet with your approval?" he demanded sullenly.

She turned, suddenly aware of her own filthy clothes, her tangled hair, and her grimy skin. Because of him she had no choice but to look this way. Because of him her home had been attacked, and she was no longer free to be Ariella MacKendrick.

"You'll do," she snapped, mounting her horse. "Let us be off."

She dug her heels into Shena's sides and galloped away, feeling a need to have distance from him, lest her hatred surface and drive him back to where she had found him.

It was nearly dusk when they reached the Mac-Kendrick border. Warm anticipation swelled within her as Ariella neared her lands. She had never been away from her clan before, and on this journey she had been gone nine endless days. Her desire to see her home made her race ahead of the others, seeking solitude as she caught the first view of her beloved castle and the cheerful cottages surrounding it.

She saw the bodies first.

They were lying in the low grasses that grew in the meadow beside the woods. She would have missed them, if not for the bright flash of yellow that suddenly caught her eye. Curious, she slowed her horse and moved toward it, wondering if someone had lost a cloak while hunting. As she got closer, she realized the yellow cloth was a shirt, and that it covered the back of a man who lay facedown upon the ground. He had been brutally stabbed, and the condition of his body indicated he had been dead for some time. Horrified, she tore her gaze from him, only to see another man lying a few meters away.

Guy and Marcus.

She wheeled her horse about, then slid to the ground and pressed her forehead against Shena's neck, fighting to stifle the sobs rising from the back of her throat.

"What is it?" demanded Malcolm, thundering forward. He reached her and dismounted as fast as his body would allow. "Are you ill?"

She swallowed and shook her head. Without looking she pointed in the direction of the bodies.

Malcolm was joined by the others as he went to investigate.

"It's Guy and Marcus," said Duncan, shaken. "The messengers Laird MacKendrick sent to speak with you."

"They have been dead for some two months," Malcolm observed grimly. "Perhaps as they returned, they came upon the band of warriors about to attack your clan. They were killed so they could not warn you."

Fresh hatred surged through Ariella. Two more deaths at the hands of Roderic.

"We must bring them with us," said Andrew. "They will need a proper burial."

"No."

All four looked at her in surprise.

Torn by her decision, she tried to make them understand. "We are returning to our clan with the mighty

Black Wolf, who has agreed to help us. It is a cause for celebration, and our people have long awaited this moment. We cannot arrive bearing the evidence of more savagery and death."

"But we can't just leave them here like this," protested Duncan. "Shall we bury them?"

She shook her head. "Marcus and Guy deserve the decency of a burial in the presence of their clan and their priest. We will cover them with a cloth and leave them to sleep under the stars a final night. Tomorrow you and Andrew will return here to fetch their bodies. That will be soon enough to let the clan know of this atrocity."

Duncan and Andrew nodded and went to fetch a blanket.

She turned to Malcolm. "It is best we do not tell my clan you are no longer laird of the Clan MacFane. It will invite too many questions and may undermine the respect you will need to train them." She disliked the idea of lying to them but knew she had little choice.

Malcolm shrugged. "You are paying for my services. Tell your clan whatever you like."

"I will ride on ahead, to announce our arrival." She mounted her horse and galloped across the meadow toward her home, hatred and loss weighing heavily upon her.

If MacFane had maintained his position as laird, this would never have happened, she reflected bitterly. He would have accepted her father's proposal, gathered a force of warriors, and ridden back with Guy and Marcus, keeping them safe. He would have slain Roderic, driven away his men, and continued on to her castle as the mighty Black Wolf, just as Alpin had foreseen it.

Blaming him could not ease the despondency that gripped her as she realized what she had done. She had set out to find the magnificent Black Wolf and bring him back to her people as their new laird. Instead she was returning with this drunken, pathetic, broken warrior, who was to train them in return for gold.

The moment her people laid eyes upon him, they would question her right to bestow the powers of the sword.

CHAPTER 3

"They have returned!"

The announcement echoed through the air as Ariella burst through the cover of the woods. Her people waved at her as she flew past their cottages, then quickly gathered their children and hurried up the green slope of land toward the castle, eager to welcome the mighty Black Wolf.

Ariella did not stop, so anxious was she to warn Alpin and the elders of MacFane's condition before he arrived. She clattered into the courtyard to find her castle in an uproar. People were pouring out of every door, hastily adjusting their best gowns and plaids, while a line of children were being given a quick

washing by the well. A wooden dais had been erected in
the center of the yard, upon which five young men were
blowing loudly into bagpipes trimmed with lengths of
colorful plaid. Trying to be heard above the racket, a
crowd was shouting directions at a group of men on the
roof who were struggling to lower an enormous gold
banner. A rope fell and the fabric unfurled prematurely,
revealing a fearsome black wolf standing guard over a
delicate white lamb. Women rushed back and forth carrying platters piled high with bread, meat, and fruit, and
great casks of wine and ale were being rolled across the
yard to a corner where dozens of cups were being assembled on tables. There were entertainers everywhere,
some juggling brightly colored balls, some reciting poetry, and others tumbling and walking on their hands.
No one took any notice of her as they hurried past, fully
preoccupied with practicing their part in the upcoming
ceremony.

She spied the eldest member of the council pacing
back and forth, his white head bent studiously over a
wrinkled leaf of paper. "Angus!" she called, dismounting.

"No time to talk now, lad, no time," muttered
Angus. "The Black Wolf will be here any moment, and I
must memorize this speech."

"Angus, it is Ariella."

He lifted his gaze in astonishment. "What are you
doing still dressed like that? Your betrothed will be here
any moment. Hurry and put on a gown, there's no need
for you to pretend to be a lad anymore."

"MacFane doesn't know I'm alive, Angus," Ariella
said urgently. "I must speak with Alpin and the rest of the
council. I have to make them understand—"

"Ariella, is that you?"

Niall was striding toward her, his face lit with relief.
At the mention of her name everyone suddenly stopped.

"Ariella!" burst out Elizabeth, waving happily from a
second-floor window. Her smile fell as she took in her

appearance. "Oh, my, you must change! Hurry and come inside!"

A group of women began to usher her toward the castle. "No, wait," she protested. "I must speak with you first—"

"How long until MacFane arrives with his army, lass?" demanded Dugald. "The men in the towers have not sighted them yet."

She turned to the second-eldest council member. "That is what I need to talk to you about—"

"Why are you still dressed like that?" asked Niall, frowning. "Does MacFane not know who you are?"

A flurry of eager questions stifled her attempt to answer.

"Is he as mighty as they say?"

"Do his warriors number a thousand?"

"Did he perform feats of great strength during your journey?"

"Will you grant him the sword right away, or will you wait?"

Her people crowded around her, unable to contain their excitement as they sought more information about their next laird.

"*Let me see her.*"

The softly spoken command had the silencing effect of a mighty crack of thunder. The crowd surrounding her parted, creating an opening for Alpin.

"Come to me, child."

Ariella obediently went to him. The ancient man leaned heavily against his cane and studied her, his black eyes sharp and assessing.

"So," he murmured after a moment, "he is not what you expected."

She shook her head.

"And you think my vision was flawed."

She did not answer, reluctant to disparage MacFane

in front of her clan. It didn't matter. Alpin could read her thoughts as clearly as if she had spoken them.

He nodded. "Let us see him, then," he said quietly. "This injured beast."

"They're coming!" cried young Colin from the tower. "Duncan, Andrew, and two others. They have ridden ahead of the Black Wolf's army!"

"Listen to me," Ariella pleaded urgently, gazing round at her people. "MacFane does not know who I am. He believes I died in the fire, and he must continue to believe that. You will treat me as the boy Rob, do you understand? And when you see him, you may notice—"

"They're here!" shouted Colin excitedly.

Everyone began to talk at once, cutting off Ariella's words as they surged forward to look.

Duncan, Andrew, and Gavin rode into the courtyard first.

Then Malcolm slowly entered.

He sat tall upon his magnificent horse, his enormous stature dwarfing the other riders. He calmly regarded the hushed crowd assembled before him, exuding confidence and power. In that silent, expectant moment he seemed every inch the mighty warrior her clan had so anxiously awaited. Ariella did not speak, afraid to break the spell that had fallen over her people. She knew this initial impression of MacFane would be fleeting.

The realization filled her with dread.

"Pipers play!" ordered Angus, waving his hand.

A grand bellow of sound filled the air. The musicians had composed a special piece in honor of MacFane's arrival, and the crowd seemed to enjoy it so much, they played it twice. When they finally finished, Angus stepped up onto the dais.

"I, Angus MacKendrick, eldest of the council, bid you welcome, MacFane, chief of the mighty Clan Mac-Fane." He squinted at his paper. "We MacKendricks are deeply honored by your presence. As you know, our troubles have been many of late. The deaths of our beloved laird and fellow clansmen have left wounds that cannot easily heal. We are relieved you have finally come, to protect us, to lead us, and most important, to marry our beloved—"

"*Pipers play!*" shouted Duncan.

The musicians instantly repeated their exuberant composition, effectively drowning the rest of Angus's speech. The elder continued to talk anyway, but several times he raised his eyes in confusion, wondering how his audience could possibly hear him over all that racket.

The music eventually ended, and Dugald slowly climbed onto the dais to recite a seemingly endless poem he had written about the history of the clan, beginning some four hundred years ago. When he finished, Elizabeth's father, Gordon, joined him on the platform to deliver yet another poem about the legendary exploits of the Black Wolf. When that was over, four jugglers and two tumblers crowded onto the platform beside the council members and began to demonstrate their skills. Their feats became increasingly more frenetic and impressive, until finally the pipers and poets were forced to step down to avoid being struck by a wayward ball or foot. The crowd applauded wildly, encouraging them to continue, which they did. The pipers then resumed playing yet another rendition of their new composition, and Dugald waved at the men standing on the castle roof. The magnificent banner unfurled once again, revealing the image of the ferocious black wolf standing guard over the little white lamb. The crowd cheered.

Ariella looked uneasily at MacFane.

At first glance his face seemed a mask of tranquillity. But on closer inspection she could see his body was taut and his hands were tightly clenched. It looked as if he longed to turn his horse and thunder away. She should have warned him, she realized miserably. She should have known her clan would prepare a spectacular welcome for the man they believed was their new laird.

Angus climbed once again onto the platform and raised his hands, finally silencing the cheering and music. "Perhaps MacFane would like to say something. Come, milord, join me on this platform and tell us how soon we can expect the arrival of your mighty army."

MacFane shifted his gaze to Ariella. Fury smoldered deep within the blue of his eyes.

You tell them.

"MacFane's army is presently engaged elsewhere," Duncan quickly explained. "It will not be coming for some time."

Her people gasped in dismay.

"And, unfortunately, he has other obligations that prevent him from accepting the chiefship of our clan," he continued, glancing uneasily at Ariella. "But we have told him of our troubles, and he has kindly agreed to help us."

"How?" called out Helen, Gordon's wife.

"By training us to fight," said Ariella. "We don't need an army of outsiders to come and protect us. We must learn to protect ourselves."

This statement was met with murmurs of disbelief.

"We are not a clan of warriors, *Rob*," retorted Gordon adamantly. "What you are proposing is impossible."

Dugald nodded in agreement. "We need to find ourselves a great army, and soon, before we are attacked again."

The crowd grumbled in agreement.

"An army is not such an easy thing to find," countered Ariella. "And we cannot wait. We must learn to fight and protect what is ours, before someone else tries to take it away. MacFane has led one of the finest armies in all of Scotland. He has trained over a thousand men.

He has much knowledge about the use of weaponry and fortifications. Until we find a new laird with an army, we will place ourselves under his guidance and let him show us how we can better protect ourselves."

Her proclamation was met with uneasy silence. It was obvious her people disagreed with her, but they had no wish to insult the Black Wolf by debating the issue in front of him. They would save the matter for discussion by the council instead.

"Well, MacFane," said Angus, recovering his composure, "we're grateful to you for generously offering your assistance. Join me up here, milord, and let us raise a cup of wine to toast your stay with us."

Malcolm hesitated. He had not expected this outpouring of adulation. But after such a flattering welcome, he found himself suddenly loath to reveal his weaknesses in front of these people. The crowd applauded politely as Angus accepted two cups of wine from a serving boy and gestured for Malcolm to join him. He had no choice, he realized. Steeling himself to the inevitable reaction, he awkwardly dismounted and began to limp slowly toward the platform.

A murmur of shock rippled through the crowd. The applause died, and puzzled whispers filled the air. Malcolm ignored them and continued his plodding, unsteady gait. He never should have come, he realized furiously. These people had expected the mighty Black Wolf to arrive with his army and save them. Their disappointment when they learned he had no army with him had been humiliating enough. But as he clumsily stepped onto the platform, their aghast pity was so profound, he did not think he could endure it.

Angus was staring at him blankly, too stunned to offer the cup he held in his hand. Malcolm turned and raked his gaze over the crowd, returning their scrutiny with apparent calm. He would not let them see the depths of his mortification, he swore darkly. To do so would unveil yet another weakness, and in this moment he felt exposed enough.

"No, Catherine!" called a plain-looking woman suddenly. "Come back!"

A pretty chestnut-haired child of about seven was threading her way through the crowd. She ignored the command and continued toward Malcolm, her brown eyes wide and grave. When she reached the platform, she thrust out her hands, demanding assistance to climb up. Not knowing what else to do, Malcolm drew her onto the dais beside him.

"My name is Catherine MacKendrick," she announced. "I made this for you." She pressed a crumpled scrap of cloth into his hand.

Malcolm opened the wrinkled fabric. A crudely embroidered wolf, stitched in black thread, lay beneath a scattering of gold stars. Beneath the wolf, in childish lettering, was the word *Welcome*.

"This is beautiful," he murmured.

Catherine nodded in immodest agreement. "The letters were the hardest part," she informed him, pointing with a dainty finger. "I had to do the last *e* twice, because it turned out much larger than the first one." She studied it a moment, then frowned. "You do think they look the same now, don't you?"

"Absolutely identical," Malcolm assured her.

Her frown curved into a smile. "Good. I wanted it to be perfect for you."

With that she slipped her tiny hand into his, as if sensing how badly he needed an ally.

The sight of Catherine holding the Black Wolf's hand snapped Ariella out of her uncertainty. She had hired him knowing exactly what his limitations were. He was here to try to help them. She had no illusions that he could turn her people into an invincible army. But he could teach them something of defense while she continued to search for the rightful bearer of the sword.

Once that man was found, she would pay MacFane and send him away.

It was as simple as that.

She climbed onto the platform beside Catherine and regarded her people solemnly.

"I ask you to welcome Malcolm MacFane, the great warrior known as the Black Wolf, and his chief warrior, Gavin. They will be our honored guests for a time. During his stay MacFane will train us to defend ourselves. We must cooperate with him in every way, so we can benefit from his vast knowledge and experience."

Her proclamation was met with silence.

"And so we shall," announced Angus, squinting with disapproval at the clan. "We will do whatever we must to make the Clan MacKendrick strong." He handed a cup of wine to Malcolm. "Welcome, MacFane," he said, lifting his cup.

A few halfhearted *welcomes* filtered through the crowd. It was clear her people were hopelessly disappointed in the man Ariella had brought home. Although they were relieved she did not intend to marry him, they had no faith whatsoever that he would be able to help them. The clan began to disperse, no longer in the mood for celebration.

"Come, MacFane," said Ariella, "let us show you the castle. Maybe you can tell us how we can make it stronger."

Malcolm nodded, anxious to escape the disillusioned stares of the MacKendricks.

Ariella bent down and brushed her grimy knuckles against Catherine's cheek. "Go with Agnes," she ordered softly. "I will see you later and tell you about my journey."

Catherine hugged her, then obediently went to find Agnes.

"She seems fond of you," observed Malcolm.

"She is my sister," Ariella replied, stepping off the

platform. "This is Niall. He is in charge of restoring the damage done to the castle."

A handsome, strong-looking young man regarded him with barely disguised hostility. He folded his arms across his chest, enabling Malcolm to see the healing scars of a burn on his hands.

"How did you burn your hands?"

"There was a fire in the south tower," Niall replied brusquely.

Malcolm looked at the charred remains of the dismantled structure, which were piled in a corner of the courtyard. The new tower was being built of stone. The rest of the hall was stone, which was why the fire had not spread through the entire building.

"That wooden tower must have belonged to the earliest part of the castle," he mused. "From now on everything must be built of stone."

"Thank you for that brilliant insight," drawled Niall.

"The attackers came through the gate," explained Ariella as Gavin, Duncan, and Andrew joined them. "Then they swarmed the castle."

Malcolm lifted his gaze to the iron bars suspended above the entrance to the courtyard. "How did they get through the gate?"

"Why, they just rode through, lad," replied Angus, as if the answer were obvious. "That opening is more than big enough to accommodate a horse."

"I mean, how did they get the gate open?" qualified Malcolm.

Angus and Dugald looked bewildered.

"It was closed, wasn't it?"

Dugald shook his head. "It's never closed, lad."

"Why not?"

"The chains are badly rusted," explained Gordon. "The last time we lowered it was, let me think—nearly twenty years ago."

"I remember that," said Dugald, chuckling. "We had

a terrible time trying to get the bloody thing back up again."

Malcolm stared at them in disbelief. "You haven't lowered the gate in twenty years?"

The three council members shook their heads.

"There's been no need, lad," explained Dugald. "We're a clan of peace. No one ever bothers us."

"Until now," observed Gavin.

"Aye," Angus agreed. "Until now."

Malcolm put the issue of the gate aside for a moment and assessed the height and depth of the curtain wall surrounding the castle. It was sufficiently high, but the parapet lining the wall head was ridiculously low, and it had no crenellations from which an archer could shoot.

"Why is the parapet so low?"

"For the view," explained Gordon. "We've put benches up there, and it's a marvelous place to sit and look at the mountains. Wonderful for writing poetry or music. You can see just about forever," he assured him enthusiastically.

"Which means your attackers can get a perfectly clear shot at you," Malcolm pointed out, trying to be patient.

Dugald looked mildly outraged. "No one ever shoots at us."

"Until now," said Gavin.

"Aye," Angus agreed, nodding. "Until now."

"Perhaps we should show MacFane the inside of the castle," suggested Ariella.

Malcolm followed as they moved toward the entrance, where a pretty honey-haired girl was waiting.

"Elizabeth, this is MacFane and his chief warrior, Gavin," said Gordon. "This is Elizabeth, my daughter."

"Welcome, milords," she murmured, curtsying. She glanced nervously at Malcolm, then Gavin. He smiled and she shyly lowered her lashes.

The group advanced into the great hall, an enormous room of gray stone with two massive, elaborately carved hearths at opposite ends. Four large arched windows flooded the space with light. A minstrel's gallery built of alternating dark and pale wood spanned one end, where a man on a ladder was carefully repairing a damaged section. At the center of the room stood the laird's table, set upon a scarlet-draped dais, with a dozen or so side tables arranged around it. Lengths of fabric lay in colorful heaps upon these tables as a group of women sat busily cutting and sewing. Others tended spinning wheels in the corners, while a little group positioned near the windows worked on intricate tapestries. The floor was covered with rushes and sweet-scented herbs, which mingled with the fragrance of roasting meat emanating from the kitchen beyond the room. The hall was not nearly as large as his own had been, Malcolm reflected, but it was far brighter and more pleasing.

"What are all these women sewing?" he asked, wondering at their industry.

"They are working to replace the banners and tapestries stolen during the attack," explained Niall. "They had hoped to have them ready in time for your arrival with your great army."

His tone was openly scornful. Malcolm chose to ignore it. It was clear this man resented his presence. Perhaps, like Rob, he believed Malcolm should have prevented the assault on his clan.

They continued their tour, which included the kitchen, the storerooms on the lower level, and the chambers above. Everywhere they went, members of the clan were weaving, painting, carving, and repairing, trying to restore the castle to its former condition. Overall, Malcolm's view of the building was heavily critical. It had not been constructed as a fortress, but as a home of beauty and light, with great attention to aesthetic detail and virtually none to defense. He grew increasingly exasperated when he made suggestions to improve its defense, only to be told that iron grilles on the windows would restrict the light, or the addition of archers' slits in the towers would let in a draft. Yet he could not help but admire the uncommon skill and artistry of these people. In every room intricate stonework framed the windows, fireplaces, and doorways, and elegantly carved panels of sweet-smelling wood covered the ceilings, lending warmth and beauty to each chamber.

"Where does that passage lead to?" he asked, pointing to an arched doorway with a heavy rope strung across it.

"That is the staircase to the south tower," replied Gordon. "It is roped off because we are still rebuilding it."

Malcolm frowned. "This tower is not a point of entry," he observed. "If your attackers just came through the front gate as you say, why did they set fire to this tower?"

The MacKendricks regarded each other uncertainly.

"Was there something in that tower they wanted to destroy?"

No one answered him.

"If I am to help you, I need to know what happened in this attack," he persisted, exasperated. "Why did the warriors burn what they were trying to capture?"

It was Rob who finally spoke. "The tower housed the room of MacKendrick's daughter," he explained. "If the warriors' leader forced her to marry him, the clan would have had no choice but to accept him as chief, because she would have provided the bloodline to our ancient chief. That would have established his son as the next blood heir."

"What you are telling me makes no sense," Malcolm argued, shaking his head. "Why would this man burn the tower if he needed this girl for his bride?"

"He didn't burn the tower," said Niall. "After mortally wounding our laird and killing many, he locked Ariella in it. He then swore to slaughter her clansmen one by one until she agreed to marry him. Ariella elected to burn to death rather than expose her people to his brutality."

Malcolm stared at the elders. "She killed herself?"

The council members looked away, clearly finding the subject too painful to discuss.

"I have seen enough," said Malcolm, appalled by this unexpected revelation. "I would rest awhile."

They led him down the corridor to an enormous chamber. A large, handsomely carved bed gleamed with the luster of fresh oil and was made up in a soft plaid of crimson and gold. The room also featured a fine table and two chairs set by the hearth, a chest, a stone sink, which was built into the wall and drained to the outside, and a doorway leading to a garderobe. Unlike the rest of the castle, the walls of this chamber were covered with glorious tapestries, each depicting a tale of one of the Black Wolf's feats. Malcolm went to the window and gazed uneasily at the valley and woods below.

He knew he was not worthy of these accommodations.

Anger flooded through Ariella as she studied the new furnishings in her father's chamber. Her clan had painstakingly prepared it for the man they assumed would be their laird. But MacFane was not that man. He was the man who had failed to come when he had been desperately needed. Now he was here as a hired warrior, nothing more. He did not deserve the honor of staying in this room. She glanced at Niall. The hostile set of his jaw told her he was thinking the same thing.

"This was MacKendrick's room," she began, struggling to keep her voice even. "I do not think—"

"He will stay here."

Alpin stood in the doorway watching her, his withered face calm yet resolute.

"Very well," she said tautly. She tossed MacFane a disapproving look, silently letting him know he had no right to this chamber. Then she left, unable to bear seeing him in it a moment longer.

"You must forgive the lad," said Angus. "He was very fond of MacKendrick."

Malcolm nodded.

Dugald gestured to the fragile stick of a man who had entered the room. He was garbed in a voluminous robe of sapphire trimmed with gold, and he leaned heavily upon a tall staff. "This is Alpin. He is our seer."

Malcolm lifted a skeptical brow at the white-haired apparition, wondering what fantasies he had told these people to make them believe such nonsense.

Alpin chuckled. "MacFane does not believe in seers," he informed them. "But you do believe in the power of fate, don't you, milord?"

His black eyes sparkled knowingly against the folds of his chalky flesh, indicating an active mind lived within that extraordinarily aged body.

"There are things that happen which are beyond our control," said Malcolm. "If some wish to call that fate, so be it."

"But there are also things that happen because we allow them to, aren't there, MacFane?" Alpin demanded. "Things that are within our control?"

"Of course. Much of a man's actions determines his future."

Alpin's sparkling eyes narrowed. "Or chains him to the past." He waved his hand and chuckled again, breaking the stillness of the moment. "How do you like your room, MacFane? Is that desk large enough to accommodate your unusual size?"

Malcolm cast an uninterested glance at the desk. "I am sure it is more than—"

He frowned.

Upon the desk sat a statue, which he did not recall

having seen earlier. It was the head of a young woman, reverently sculpted in luminous gray rock. Her features were delicate, almost childlike, yet Malcolm knew she was no child. Her eyes were large, her cheeks high, her nose small and straight. Her lips were soft, even in stone, and her chin was thrust slightly forward, a pose of defiance, or perhaps playfulness, suggesting she had found the task of sitting for the sculptor rather silly. He felt a strange, instant affinity toward her, as if she were an old friend, yet Malcolm knew he could not possibly know her. Long curls were etched around her face and over her shoulders. He found himself contemplating her hair's color and weight, and wondering what it would be like to plunge his hand into that silky mass, were it not stone.

"Who is this?" he demanded.

"That is Ariella," Alpin replied quietly. "MacKendrick's daughter."

"Our laird had that statue sculpted just over a year ago," said Gordon. "It was one of his favorite possessions." His brow furrowed in confusion. "I thought it was stolen during the attack," he remarked, looking pointedly at Alpin.

Ariella. The girl he was supposed to marry. The girl who had expected him to come with his great army, certain he would rescue her and her clan from their brutal assault. How long had she waited for him, Malcolm wondered, before setting her room afire? Five minutes? Ten? How long had she stood at her window and desperately searched the horizon for some sign of the Black Wolf? An hour? No, not an hour, he realized grimly. The attackers' leader had murdered her father and threatened to slaughter her clansmen one by one until she submitted to him. This woman before him would not have waited an hour to kill herself.

She would have done it immediately, praying her death might spare just one life.

He had thought himself steeled to the torment of

guilt. He had endured so much of it for so long, he had believed nothing could make him suffer more when it came to his failings. But as he stared at this beautiful girl who had burned to death for her clan, a surge of self-loathing engulfed him, robbing him of his ability to speak. Even worse was the knowledge that there was nothing he could have done to prevent it. If he had arrived before the raid to accept their offer, the MacKendricks would have simply laughed and turned him away.

Just as they were tempted to do today.

Everyone was watching him, wondering at his thoughts. It was clear they did not believe there was anything he could do for them. They had expected a powerful warrior and an army. Instead, all they had gotten was him. He knew he could not turn this gentle clan of poets and jugglers into an army. But at the very least he could improve their fortifications. No one would ever find this holding so easy to attack again. He owed MacKendrick and his daughter that much, at least.

"Come," he said suddenly, ignoring the throbbing in his back and leg as he limped to the door. "I wish to make a tour of the outer wall."

Yellow light flickered from the smoky torches, casting a glow over the revelers. The entire clan was invited to dine in the great hall that night, and to share in the food and drink that had been prepared for the Black Wolf's army. The men arrived in their finest shirts and plaids, the women in their best gowns, and despite their disappointment in the warrior Ariella had returned with, the mood was generally merry. It was as if her people had long needed a reason to celebrate, and although this was not the great moment they had foreseen, they were anxious to take advantage of it. Musicians played bagpipes and harp from the gallery above, while jugglers, tumblers, and dancers wandered through the hall. MacFane sat at the laird's table, as befitted an honored guest, with Gavin, the council members, Niall, Alpin, and Rob. Before MacFane had entered the hall, Ariella had vehemently protested this seating arrangement. It had pained her to see him standing in her father's newly furnished chamber, as if he had a right to be there. She had no desire to sit with him tonight, and had asked to be moved to another table. Alpin had refused, leaving her no choice.

"Don't you ever wash?" MacFane demanded when he came to the table.

"If you don't like it, sit somewhere else," she returned sourly.

Angus, Dugald, and Gordon looked up from their trenchers in shock, unaccustomed to hearing her speak so rudely.

"Rob has long been a stranger to soap and water," declared Alpin cheerfully. "We expect he will outgrow his aversion in time."

Ariella sullenly lowered her gaze to her food. It was because of MacFane that she had to look this way. If she cleaned herself even a little, he might notice that her features were more feminine than boyish. She could not risk an outsider discovering she had not died in the fire. She told herself she didn't care about her appearance. Even so, she felt strangely out of place as she sat amidst her clan, who were all freshly scrubbed and dressed in their finest.

MacFane had brought paper, a quill, and ink to the table with him, and during the meal he rudely ignored everyone and made notes. Angus, Dugald, and Gordon were confounded by his conduct, which was clearly unbecoming of an honored guest. Several times they tried to draw him into conversation, only to be answered with a preoccupied grunt, until finally they gave up. Gavin, however, was eager to entertain them with tales of his adventures with MacFane. Each story grew more incredible than the last, until Ariella found herself irritably wondering if any of the accounts were true. A few times Malcolm raised his head and scowled, but Gavin continued, blithely unconcerned with the fact that he was annoying his friend.

Before the meal was finished, Malcolm put down his quill and rose from the table. A hush descended over the hall.

"Tomorrow we will begin to train and work on fortifying this castle," he announced. "The men will be divided into groups so some can work while others are training. There will be four training sessions each day, and all the men will train for at least one session."

"What about the women?"

Malcolm looked at Rob in confusion. "What about them?"

"The women should also train," the boy said. "They need to know how to defend themselves if they are attacked."

"Absolutely not," stated Malcolm flatly. "I will not have women participating in warfare."

"It is our homes that are attacked as much as the men's," argued Helen. "We need to know how to help."

"You're talking foolishness, wife," said Gordon. "A woman cannot fight a man. Be quiet and let MacFane continue."

"It is not foolishness," protested Rob. "While we were traveling home, MacFane spent time each day training me to fight. Because I am small, he showed me methods that do not require great strength."

"Teaching a rough, angry young lad and a delicate, gentle woman are two entirely different things," pointed out Malcolm. "I would never expect a lady to attack a man in the manner I showed you. It is out of the question. Now, then, tomorrow morning the men will be divided—"

"If Rob could do it, I can do it," announced Elizabeth, standing so she could be seen.

"Elizabeth MacKendrick, I order you to take your seat and stop shaming me before this clan," thundered Gordon.

"No, Father," she returned, shaking her head. "You taught me to argue for what I believe in. Well, I believe I must help fight if we are attacked again."

"And so do I," stated a pretty red-haired girl, who also rose from her table.

"Sit down, Meagan!" ordered an astounded father with matching hair. The girl paled considerably but remained standing.

"And I," called another woman.

"And I."

"And I."

Malcolm gazed around the hall in astonishment as every woman, including those with gray hair and creased faces, rose and added her voice. He had never known of women eager to fight. Perhaps, he reflected, he was being too hasty in dismissing the idea. The MacKendrick men numbered less than 150, and that included elders like Angus and Dugald, who were far too old to wield a sword. Their paltry number virtually condemned them to defeat if they were attacked by even a modest army. By adding the women to this force, the MacKendricks just might be able to tip the balance of an assault in their favor.

"You don't have to teach them everything you taught me," Rob pointed out. "But they have a right to learn some way of defending themselves. And since women could make just as fine archers as men, they should be trained in the use of a bow and arrow. That would leave more men on the ground to fight with swords."

Reluctantly, he contemplated the logic of the lad's argument. The idea of women participating in warfare did not appeal to him. But Malcolm was acutely aware of the particularly vile atrocities routinely inflicted on them during an attack. The women of his own clan had had no knowledge of how to protect themselves on the day he had left them so unforgivably vulnerable.

Rob was right, he realized, stifling the memory. These women had a right to know how to fight back.

"Very well," he relented. "Any woman above the age of fifteen who wishes to be trained in defense will participate in a separate training session, to be led by Gavin. Is that satisfactory to you?" he demanded, looking at Elizabeth.

A rosy stain colored her cheeks. "Yes," she replied, suddenly sounding shy and uncertain. She lowered her gaze and took her seat, baffling him with her change in manner.

"While one group is training, the others will work on strengthening the castle," continued Malcolm, referring to his notes. "First, the parapet is to be raised to a height of six feet six inches—"

"That will block the view!" burst out Dugald, clearly horrified.

"Six feet six inches," repeated Malcolm firmly, "with regular merlons and crenelles every three feet. That will allow the archers a shield as they reload their weapons. A new iron portcullis is to be forged, which will be raised and lowered by well-oiled chains. When lowered, it will be secured by two heavy iron bars that slide deep into the stone wall on either side. In addition, a thick oak door is to be built in front of the portcullis, which will also be secured by two heavy iron bars."

"That's a waste of time and wood," stated Niall scornfully. "If we have a portcullis, we hardly need a wooden gate as well."

"Neither gate is impenetrable," explained Malcolm, trying to ignore the contempt in the young man's tone. "But keeping an attacking army stalled at the gates will give you time to prepare yourselves as you shower arrows, rocks, boiling water, and boiling oil on their heads."

"Did he say boiling oil?" asked Angus, frowning as he cupped his hand to his ear.

"You will transform no fewer than four of the windows in each tower into narrow slits, from which archers can shoot their weapons," continued Malcolm. "A room will be created behind the slit, large enough for two men, with ample area to store a supply of arrows."

"There are already bedchambers in the towers," protested Dugald. "There is no room for these archer chambers you speak of."

"Your towers should be for defense, not bedchambers," Malcolm informed him. "If you wish to continue sleeping there, you must learn to live in a smaller area."

Dugald looked at Angus in astonishment. "He's turning our chambers into storage room for weapons."

"The base of your curtain wall is perpendicular to the ground, which means during a siege an attacking army can easily hack an opening through the stone, or burrow underneath it," Malcolm continued. "You will extend the base so it slopes out an additional three feet. This will place the sappers farther from the wall as they work, making them more exposed to the heavy stones you will drop on them from the battlements."

"Did you hear what he said?" demanded a thickly bearded man from a nearby table. "He's saying we should crush a man like a bug with a rock."

"I have other plans for the fortification of your castle, but they can wait," finished Malcolm, curling his notes into a scroll. "For now, you will concentrate on the gate, the curtain wall, and the towers. Those who are not working on these improvements will either train or produce weapons. You need an ample stock of bows, arrows, swords, axes, dirks, spears, and shields. Large quantities of food must also be preserved, to be stored in case of siege. Many a fortress has remained impenetrable to all but the weapon of starvation."

The clan was staring at him blankly, overwhelmed.

"You will assemble in the courtyard at first light, so I can separate you into groups and organize your work and training. Bring your weapons, and whatever armor you may have. Until then I suggest you get some sleep. Tomorrow will be a long day."

He bent down and whispered his need for wine in Gavin's ear. Then he began to walk toward the staircase. He tried to exit the hall with the same power and confidence he had demonstrated during his speech, but the pain in his leg defeated his attempt to control his limp. Aware of everyone's eyes upon him, he crossed the room with slow, stiff dignity, wondering if it was pity or contempt that rendered his audience silent.

The corridor outside MacFane's chamber was empty when Ariella knocked against the massive oak door.

"Enter."

He rose from his chair as the door swung open, effecting an ease of movement she had not witnessed before. On seeing it was only Rob, he grunted and collapsed back into his seat, abandoning his pretense. He raised the jug on the desk and took a deep swig, oblivious to the wine that dripped onto the fine fabric of his shirt. Then he regarded her with weary indifference, his lids heavy over the dullness of his eyes. Gone was the experienced commander who had stood tall before her clan, outlining in precise detail what must be done to make their castle secure. Here again was the pain-racked, alcohol-dependent cripple. Ariella berated herself for falling victim to the illusion he had fleetingly created. How many others had believed in him for that brief moment, before he had reminded them of his decrepitude by limping across the hall?

"What the hell do you want?" he snapped.

She crossed her arms over her chest and leaned casually against the door. "You shouldn't drink so much while you're here, MacFane. If my clan sees you drunk, they won't respect you."

He shrugged. "They don't respect me now," he observed darkly.

"They are judging you by the tales of your past." She glanced at the tapestry hanging on the wall behind his bed. It showed the Black Wolf leading a small band against an army of Munro warriors, who were savagely attacking a village. Gavin had recounted this tale at dinner, unaware her people already knew it well. Her gaze moved back to the self-pitying drunk seated in the chair. "If you want their respect, show them you deserve it."

He took another swallow of wine and stared moodily into the flame of the candle burning on the desk. "I don't give a damn whether they respect me or not."

"You can't train men who don't respect you."

His expression grew incredulous. "Do you actually believe I can make warriors out of these musicians and jugglers and poets?" He laughed, a harsh, ugly sound. "Your people are like children. They have no comprehension of what it takes to fight an invading army. They are consumed with worries of blocking the view, and losing room to an archer, and how nasty it will be for their enemy to be hit by a falling rock." He leaned back in his chair and closed his eyes, the jug of wine cradled on his lap. "The next time you are attacked, surrender immediately and be done with it. At least that way no one will get hurt."

She moved to stand in front of him, her hands clenched into fists. "You're wrong, MacFane," she said coldly. "Just because we are skilled at music and carving doesn't mean we can't learn to apply those skills to defense. And the fact that we take pleasure in a magnificent sky, or feel compassion for another person, doesn't make us weak. It makes us whole and strong. But of course," she finished, her voice dripping scorn, "being so obsessed with yourself, how could you possibly understand?"

The insult forced his heavy lids open. Rob's gray eyes were burning with a fury that Malcolm found disconcerting in a mere lad of thirteen.

"You have been hired to teach us to defend ourselves, and you're being well paid for your trouble," the boy continued fiercely. "Since you ordered everyone to assemble at first light, I suggest you quit drinking and get some sleep. In the morning I will wake you."

"I can bloody well wake myself," Malcolm snapped.

"Not at dawn you can't," Rob scoffed.

The door slammed shut before Malcolm could further argue. His mind clouded with alcohol, he took another drink, dismissing the insolent lad. His eyes fell upon the tapestry hanging above his bed. The Black Wolf was defeating an army of fifty warriors with only ten men. He stared at it in sudden fascination, wondering if he had ever really performed such an incredible feat. He could not remember. Depressed by his inability to recall it, he pulled himself out of the chair and doused the candles, veiling the tapestry in darkness.

Then he collapsed against the bed and finished his wine, bitterly wondering if all the stories about him were so exaggerated, none of them were true anymore.

CHAPTER 4

Her fist pounded against the dark panel several times. Finally she jerked up the latch and threw the heavy door open, prepared to drag MacFane from his bed if necessary.

He was not there.

Frowning, Ariella moved along the corridor. Muffled yawns and the splashing of water filtered from behind each door she passed. Downstairs she found Duncan and Andrew grabbing a chunk of bread from a table as they hurried outside. She followed them into the smoky light of early morning, where the rest of her clan were yawning and adjusting their clothes as they sleepily gathered before MacFane.

He sat high atop his powerful black charger, calmly watching the MacKendricks slowly appear. Once again he was dressed in his neatly arranged plaid, oiled-leather jerkin, and saffron shirt, which bore no trace of the wine he had carelessly spilled on it the previous night. His chiseled face was freshly shaven, his dark hair combed, his bearing utterly awake and sober. If anything, he appeared far more alert than her people, who were unaccustomed to assembling at this early hour and were obviously feeling the effects of last night's merriment. Ariella studied him in confusion, unable to comprehend how he had managed to rise and prepare himself so early when he had been so sodden with alcohol the night before. MacFane had always been the final one to rise during their journey home. Gavin rode over to him, and the answer was suddenly clear. MacFane had not risen unassisted. His friend had roused him early, so the proud Black Wolf would not further humiliate himself in front of her clan.

"He is a fine-looking man, is he not?"

Ariella regarded Elizabeth in surprise. "I wouldn't have thought you would be attracted to one so harsh looking."

"I don't find him harsh at all," Elizabeth countered, her eyes dreamy. "I think he has a kind, gentle face—especially when he smiles."

Ariella returned her attention to Malcolm, bewildered. His expression was calm, but even in calmness his features remained hard and heavily creased. It was the face of a man who found no pleasure in life, and it bore no trace of gentleness. "You have seen him smile?"

"Of course," Elizabeth assured her. "He smiled when we were introduced, and my heart very nearly stood still. Then he smiled often during the meal last night, and each time I felt as if I couldn't draw another breath." She raised her hand to her throat and sighed.

"You are imagining things, Elizabeth," Ariella told

her, shaking her head. "I traveled with the man for three long days, and I promise you, MacFane never smiles."

Startled laughter bubbled from Elizabeth's throat. "I don't mean MacFane. I'm sure that man never smiles, especially since those horrible injuries destroyed his body. I am speaking of his chief warrior, Gavin."

A stab of irritation pierced Ariella at hearing Mac-Fane described so. She quickly suppressed it, wondering why it should bother her when she had thought the same thing many times. She focused her attention on Gavin, who was speaking to MacFane as people continued to stream through the gate. He was pleasant enough to look at, she supposed. He had good, even features, straight teeth, and thick black hair that was lightly threaded with gray. There was certainly nothing unattractive about him. And he did smile often. But fine?

"He is far too old for you, Elizabeth," she observed. "He is well past forty years, and you have only reached twenty-two. Besides, when MacFane leaves, he will go with him. You must be careful to guard your heart."

"My heart has been guarded far too long," Elizabeth murmured. "And no MacKendrick has managed to capture it." A faint smile curved her lips as she continued to watch Gavin.

Ariella contemplated her pretty friend in silence. Because the MacKendricks kept themselves isolated, the young women and men found their mates within the clan. When she was a little girl, Ariella had wondered which of the boys she played with would ultimately become her husband. But after her mother died without giving birth to a son, Ariella had learned she had an enormous obligation to her clan in the selection of her husband. Quiet and headstrong as a boy, Niall had grown into a tall, handsome, rather serious young man, and Ariella knew his fondness for her was deep. The moment she realized his feelings were evolving into more than friendship, Ariella had gone to Alpin and asked if Niall was the next bearer of the sword. Alpin informed her the next MacKendrick would not be found within the clan. Although they remained good friends, no other woman had since captured his eye, and Ariella knew Niall was not anxious for her to find a husband, even though it was her duty to do so. The day she found Roderic wounded in the woods and brought him back to the castle, Niall had instantly sensed her attraction to him. After a brief meeting with Roderic, he had taken Ariella aside and told her this comely stranger was not to be trusted.

Ariella had foolishly dismissed his advice as jealousy.

"Men move to the west side of the courtyard, women to the east," ordered Malcolm.

The bleary-eyed MacKendricks slowly complied, unaccustomed to moving sharply at this ungodly hour of the morning.

As was he.

"Now, both sides divide into four equal groups. The first three groups of men are assigned to the duties of constructing the new gates, building the parapet, and making weapons. The first three groups of women will prepare food for storage, make bows and arrows, and attend to household duties, including the preparation of the day's meals and watching over the children. The rest of you will remain here for the first session of training."

If any of them questioned his orders, they did not use this moment to debate it. Nevertheless, their expressions were sullen as they dispersed to carry out his bidding.

"Those of you who have brought bows and arrows, give them to the women," Malcolm continued. "They will begin their training by practicing archery outside the curtain wall with Gavin."

Once they were armed with their new weapons, the women proceeded to file out the gate. Rob casually slung his bow over his shoulder and began to follow them.

"Where do you think you're going?" demanded Malcolm.

"I'm going to assist Gavin instructing the women," Rob told him.

"Gavin is quite capable of handling the women on his own. You will train with the men."

"He can't train with us," protested Niall, looking outraged. "He is just a lad."

"He will train with the men," repeated Malcolm firmly.

Rob hesitated, then reluctantly moved to join the rest of the men.

"Now then," began Malcolm, "the first thing I want to do—"

"Don't start!" shouted Angus as he emerged from the castle, dragging an old sword. "We're coming!"

A puffing Dugald followed slowly behind him, wielding his rusted sword only marginally better than Angus. Finally Alpin appeared, garbed in a magnificent emerald robe, bearing no weapon other than his staff. Angus and Dugald took their place in front of the men and immediately began to quibble over who carried the heavier sword. Alpin waved cheerfully at Malcolm, then moved to the side to watch.

Malcolm stared at the snowy-haired elders in disbelief. "What on earth are you doing?"

Angus and Dugald looked up in surprise.

"We're here to train, lad," Angus informed him, as if the answer were obvious.

"To be warriors," clarified Dugald, lest Malcolm think they were training for something else.

His pale, brown-spotted arms straining with effort, Angus raised his ancient weapon for Malcolm to see. "I brought my father's sword, lad," he announced proudly. "Over one hundred years old, and it's never been used."

"Mine is heavier," boasted Dugald. He grunted as

he attempted to lift the weapon, his bent frame quivering. Unable to raise it past his waist, he gave up, allowing the dull tip to fall heavily to the ground. "They were making swords far better sixty years ago than they were before."

"You don't know that," Angus retorted, "since you've never had cause to use it."

"I have cause now, and any fool can see it's a heavier sword," declared Dugald testily. "Just ask MacFane."

The two men looked at him, expecting him to resolve the matter.

Malcolm stared back at them in bewilderment. The two old men regarded him with utter gravity, forcing him to accept the fact that they were serious about training with the others.

"Your desire to train pleases me," he began, swiftly searching for a way to exclude them without injuring their feelings. "It inspires the determination of every man here who thinks he cannot learn to fight because of his size, or strength, or fear." He was careful to avoid the mention of age. "However, you would honor me far more, Angus and Dugald, if you would join me at the side and help direct the training. I am certain we can all benefit from your many years of experience, and the wisdom that comes with it."

A beam of pleasure lit Angus's wrinkled face. "Of course, lad. Excuse me, Dugald, but the Black Wolf needs my help." He shuffled forward, carelessly dragging his father's sword behind him.

"I can help the lad just as well as you," huffed Dugald, whose weapon was instantly relegated to a crutch.

"Let's stand up on the platform, so we have a good view," suggested Angus.

"You know I can't stand for long," Dugald reminded him. "It makes my ankles swell."

"Someone bring them chairs," ordered Malcolm, trying to remain patient.

Three chairs were quickly procured. When Angus, Dugald, and Alpin were finally settled on the platform, Malcolm returned his attention to the group of would-be warriors before him.

They were of every size and shape imaginable, ranging in years from twelve to sixty. As instructed, the MacKendricks had rooted through their cupboards and chests for any weapon they could find. The result was not auspicious: rusted, pitted swords that had probably been wielded by their great-grandfathers, axes blunted by years of chopping wood, dirks with blackened blades well used in the skinning of animals and carving of furniture. A few particularly industrious men had created colorful shields from twig frames covered with brilliant, if useless, swatches of fabric. Others wore assorted buckets and bowls on their heads, which kept slipping down and covering their eyes. The entire assemblage was so thoroughly ridiculous, Malcolm had to lower his gaze and cough, suddenly fearing he might actually laugh.

"To begin, we will train without armor or weapons," he announced, deciding that was a way around the problem. "Put them aside, and divide into two lines, facing each other from a distance of ten paces."

Disappointment washed over their faces, followed by some grumbling. Evidently they believed they were ready for swordplay. Malcolm did not know whether to be encouraged by their enthusiasm, or appalled by their naïveté.

"When I give the command, I want you to charge each other and bring your opponent to the ground." He paused, making sure they were ready. "Attack!"

The two lines of MacKendricks charged.

In the crash that followed most of them simply bounced off each other and dropped to the ground.

Others fell and, in a surge of profound irritation, grabbed their opponent's ankles and brought him down as well. This led to much rolling and scrabbling in the dirt, and a few cross words. One man repeatedly shouted he was winded, and had to be carried away. Another claimed to have hurt his shoulder in the fall and was instantly surrounded by a sympathetic group of onlookers, each offering to rub it for him.

"Can't see how that taught them anything, lad," commented Angus, shaking his head. "I say let them take up their weapons and really go at it."

"Don't tempt me," muttered Malcolm.

"What's that?" asked Dugald, cupping his hand to his ear.

"I said not just yet." Malcolm returned his gaze to his men, who were pulling themselves up and meticulously dusting off their shirts and plaids.

"Separate yourselves and try again," he ordered. "And remember, your partner is your enemy. When you attack, be determined it is you who will emerge the victor."

The two lines charged once more, only this time with far more aggression. The results were impressive. Over a dozen men lay upon the ground, groaning, while their partners inundated them with apologies and asked how badly they were hurt. Two men hobbled swiftly away, neither seriously injured, but clearly unwilling to continue. The rest were absorbed with examining a bevy of minor scrapes and scratches, and in one case a badly torn sleeve.

"A terrible thing for that to happen," commented Dugald, clicking his tongue sympathetically. "That was Kenneth's best shirt."

"Glynis will fix it for him," Angus assured him. "The woman is wonderful with a needle."

"You will try again," said Malcolm, struggling for patience, "only this time—"

A barrage of arrows suddenly flew over the outer wall, cutting short his directive. The astonished Mac-Kendricks turned and ran, yelping as the shafts rained down on them. Unfortunately, Gordon did not move fast enough and was hit in the backside. Another arrow skewered the earth scant inches from the front hoof of Malcolm's horse, causing the animal to toss his head and dance backward.

"What the hell is going on?" roared Malcolm, laying a calming hand upon Cain's neck.

The shower of arrows stopped.

After a moment a sheepish-looking Gavin appeared through the gate.

"Sorry about that. The women kept shooting too low and missing the targets. I told them to aim higher than they thought they needed to." He shrugged his shoulders. "And they did."

"Well, now, you can't blame them for that, lad," said Angus.

Dugald nodded in agreement. "After all, they were only doing as they were told."

"It seems they take instruction very well," remarked Alpin brightly.

"You're right," said Angus, suddenly elated. "Who would have thought the lassies would shoot so high on their very first lesson?"

His jaw clenched, Malcolm watched as Gordon was slowly helped off the field. There were now four men gone, and they had been training for only ten minutes.

At this rate the entire clan would be incapacitated by the end of the day.

"I say we don't need him," announced Niall flatly. "What did we learn today, except that endlessly lifting and thrusting a weapon makes your arm throb?"

"I learned that women are better suited to a needle

than to a bow," grumbled Gordon, shifting painfully on his cushion.

"We were doing much better by the end of our session, Father," pointed out Elizabeth defensively. "Once the targets were moved away from the castle wall."

"He is trying to make archers of women, while he has us hacking and thrusting at empty air," continued Niall, his tone thick with scorn. "Now every one of you is aching and weary, and what do we have to show for it? Does any man here feel better prepared to face an attacker?"

"I'm too tired to face anything but my bed," grumbled Ramsay.

"My arms are as weak as a babe's. If someone came through that door right now, I doubt I'd be able to lift my sword," said Graham.

"A sore arm?" scoffed Hugh. "That's nothing. You should see the scrape on my thigh." He began to raise his plaid. "I'd wager it's longer than—"

"You call that wee scratch a scrape? I've a cut on my shoulder as wide as a loch," declared Bryce, loosening his shirt.

"A cut? Why I've a broken rib, I'm sure of it, and you don't hear me crying about it," boasted Ramsay.

"You were crying hard enough when I ran into you," pointed out Graham. "I thought I was going to have to fetch your mother."

"This training is a waste of time," continued Niall, trying to recapture their attention. "We are deluding ourselves if we think MacFane can turn us into warriors."

"It's not our business to fight," agreed Gordon irritably. "We should leave it to others."

"Exactly," agreed Niall. "So what is MacFane doing here? One only has to look at him to know he is not the next laird—"

"He's not, is he, Alpin?" demanded Bryce, sounding horrified by the possibility.

All eyes turned to Alpin, who was seated at the laird's

table. A hush descended over the hall as they anxiously awaited his response.

Alpin rose from his chair and calmly regarded the clan, his black eyes sharp and knowing. "If I showed you a single, tiny seed, and told you that within its fragile walls lay endless shade in the summer, bushels of fruit in the autumn, and ample wood to furnish your homes and warm you in the winter, would you believe me?"

The silent clan stared at him, awestruck, contemplating the wisdom of his words.

Alpin nodded with satisfaction and slowly left the hall, his scarlet robes dusting the floor behind him.

The moment he was gone, the clan erupted in a baffled cacophony of questions.

"What did he say?" demanded Angus.

Dugald shook his head, bewildered. "Something about seeds."

"I think he means we need to collect more seeds to replant what we felled last autumn," suggested Graham.

"Seems an odd time to be concerned about seeds," mused Angus. "I thought we were talking about the Black Wolf."

Dugald leaned into his friend and whispered loudly, "He's not the same as he used to be, you know. Getting older. I've noticed quite a difference since he turned one hundred and forty."

"The Black Wolf was supposed to come with his great army," declared Niall, trying to regain his audience's attention. "Instead he arrives alone, weak, and pathetically unfit for the role of laird. Because of him, MacKendrick and many others were slain, including poor Guy and Marcus, who were finally buried just today. Why are we dishonoring their memory by wasting our time with this man?"

"Even Ariella realizes he's not the one, or she would have given him the sword," pointed out Agnes hesitantly.

"Why did she bring him, then?" wondered Helen.

Duncan rose from his chair and solemnly regarded the clan. "She brought him because she believed he could be of help," he explained. "And although he is scarred, MacFane is not as weak as you seem to think."

"That's true," agreed Andrew. "On our journey home we were—"

"If he's not the one," interrupted Niall, "then we should be spending our time trying to find the right laird, not performing foolish antics in the courtyard. We need a chief who leads a strong army that can defend us. And if we must train, let us find someone who is not so crippled with injuries, he can barely limp across the hall without eliciting pity."

"Then don't pity him."

All eyes turned to Ariella as she descended the staircase. She swept her gaze disapprovingly over her clan before fastening her attention on Niall.

"I realize you mean well, Niall, with your attempt to incite the clan to reject MacFane," she began, her voice reproachful. "But as I made clear yesterday, I have not brought him here to assume the position of laird. I have brought him here because I believe he can train us to better defend ourselves."

"How is he training us by having us knock each other down and stab at empty air?" demanded Niall.

"You don't see him running and jumping and fighting air," added Ramsay. "How can he teach us to do things he can't even do himself?"

"MacFane has fought countless great battles and never lost one," stated Ariella boldly. She had no idea whether that was true, but the amazed faces surrounding her told her she had captured their attention. "He has trained thousands of men," she exaggerated, "turning the simplest of farmers into the finest warriors in all Scotland. These things more than qualify him to be our teacher." She paused, allowing her remarks to penetrate their disgruntlement.

"Yes, his once perfect body has been weakened by the terrible toll of fighting many successful battles," she admitted. "But do not think for a moment MacFane is in any way helpless. On our journey home Andrew, Duncan, and I were attacked by eight savage thieves. At the very moment we were to be brutally slaughtered, Mac-Fane burst from the darkness on his magnificent horse. He expertly killed all eight of the murderers before any of us could so much as lift a sword to come to his aid." She paused again, giving her people time to imagine the highly exaggerated but glorious scene she had described.

"So, you see, even with his scars, even with his body racked with pain, with his injured arm and leg, the Black Wolf is still a great warrior. He could easily defeat five of you at the same time, with or without a sword. Given this extraordinary ability, I have no doubt he will be able to train us to defend ourselves, until we find the next rightful laird of our clan."

Her clan stared at her in spellbound silence, their eyes wide and grave. Ariella nodded with satisfaction. It was clear she had been exceptionally convincing.

"I am flattered by your faith in me."

She gasped and whirled about.

MacFane stood tall on the steps behind her. Anger chiseled the lines of his face into deep grooves, and his eyes smoldered with fury. Whether it was directed at her or her clan, she could not be sure.

He jerked his gaze from her to address the others. "Training will resume at dawn," he announced harshly. "I suggest you get some rest. Tomorrow will be another long day."

He gave her a scathing look before turning and slowly mounting the steps, leaving Ariella no doubt he had heard far too much of their discussion.

"Go to bloody hell."

The knocking continued, loud and determined.

"I have retired for the evening," snarled Malcolm thickly. "Whatever it is, it can goddamn wait until morning."

The heavy door swung open. Rob eyed him warily from the corridor.

"Gavin already brought me a tray," Malcolm said, gesturing at the untouched food on the desk. He drained his cup and collapsed against the pillows propped behind his aching back. Suddenly he noticed a pitcher on the tray the boy carried. "Is that wine?"

"Water," replied Rob, placing his tray beside the other. He peered into the three empty jugs on the desk. "It seems you've had enough wine for the evening."

"I'll decide what's enough," Malcolm snapped. "Next time you feel sorry for me, bring wine or don't bother me. Is that clear?"

"I don't feel sorry for you, MacFane."

His expression, or what one could see of it beneath the layers of dirt streaking his face, was intense. Malcolm fixed a bleary stare on those cool gray eyes, determined to root out the pity he knew was buried beneath their depths. Rob folded his arms across his narrow chest and returned his scrutiny with utter indifference. He was telling the truth, Malcolm decided after a moment. The lad did not feel anything akin to pity for him. Contempt, certainly. But not pity. He grunted with satisfaction and closed his eyes.

Contempt was far easier to endure.

"You should have left me where I was," he growled, shifting uncomfortably on the bed. "As soon as you saw what I had become, you should have just left and let me be."

"I did leave you, MacFane. You came after us."

Malcolm frowned, trying to remember. "I came after you?"

"Actually, it was Gavin who was worried something

might happen to us," Rob qualified. "You just decided to go with him."

Malcolm considered this a moment. The memory swirled within his pounding brain, just eluding his grasp. It seemed logical, though. Finally he nodded. "I went after you because of Gavin." He closed his eyes again, satisfied that the matter was now clear. Then his brow creased and he lifted his lids once more. "But you convinced me to come here. You made me think it didn't matter about—this." He gestured in disgust at his battered body. "But it does matter. They look at me, and they know I am unfit. They watch me move, and their eyes are filled with pity." Anger flooded through him. He hurled his empty cup against the room. It did not shatter as he had hoped. The wooden vessel hit the wall and fell whole to the ground, making him feel even more impotent.

"You should have bloody well left me alone," he finished bitterly.

"So," drawled Rob, his voice steeped in scorn, "this is how the mighty Black Wolf rises to a challenge. Tell me, MacFane, did you always feel this sorry for yourself when you faced something you could not immediately overcome? It's a wonder you were able to forge such a magnificent reputation for yourself. Or did each legendary feat of the Black Wolf happen easily, with no effort on your part?"

"There were no legendary feats!" roared Malcolm, infuriated by the youth's insolence. "It's all lies! What once might have been truth is so buried beneath fantasy and exaggeration, even I can't goddamn well remember what really happened."

He paused, fighting to stifle the despair rising fast in his chest. Finally he murmured in a hollow voice, "Was the truth of my past so inconsequential, it had to be embellished until even I don't believe it anymore?"

"No," said Rob quietly, shaking his head. "It was not."

Malcolm considered this a moment, wanting to believe him. Then his eyes narrowed. "You say that, yet you did not tell the truth to your own clan."

"That was wrong," he admitted. "But if they are going to permit you to train them, they have to respect you. That is why I made it eight thieves, instead of four."

"Three," Malcolm corrected. "Gavin killed one." He snorted. "Hardly the tale of a great warrior." He flung his arm over his eyes.

"If you don't like that one, MacFane, and if your victories in battle do not count, then look at that tapestry above the bed," Rob suggested. "It shows you and a party of ten men coming upon a village under attack by nearly fifty Munros. The people of that village were not part of your clan. You were vastly outnumbered. Yet you and your warriors drove the Munros away with such ferocity, no one has dared harass that village since."

He paused, waiting for some kind of response. Malcolm lowered his arm but refused to look at the tapestry. The story was familiar, but the actual memory was veiled.

Was it really only ten men he had led that day?

"Then there was the night you came upon a burning house," continued Rob, gesturing to the tapestry hanging on the opposite wall. "Five children and their parents lay sleeping within. Do you remember that night, MacFane? They say the flames parted each time you went in, allowing you to carry the children into the night without the fire so much as scorching their nightshirts. Finally the building began to collapse. Yet you went back and fetched the last child, shielding him with your body as you carried him outside. The child emerged unscathed, but you suffered a bad burn to your hands."

Rob stood in front of the fabric rendition of the

scene, his fists on his small hips as he waited for Malcolm to confirm or deny the tale. Malcolm resisted the impulse to look at his hands, afraid the scars would not be there.

"Or perhaps you will recall the afternoon you were riding in the woods and found four men ravishing a helpless young girl," continued Rob. "You killed all four. When you later learned the girl's father beat her for shaming the family, you struck the father with your fist and took the girl back to your castle to live as a MacFane, under your protection. Do you remember?"

Malcolm stared wearily into the boy's gray eyes, which were burning with a haunting mixture of admiration and disgust. It was as if he had learned these tales too well and could not bear his disappointment in the man about whom they had been spun.

"No," he confessed, disgusted by his inability to recall his supposedly heroic past. "I don't."

Rob shook his head, whether in frustration or anger, Malcolm could not tell.

"Then there was the day you killed the boar as it charged those lads—"

"How do you know about that?" he demanded suddenly, startled. "I didn't reveal myself. Those boys never knew how close they were to death."

"Alpin told me. He saw it."

Malcolm snorted in disbelief.

"He saw it," Rob repeated adamantly. "Just as he saw you coming here."

"If he saw me coming here, then why are the MacKendricks so appalled by my condition?" Malcolm demanded dryly.

"He didn't see you coming like—this," Rob admitted. "Sometimes Alpin's visions are rather hazy."

"Convenient to have you think so when things don't turn out as he anticipates," observed Malcolm.

"It doesn't matter whether you believe in Alpin's

abilities or not," the boy retorted impatiently. "All that matters is your ability to train my clan to fight."

"After what I saw today, I don't believe anyone could train your clan to fight," Malcolm scoffed. "Not even the Black Wolf when he was at the height of his abilities."

"The MacKendricks do not have a penchant for fighting," Rob acknowledged. "But surely when you led your army, you did not always have the strongest and fittest men to train, did you?"

"They were not always strong and fit when they began, but at least none of the MacFanes was afraid of giving or receiving a few scratches."

Rob frowned as he considered this. "Then that is something you must overcome. How do you train men who are afraid of getting hurt, or of hurting each other?"

"You don't," snapped Malcolm. "You put them to work making weapons, or improving fortifications. Unless—"

He stopped. Perhaps there was a way around the MacKendricks' faintheartedness. He fought to clear the mists clouding his brain as he rose from the bed. At the desk he found a quill and paper, and he quickly began to make a sketch. When it was finished, he added a few instructions detailing its measurements and the materials to be used.

"Take this to Duncan and Andrew," he commanded. "Tell them to organize the construction of two of these tonight, in time for training tomorrow morning. Given the skill of your carpenters, I don't think it will take them more than a few hours. Maybe with these I will be able to incite some aggression in the MacKendricks tomorrow."

Rob reached out to take the sheet. Suddenly he paused, his expression unreadable.

"What's wrong?" demanded Malcolm impatiently.

"Nothing." The boy took the sketch and opened the

door. "I was just looking at your hands." The door closed.

Mystified, Malcolm raised his hands.

Faint, pearly scars stretched across them, where flames had forever seared the skin.

CHAPTER 5

Ariella sighed and buried her head deeper into her pillow, trying to escape the gray shadows seeping across her bed.

The steady crack of hammering pierced her slumber, forcing her eyes open. She rose from the bed and padded across the cool stone floor to the window, where she cautiously peeked at the courtyard below. Gavin, Duncan, and Andrew were directing a dozen men in the construction of two wooden structures, which she recognized from the sketch MacFane had drawn the night before. Curious to find out how he intended to use these scaffolds, she pulled her chemise over her head and tossed it onto the bed. Then she quickly dressed in Rob's grimy shirt, plaid, and well-worn boots, swallowing her revulsion as she rubbed her hair, face, hands, and calves with ashes from the hearth.

The door swung open. Ariella instantly cocked her head to one side and slumped her shoulders slightly, affecting the indifferent stance of a thirteen-year-old boy who needed to be told to stand up straight.

"Duncan won't let me play with the big dolls," complained Catherine petulantly. "I don't think he's being nice."

"What big dolls?" asked Ariella, abandoning her boyish demeanor.

"The big dolls he ordered Agnes, Elizabeth, and Meagan to sew last night," Catherine explained. "This morning I found them lying on tables in the hall. Elizabeth said they were finished. But they had forgotten to put faces on them, and they looked *so* sad. So I got some paint and drew nice faces on them, with big smiles. Then I realized they had no hair. Can you imagine?" she demanded, her little face incredulous. "So I painted that on them as well. I thought Isabel should have dark hair, like you, and Flora should have lovely blond hair, like Elizabeth. It came out very nice, but now that they had faces and hair, you could tell they were both *naked*. Downstairs in the hall, where just anybody could see them! They were too big for my clothes, so I fetched some of Agnes's things, knowing she wouldn't mind. And just as I was dressing Isabel in the prettiest purple chemise, Duncan came in and yelled what on earth did I think I was doing. Those were his very words. I told him it was mean to leave naked dolls lying in the hall, and he shouted that they weren't dolls, and I was not to touch them. Now, then," she finished, flouncing onto the bed, "what do you think of that?"

"I'll speak to him about it," Ariella promised, trying

her best not to laugh. She had an awful suspicion regarding the purpose of those "dolls." "But really, Catherine, you should know better than to touch things that do not belong to you."

"They were so sad, lying there with those plain white heads," protested Catherine. "They couldn't see."

"Even so," said Ariella, "they were not yours. How would you like it if someone came along and decided that Matilda needed to have her hair cut, or that it should be a different color?"

She hugged her little doll tight. "I wouldn't," she admitted.

"Well, it is the same with Duncan. He wanted those dolls made a certain way, and it was not up to you to decide they should be different. Do you understand?"

Her sister nodded glumly, obviously upset that Ariella had not taken her side.

"Good." Ariella sat down beside her and gave her a hug.

"How much longer do you have to dress like that?" demanded Catherine, wrinkling her nose.

"As long as MacFane is here," replied Ariella. "Until I find the next laird, no outsider can know I'm still alive, or word would spread and Roderic might return."

"I thought MacFane was to be our new laird."

"I thought so too. But he is not suitable." She ruffled her fingers through her sister's hair. "Now, I'm going to take you to the kitchen to help Agnes. And tonight we will finish the story about the kelpie who took the little girl to live in the sea."

"He's not mean, you know," Catherine said, placing her clean little hand in hers.

"The kelpie?"

"The Black Wolf."

"How do you know?" asked Ariella.

"I could tell by the way he looked when he first came here," Catherine explained as they descended the stairs.

"He seemed so sad. That's why I gave him my embroidery right away."

"That was very thoughtful of you."

She nodded in agreement. "He said my stitching was beautiful." Suddenly she smiled. "I wonder what Mac-Fane will think when he sees how nicely I painted Duncan's dolls?"

Malcolm stared in furious disbelief at the ridiculously grinning sack figures being hanged from the gallows.

"Is this supposed to be a joke?" he demanded.

"I'm afraid little Catherine decided they needed faces," explained Duncan, apologetic. "I was barely able to stop her before she had them both outfitted in ladies' gowns."

"I think it's rather nice," said Gavin. "Makes them look cheerful."

"Let's hope the MacKendricks don't find them too bloody cheerful to attack," muttered Malcolm, directing his attention to the clan.

"Today we will begin by learning to charge an opponent," he announced. "But instead of charging each other, you will attack the figures you see hanging before you. They will be swinging as you run, so you must anticipate their movement. Hit them as hard as you can, then get out of the way to make room for the next man. For the moment you will use only your bodies. The figures have been tightly stuffed with cloth and sand, so they are heavier than you think."

The MacKendricks looked at each other uncertainly. It was obvious they didn't think much of his instructions.

"Duncan and Andrew, you will swing the figures hard as the men approach. The rest of you divide into two lines and begin."

"Forgive me, lad, but I can't see how this is going to teach them anything," remarked Angus doubtfully.

"Attacking a sack man is not at all like attacking a real man," pointed out Dugald. "A sack man can't hit back."

"I know."

Alpin chuckled. "I believe that's what MacFane intended."

"What good does it do to teach them to hit over-stuffed dolls?" asked Angus, bewildered.

"Your clan is consumed with the fear both of getting hurt and of hurting each other," Malcolm explained. "That makes it impossible for them to engage in combat, with or without weapons. Since these stuffed figures cannot harm them, and since they won't feel any pain, I believe the men will gradually lose their fear and become more aggressive in their attack. I want them to learn what it is to have aggression pounding through their veins. Then we can move on in the training. As for the women, I believe Gavin has placed the targets away from the castle, so we need not worry about arrows showering down on us."

"Some of the women actually have a very good eye," remarked Gavin, urging his horse toward the gate. "I believe they are going to make fine archers."

"Then let's hope we get some slits cut into the towers, so there is a place from which they can shoot," drawled Malcolm.

Having slowly formed their lines, the MacKendricks were ready to begin. Bryce went first. As he ran, Duncan heaved the sack figure at him. Startled, Bryce yelped and dodged to the side, missing the grinning mannequin entirely.

Malcolm controlled his impulse to bark out an insult. "Not too fast," he instructed. "Wait for him to come to you."

"She looks more like a girl to me," observed Ramsay.

"And an ugly one, at that," snorted Hugh.

The other laughed.

"Think of it as your greatest enemy," suggested Malcolm, ignoring their unruliness. "He is unarmed, just like you. He is big, but even a big man has weaknesses. One solid blow to his knee will shatter the bone, instantly bringing him down. A hard strike to the groin will reduce the deadliest opponent to tears. If you ram him just below his ribs with both your fists, you will knock the air from him. If you grab his arm and twist it hard around his back, you will wrench his shoulder from its socket. Plan your attack as you run, but don't give it away with your eyes. Then hit him where it will count."

The MacKendricks stared at him blankly. Malcolm realized he had made an error by telling them so much. Clearly his suggestions had shocked them.

"Let me at him!" roared Graham suddenly, racing toward the grinning figure. He plowed into the swinging mannequin full force, sending it flying.

"Very good, Graham," said Malcolm, surprised. "Next time try to hit him a little lower. That will force the air out of him."

"My turn," said Ramsay. He crouched low, then ran at the figure and rammed both his fists into its abdomen. "Take that, you cowardly dog," he huffed.

"Your aim was excellent, Ramsay," praised Malcolm. "A blow like that would have doubled him over. Next time lock your hands together into one fist to make them even more powerful."

During the next two hours Malcolm watched with increasing amazement as the MacKendricks gradually overcame their uncertainty and repeatedly attacked the grinning sack figures. He used Rob, Andrew, and Duncan to demonstrate some of the techniques he had taught them during their journey there. Because the stuffed dolls were impervious to pain, the men soon abandoned their inhibitions and attacked them with considerable fervor. When the session came to an end and the next group arrived, the first group boasted to them of their prowess and challenged them to do better. After only an hour his new pupils were ready for Malcolm to demonstrate more complex methods of attack.

Dismounting from his horse, he stood in the center of the courtyard and invited anyone forward who thought he could best Malcolm in an attack. No one volunteered. Malcolm knew it was not because they were uncertain of the outcome. The MacKendricks were convinced Malcolm was little better than a cripple. No one wanted to shame himself by fighting a man they believed was defenseless. Finally he ordered Duncan and Andrew to attack him. The MacKendricks watched in astonishment as Malcolm deftly overwhelmed them both. After that others tried charging him. Every one ended up flat on the ground, but Malcolm was careful to commend the efforts of each man. He had learned that the MacKendricks responded far better to praise than to insult or criticism, and it seemed with every encouraging word they wanted to try again. By the time he announced that training was finished for the day, his pupils were reluctant to quit.

As for him, his body was stiff and aching, and he was anxious to retreat to the privacy of his chamber.

"Did you see how hard I hit that thing today? I thought for sure its head was going to come flying off," boasted Ramsay as he took a second helping of salmon.

"That's nothing," scoffed Hugh. "I smashed it with my fists together, and I know I heard the fabric give way. If it hadn't been woven so tight, the sand would have spilled right from its belly."

"You heard it give way because I went before you and had already weakened it," Graham announced. "You were just finishing what I had started."

"My shoulder is purple from knocking into it so

hard," said Bryce, drawing his shirt down so they could see. "Had that thing been a man, his ribs would have cracked."

"Cracked? I drove my elbow into it so hard, a man's rib would have snapped in half and pierced an organ. I'd like to see one of Roderic's warriors get up after that," Hugh declared ominously.

"If Roderic or anyone else attacks the castle again, they won't have the chance to get to you," Elizabeth assured them. "Three times today I hit the target right in the center. Meagan and Agnes hit it twice. By the end of the week our aim will be as straight and true as anyone's, man or woman."

"Young lassies today have such spirit," declared Angus cheerily. Then he frowned. "Do you suppose that's a good thing?"

"The lass takes after her father," declared Gordon proudly.

Helen swatted her husband's shoulder. "And I suppose I had nothing to do with raising her?"

"That's a fine-looking scrape you've got there, Ramsay—"

Ariella listened in astonishment as her clan boasted of the day's feats. The night before, they had done nothing but complain of their aches and grumble that they were not born to be warriors. Tonight they were brandishing their bruises like trophies and making threats about what would happen to anyone who dared attack them. Somehow MacFane had evoked a profound change in their attitude. Although the MacKendricks were nowhere near as dangerous as they seemed to think, it was an excellent beginning.

"Good evening."

The hall grew hushed as all eyes turned to MacFane. He stood straight and tall at the bottom of the staircase. His expression was calm, but Ariella thought she detected a faint clenching of his jaw.

"I am pleased by everyone's accomplishments to-day," he began. "Not just in training, but also in the work done on the castle. I have given Duncan orders to arrange for the production of wooden swords and shields, so that tomorrow we can begin the basics of swordplay. When you have mastered your technique, we will graduate to real swords, which will be newly forged."

A murmur of excited anticipation rippled through the hall.

"Eat well tonight, and get some sleep," he advised. "Tomorrow's training begins at first light."

He turned, grimacing slightly, as if the action cost him more than he had expected. Using the wall for support, he moved up the stairs with slow deliberation, manfully trying to minimize his limp. The MacKendricks watched him in awkward silence. Finally the door to his chamber closed.

"It seems the day's training has taken its toll on our revered teacher," drawled Niall.

"If I didn't know better, Niall, I would think you actually enjoyed seeing him in pain," Ariella snapped. "Either that, or you are hoping he will fail in his attempt to train us."

She grabbed a pitcher of wine from the table and hurried up the stairs, unwilling to hear any explanation he might choose to offer.

"Enter."

She found him standing before the low fire burning in the hearth. Once again his carriage was strong and upright, his body betraying no sign of the discomfort he had endured only moments earlier. As soon as she closed the door, he braced his hand against the mantel and painfully lowered himself into the chair, all attempts to pretend he was fine abandoned now that he knew it was only Rob.

She went to the desk and poured him a generous cup of wine. "The clan seems very pleased with their training today. You made them feel able, whereas yesterday they felt incompetent."

Malcolm drained the cup, desperate to numb the pain streaking through his leg and back. "More," he demanded, holding out the vessel. Rob filled it again, and Malcolm emptied it. Soothing liquid heat began to spread through his chest. It did not ease his discomfort, but the faint promise of relief was there. "Again."

The boy hesitated, then filled the cup. This time Malcolm limited himself to just a swallow.

"I was accustomed to training men who dreamed of nothing other than becoming warriors," he began, shifting to ease the weight of his left side. "Men who had lifted toy swords and axes from the time they could walk. Their fathers demanded that they be bold and hard, and punished them severely if they showed any sign of weakness or fear. Yesterday it became clear I could not expect the same behavior from gently reared artisans and poets who have been taught from infancy that a wall head is a place from which one can admire the sky."

Ariella watched him as he stared pensively into the amber flames of the fire. His dark brows were clenched, and the lines of his face seemed more deeply etched. Tonight she recognized his expression not as one of anger, but a reflection of the battle he constantly waged against the torment of his body. The clear blue pools of his eyes were shadowed, as if he were recalling some memory that stirred him. He was not talking about the warriors he had trained, she realized.

He was talking about himself, and the unyielding demands of his own father.

"The MacKendricks encourage their children to look for beauty in the world, and then find a way to add to it," she said. "I never understood how clans who war all the time can accomplish anything. Being at peace allowed us to focus on creating, rather than destroying."

"It has also made you vulnerable."

"For the moment," she agreed. "But should we have spent a hundred years training for war, just for this one moment?"

He stared into the fire, considering. "You are asking a man who was a warrior. For me, the answer must be yes." He shifted his body again, then grimaced as pain pierced his back.

"Where does it hurt, MacFane?"

A bitter laugh escaped his lips. "It would be easier to say where it doesn't hurt."

"How long has it been like this?"

He took a deep swallow of wine. "Over three years, now. I led my men in a battle for King William against a troublesome English baron. A warrior ran his spear through my horse's belly. I was caught beneath the animal as he fell, shattering the bone in my leg and injuring my back. I continued to fight, but I was trapped. That made it easy for the bastard. He slashed at me with his sword a few times, but just as he was about to finish me, Gavin killed him." He stared at the flames, remembering how the ground had grown warm and wet with his blood. Then he shook his head, banishing the memory. "The next thing I knew, Gavin was stitching me closed."

"Did he set your leg right away, or did he wait?"

"I don't remember. I assume it was a few hours after it happened."

"What about your arm? Did anyone do anything for it after Gavin stitched it?"

Malcolm regarded the boy over the rim of his cup. "Why this sudden interest in my wounds?"

He shrugged. "I told you before, MacFane, I'm skilled in the art of healing." He slouched in the chair opposite him. "You saw how well I stitched your arm the night you killed the thieves. Your other injuries are old, but there are ways we might try to ease your discomfort, if you're willing."

"When we got home, our healer attended to me. My body was on fire, so he bled me, to rid me of the unhealthy blood. Then he covered my wounds with some foul-smelling potions and herbs. I was unconscious for a while, so I don't know what else he did. When I was finally lucid again, he just told me to rest."

"For how long?"

"I don't know. Until I felt better."

"I mean, how long until you began to work your arm and leg again?" Rob persisted.

"The gash to my arm had severed the muscles. When I tried to work it, the pain was intolerable. The healer told me I had to accept the fact that my right arm would always be smaller and weaker than the other."

"You should have worked it anyway," the boy informed him impatiently. "The sooner the better. What about your leg?"

"You can see for yourself," snorted Malcolm. "It's the leg of a cripple."

"But when did you begin to exercise it after the bone had healed?"

"I began to walk as soon as I could stand the pain. Gradually the pain eased somewhat. But never enough to allow me to walk normally again."

"I don't just mean walking, MacFane. Didn't this healer have you perform exercises to strengthen the muscles?"

"Walking and riding should have strengthened them."

"Walking and riding are not enough," the boy retorted. "My mother taught me that when a limb is broken or badly injured, you must perform specific exercises just for those muscles. These exercises should be done many times a day, for short periods of time. Gradually, as the muscles strengthen, you can increase the amount of exercise. That's how you repair the damage."

"I have accepted that the damage can never be repaired," drawled Malcolm wearily. "At this point, I just want the pain to stop." He took another hearty swallow of wine.

"Then it's time to try something other than drunkenness."

Malcolm raised his eyes to the insolent lad. He did not understand why he tolerated the boy's rudeness. Perhaps it was because young Rob was so disarmingly honest. Strangely, Malcolm found comfort in the fact that Rob always said exactly what he felt.

"What did you have in mind?"

"A hot bath," announced Rob. "To relax your muscles."

"I don't find baths relaxing," countered Malcolm.

"Because you are accustomed to bathing in the cold water of a loch or river," said the boy, heading toward the door. "This will be different."

He was gone before Malcolm could protest further. After a few minutes Graham and Ramsay appeared, bearing a heavy tub. A parade of MacKendricks followed, carrying wooden buckets filled with hot water. The girl named Agnes brought him soap and towels, which she deposited on the chest before nervously curtsying and hurrying from the room. Malcolm remained in his chair and regarded the steaming tub with indifference, certain it could do nothing to ease his suffering.

After a few minutes Rob returned.

"You're supposed to get in it while it's still hot," the boy complained, looking exasperated. He went to the tub and emptied the contents of a brown bottle into it. A sweet, pungent aroma drifted through the air. "The herbs in this oil will help ease your pain," he said, stirring the water with his hands. "You must stay in the water until it grows warm, but not cool. Once you are out and have dried off, I will return to—"

His gray eyes grew wide with shock.

Malcolm limped naked past him and stepped into the tub, bothered by the fact that the boy found the sight of his battle-scarred body so disturbing. Obviously the lad had never seen a man with such extensive injuries. Rob turned away and began to snatch up the clothes Malcolm had carelessly shed onto the floor. Malcolm closed his eyes and leaned back, allowing the water to close over his head. Surprisingly, it actually felt good to have his body surrounded by liquid heat. When he emerged again, Rob was carefully folding his plaid. His small hands moved expertly over the woolen fabric, reducing it to a neat square within seconds. Malcolm found the care he took with the clothes peculiar in a lad, particularly one who showed such a complete lack of interest in his own bedraggled appearance.

"I'll leave you to your bath," said Ariella, risking a glance at MacFane now that his enormous body was safely hidden in the tub. She had planned to rub his back and leg with soothing liniment. But the sight of him standing powerful and naked before her had left her strangely flustered. All she wanted at that moment was to be away from him.

"Wash my back before you go."

"I—I'll send Agnes to do it," she stammered.

"Agnes acts like a frightened hare when she is near me," grumbled Malcolm. "I do not want her tending to me. Here," he said, holding out a dripping cloth.

She didn't move.

"Are you so afraid of getting a little soap and water on you?" he snapped.

Reluctantly, she went to him and took it.

"God forbid I might see your hands clean," he

muttered as she dropped the cloth into the water beside his hip.

"You didn't look much better when I first met you, MacFane," Ariella reminded him, rubbing soap into the cloth. "I hardly think you'd be one to complain about my appearance."

"My standards have changed since then. And I don't see anyone else here, children included, looking nearly as dirty and tangled as you."

"How I look is my affair, not yours." She slapped the hot cloth against his back and began to scrub vigorously at the broad, scarred expanse of muscle.

"Jesus Christ," he swore, his jaw clenched.

Ariella saw his muscles lurch beneath the taut skin. "Forgive me," she murmured, instantly lightening her touch.

She dipped the cloth into the water and slowly drew it up his back, trailing a soothing stream across the sun-bronzed skin. When the stream eased, she moved the cloth down his back and soaked it in the water again, then pulled it up once more, skimming across his aching, injured flesh in gentle swirls. The water was hot and fragrant with herbs and soap; it trickled down his neck and across his shoulders in silvery beads that dripped into the pool at his waist. MacFane leaned forward slightly and sighed. Ariella repeated the motion again and again, washing away the tension and the pain, covering him with fragrant heat and wet until she began to feel the grip of his pain ease slightly. Beneath the fabric of the cloth she was acutely aware of the structure of him, the even ridges of his ribs, the rippled chain of his spine, the firm depth of his flesh. The muscles of his upper back were so locked in spasm, she could almost imagine it was warm stone beneath her fingers rather than a man. Knowing this area was one of great pain, she let the cloth slip from her fingers so she could massage the knotted tissue. Her mother had taught her well—how to apply pressure without discomfort, how to use her fingers to knead the tension from the fibers, how to bring blood to the stiff flesh, reminding it what it was like to be relaxed. And so she leaned closer and shut her eyes, letting touch be her guide, pressing and caressing the rigid muscles, slowly, gently, feeling the damage of years of spasm, and listening to the low, suppressed groans MacFane made as she administered this soothing mixture of pleasure and pain.

Little by little the spasm began to ease, at first almost imperceptibly, like a pinprick of air escaping from a massive stone wall. Her touch grew firmer, more demanding, encouraging the muscle to relent, to let go of the tight clutch it had maintained for so long. And then, knowing she could not possibly erase the spasm in one night, she allowed her hands to seep outward, kneading and caressing the surrounding flesh of his scarred back, which shifted and rippled beneath her touch, as if starving for the relief she offered. Down his spine, up his sides, across his massive shoulders, she allowed herself to explore him, listening to the soft groans he made as she brought the heat and gentle persuasion of her hands to his battered, angry body.

Malcolm sighed with pleasure as Rob expertly massaged his tired, aching muscles. He had never been touched with such gentle, confident skill, not by any healer, and certainly not by any woman. It was as if the boy knew exactly where the pain was in every area of his back. He also understood just how much pressure to apply, and for exactly how long, to make the muscles respond, not with more pain, but with something akin to a sigh. It was as if they had long awaited for someone to soothe them in this firm, healing way, to release them from the bondage of their ache. He sat there with his eyes closed, inhaling the fragrant steam of the scented water, his naked body drenched in liquid heat. Slowly his flesh began to waken, not just to the gentle touch being ministered on his back, but to the unexpected sensation of being stroked in a way that was gradually becoming more tentative and searching.

He shifted slightly, told himself he was being ridiculous, and tried to recapture the tranquillity he had enjoyed only a moment earlier. But something had changed. The massaging of his back seemed less firm and therapeutic, and somehow had become more of a caress that was almost sensual, as if it were a woman exploring his back instead of a young boy. Rob leaned closer, until Malcolm could feel the sigh of the lad's breath against his wet skin as Rob's small hands trailed over his shoulders.

Appalled by the sensations flooding through him, Malcolm jerked away, sloshing water onto the floor.

"That's enough," he commanded brusquely. "Leave me."

The boy looked at him in confusion. "But I haven't finished. I brought a liniment—"

"I don't want your liniment," Malcolm snapped. "I want you to get the hell away from me. Now."

His face was dark with fury. Ariella stared at him in bewilderment, unable to comprehend what she had done to make him so angry. She had felt his muscles relax beneath her touch. Yet now he sat there, his body taut, as if he were in great pain.

"Fine, MacFane," she shot back.

She stomped across the chamber and slammed the door behind her.

Something had changed between them, she realized. Because at some point in that hot, herb-scented chamber, she had gone beyond merely trying to alleviate his pain. Her touch had evolved into a forbidden exploration of his body, which was heavily scarred but still warm and firm and seething with power.

And although loath to admit it, she had enjoyed touching him.

CHAPTER 6

"What has happened between you and MacFane?"

Ariella shifted uneasily in her seat. "Nothing."

"Nothing?" repeated Dugald in disbelief. "You used to be the one person he would talk to. Now he goes directly to his chamber after training and sees no one at all."

"He sees Agnes," pointed out Andrew. "She brings him his dinner and attends to his bath."

Irritation pricked Ariella. Since the night she had massaged his back, something had changed between her and MacFane. The following day he had completely ignored Rob, as if he were angry with the boy. Annoyed by Malcolm's rudeness, Ariella had sent Agnes to organize his bath that night, knowing he did not want the girl around him. Instead of turning Agnes away as she had anticipated, MacFane had welcomed her in and insisted she attend him each night as he bathed.

"He won't take his evening meal in the hall anymore," remarked Gordon. "He trains the clan all day, then shuts himself in his chamber and doesn't come out. What is he doing there?"

Niall snorted. "Probably drinking."

"You don't know that," countered Duncan, irritated. "And even if he was, what does it matter, so long as he is up and training us the next morning?"

"The lad should dine with the clan and enjoy himself a little," said Angus. "When I was young—"

"If MacFane wants to stay in his chamber, that is up to him," interrupted Ariella. "It has no bearing on his ability to train us."

She did not want the council to know the extent of MacFane's dependence on alcohol. This past week he had gradually lifted her clan's confidence, making them believe that perhaps they could actually fight back if they were attacked. Each time he demonstrated some new movement or taught them a different tactic, he won another scrap of their admiration. The knowledge that he collapsed in a drunken stupor of self-pity every night would certainly erode that newfound respect.

"I don't understand why we are wasting our time with this foolishness," complained Niall. "We could be attacked again at any moment, and we are heaving ourselves at oversize dolls and waving wooden swords at each other. How much longer before we find a real warrior with a strong army to protect us?"

"I suppose until that man appears, or Alpin has another vision," returned Ariella shortly.

Dugald looked at Alpin. "You haven't had another vision, have you?"

There was a moment of expectant silence. Alpin

stared at them knowingly, enjoying being the center of attention. Finally he sighed and shook his head. "No."

"As we have no way of knowing when either event might happen, we must continue to have MacFane train us," concluded Ariella.

"I don't believe this," growled Niall. "Ariella has to dress as a boy to stay alive, while we train under the direction of a cripple. It is ridiculous."

"He is *not* a cripple," retorted Ariella.

"We are forgetting about MacFane's great army," said Angus brightly. "Perhaps they will soon be able to join him here. Then we will have nothing to fear, from Roderic or any other."

"They are engaged elsewhere," Ariella reminded him. "We cannot depend on them to assist us."

"Rather odd, isn't it?" remarked Niall. "That the Black Wolf's army would be off fighting without him?"

"Ariella has determined he is not the next laird," said Duncan, "so it is irrelevant where his army is. He is here to help us temporarily, nothing more."

"And as it is obvious we will never be able to fight off an attack, we should stop this nonsense and apply ourselves to finding the next MacKendrick," asserted Niall impatiently. "Our clan will not be safe until Ariella marries and bestows the sword."

Silence fell over the hall as the elders considered this.

"You may be right," allowed Gordon finally.

Ariella's spirit sank. If Niall and Gordon felt this way about MacFane and his training, how many others in her clan did as well?

Malcolm leaned low against Cain's neck, trying to ignore the pain the movement cost him as he rode deeper into the green and gold of the forest. The woods trembled as Gavin, Ramsay, and Hugh thundered past, their bows clutched in their fists, racing after the handsome red deer they had spotted. Malcolm steeled himself and urged Cain faster. But his body rebelled, and he was forced to succumb, slowing his mount to a walk.

He shook his head in disgust.

It was not easy, accepting these limitations. It was frustrating, demeaning—unmanning, even. Especially since coming here, where his every movement was watched with an insufferable mixture of pity and disappointment. He felt as if he were constantly being appraised and found pathetically lacking.

Which was not surprising, as he judged himself the same way.

He inhaled deeply, savoring the scent of earth, horse, and leather, trying to enjoy the simple pleasure of slowly riding in the woods on this fading summer afternoon. Since his arrival there two weeks ago, he had ventured no farther than the castle's courtyard, preferring to attend to his duties, then retreat to the privacy of his chamber. But the MacKendricks had worked hard this past week, and because they responded well to compliments, he reasoned they would also appreciate a reward. And so he had offered a day away from the rigors of training and building, in which they could either rest or join him on a hunt. To his surprise, this morning most of the men had assembled in the courtyard at their now customary early hour, eager to demonstrate their skills at riding and shooting. The surrounding woods were rich with wildlife, and they had killed several dozen rabbits and birds, and three red deer. Tonight a hearty feast would be prepared, and there would be music and dancing to celebrate the success of the day's hunt.

A pity he would be too racked with pain by then to attend.

He soaked in a hot bath each evening, as Rob had suggested. Although this did relax him somewhat, it could not begin to match the effects of several pitchers of wine. So he indulged in both, hoping that together they might ease the ache of his tortured muscles and bones. Shy, plain Agnes dutifully brought him soap and towels, kept her eyes modestly averted as he stripped and stepped into the tub, then asked in a trembling voice if he needed anything else. On the first night she appeared, Malcolm realized Rob was purposely trying to annoy him for having ordered the boy out the evening before. Instead of dismissing Agnes, Malcolm ordered her to wash his back. Her small brown eyes grew wide, but she obeyed. As he endured the frightened, tentative skim of her wet cloth, he wearily wondered why he had made the request. Perhaps because it had been so long since a woman had touched him, and he longed to remember what it was like to feel slim, gentle fingers sweep across his flesh. Surely that was why he had experienced those disturbing sensations when Rob touched him the other night. His mind had been languid, his body soothed, and in that quiet, liquid moment he had imagined it was a woman's hands gently pulsing over him, instead of the hands of a filthy slip of a boy. Shocked by his reaction, he had treated Rob harshly the following day, as if the lad were somehow to blame. He knew it was wrong to punish the boy for his own bizarre response. But he felt a need to distance himself from him, thinking this might eradicate that unsettling moment. He ignored the lad completely during training and managed to avoid him the rest of the time. At night he retreated to his chamber, and Rob never came to speak with him as he used to.

He found he missed his prickly little friend.

The earth began to vibrate, signaling the approach of another rider. A pearly-gray mare burst through the leafy curtain of trees, a small form pressing low against her back. Rob did not see Malcolm at first, so focused was he on whatever prey he was hunting. After a few seconds the boy realized his quarry had not come that way. He reined in his horse and stroked her neck, smiling as he praised her in an unexpectedly soft and gentle tone. The wind had blown his ragged brown hair off his face, revealing a delicate bone structure that seemed almost feminine, and his gray eyes were sparkling with pleasure, a sensibility Malcolm had not witnessed in the lad before. The mare tossed her head and snorted, then cast her gaze toward Cain. Rob's eyes followed.

If his first reaction at seeing Malcolm was surprise, he was quick to master it. His slim body slouched, not suddenly, but by slow, nearly imperceptible degrees. This caused the boy's hair to fall forward and veil the sculpted form of his cheeks. Malcolm watched in fascination as Rob's expression closed, and the smiling youth who had appeared a moment earlier vanished. He was vaguely disappointed as he realized that his own presence had caused this transformation.

Awkward silence stretched between them.

"Good hunting?" Malcolm finally asked, trying to fill it.

Rob shrugged. "Good enough."

Malcolm waited for the boy to say something else. When the silence grew between them, he persisted, "I didn't see you when we left the castle this morning."

"I joined the hunt later," returned Rob shortly. *After you were gone,* his gray eyes finished.

It bothered him, this coldness—even though he had invited it with his own surly behavior. A chasm divided them—a strange turn of events, Malcolm thought, as he had never really considered them friends. But he now realized that a bond *had* existed, and he had severed it.

"Your clan has been performing well," he offered, seeking to repair some of the damage.

Rob snorted. "And what of Agnes?" he drawled sarcastically. "Has she been performing well also?"

Malcolm felt himself on the verge of a smile. The reason for the lad's animosity was suddenly clear.

"You sound like a jealous wife," he observed wryly. "If you fancy her for yourself, why did you send her to me?"

Rob looked astounded. "I don't fancy her!" he sputtered.

"Why not?" prodded Malcolm, enjoying teasing him. "She is comely enough." In face, Agnes was quite plain, but he suspected that, to a thirteen-year-old boy, her scrubbed face and ample figure might be appealing.

"I just don't."

"Then why does it bother you that she tends to me?" persisted Malcolm, trying to hide his amusement.

Rob glared at him. "It doesn't."

"She doesn't have your skill at healing," he admitted, "but then, she doesn't have your nagging tongue either." He pretended to consider this a moment, then sighed. "I suppose I must accept her flaws for the supreme pleasure of the quiet."

"You have been hired to train my clan, MacFane," Rob reminded him sourly, "not to bed the women."

His mouth was set in a prim line, and his gray eyes were cool with disapproval. Unable to control himself, Malcolm tilted his head back and laughed, a low, forgotten sound that spread tremors of warmth through his chest.

Suddenly Rob plowed into his chest, knocking him backward. Malcolm grunted and instinctively wrapped his arm around the boy as they crashed in a tangled heap on the ground.

Pain blazed through him, as if every nerve had been set afire.

"Jesus Christ," he swore, roughly throwing Rob aside, "what the bloody hell did you do that for!"

The pounding of a horse's hooves distracted him. He glanced at the trees and saw a cloaked figure galloping into the shadows. Frowning, he looked at Rob, who lay curled on the ground beside him.

An arrow was buried in his upper arm.

Malcolm yanked his dirk from his belt and stood, listening hard as he raked the surrounding woods with his gaze. Convinced they were alone, he knelt beside the lad.

"Don't touch me!" Rob hissed.

"I need to see how deep it is," Malcolm told him firmly. "Let me open your shirt—"

"No!" cried Rob, shoving his hands away. "Just leave me alone!"

"If the arrow isn't buried deep, it's better to pull it out now rather than ride with it back to the castle," Malcolm explained, trying to be patient. "Otherwise it will only delve its way in farther."

"Don't touch me, MacFane," the boy warned, his eyes shimmering with tears.

"Oh, for God's sake." Before Rob could protest further, Malcolm took hold of his sleeve and sliced the fabric open, revealing the torn flesh from which the arrow protruded.

"It's not in deep," he concluded, studying the wound. "I can take it out here."

"No!" gasped Rob, horrified. "Don't you—"

Firmly holding his arm, Malcolm pulled the arrow out in one quick motion. A startled cry of pain cut the air.

"There," he said gently. "It's out." He tossed the arrow away and began to bind the boy's arm with the torn linen of his sleeve. "Are you all right?"

Rob took a shuddering breath and nodded. Tears began to slip down his smudged cheeks.

"Good. When we get back to the castle, we will have someone stitch it and bandage it properly. You will ride with me."

"I can ride my own horse," the boy told him, his voice shaking.

"I know you can," agreed Malcolm. "But you have been injured, and I would prefer you ride with me."

He stood and helped the lad to his feet. Then he placed his hands on his waist, to lift him onto Cain. Instead of feeling the lean, bony quality of most lads his age, Rob was surprisingly soft beneath his touch. Frowning, Malcolm adjusted his grip. The gentle curve of hips flared beneath his fingers.

"Take your hands off me!" snapped Rob. "I said I can ride my own damn horse!" He stalked over to the animal, took a deep breath, then awkwardly hoisted himself up.

Deciding not to argue the matter, Malcolm mounted Cain. Cool darkness wrapped around them as they silently rode through the woods. Malcolm was careful not to ride too fast, for fear his pace would prove overly difficult for his small, wounded friend. This gave him time to reflect on what had happened.

And to accept with absolute certainty that the arrow had been meant for him.

Laughter and music wafted merrily toward them, indicating that the feast was well under way. Amber light spilled from the castle's windows, and the spicy aroma of roasting meat pervaded the evening air. Malcolm swung himself down from his horse.

"We must minimize this event to the clan, Mac-Fane," Rob said, his expression grave.

Malcolm looked at him in disbelief. "You were shot. With an arrow meant for me."

"It will not help for the clan to know that," the boy argued. "It will only make everyone worry."

"They goddamn well should worry," growled Malcolm. "You could have been killed. And I don't enjoy being shot at."

Rob shook his head impatiently. "If we hope to find out who did it, we can't have everyone watching everyone else. It would be better to let the attacker think we believe I was hit by a stray arrow."

Malcolm considered a moment. Perhaps the lad was right. An attacker who believed he had escaped detection was less likely to exercise caution. And would probably try again. "Very well." He raised his arms to help the injured boy off his horse.

"I can get down myself," Rob told him tautly. His brow creased with effort, he dismounted, leaned against his mare a moment, then stepped away.

Malcolm caught him as he collapsed to the ground.

"Your injury has bled and made you weak." Grunting against his own pain, he awkwardly hoisted the lad into his arms.

"I don't want you to carry me," protested Rob.

"I don't really see a choice in the matter," observed Malcolm as he slowly limped toward the castle. "Next time you can carry me."

The great hall swirled with gaiety and music. When Malcolm entered carrying Rob, everyone stopped and stared at them in shock.

"No!" cried Elizabeth, dropping the cup of wine she had been offering to Gavin into his lap. She rushed toward them, with Agnes, Helen, and little Catherine following close behind.

"Where are you injured?" demanded Duncan.

Gavin rose from his chair, heedless of his wine-soaked plaid. "What happened?"

"It is nothing," Rob assured them as Malcolm carefully stood him on his feet. "A stray arrow during the hunt. It struck me in the arm, and MacFane took it out." He took his little sister's hand and gave her a weak smile. "I'm fine."

Relief washed over the room. Malcolm studied the expressions around him, searching for a hint of guilt— or perhaps regret that the arrow had not found its intended target. All he saw were surprise and concern—

except from Alpin. His keen black eyes returned Malcolm's perusal tranquilly, as if he had always known this would happen and was not disturbed by it.

And from Niall, whose face was twisted in fury.

"The wound will need cleaning, and a few stitches," Malcolm informed Duncan. "Take the lad to my chamber and strip him of these filthy clothes. Let us use this as an opportunity to finally bathe him."

The women in the hall gasped.

Malcolm frowned, not understanding their reaction.

"Perhaps, MacFane, it would be better if Rob stayed with me and Andrew," Duncan suggested. "We have ample room, and we can take turns watching over him tonight, in case he needs anything."

"Yes," agreed Rob quickly. "That would be better."

"Agnes and I will look after his wound," offered Elizabeth.

"And I'll tell him a story to make him feel better," declared Catherine, clinging fast to her brother's uninjured arm.

Malcolm shrugged. What did it matter who tended the boy, as long as he was looked after? "Very well."

"Well, now, seeing as the lad is going to be fine, there's no reason we shouldn't continue our festivities," remarked Angus as Rob was led away. He regarded Alpin uncertainly. "Is there?"

"No reason," Alpin agreed brightly. He lifted a gnarled hand into the air. "Musicians play!"

A deafening blast of bagpipes assaulted Malcolm's ears. He glanced at Gavin, who nodded. Then he turned and slowly headed toward his chamber.

"You believe the arrow was meant for you?"

"Rob saw the fellow taking aim," Malcolm told him. "That's why he tried to knock me out of the way."

"But once the attacker realized his mistake, he didn't

shoot again," pointed out Gavin. "It could be he was just trying to scare you, not actually kill you."

"Then he is exceptionally confident of his aim," observed Malcolm darkly. He took a deep swallow of wine. "Either way, someone wants me gone. If he didn't intend to kill me, then he was hoping I would decide to leave. The question is, Why does he want me to go?"

Gavin gazed pensively into the fire. "From what I can see, the MacKendricks are beginning to accept you as their military adviser. Not knowing you were hired to come here, they believe you genuinely want to help them. And most of them accept that they need your help, at least until they find their new laird. But," he continued hesitantly, "Elizabeth has told me there are those who blame you for the attack on the clan."

Malcolm looked at him in disbelief. "Why the hell should they blame me?"

"MacKendrick promised his people you were coming with your army, to marry his daughter and assume the position of laird, as Alpin had foreseen," Gavin explained. "Everyone had heard the tales of your past, and they were excited by the prospect of having the great Black Wolf as their chief. When the clan was attacked and MacKendrick and his daughter were killed, the people were devastated. They adored the old laird and his daughter. Apparently she was exceptionally beautiful."

Malcolm stole a glance at the sculpture on the desk. If that elegant carving was any indication, then Ariella must have been exquisite.

"She was also a girl of some courage," mused Gavin, "to sacrifice herself for her people the way she did."

Malcolm returned his gaze to the fire, unable to look at her. Instead of finding comfort, he was tormented by the image of her lovely face slowly being engulfed by flames.

How long did she wait for me?

"I find there is a reluctance to talk about her," Gavin continued. "Elizabeth says it is because the memory is still too painful."

Of course it would be. Just as the death of Marrian had been an agony for him. Marrian's death, and all those other helpless MacFane women and children who had died because of his drunken ineptitude.

He took another swallow of wine, loathing himself.

"It could be whoever shot at you wants to punish you for failing to come," Gavin suggested. "The MacKendricks were brutally awakened from a peaceful slumber that had lasted nearly a hundred years. Perhaps one of them blames you for their loss of innocence. He wants you to leave because he thinks you failed them and have no right to be here."

"He is right."

Gavin cast him an irritated look. "You did not come here because you thought it was your right, Malcolm. You came because you were asked."

"No," he countered, his voice thick with contempt. "I came because I wanted the gold they offered."

"Even so, your reasons for coming have nothing to do with what you accomplish while you are here. If you can help the MacKendricks, what does it matter if you are paid for doing so?"

Malcolm was silent as he contemplated this. Perhaps the fact of being hired would not have bothered an ordinary warrior. It certainly hadn't bothered him when Duncan had made the offer. But he was not an ordinary warrior. He had been the Black Wolf, and laird of the mighty Clan MacFane. A few years ago he would have given his help solely because it was right to do so, not because he expected payment in return.

"There is another, more disturbing possibility," he mused, pushing aside the thought of how low he had sunk. "It could be someone wants me gone because he is concerned that the clan is becoming stronger."

Gavin frowned. "Who would want the clan to remain weak?"

Malcolm drained his cup, then regarded his friend grimly. "Someone who knows it will be attacked again."

The fire was a mound of pink and gray embers as Malcolm vainly tried to coax a last drop of wine into his mouth. Irritated at finding the jug empty, he hurled it aside, listening with complete indifference as it shattered against the stone floor. Blinking wearily, he focused his gaze on the candle, which was perilously close to drowning in a yellow pool of wax. He did not want it to go out. If it went out, there would be nothing left to illuminate the smooth, high cheeks and small, straight nose of the girl who might have been his wife. But then, if he had still been laird of the Clan MacFane, she wouldn't have been his wife, he reminded himself dully. Because if he hadn't been injured, if he hadn't been so tortured by pain, if he hadn't become so dependent upon alcohol just to get through the endless days and hours and minutes, he would be married to Marrian now, with a child born and perhaps another growing deep within her.

He lay his head against his aching arm and studied the red-gold flame, which reminded him of the color of Marrian's hair. His little cousin had worshiped him for as long as he could remember, traipsing around after him from the time she had begun to walk on her chubby little legs. Shy Marrian blossomed into a tall, lush beauty, and he had considered himself lucky indeed when his father arranged a marriage between them. She had been but sixteen and Malcolm twenty-eight, and it was agreed they would not marry until Malcolm returned home to stay. Often when he had camped at night, he would imagine that moment, of the Black Wolf returning proud and strong at the front of his great army, and Marrian running across the meadow to greet him, her cheeks flushed and her sunlit hair floating behind her.

Instead Gavin had brought him home in the back of a cart, broken and bleeding and dazed with fever. Not so dazed, however, that he couldn't see the horror clouding his betrothed's lovely face as he'd been carried into the hall. Horror, and pity, and even a shade of revulsion.

In that moment he knew he would never marry.

The stone face of the girl named Ariella regarded him silently. He looked away, embarrassed by his self-pity. He was alive, while both the women he might have married were dead. Marrian had been slaughtered while he was drunkenly leading his men away from his castle, leaving it hopelessly vulnerable. And Ariella, who had loved her clan so selflessly she would sooner die than permit them to suffer, had finally accepted that he would not come and killed herself. Had she hated him, in that terrible moment? Had she stolen one last, desperate glance at the horizon, searching for some sign of the man Alpin had promised would save them? He experienced a suffocating wave of guilt; it choked the room, making it hot and small and airless. This was MacKendrick's chamber, he reminded himself harshly. He had no right to be in it. The candle sputtered and drowned, abandoning him. He pulled himself to his feet and staggered through the darkness, fumbling for the door. Then he limped along the corridor, down the stairs, and out the front door, searching for the cool, clean air and endless black of night to steady his reeling senses.

A velvet sky stretched above him, silent and unfathomable. He stumbled forward, searching for a star to focus his gaze on. There was only the moon, and it seemed too large, too brilliant, nearly blinding him with its aura. He closed his eyes and sank to the ground, drawing comfort from the feel of hard earth beneath his knees. His body ached, but the pain was dulled by the wine flowing through his veins, enabling him to think of other things. He thought of Marrian, and what it had been like to chastely press his lips against her sweet, smiling mouth. And Harold, his cousin and Marrian's half brother, teasing him about what he would do if anything ever happened to his sister. *He should have killed me,* Malcolm thought bitterly. *He believed he was being merciful by letting me go.*

He should have run me through with his sword and been done with it.

A sound escaped his lips, a sob or a groan, he was not sure. Startled, he searched the darkness to see if anyone had heard. The castle was asleep, its windows yawning caverns of black—except for a shaft of gold spilling from an opening high in one of the towers. He gazed at it, vaguely consoled by the idea that he was not alone, that someone else could not rest on this lonely summer night. Suddenly a woman stepped into the amber beam. Her face was shadowed, her silhouette small and fine, but the unhurried grace of her movements left no doubt it was a woman he saw, not a child. She leaned forward, searching the sky for something, or perhaps to feel the coolness of the air upon her cheek. Moonlight splashed across her face, revealing her features in a shower of silvery light.

Malcolm's breath froze.

His mind was playing tricks on him, he realized numbly. It was the alcohol, combined with guilt and exhaustion, that made him think this was Ariella. He did not believe in ghosts or spirits. He did not even believe in seers, or any of the other superstitious nonsense the people of the Highlands so delighted in. Yet he stood there, unable to pull his gaze away from the woman contemplating the moon, afraid if he blinked, she would vanish forever. Finally he did blink, and still she remained. Relief swept through him.

Then she turned and disappeared, leaving him alone in the shadows of the courtyard.

He could not let her go. Not without telling her how deeply sorry he was for all that had happened. She had died because of him. She had set her chamber afire and allowed herself to be engulfed by the flames. A hideous, painful death. He did not expect her to forgive him. He was not worthy of forgiveness. But he needed to beg for it all the same. He wanted her to know he had never meant for these terrible things to happen.

And that had he been able, he would have come.

The sleeping herb fell in a pale cloud onto the crimson surface of her wine.

Ariella picked up the goblet and swirled it around a few times, watching the powder dissolve. Her arm was throbbing badly, preventing her from lying upon those clean sheets and falling asleep. Elizabeth had carefully stitched and bandaged her wound, while Agnes had arranged for a hot bath to soothe her aching muscles. Together her friends had washed her filthy hair, giving her a brief respite from the ashes she would rub into it again tomorrow, and dressed her in a soft linen chemise. Realizing her injury would make sleep elusive, Ariella then took a special mix of herbs to help her rest. But several hours had passed, and she remained frustratingly awake. She seated herself before the fire and sipped her wine, waiting for her mind to relinquish her body to the comfort of sleep. But try as she might, she could not quell her horror over what had happened that day.

Someone had tried to kill MacFane.

At first she had tried to convince herself it was an accident. But she had seen the cloaked rider emerge from the woods, slowly, stealthily, a hunter closing in on its prey. The woods had been filled with the sound of MacFane's laughter. No one could have missed it.

The rider had known they were there, had wanted to find them. And when he appeared, his arrow taut against the string of his bow, he took swift but careful aim. Ariella had barely had time to throw herself at MacFane as the shaft cut through the air. It had pierced her arm, but the wound was nothing. Nothing compared to the terrible fact that someone had tried to kill the Black Wolf.

Someone from her clan.

She knew they did not want him here. Their aversion to being trained by the man who had failed them so profoundly was easy to understand. And in his current condition MacFane was far from the magnificent warrior they had dreamed would come to save them. But she was keeper of the sword, and her clan was expected to abide by her decisions. The idea that someone would try to injure MacFane, even if that person had meant only to frighten him away, was shocking. At this moment he was their only hope of learning how to fend off another attack by Roderic, or someone else like him. Until she found the rightful laird and gave him the sword, the MacKendricks were dangerously vulnerable. What could anyone possibly hope to gain by getting rid of MacFane?

She sipped her wine and gazed pensively at the fire, struggling to think clearly as the sleeping herb began to dull her senses. Perhaps, she reflected, there was someone in the clan who worried she might give the sword to MacFane. The idea was ridiculous. Although he was proving a reasonably able teacher and adviser, MacFane's battered body, his failure of his own clan, his addiction to alcohol, and his lack of an army made him hopelessly unfit for the honor and responsibility of becoming the next MacKendrick. Choosing MacFane would condemn her clan to suffering and destruction. But her people did not know the extent of his injuries, or that he had been cast out as chief of the Mac-

Fanes, or that his mighty army was now led by another. Or that he drowned himself in a vortex of alcohol each night. No man with such overwhelming weaknesses could wield the MacKendrick sword. What might have been, she wondered, if she had met MacFane when he'd been at the pinnacle of his physical power and ability? Could the sword have saved him from his own destruction?

It was irrelevant, she reminded herself bitterly. He was here now, not out of any noble desire to help her people, but because she had bribed him with gold. Their arrangement was simple. She would use him for his knowledge of training and fortifications, and see that her clan worked hard to benefit from that knowledge.

The minute he was no longer needed, she would send him away.

The door creaked softly. She glanced up, wondering who could be needing to speak with her at this hour.

At the sight of MacFane she leaped to her feet, spilling her goblet of wine across the front of her nightdress.

Malcolm stared in horrified fascination at the exquisite apparition standing before him. Her hair was the color of the richest, glossiest wood, threaded with coppery highlights that gleamed in the light of the fire. It was thick, as he had known it would be, and fluid with the waves he had previously seen carved in stone. Only its length surprised him. Instead of cascading down to the small of her back, it fell barely past her shoulders. It must have burned off in the fire, he realized, experiencing a stab of loss. Her skin was pale, her features delicate and fine. How well he knew the contours of that face: the small, straight nose, those elegant cheekbones, that sweetly determined thrust of a chin. Everything about her was painfully familiar, from the lush curve of her lips to her wide gray eyes. She stared at him in dismay, as if she feared him, although he could not imagine why she should. The apricot pulse of firelight reduced her linen gown to the most transparent of veils, revealing the slender, round lines of her form. A hot surge of desire flared within him. Appalled by his unseemly reaction, he moved his gaze down. Only then did he notice the splash of scarlet staining the front of her nightdress.

She was covered in blood.

"Forgive me," he managed, his voice a rough crack against the hush of the chamber.

She regarded him uncertainly, as if she did not understand.

"I—I didn't know," he continued, feeling helpless and ashamed. "I didn't understand the danger you were in."

She said nothing. But her silence was condemning.

"Even if I had," he admitted, despising himself as he wrestled with his confession, "there was nothing I could do. I had no army to lead to your rescue. No arsenal of weapons and shields and horses." He gestured in disgust at himself as he added, "Not even a sound body with which to fight."

Her gray eyes grew shadowed. She stayed there watching him, her small form rigid, as if she found his pathetic excuses cowardly.

And they were.

"You are right, milady," he admitted finally, his voice a raw whisper. "I should have come."

The guilt of it was more than he could endure. Sick with remorse, he closed his eyes, blocking out the terrible bloodstained sight of her. He wished he could exchange his life for hers. She, at least, had had a life worth living, with people who had loved and needed her. Instead she had burned, condemning him to carry the excruciating burden of yet another death upon his conscience.

He did not think he could bear it.

"Ariella," he whispered, the name haunting and bittersweet, "I am so goddamn sorry."

Ariella stared at him in stunned surprise. She had never seen MacFane like this. Often he appeared tormented, but she had judged it a selfish torment, with roots that drank deep of self-pity. The man standing before her was not the MacFane who got drunk and bitterly wondered if he had really performed the reputed feats of the Black Wolf. This man was intoxicated, yes, but not self-pitying. Instead he was consumed by the single thought that he was responsible for a woman's death. And the thought of it rendered him so guilt ridden, he could not bring himself even to look at her spirit.

She had every reason to despise him. He had failed her, her father, her people. Yet in this solemn, silent moment she could not hate him. She was far too shaken by the depths of his suffering.

He could not stay there much longer, she realized, or he would soon start to wonder why her spirit didn't fade into the air. She poured him a goblet of wine, liberally dosed with sleeping powder.

"Drink, MacFane," she ordered, holding the goblet out to him. "All of it."

He opened his eyes and looked at her. If he was surprised by the fact that an apparition could speak, he made no comment on it. Instead he reached for the goblet. His fingers brushed hers as he took hold of it, a flash of warmth against her cool skin. Keeping his blue gaze locked upon her, he tilted his head and obediently drained the glass. Then he wiped his mouth against the back of his hand and carefully placed the goblet on the table.

"Do not torment yourself over my death," she murmured quietly. "It is done."

He shook his head. He did not deserve absolution.

"You died a hideous death because of me. You watched your father die, saw your fellow clansmen cut to pieces as they fought to protect their home. All the while clinging to the hope that maybe I would come. But, Christ," he swore, suddenly angry, "couldn't you have waited a while longer? If you had but agreed to wed this warrior, then you would have lived. You could have sent word to me again. I would have found some way to help."

"I could not wed him," Ariella replied. "I could not make him laird of my people. Their suffering would have been—unimaginable."

"Even cruel, oppressive lairds can be killed," Malcolm argued. "They are not invincible."

With the sword he would have been. As my father would have been, had he only thought to keep it close. She knew the weapon alone could not have saved her clan. But at least her father would not have fallen beneath the blade of Roderic's sword.

"I could not wed him," she repeated stonily. Terrible memories began to unfurl, images of the suffering she had witnessed that day. "After all he had done, I would rather die than have him touch me." She wrapped her arms around herself, trying to shield herself from the horrors eddying through her mind.

That he could understand. "Of course," he said, feeling brutish and stupid for even suggesting it. He moved closer. "He had no right to touch you."

He reached out and unthinkingly laid his hand against her cheek, forgetting she was a ghost and would have no substance. To his surprise she was decidedly solid beneath his touch. Solid, yet small and delicate. And cool, he mused, feeling her tremble slightly. Despite the fact that she stood before the hot flames of the fire, which were warm upon his skin. She did not move away from his touch, nor did she lean into it. Instead she remained utterly still, staring at him, her eyes silvery in the amber wash of firelight. Desire poured through him, clouding his thoughts. This was the woman who might have been his. The woman who had been offered as his wife, if only he had been man enough to come and protect her. The woman who would have lain beside him at night, wrapped in his arms, her cheek a scrap of pale silk against his aching chest. Overwhelmed with loss, he trailed his fingers along the fragile line of her jaw, across her small chin, down the creamy column of her throat. The rapid beat of a pulse fluttered against his fingertips, faint as the whisper of a moth's wings. In his mind he knew she was dead. Yet to him she was as filled with life as his own flesh, or the ripple of flames behind her, or the air gusting softly through the window.

"Ariella," he murmured, his voice rough with need. He sank his fingers deep into the coppery silk of her hair and leaned closer, inhaling the scent of soap and heather. Her eyes were shimmering with uncertainty, but she did not retreat. And in that moment she somehow ceased to be a ghost, or a mere trick of his imagination. His mind reeling with wine and desire, he wrapped his arms around her.

And then, accepting the fact that he had gone absolutely insane, he bent his head low and took her lips in his.

Ariella held her breath, so startled was she by the feel of Malcolm's mouth pressed warm and hard against hers. She knew she should push him away. He had no right to touch her so, no right to pull her against the solid heat of his body, no right to hold her fast against him as his mouth invaded hers with a terrible, frightening desperation. But somehow she could not bring herself to resist, to raise her arms and shove against his chest and step away. A strange sensation began to grow within her, slowly at first, a tiny ember glowing deep in the pit of her stomach. She tried to force it from her mind as Malcolm's hands began to possessively stroke her back, her shoulders, her waist, her hips, exploring the curves and valleys of her as if he could not quite believe she was real, and needed to see for himself. His kiss grew bolder and more demanding, suckling her lips, then tasting her with his tongue, until she gasped in surprise at the dark pleasure flooding through her. This enabled him to kiss her deeply, thoroughly, stripping away the last vestiges of her resistance. The ember in her stomach burst into flame. Unable to restrain herself, she reached up and wrapped her arms around his neck. His immense height forced her to raise herself on her toes, causing her to lean against the hard breadth of his body. He tightened his embrace, wrapping her in his strength and power and need, touching her and tasting her and holding her until she was dizzy from it, until she felt as if she were coming to life for the first time, that everything before this moment had been but a shadow of the sensations pouring through her as she kissed the man who had been destined to be her husband.

The man who had failed to come when she needed him, leaving her clan to suffer.

Shame pierced her senses. In that same instant Malcolm squeezed her injured arm, causing her to cry out. He instantly released his hold and drew back.

"Did I hurt you?" he demanded, astonished by the possibility.

"No," she murmured, shaking her head. "It was nothing."

His gaze was bleary with the effects of drink and the sleeping herb. Still, he was lucid enough to find her discomfort peculiar. Frowning, he reached out and jerked her gown off her shoulder, revealing the white linen of her bandage. He stared at it a moment, mystified.

And then his eyes narrowed.

"What the hell is this?" he growled thickly.

Her mind racing, she searched for some plausible explanation.

Before one came to her, he sighed, as if the matter no longer interested him.

Then his eyes closed, and he collapsed heavily onto the floor in a deep, drugged sleep.

CHAPTER 7

Someone was calling him. The voice had a languid, muffled quality to it, as if the person were shouting into the wind. Malcolm did not know what the fellow was going on about, but he wished he would shut the hell up. His mind was wrapped in layers of soft wool, sheltering him from pain, and from anything else he might feel if he allowed himself to waken. He sighed and buried his head deeper into his pillow. If he just ignored this irritating noise, surely it would go away.

The next thing he knew, his blankets were gone, exposing his naked body to the chill morning air.

"What the *Christ*—"

"Time to get up, Malcolm," announced Gavin cheerfully. "Jesus, you look like hell. How much did you drink last night?"

Malcolm blinked and tried to focus. "I don't know," he mumbled. His tongue felt strangely thick and slow, forcing him to concentrate as he formed the words. "Whatever you brought me."

"I brought you three pitchers," said Gavin, glancing at the empty vessels on the table. "The same as always."

Malcolm rubbed his eyes and tried to sit up. His body was weak, making every movement an effort. "That wine must have been unusually strong. I don't remember falling into bed."

"Well, you were exceptionally neat about it," observed Gavin. "I've never known you to fold your clothes, drunk or sober."

Malcolm frowned at the tidily arranged garments piled on the chest at the foot of his bed. It was not his habit to fold his clothes. Usually he left them strewn over the floor, because by the time he was drunk enough for sleep, that was all he was capable of.

"Agnes must have folded them." But that didn't seem right. Agnes never did more than bring him towels and soap, and he couldn't remember having had a bath last night.

"Most thoughtful of her," teased Gavin, tossing him his shirt and plaid. "Perhaps she fancies you and is trying to impress you with her womanly touches."

"Agnes is afraid of me," snapped Malcolm. He had long accepted the fact that no woman could find his battered, crippled body attractive. Which didn't bother him, as he had never desired a woman since the moment Marrian looked at him with pity and revulsion.

Until last night.

He stopped adjusting his plaid. "Did anyone come to see me last night?"

"Not that I know of," replied Gavin, seating himself. "But after I brought you your dinner, I returned to the hall to enjoy the company of some lovely MacKendrick ladies. Why?"

A memory was shrouded in the mists of his mind. There was a woman, and heat, and the pulse of flames. He drew his brows together, struggling to see more. Her hair was strange, because it was short, which he had found troubling. *Why?* he wondered. Gradually the mist began to dissipate, making the image of her clearer. She was sculpted in shadows before a fire, wrapped in a gown of white linen. He had been drawn to her, but there was something about the gown that had bothered him. Something disturbing—

"What's the matter with you, Malcolm?"

"I don't know," he muttered, shaking his head. "I think I was with a woman last night, but I can't remember who she was, or where she was, or if the whole thing was just a dream."

"Maybe you haven't managed to scare all the Mac-Kendrick girls as thoroughly as you like to think. What did she look like?"

Malcolm tried to remember as he belted his plaid. "She was small," he began, recalling her slim form before the hearth. "And her hair was the most glorious color. Not brown, and not red, but more like . . ." He paused, searching for the right words. "Like mud and rust," he said finally.

"An unusual choice of words," commented Gavin. "These MacKendricks may make a poet of you yet."

Malcolm scowled. "Her hair isn't important," he said impatiently. "What is important is the fact that I knew every detail of her. Her cheeks, her chin, her nose—it was as if I had studied them at length—but I had never seen her before."

"Then she was a dream or an apparition," concluded Gavin, "because during the two weeks you have been here, you've seen all the MacKendrick women at one time or another."

"I suppose so." He sat on the bed and pulled on his boots. "But she seemed so real. I can remember how soft she felt in my arms, and when I leaned close, she smelled sweet, like heather and—something else." He closed his eyes, trying to remember.

"Roses?" suggested Gavin. "Silverweed? Violets?"

"Soap."

Gavin nodded approvingly. "I like an apparition who bathes."

"I don't know why I'm telling you this," Malcolm grumbled.

"Did she say anything to you?" prodded Gavin, ignoring his irritation.

He thought for a moment. She had spoken, he was certain of it. He stared into space, picturing her standing before a fire, her gown a filmy veil against the flames. Her hair reached just past her shoulders. And somehow that was his fault. He moved his gaze down, re-creating her. Blood. There was blood on her dress.

Do not torment yourself over my death.

That was what she had said. Because he was responsible. She was dead because of him. But it wasn't Marrian, or any of the other MacFane women who had died that hideous night he had failed his clan. It was another. His gaze shifted, suddenly drawn to the sculpture on the desk.

Ariella.

"It can't be," he murmured, stunned. But the memory began to grow clearer. He could see her leaning out the tower window while he stood in the courtyard. And then he went to her. To apologize. He found her in the tower room, and she had been more beautiful than any woman he had ever known. Just as MacKendrick had promised. Desire had surged through him, raw and powerful.

Desire for a ghost.

"She isn't dead."

Gavin looked at him in confusion. "Who?"

"MacKendrick's daughter." He went to the door and threw it open.

Gavin hurried along the corridor beside him. "How do you know?"

"Because I saw her last night," Malcolm snapped, furious that some trick was being played on him. "She's been hiding in this tower. And I intend to find out why."

His limp prevented him from moving as quickly as he would have liked. Still, he advanced with considerable speed up the narrow tower stairs, impatient to confront this woman and demand why she had played this game. He wrenched down the latch and hurled the door open. She lay on the bed, huddled beneath a mound of blankets. Malcolm stalked over and violently jerked the coverings off her.

"*What in damnation—*"

Angus frowned as his gnarled hand groped for the missing blankets. Finding only cool air, he opened his eyes and regarded Malcolm with sleepy irritation.

"What's amiss, lad?" he demanded. "Are we under attack?" He sat up suddenly, his expression brightening. "Shall I fetch my sword?"

"What are you doing here, Angus?" demanded Malcolm, torn between confusion and exasperation.

"Why, I'm sleeping, lad." He scratched his white head and glanced uncertainly at Gavin, as if wondering what was wrong with MacFane. "What are you doing here?"

"I mean, what are you doing in this room?" clarified Malcolm tautly.

Angus looked at him in bewilderment. "I *was* sleeping, and now I'm talking to you."

Malcolm closed his eyes and prayed for patience. "Why aren't you in your own room?"

"This is my room, lad. Has been for nearly twenty years now."

"No, it isn't," countered Malcolm. "This is Ariella's room."

"Ariella's room was in the other tower, lad," Angus corrected. "The one that burned when she set fire to it."

"Yes, but this is her room now. I saw her here last night."

Angus stroked his white beard, contemplating this. "That's odd. I came up here right after dinner, and I don't remember seeing either of you. Of course," he continued, looking at Gavin, "Ariella is dead, so I wouldn't expect to see her."

"I came to this room last night," growled Malcolm, "and she was sitting right there—"

He paused, searching the room for the elegantly carved chair she had been seated in when he had opened the door. It wasn't there. Instead he saw a chair that was heavy and roughly cut. Confused, he scanned the room. Gone were the intricately woven tapestries that had covered the walls, the delicate table that had held her wine, the small, polished bed with the scarlet plaid. All the furnishings in the chamber now were worn and distinctively masculine, the aged, shabby furniture of a man who has had it for years and sees no reason to change it.

"You say you saw her sitting in my chair?" asked Angus, clearly intrigued. "Did you see MacKendrick as well?"

"No," said Malcolm, shaking his head. He was almost certain he had been in this room. But if he had been, why was everything different this morning? And what was Angus doing sleeping here?

A dull pounding began to split his head, reminding him of how much wine he had consumed.

"Forgive me, Angus," he murmured, rubbing his temple. "Obviously I overindulged last night. I did not mean to disturb you."

"Not at all, laddie," said Angus good-naturedly. "I

don't get many visitors up here. Come and see me any-time." He lay back and pulled his blankets up to his chin.

His head throbbing, Malcolm slowly made his way back down the narrow tower stairs. What the hell was happening to him? Was he drinking so much he could no longer distinguish dreams from reality? The thought disgusted him, but it was the only answer.

Either that, or he had seen a ghost last night.

He descended to the great hall, where Duncan, Andrew, Niall, and Rob were seated at a table eating their morning meal. Rob sat hunched over his plate, ignoring everyone. He did not look up as they approached, but Malcolm could see that the boy was just as filthy as always. If it was possible, his dirty, matted hair looked even worse than it had the day before.

"For God's sake, Duncan, why didn't you see that he took a bath?" Malcolm demanded irritably.

Rob barely lifted his head to scowl. "I don't see how it's any of your business if I bathe or not, MacFane," he informed him testily.

"He didn't want to take one," intervened Duncan. "But Elizabeth and Agnes made sure his wound was well cleansed before they stitched it."

"Wonderful," drawled Malcolm. "I am relieved to know there is at least one patch of him that is not crusted in grime and vermin. My God, Rob, how can you let yourself look like that?"

"If you don't like it, then stay away from me!" Rob snapped, banging down his cup.

Duncan and Andrew looked at him in surprise.

"Lads are like that," remarked Gavin, attempting to ease the tension. "Then they discover lasses, and you can't get them to stop fretting over their appearance."

"Let's hope he discovers them soon," grumbled Malcolm, "so we can all breathe fresher air."

"Fine!" spat Rob, shoving his chair out from the table. "I won't be training with you today, MacFane," he announced fiercely as he stalked toward the door. "So breathe all the fresh air you like." He slammed the door behind him.

"I don't know why you bother the lad so much about his appearance," remarked Gavin. "The day you two met, you didn't look much different."

"He's not feeling well today," added Duncan. "His arm is aching from that arrow."

He and Andrew gave Malcolm disapproving looks, revealing that Rob had told them the truth about the attack on MacFanc. Obviously the boy trusted them enough to believe they had nothing to do with it. Malcolm glanced at Niall to measure his expression. It was more contemptuous than annoyed, as if he were pleased with the fact that Rob was angry with him. Irritated at being the object of everyone's censure, he turned and headed toward the door.

"Morning drill begins in one minute," he said tautly. "Don't be late."

Malcolm's patience was dangerously thin that day. He did not know if it was due to the pounding in his head, the attempt on his life, or his fight with Rob. Whatever the reason, the MacKendricks struck him as hopelessly inept at each exercise they attempted, and it took every shred of his self-control not to erupt and order them all to go back to their juggling and poetry. By midafternoon, when Graham and Ramsay got into an argument over who got to use the bigger of two swords they had been given, Malcolm had reached his limit. He abruptly ordered Gavin to take over and headed to his room, seeking solitude.

Instead he found himself deep in the lower recesses of the castle, his fist poised over the scarred wood of Alpin's chamber door.

"Come in, MacFane," called Alpin cheerfully.

Startled, Malcolm pushed the door open. The room

was dark and cool, lit only by a few yellow candles dripping onto the tables crowding it. He stepped inside and was immediately forced to duck as an enormous owl swooped over his head before perching on a shelf just above him. A small fire burned in the hearth, with three rapidly boiling cauldrons hanging over it. The air was heavy with an odd, dank smell, a mixture of smoke and herbs and things Malcolm did not want to contemplate. Alpin was bent over a table in the far corner. Malcolm approached him slowly, wondering how the old man could possibly have heard him before he knocked.

"I didn't hear you," Alpin assured him, chuckling. "At my age I can't depend on my ears the way I used to."

Malcolm refrained from questioning him further. He did not want to hear some idiotic tale about how Alpin had "seen" him.

"What are you doing?"

"Preparing a cure for nausea," Alpin replied, filling a jar with dark lumps.

Malcolm leaned a little closer, intrigued. "What is it?"

Alpin lifted the jar to Malcolm's nose, offering him better access. "Wild boar droppings."

Malcolm coughed and stepped back.

"I collect them in the woods and dry them over the fire. When ground and taken with water, they are a splendid purge for an unsettled stomach."

"I can imagine," said Malcolm, revolted.

Alpin pressed a lid onto the container and placed it on a shelf, beside a jar filled with leeches. "So, MacFane," he said, his black eyes suddenly sharp and assessing, "what brings you to me?"

Malcolm hesitated. He did not know why he had come here. He was starting to feel like a fool for allowing what had obviously been a dream to unnerve him. Still, since he was here, perhaps there was no harm in telling the old man about it.

"I had a dream."

Alpin nodded, as if this information did not surprise him.

"But that in itself is strange," he qualified, "as I never dream."

"Because you are afraid."

The statement was ridiculous. "I am not afraid of anything," Malcolm assured him harshly.

"Of course you are, MacFane," Alpin chuckled, not bothered in the least by his anger. He retrieved his staff, then moved to the fire and sprinkled something from his pocket into one of the steaming cauldrons. "We are all afraid of something. You are afraid of dreaming, because you cannot bear to witness what you might see in your dreams. This is what forces you to keep your mind blank night after night."

He was right, Malcolm realized. Dreaming might bring back a vision of Marrian, lying still upon a cold stone floor, her lovely white throat slashed and leaking blood. Of Abigail crumpled on the stairs, and Fiona huddled in a corner, and little Hester lying sweetly in her bed. All with ashen, bloodless faces, because the blood had flowed from their wounds and soaked their clothes. Over two hundred women and children had been slaughtered that night, he reminded himself savagely.

Because of him.

"We were speaking of your dream," Alpin reminded him, his voice gentle.

Malcolm inhaled sharply, banishing the memory. "There was a woman," he began. "And although I had never seen her before, I knew she was Ariella."

Alpin looked up from stirring his pot. "How did you know?" he asked, curious.

"I knew her face. From the statue in MacKendrick's chamber."

The old man nodded and continued stirring.

"She was beautiful," Malcolm murmured, recalling

her image before the fire. "Even though her hair had burned off, and her gown was splattered with blood."

Alpin frowned. "Why? Had she cut herself?"

"I don't know. I suppose it has something to do with the terrible nature of her death."

Alpin considered this a moment, then shrugged and turned his attention to another pot. "Go on."

"She told me not to torment myself so much over her death—"

"She did?" sputtered Alpin, amazed.

Malcolm's eyes narrowed. "Does that surprise you?"

"No, of course not," he said, quick to recover. "At my age very little surprises me. It's just that I did not foresee Ariella offering you forgiveness."

"She didn't forgive me," clarified Malcolm. "She simply told me not to torment myself over it. It is not the same thing."

Alpin nodded thoughtfully. "Of course not." He went over to a table and began to pour a dark liquid carefully into a bottle. "What happened then?"

Malcolm thought for a moment. "We talked awhile, but I can't remember what we spoke of. And then I took her in my arms and kissed her."

The bottle crashed to the floor, causing the owl to spread its great wings and hoot noisily.

"I'm fine," Alpin assured him, waving him away as he picked up the shattered pieces. "At my age you get to be a bit clumsy, that's all. Nothing to worry about. You say you kissed her?"

He nodded.

"And she let you?"

"Of course she let me," replied Malcolm impatiently. "I'm not in the habit of forcing myself on women—even ones that exist only in my imagination."

"Was it a long kiss, or just a quick peck?" prodded Alpin.

Malcolm raised a brow. "Why are you so interested?"

"No reason," he told him, shrugging. "Just an old man's curiosity. Perhaps I am recalling the long-faded memories of my lost youth. Don't bother indulging an aged seer with an answer if you don't want to."

Malcolm sighed. "It was not a quick peck."

"Wonderful!"

"I fail to see why," drawled Malcolm aridly. "I have a dream for the first time in years, in which I kiss a dead woman with burned-off hair who is covered in blood, and this is something wonderful?"

"No, it's terrible," amended Alpin, his tone sympathetic. "I mean, it's terrible that this dream, if that's what it was, has disturbed you so."

"What do you mean, 'if that's what it was'?" demanded Malcolm. "What the hell else could it be?"

Alpin regarded him a long moment, as if debating whether or not to answer. Finally he sighed. "I know you do not believe in things that cannot easily be explained, like ghosts and seers," he began. "And I have no reason to try to convince you. All you need to understand, Mac-Fane, is that MacKendrick's daughter loved her father, her clan, and her home more than life itself. She loved them so she could not bear to see them come to harm. And when we were attacked, she would have done anything to spare the suffering of any clan member. More than any of us, Ariella was a fighter."

"Why are you telling me this?" asked Malcolm. "Do you think I haven't agonized enough over what happened?"

"I do not say it to further punish you," he assured him. "I am telling you because I want you to better understand the woman who was to be your wife."

"Marrian was to be my wife," Malcolm countered harshly. "If you truly have the ability to see things, you must know that."

"But your path changed, MacFane. Marrian was

killed that night, but you were alive. Much as you would have liked to, you did not die with her."

Part of me did, he thought bitterly.

"Yes," agreed Alpin, nodding. "But not all."

He looked at him in surprise.

"Perhaps the same can be said for Ariella," Alpin continued. "She set the tower afire, and part of her died. But she was too much a part of this clan, this castle, these lands, to let go completely. And so she remains, watching over us, trying to guide us along the next path."

"If you are trying to convince me that her ghost is haunting this castle, you're wasting your time," Malcolm growled. He began to limp toward the door. "It was just a dream, Alpin. Made to seem real by the vast quantity of wine I had consumed."

"Are you sure, MacFane?"

"I do *not* believe in goddamn ghosts," he swore, banging the door behind him.

The wind blew cool and clean against him as he raced across the moors. He battled the pain in his back and leg as he urged Cain faster, enjoying the sensation of thundering across the dry grasses toward the sapphire sparkle of loch ahead. His muscles were taut and aching with effort, his breathing heavy and deep, but the exertion brought more pleasure than discomfort. He had not ridden this hard since the day he had set out to find young Rob and his friends before they got themselves killed. Already his body was warning him he would pay dearly for it. Tomorrow he would rest, and then he would ride hard and long again the following day. Perhaps, if he pushed himself enough, he would learn to get past the infuriating feebleness of his body.

He slowed Cain to a walk, not because he was tired, but because he wanted to study his surroundings. The MacKendrick castle sat high in the distance, its creamy stone structure gracefully rising from an emerald slope of hill, spattered with brilliant bouquets of wildflowers. The burned tower was still under construction, an ugly reminder of the attack, but other than that the view was remarkably pleasing. Below the castle lay a tidy arrangement of small white cottages, each puffing a thin stream of smoke. Flocks of geese and chickens squawked as a group of laughing children ran up the hill, scurrying to greet the men returning home for their evening meal. Work and training were finished for the day, and they were gathering with their families to laugh over dinner while sharing stories about what had happened while they'd been apart. Malcolm watched as the men lifted their squealing children high into the air, then ruffled the windblown locks of the older children and took their hands, letting the young ones lead them down the hill to where wives and mothers waited.

He abruptly turned his horse and rode away.

He had accepted the fact that he would never know such simple pleasures. His chance of being a husband and a father had been destroyed long before the night Marrian died. It had vanished the moment she had looked at him lying broken in the hall. She had tried her best to hide her aversion to him in the long months that followed. But every time he had drawn near, Malcolm had felt her recoil. When it had become apparent that he would never fully recover, that he was destined to live within this scarred, broken shell for the rest of his life, he had realized he could not sentence pretty, vibrant Marrian to the role of a cripple's wife. But neither could he bring himself to formally dissolve their betrothal. The humiliation of such an act would have been unbearable. The great Black Wolf, laird of the Clan MacFane, was unable to make his chosen bride desire him. His pride was slashed deep, and he could not aggravate the wound by releasing Marrian to the arms of another.

Instead he merely postponed their wedding, telling her he was not ready.

She had accepted his decision in stoic silence, her face betraying none of the relief he had anticipated, nor the disappointment he had hoped for. Anger had surged through him, anger with her for not throwing her arms around him and telling him it didn't matter, that she longed to be his wife, no matter the condition of his body. Instead she had sat there, her head serenely bowed, saying nothing. Sweet, dutiful Marrian, who had been raised to accept whatever decision her father or laird or husband made for her. She had patiently waited for over a year for Malcolm to tell her when they would wed. She never pressed him on the matter. After that meeting Malcolm openly ignored her, as if the subject of their betrothal was of no interest to him. But every day he had watched her from a distance, taking bitter pleasure in her loveliness, her grace, torturing himself with the knowledge that at any moment she could be his, if only he were willing to command it. He suspected she had given her heart to another. A young woman as beautiful as she would have caught the eye of every man in the clan, married or not. His conviction that she had betrayed him helped to justify his callous rejection of her.

Only after her death had Harold harshly informed Malcolm how wrong he had been.

He had come to the end of the moor, where it ringed the shimmering blue of a deep loch. Rob's pretty gray mare was standing at the water's shallow edge, her ears pricked as she listened for Cain's approach. A small figure sat perched on a log just beyond her. Rob was idly tossing stones as he cooled his bare feet in the water. Malcolm dismounted and slowly limped toward him. He realized he had been unnecessarily hard on the boy that morning, and he wanted to make amends.

"May I join you?"

Rob cast him a surly look.

Interpreting that as slightly better than a no, Malcolm sat down and gathered a few stones in his hand.

"We missed you at training today," he said, throwing one of them into the loch.

Rob didn't spare him a glance. "Who's 'we'?"

"I missed you," he admitted. "Either I was in the foulest of tempers, or the clan was performing unbelievably badly."

"Given your black mood this morning, I'd say the problem was with you, MacFane."

"You may be right." He hesitated, then threw another stone into the water. "I hope we can put the matter behind us."

The boy turned to him, incredulous. "Are you apologizing to me?"

His face was heavily streaked with dirt, and his hair fell in ratty clumps over his shoulders. But it was his eyes that suddenly captured Malcolm's attention. They were large and intense, their color the clearest of grays. Malcolm stared at them, bewildered. "I—I guess you could call it that."

Rob turned to study the loch again. "Fine," he grumbled. "I accept your apology."

"Good," said Malcolm, feeling strangely unsettled.

They contemplated the view in silence. After a moment, Rob demanded "How much longer until the castle is secure?"

Malcolm skipped a stone across the water. "Your clan has been working hard, and they are unusually skilled at building. The new gate will be ready shortly. The wall along the parapet is coming along well, and Duncan assures me it will be completed before the end of summer. Archers' slits have already been created in two of the towers. Extending the base of the curtain wall will take a long time, but the stone is being cut and the work will begin as soon as everything else has been completed."

"How much longer until we can defend ourselves and you can leave?"

Malcolm lifted a brow. "You make it sound as if you are anxious for me to go."

"You didn't want to come here, MacFane," he reminded him tersely. "You only came for the gold, and you said you wouldn't stay longer than three months. After last night I thought you would be more anxious than ever to leave."

"How do you know about last night?" demanded Malcolm, stunned.

Rob gave him a dry glance. "I was hit by the arrow. Remember?"

Of course. The arrow. What the hell was the matter with him?

"If you think I will be driven away by fear, you can put your mind at ease. I'm not going anywhere."

Rob's jaw tightened. If Malcolm hadn't known better, he would have thought his answer displeased the boy.

"As for your clan," he continued, "I don't believe they will ever be able to defend themselves. At least not against a seasoned force. Your people are learning well, now that they have decided they want to learn. But they lack the ruthlessness it takes to be a warrior. And brutality isn't something I can teach them."

"Are you saying we're just wasting our time?"

"No. At the very least I can train you to fend off a small attack. But for anything more than that you're going to need help. Which is why you must make alliances with the surrounding clans."

Rob shook his head. "We MacKendricks have never made alliances. An alliance means we would be forced to go to war whenever the other clan demands it. We have always been a clan of peace. I could never ask my people to consent to such an agreement."

"It is not your decision to make," pointed out Malcolm. "This is a matter that must be put before the council."

"Then present it to the council," said the boy, shrugging his slim shoulders. "They will never agree."

He was probably right, Malcolm realized. The peace-loving MacKendricks might be willing to learn to defend their own homes, but going out to fight for others was another matter entirely.

"If you won't make alliances, then you'd better hurry and find yourselves a new laird with an army, before you are attacked again."

"It's not that simple. He has to be the right one."

"The right one for what?"

"To lead my people," said Rob impatiently.

"At this point I would think anyone who was a relatively decent sort with a good-sized army would do."

"Perhaps for some clans," declared Rob scornfully. "Not for the MacKendricks." He turned to study the loch again. "The next MacKendrick laird must be far greater than that. He has to be exceptionally strong, relentlessly brave, and driven by his innate sense of honor."

"As I was?" asked Malcolm, half joking.

"Yes, MacFane," he agreed tautly, hurling a stone at the water. "As you *were*."

The insult cut far deeper than Malcolm had expected. Why was he sitting there taking abuse from this filthy slip of a boy? he wondered angrily. He had better things to do with his time. He rose and began to limp toward his horse.

Ariella regretted the words the instant they were out of her mouth. She did not know why she had tried to hurt him. But something had changed between them since last night. He had wrapped his arms around her and drawn her close, and she had felt life and heat quicken within her. Somehow, despite his battered body and his drunken, drugged state, he had kindled a flame of desire in her. For one brief, impossible moment she had felt safe as she'd stood shielded against the power of his body— she, who was keeper of the sword and had a solemn duty

to give her heart to none other than the next Mac-
Kendrick. Her behavior was as incomprehensible as it
was shameful. That was why she wanted him to go. From
the moment he had seated himself beside her, she had felt
an overwhelming need to drive him away. Yet now he
was leaving, and she was gripped with loss.

"MacFane."

Malcolm stopped.

"I—I didn't mean that the way it sounded."

"Really? How did you mean it, then?" His tone was
heavily mocking.

She paused, trying to choose her words carefully.
"You did not come here because you wanted to help us.
You came here for the gold. All I meant was, the true
MacKendrick would not be motivated by thoughts of his
own reward."

"You are deluding yourselves if you believe such a
man exists," Malcolm stated harshly. "Any warrior who
becomes your laird will do so because he wants control of
your lands and your clan. Once here, he will see how
skilled your people are at making beautiful objects, and
he will want those as well, to sell to other clans and vil-
lages for more gold. He will take a pretty girl to his bed
and father children. And as the years go by, if he is fair
and just, no one will remember why he originally became
laird. At some point it will cease to matter. But I tell you
now, any man who comes to rule your clan will do so not
because of what he has to give, but because of what he has
to gain."

"You're wrong!" spat Ariella, jumping to her feet and
closing the distance between them. "There was a time,
MacFane, when you would have come only because you
were needed. That would have been more than reason
enough. You found ample reward merely in the act of
helping someone. Maybe you have changed, but you
cannot make me believe there is not another out there,

somewhere, who lives his life by the same standard of honor you once revered."

"Then you better goddamn well find him," drawled Malcolm, "before you are attacked by another who decides to butcher you one by one until he gets what he wants."

Vivid, brutal memories rose to Ariella's mind. She wrapped her arms around her body, trying to protect herself from those chilling images. "I will find him," she vowed in a trembling voice.

Malcolm stared at Rob in surprise. His arms were closed tightly around his small frame, as if he found the gesture comforting. Malcolm's memory of Ariella returned: She stood before him once again, her slim form taut with anguish as she wrapped herself in her arms. Her height had been about the same as the lad's, her head barely reaching the middle of Malcolm's chest. Disconcerted, Malcolm studied the slight figure before him. Rob's shoulder-length hair was tangled and dirty, making it impossible to assess its color, other than the fact that it was dark. He focused his attention on the face, trying to see beneath the layers of grime. The boy's grubby cheekbones were high, his nose small and straight, his chin a determined little thrust—a delicacy of structure Malcolm knew well, for he had studied it endlessly as he'd gazed at the statue of Ariella in his chamber. But, he reminded himself impatiently, this filthy, insolent pup was not the woman who had awakened such desire in him last night. He shook his head, wondering what the hell was the matter with him. If there was a resemblance, it was probably because they were somehow related. Ariella MacKendrick was dead. Hadn't Alpin assured him of that?

And so she remains, watching over us, trying to guide us along the next path.

No, he realized suddenly. Alpin hadn't told him she

was dead. He had said a part of her had died. And that, more than anyone in the clan, Ariella was a fighter.

If there was one thing Malcolm knew, it was that fighters didn't kill themselves.

He frowned.

There was something strange, Ariella noticed, about the way MacFane was staring at her. His expression was hard, and his blue eyes burned with intensity, as if he were trying to see deep within her. Unnerved, she turned away, fearing she had revealed too much to him.

"Believe what you like, MacFane," she finished indifferently, scratching her hip. "The matter is no concern of yours." She spat upon the ground for effect, pulled on her boots, then slumped her shoulders and began to stalk toward her horse.

He grabbed her by her wounded arm, causing her to cry out.

Malcolm eased his grip, but he did not release her. Instead he grasped the neckline of her shirt and tore it down with one quick motion, exposing her bandaged arm and part of her chest. Ariella gasped in outrage and jerked the fabric up, but she knew it was too late. He had seen the swath of linen binding her breasts flat. If that weren't enough, she could see that the sight of her bandage was bringing back the memory of the night before.

Malcolm stared at the girl before him, dumbfounded. She was as filthy and ragged as she had been an instant earlier, but suddenly he could not imagine mistaking her for a boy. Her features were too fine and delicate, her gray eyes too wide and beautiful. Anger had eradicated her slouched, boyish stance, straightening her spine so she could face him with the full height of her fury.

"My God," he breathed, overwhelmed, "you're alive."

"Yes!" she spat, casting him a look of pure rage. "With no thanks to you, MacFane!"

"But why?" he demanded, still struggling to believe the boy he had befriended was actually a woman. "Why did you pretend you were dead?"

"I had no choice!" she hissed. "Roderic attacked and murdered my father because he wanted me for his bride, even if it meant he had to kill every one of my people to force me to agree. Only my death would make him stop his brutality."

Roderic.

"Once I realized you weren't coming, and my clan could not possibly defeat his warriors, I set the tower afire, knowing I could escape through a secret passage that led to the lower level of the castle."

It couldn't be the same Roderic.

"What clan was this Roderic from?" demanded Malcolm brusquely.

"He said he was a Sutherland. But most of what he said was lies," she finished bitterly.

"How is it that he came to your lands?"

Ariella looked at him in confusion, not understanding his intense interest. "I found him two months before the attack, lying wounded near the MacFane border. He told me he had been fighting in King William's army, and that when he had returned home, he'd discovered his parents had died. He claimed he was on his way to Inverness to find work when he was attacked by thieves who stole his money, his sword, and his horse."

A compelling story, thought Malcolm. Bound to elicit nothing but compassion from a people as ingenuous as the MacKendricks.

"But his wounds were not life threatening," he drawled.

"No," said Ariella, shaking her head. "He had been stabbed in the shoulder and leg. He required stitches and rest, but nothing more."

Nothing serious. Just enough that a guileless girl

would take him home and care for him—giving him the opportunity to assess her clan's castle and its defenses.

"What did this man look like?"

She snorted in disgust. "Some thought him handsome." She paused a moment, then shrugged her shoulders. "I thought him handsome," she admitted reluctantly. "He was a tall man, with a broad, muscular body that spoke of endless hours working outdoors."

Or endless hours spent training.

"His hair was long and fair, and you could tell he was most proud of it. His features were fine, but it was his eyes that captured your attention. They were a most unusual color—"

Green.

"—a dark shade of green—"

A dull roar began to fill his ears.

"—really quite vain, which is why he was so furious when I cut his face," she finished scornfully.

"You cut his face?" he demanded, astonished.

"When he was dragging me up to the tower. He told me he had mortally wounded my father, and threatened to kill everyone in my clan if I didn't marry him. His words were horrible, so I took my dirk from under my gown and carved open his cheek."

"Christ almighty, he could have killed you!" thundered Malcolm, by now fully convinced this man was the Roderic he knew.

"Or I could have killed him," countered Ariella. "I was aiming for his throat. Unfortunately, he grabbed my wrist."

Malcolm shook his head, trying to absorb everything she was telling him. Roderic had assessed the Mac-Kendrick clan and decided he wanted it. So he had attacked, killed their laird, then tried to force his daughter to marry him. But she had killed herself, and he'd left.

"If Roderic wanted control of your clan, and you

were just a means of gaining that control, then why didn't he stay after you supposedly burned to death? He could have wed your sister instead." Catherine was young, but not so young Roderic couldn't have forced her to marry him.

"Catherine is not a direct descendant of the founder of our clan," explained Ariella. "Her parents died of a fever when she was two, and my father brought her to the castle to live with us. Marriage to her would not have given Roderic a blood tie to our original chief."

"Even so, he could have stayed and simply forced your clan to submit to him," argued Malcolm. "He didn't need you for that."

Ariella hesitated. She couldn't possibly tell him about the sword. If MacFane knew of its powers, he would want it for himself.

And he was not the one.

"He could have forced them to a point," she allowed, "but not in their hearts. Roderic had murdered their laird, as well as a dozen other men, and caused me to kill myself. No MacKendrick would ever forgive him for that. If he was foolish enough to stay here, it would only be a matter of time before poison was placed in his food, or his throat was cut as he slept. No matter how many warriors he brought to guard him, he would never have an easy moment. He must have realized this, so he just stole what he could and left." She shrugged her shoulders dismissively.

There was something she wasn't telling him. Roderic was not a warrior who retreated from something he wanted. And he could hardly have believed he had much to fear from these pipers and poets. If he had thought he might be poisoned, he would have forced a child to taste his food for him first. No, there was something else Roderic had wanted. Something that Ariella's death made him believe he could no longer have.

"Is this why you have pretended to be a boy?"

Malcolm asked, putting the matter aside. "Because you think if Roderic learns that you live, he will return?"

She nodded. "He will be furious when he discovers I tricked him. With neither a laird nor an army, he knows how vulnerable we are. My clan knew I was alive, but I could not risk letting any outsiders know."

"So this entire masquerade has been put on for my benefit," he drawled.

"Yours and Gavin's. Once you left, I could return to being myself. If a stranger came to the castle, I would change back into Rob."

Malcolm clasped his hands behind his back and watched the sunlight shimmer across the loch, contemplating everything she had told him. MacKendrick's daughter was alive. The terrible weight of her death had been lifted from his shoulders, but another burden had taken its place. Roderic could return at any moment, deciding he would assume control of the clan with or without Ariella. Or he could boast of his exploits to another, sending a new army to see what they could plunder. Either way, the MacKendricks were in imminent danger and needed a laird who could protect them.

The recognition that he was not that man cut his pride deep. But he was realistic enough to recognize that he had neither the strength, the stamina, nor even the respect to consider assuming such a position. Not that he wanted it, he reminded himself harshly. He had been a laird, and he had failed his people, resulting in scores of deaths.

He could not endure the possibility of such an agony again.

"Like it or not, the MacKendrick clan is not strong enough to repel another attack for long. You will have to make alliances, at least until you find this mythical laird and army you are waiting for. I am experienced in this kind of negotiation, so I can help you. Perhaps I can limit the reciprocal nature of the agreement. I will also stay and continue to make your clan as strong as possible, either until your new laird is in place, or until I have secured sufficient alliances that I believe you safe."

"How much gold will you expect for these services?"

Her question was insulting. "For no more than we initially agreed upon."

She looked at him in surprise.

"I am in a generous mood," he muttered tautly. "And now that I know who you are, there is no reason for you to crawl into the hearth every morning for my benefit. You will wash and resume dressing like a woman immediately—in something that covers your legs," he added, frowning with disapproval at the smooth curve of her grimy calves.

"But if a stranger comes—"

"If a stranger comes, you can put on whatever ridiculous disguise you feel most comfortable in," he snapped impatiently. "Until then you will resume your role as Ariella MacKendrick and conduct yourself accordingly." He began to limp toward his horse. "Which means no more training with the men," he added, shaking his head in disbelief.

"Why not?" she demanded. "I was doing very well."

"I will not have you wrestling with men," he growled, appalled that she had been doing so for over two weeks. "In a bloody plaid, no less." He hoisted himself onto Cain. "It is most unseemly."

Ariella cast him an exasperated look. Although anxious to rid herself of these wretched clothes and be clean again, she had begun to enjoy her daily training. "And how unseemly will it be, MacFane, if I am attacked by a man and don't know how to defend myself?" she challenged.

"No man will ever get that close to you, Ariella," he swore, his voice low and harsh. "Not while I am here."

His expression was ruthless, causing a shiver of fear to ripple through her. She was suddenly reminded of the warrior who had boldly thundered into her campsite, his sword swinging with merciless accuracy at the thieves who had tried to kill her. She was well aware of the extent of his physical weaknesses—yet as he sat upon his magnificent black mount, towering over her, she was convinced that were it only one man MacFane faced, he would surely win. In moments of fury the limitations of his broken, abused body no longer seemed to matter. She found that thought strangely comforting as she watched him turn his horse and ride away.

Until she remembered: If they were attacked, it would be by an army, not by one man.

CHAPTER 8

Clutching the sheets close to her chest, Elizabeth took a deep breath and opened the door.

"Oh!" she gasped, feigning surprise at seeing Gavin seated by the window. "I didn't know you were in here. I was going to change your bed linens, but I will come back later."

"Do it now, if you like," said Gavin as he continued to polish Malcolm's sword. "You aren't disturbing me."

Her mouth curving into a smile, she closed the door behind her.

"Perhaps you should leave the door open, Elizabeth," Gavin suggested. "Your father might not approve of your being in here with me alone."

"Agnes and Meagan are sweeping the corridor, and the dust is terrible. I would not want it getting into your room. Besides, I won't be but a moment." Not waiting for him to argue, she went to the bed and began to strip off the blankets. "You know, I'm sure I could get one of the lads to do that sharpening and polishing for you," she offered, nodding at the other sword, ax, and dirks lying on the floor.

He shook his head. "A warrior is responsible for his own weapons. Besides, I've been doing this for so many years, I could never be satisfied if another did it for me." He sighed. "When you get to be my age, you become set in your ways."

"So you're as ancient as all that, are you?" teased Elizabeth.

"Old enough to be your father."

"You're not!"

"I am," he assured her. "Forty-two, and starting to feel every day of it."

"Well, I'm twenty-two, so you would have had to wed as barely more than a lad to be my father," she scoffed, pulling off the sheets. A startling thought occurred to her. "You're not wed, are you?"

He became intently absorbed with some mark on the blade. "No."

"Were you?" she prodded, sensing he wasn't telling her everything.

"Yes."

"What happened?"

"She died." His tone was abrupt, indicating he did not want to discuss it.

"I'm sorry." She turned back to her task. "Was it recently, then?"

"No."

"Do you have any children?"

"Elizabeth, did you come in here to change the bed, or to interrogate me?"

"Why, of all the rude things to say!" She dropped the sheets to plant her hands on her hips. "It just so happens, Gavin MacFane, that we MacKendricks believe in making polite conversation with our guests. But I suppose after spending so much time fighting with MacFane and his army, you don't know anything about that."

"Forgive me," Gavin apologized, enjoying the flush that had risen to her cheeks. What a delightful creature she was, with her honey-gold hair falling in thick waves over her shoulders, and her pale-blue eyes sparkling with indignation. "I did not mean to insult you. Please continue with your quest—conversation."

"There's nothing more I wish to know," she assured him tartly, snapping the sheet over the mattress.

The room fell silent except for the whisper of the bedclothes being spread and tucked under the mattress. Gavin suddenly wished he hadn't offended her. In a moment she would be finished and leave. Which was for the best, he reminded himself. He was not there to indulge in a dalliance with a girl nearly half his age, regardless of how tempting the thought might be. He and Malcolm would be leaving in a few weeks. He did not want their departure complicated by Elizabeth Mac-Kendrick's tender feelings.

Or Gordon MacKendrick's wrath.

Still, he could not help but admire her as she leaned low over the bed, smoothing the ripples in the covers with her pale, slender hands. Her thin summer gown clung to her as she bent to adjust one corner, accentuating the fullness of her breasts. She was barely more than a girl, at least to him, who was so much older and battle worn and weary, and had already loved and buried both a wife and an infant. But as her fingers expertly caressed the fabrics on his bed, she seemed every inch a woman, all lush curves and soft skin, and brimming with laughter and life. He could not understand why one of the MacKendrick lads had not taken her as his bride. He smiled as he recalled the night she had boldly stood before the clan and announced she wanted to learn to fight. Not even her father had been able to stop her. A woman like that would need a strong man to match wits with her. A man experienced enough to understand her needs, and wise enough to let her explore them. He quickly considered the eligible MacKendrick youths, and just as quickly dismissed them.

"There, now," she huffed, gathering the old linens into a bundle. "I've finished." She started for the door, her hips swaying gently beneath her gown.

"Thank you, Elizabeth."

She stopped. "The next time you're needing your bed changed, Gavin, I'll be sure to send Ada. I can see you'll be more comfortable being tended by a woman nearer your own age." The door was almost closed as she sweetly added, "Of course, she's well past seventy, but you'll find she's as spry as ever." The door slammed shut.

Gavin smiled, his amusement tempered with regret. There was no one there, he suspected, who would make a suitable husband for Elizabeth MacKendrick.

Malcolm watched as the MacKendrick men cautiously practiced fighting each other with their gleaming new swords, shields, and axes. Their movements were tentative, making it easy for their opponents to anticipate the next point of attack.

"Faster," he commanded impatiently. "God help me, I've seen old women fight with more spirit."

"You're right, lad," agreed Angus. "Do you want Dugald and me to go in there and show them how to do it?"

"Thank you, Angus, that won't be necessary," said Malcolm. "I would prefer they learn to do it on their own."

"If you change your mind, we're more than willing to

oblige," Angus assured him. "I brought my father's sword." He patted the ancient weapon propped against his chair.

"Mine is heavier," boasted Dugald.

"Doesn't make it better," retorted Angus.

Alpin regarded them curiously. "Where is your sword, Dugald?"

"I left it in my chamber," he admitted. "It's far too heavy to carry around for no reason. But I could get it if we needed it," he hastily added, not wanting MacFane to think he couldn't participate in the training if he was asked.

"By the time you dragged it out here, training would be over," scoffed Angus.

"I could go and come back before you had time to climb off this platform," Dugald assured him testily. "After all, I'm three years younger than you."

"Two and a half."

"Three."

"I remember very clearly that it's two and a half."

"It's *my* age," pointed out Dugald, "so I think I know it better than you—"

Malcolm shook his head and turned his attention back to the men. The MacKendricks were progressing well, but they were still no match for a trained army, or for anyone who was not overly disturbed by the prospect of hacking off an arm or splitting a head open with an ax. If Roderic decided to return, these people had no hope of defeating the brutal warriors he would bring with him.

His jaw tightened with frustration.

Since learning over two weeks ago that it was Roderic who had attacked the MacKendricks, Malcolm had intensified the level of training for everyone. The wooden swords and shields were abandoned, and the men had begun training with real weapons. To prevent injury, they had started by slicing and thrusting into the air, so they could learn the weight and balance of their newly forged instruments. But Malcolm did not indulge them in this activity for long, ordering them to face each other as soon as they seemed capable. Unfortunately, training with real weapons had made them all terrified of hurting each other again. When he saw how timidly they clinked their swords together, he was forced to put them back to charging the sack figures once again.

He also asked Duncan to extend the hours on which the clan worked on the castle's fortifications. The work had been progressing at a reasonable pace, but that was no longer good enough. The new portcullis was still not completed, the parapet was only about two-thirds finished, and archers' slits had not been cut in all the towers. If attacked, the castle must be sufficiently secure that the invaders could be kept out for as long as possible. That would give the MacKendricks time to shoot as many of them as possible before they breached the curtain wall.

He did not want to contemplate what would happen once they were actually inside.

"Could we speak with you a moment, lad?" asked Dugald, interrupting Malcolm's thoughts.

"What is it?"

"We were thinking it might be a good time for you to order a feast," said Angus.

"Why?"

"To celebrate."

Malcolm looked at them blankly. "Celebrate what?"

"Why, the return of our Ariella," Dugald replied. "It's already been over two weeks."

"But she has always been here," pointed out Malcolm, "and everyone knew."

"The clan is pleased their mistress has been able to abandon her disguise and resume her rightful position as

MacKendrick's daughter," explained Alpin. "They would enjoy some kind of festivity to mark this event."

"Of course, if that doesn't seem reason enough, there are other things we could celebrate," allowed Angus. He drew his white brows together, thinking. "We could celebrate the marvelous progress the clan has made in its fighting skills."

"God's ballocks!" bellowed Ramsay from the courtyard. "What the hell are you trying to do, Graham, *kill me?*"

With great effort Malcolm refrained from pointing out that the MacKendricks had not yet reached a level that merited celebration.

"Then there is the work on the castle," added Dugald. "The lads have been laboring hard, and even though the parapet now blocks the view, the stonework is impressive."

"Really first-rate," agreed Angus enthusiastically.

"And the harvest is promising to be a good one," said Dugald, grasping for other reasons.

"And I just developed a particularly effective cure for stomach ailments," added Alpin. "One that works even better than boar droppings—"

"Fine," said Malcolm, not wanting to hear any more. "Order a feast if you like. As long as it doesn't interfere with training or work."

"Excellent," Angus said, beaming. "All you need do is tell Ariella, and she will organize it."

"Why can't you tell her?" demanded Malcolm.

"Why, we thought you might like to, lad," said Dugald.

MacFane turned abruptly to watch the clan. "I don't have time for that."

Angus looked surprised. "It will only take a minute—"

"I don't have time for it," he snapped. "If you want a feast, tell her yourselves."

"Very well, MacFane," agreed Alpin calmly. "We will tell her."

Malcolm knew they must think his behavior strange, but he did not care. The day he had discovered Rob was actually a girl, he had still been able to talk to her, because in her filthy, tattered, shapeless state, she retained the appearance of a thirteen-year-old lad. But that night she had appeared in the hall, bathed and dressed in a gown of forest green, which poured over her slim curves like water, leaving no question this was a woman he beheld. Her skin was radiant, her red-brown hair spilling like fire over her shoulders, its shorn length a bitter reminder that she had been forced to cut it because of him. And he had been overwhelmed by her. By her extraordinary beauty, which surpassed that of any woman he had ever known. By the knowledge that beneath that beauty was a woman of tremendous courage and strength, who had put her own pain aside to risk herself for her people. By the memory of the woman trembling in his arms as he had pulled her against him and felt desire surge through his veins.

And by the unbearable knowledge that she could have been his, if only he had not failed her so absolutely.

"And so the kelpie took the little girl to live in the sea with him, where they made a home in a cave of pink and white rock, and they slept on beds of feathery-soft water weed."

"What did they eat?" prodded Catherine, not ready for the story to end.

Ariella rinsed her gutted salmon in the bucket of cold water beside her. "They ate fish."

Catherine considered this a moment. "Was it smoked?"

"No," she replied, slicing open the belly of another

salmon. "Unfortunately, the kelpie didn't have a smoke-house in the ocean."

Catherine's eyes went round. "Was it raw?" she demanded, horrified by the thought.

"No, it was cooked," Ariella assured her.

"But how did they cook it if they were living in the ocean?"

Ariella scooped the entrails of another fish into a bucket as she grasped for an explanation. "The kelpie had magic powers," she finally supplied. "All he had to do was cast a spell, and he could make a fire that would burn in the ocean."

"Oh," said Catherine, nodding with satisfaction. Then she frowned. "Did they have bread?"

"Yes, they had bread," replied Ariella. "The kelpie had a big oven that baked the finest loaves you've ever seen, big and crusty and golden."

Catherine shook her head. "That doesn't make sense. If they could make a fire, and they could make an oven, then why couldn't they make a smokehouse?"

"I was wondering the same thing myself," said Elizabeth, smiling.

"I suppose they could have made a smokehouse if they wanted to," said Ariella, "but with all that fresh fish swimming around them, what did they need to smoke it for?"

"Because it tastes good," suggested Agnes.

"That's right," agreed Catherine. "Because it tastes good."

"Very well," Ariella conceded. "The next time I tell the story, I'll have the kelpie build an enormous smoke-house to smoke his fish in."

"I thought kelpies devoured the women and children they lured into the water," said Agnes, sawing off a fish's head.

Catherine gasped in shock. "They don't, do they, Ariella?"

"Not in my stories, they don't," said Ariella, mildly annoyed with Agnes for bringing up the point.

"How many fish do you think we've cleaned so far?" asked Elizabeth, changing the subject.

Ariella rubbed her forehead on her sleeve, careful not to let her hands touch her face. "About a thousand," she exaggerated wearily.

"My hands are going to smell for days," sighed Agnes.

"I have a special essence that will get rid of the smell, Agnes," Ariella assured her. "You mix it in hot water and soak your hands in it, and it takes the odor away."

"Just think, Ariella, if you were still pretending to be Rob, you wouldn't be stuck here gutting fish," remarked Elizabeth. "Did you prefer working on the castle with the men?"

"MacFane has even the women helping with the fortifications and the weapons," Ariella reminded her. "Except for the very heavy work."

"True. But I don't see any men helping with the preparation of food in case of siege, do you?"

"No," Ariella admitted. "I guess they reason if they catch it, they shouldn't have to clean it as well."

"If I had a choice in the matter, I would rather catch it," said Elizabeth. "Being out on the loch on a fine morning pulling in fish doesn't compare to this."

"I don't understand why MacFane is so intent on having us store so much food," complained Agnes, hacking open another creamy belly. "I mean, if we are attacked, won't he just send for his army?"

"He might," replied Ariella carefully, "assuming he was here."

Agnes looked up in surprise. "Is he leaving?"

"Not right away. But he will stay only until we have a new laird in place."

"How long do you think that will be?" asked Elizabeth, careful to mask her anxiety. When MacFane left, Gavin would be going with him.

Ariella shrugged. "I don't know. Not much longer, I hope. I keep thinking Alpin is long overdue for a vision. The sooner the sword is bestowed, the safer we will be."

"Why don't you just give MacFane the sword?" asked Catherine. "You and Papa always said the Black Wolf was the one."

"That was before I met him."

Catherine gave her sister a disapproving look. "Is it because he limps?"

"That is part of it," she admitted. "But there are other reasons."

"Like what?"

"Reasons you are too young to understand, Catherine," Ariella replied firmly, putting an end to the subject.

"So you are absolutely certain he is not the one?" persisted Agnes.

"Yes."

Elizabeth sighed. "It's a shame."

Ariella looked at her in surprise. "I thought you didn't like him."

"He scares me a little," Elizabeth confessed. "But it seems the clan is actually coming to like him, despite his temper and his physical weaknesses. He is an able teacher, and his recommendations for fortifying the castle have been good. He even settled a dispute this past week, and everyone was very content with the way he handled it."

"What dispute?" asked Ariella.

"Ewen's dog went digging in Thomas's garden and ruined all his summer vegetables. So Thomas went to Ewen about it, demanding payment and ranting that the dog should be killed. Ewen refused, saying it wasn't his fault that Thomas insists on burying old bones and food in his garden, which makes the dog want to dig.

Well, the two were about to come to blows, but they decided to talk to MacFane instead. He listened to both sides, then told Ewen his dog was his responsibility, and he would have to make amends when the dog did something wrong, or else keep him tied up. As for the dog, MacFane wouldn't hear of his coming to harm, saying it was only natural for him to want to dig, especially if someone was burying bones under freshly turned earth."

"Why wasn't I informed of this?" Ariella demanded, hurt that her people were going to MacFane for advice rather than to her.

"I don't know," said Elizabeth. "I suppose they thought MacFane had settled the matter to everyone's satisfaction, and there was no need to bother you with it."

"It is not a bother," she assured her. "My father did it, and now it is my duty to do it, *not* MacFane's."

"If it upsets you so much, why don't you speak to him about it?" suggested Agnes.

"I will." She buried her knife deep into another salmon. "When I get the opportunity," she qualified.

In truth, she was not certain when that would be. She and MacFane had not spoken to each other in the weeks that had passed since he had discovered who she really was. At first Ariella believed that because they were both exceptionally busy, their paths had simply not crossed. But then she began to notice MacFane retreating from a room the moment she entered, and she realized he was purposely avoiding her. It seemed now that he knew she was not a boy, he wanted nothing more to do with her. Initially, she had been insulted. Why should the fact that she was a woman eradicate their previous relationship? She angrily tossed her gutted fish into the bucket of rinse water.

And then she remembered the night he had discovered her before the fire in her chamber. She recalled how he had looked at her, his blue eyes burning with desire as he'd struggled to convince himself that what he saw could not possibly be real. He had pulled her hard against the solid frame of his body, enclosing her in strength and heat and need as he bent his head and took her lips in his. His cheek had been rough against her skin, his mouth sweet with wine, and he had seemed large and powerful and fearless, a man who could protect her from anything. And she had kissed him back, had wrapped her arms around his neck and pressed herself farther into him, wanting to feel the muscular, unyielding wall of his chest and waist and thighs against her own softness. With a trembling hand she raised her knife and sliced open the next fish.

Perhaps, she reflected, it was she who was avoiding MacFane.

"Drop rocks on them!" commanded Malcolm as he watched the first line of attackers attempt to climb the scaling ladders. *"Now!"*

A shower of sacks stuffed with earth were hurled off the battlements onto the men below. These were followed by some stale loaves of bread, a few wooden bowls, and several pairs of old boots.

"Now the boiling oil!" he ordered. "Hurry!"

The great cauldrons positioned on the timber platform above the gate were tilted forward.

"Bloody hell!" gasped Gordon as the liquid gushed over him. "That water is freezing!"

"Archers shoot!" commanded Malcolm. "Keep them away from the wall!"

The women positioned along the battlements and in the towers obediently sent a flurry of padded arrows into the air.

"I'm hit!" yelled Bryce, grabbing his chest. He staggered a few steps, then collapsed onto the ground.

"All those who are dead, go to the back of the line

and attack again," ordered Malcolm. "The rest of you, get up that wall! And you archers, keep shooting!"

"I'm nearly there!" shouted Duncan triumphantly. Leaning close against the wall, he continued to climb the ladder.

"Ramsay, Graham, don't just stand there!" yelled Malcolm. "Grab the ladder and throw it backward!"

Duncan's eyes widened in dismay as Ramsay and Graham obeyed their orders, pitching the ladder back with Duncan clinging desperately to it.

"Keep dropping those rocks!" shouted Malcolm. "Don't let them get up to the battlements!"

More loaves of bread were dropped between the merlons of the newly heightened parapet.

"You've got men at the gate with a battering ram!" warned Gavin as a group of MacKendricks rushed forward carrying a small tree trunk. "Pour boiling oil on them!"

A shower of water fell from the platform over the gate, but the tree-bearing MacKendricks were able to retreat in time to avoid it.

"Wait for them!" thundered Malcolm. "Watch their movements. And don't forget to guard the back, as well—it's just a matter of time before they discover the curtain wall is lower in the back."

A dozen MacKendricks instantly retreated to the back of the wall head to watch for invaders. Malcolm folded his arms across his chest and calmly waited for them to discover that they had now left too much of the front unguarded.

During the past two weeks the MacKendricks had overcome their fear of their new swords sufficiently that Malcolm had decided they were ready to fight a mock battle. The clan was divided into two teams, attackers and defenders. The object of the first phase of the battle was to keep the attackers out for as long as possible. Considering they were fighting with loaves of bread, cold water, and padded arrows, Malcolm thought they were doing a commendable job.

He could only hope they would do as well facing an actual army.

"Open the gate!" he shouted, limping toward his horse. "The attackers will gain entrance to the courtyard, and you must keep them out of the castle. Women, shoot only if you are well shielded, and only the men are permitted to go into the courtyard to fight. Move!" He swung himself heavily into his saddle.

In a sudden, terrified reaction Cain whickered and violently reared, throwing Malcolm hard against the ground.

The pain was excruciating.

The MacKendrick invaders immediately abandoned their battle and ran toward him, while the defenders watched anxiously from the battlements.

"Are you all right?" demanded Gavin tersely as he knelt beside Malcolm, his face creased with concern.

"Are you hurt, MacFane?" called Duncan.

"He's fine," Gavin assured him before Malcolm could answer. "He just needs a moment to recover."

"Are you sure?" asked Gordon doubtfully. "If he's hurt, we could carry—"

"That was a nasty fall," interrupted Niall, wandering up behind them. "Do you often have trouble staying on your horse?"

"Get the hell away from me!" bellowed Malcolm, suddenly enraged. *"All of you!"*

The MacKendricks slowly withdrew to the castle wall.

Mortified that they had witnessed such a humiliating incident, Malcolm struggled to pull himself off the ground. Gavin offered his hand, but Malcolm ignored it. Forcing himself to conquer his pain, he awkwardly rose, then hunched against Cain for support. His horse lowered his massive head and gently nuzzled his shoulder, neighing softly. Malcolm stroked Cain's nose, wondering what had happened to make the animal throw him off. Cain was a superbly disciplined mount, who remained calm even in the bloodiest of clashes. Malcolm quickly ran his hands over Cain's back and sides. Finding no apparent injury, he loosened the animal's girth and lifted his saddle.

Blood trickled from where a metal spur was embedded deep in the horse's flesh.

"Jesus Christ."

"What is it?" asked Gavin.

"Who saddled Cain this morning?" he demanded tautly.

Gavin stared at the spur in disbelief. "It was young Colin, the same as always, but he would never—"

"Colin!" thundered Malcolm.

Colin hesitantly came forward. "Yes, MacFane?" he said, his voice trembling.

"Do you know anything about this?"

Colin's eyes grew wide with horror.

"When did you saddle Cain?" asked Gavin gently.

"I saddled him first, like I do every morning." He glanced nervously at Malcolm. "I want to make sure he's ready for you when you come down for training."

"And then you leave him in his stall?"

Colin nodded.

"Thank you, Colin. You may go," said Gavin.

"Wait," commanded Malcolm. Holding on to the horse's reins, he quickly extracted the spur. Cain let out a pained protest but remained still. Malcolm stroked him, murmured a few words of praise into his ear, then stiffly handed the reins to Colin.

"Take him to the stables and clean his wound. See if you can get some ointment from Alpin to apply to it. I will not be riding him again until the wound has healed."

"Yes, MacFane," said Colin solemnly.

Malcolm watched as the boy led Cain away.

"He didn't do it."

"No," Malcolm agreed. "But when I find the bastard who did, I'm going to kill him." Inhaling deeply, he took a step toward the castle. Pain streaked through his leg and up his spine. "Mother of God!" he gasped, bending over.

"Here," said Gavin, moving beside him, "lean on me."

"No," ground out Malcolm. "I will not have them watch me hobbling toward them on another man's arm like an old woman."

"For God's sake, Malcolm—"

"*Leave me be!*"

He took a deep breath, steeling himself against the pain.

Then he slowly limped into the courtyard, burning with humiliation, and unable to straighten his back.

Ariella shifted her basket to her other arm as she wearily climbed the hill. She had been with Glynis since late the night before, helping her endure the long hours of her birthing pains. Finally the baby had decided it had kept its mother waiting long enough, and out came the sweetest little boy Ariella had ever seen, with a scowling face and a brilliant thatch of red hair. Glynis seemed to recover from her ordeal almost instantly, and the two women laughed as they examined the baby's tiny fingers and toes, and debated whether he resembled his father or his mother more. Ariella stayed with them until they fell asleep, then quietly left the cottage. She was anxious to find Kenneth and tell him his little family was waiting to see him.

MacFane's training must have ended for the day, for there were no sounds of fighting as she approached the castle. She entered the courtyard to find the clan milling about, speaking to each other in hushed voices. Evidently they had been overly concerned about Glynis's long labor. Kenneth hurried toward her, followed by Duncan, Andrew, Angus, and Dugald.

"It's a boy, Kenneth!" she announced happily. "A fine, healthy boy. Glynis is tired, but well. You may go see her now."

Relief lit his face. "Thank you, Ariella!" he called, racing out the gate.

She gazed round at the solemn faces of her clan. "I don't know why you all look so gloomy," she teased. "Tonight we must celebrate the arrival of a new MacKendrick!"

"Ariella," began Duncan grimly, "MacFane is hurt."

Her smile vanished. "What happened?"

"He fell off his horse, lass," said Angus.

She looked at him in disbelief. "He fell off?"

"Actually, he was thrown off," qualified Dugald.

"There was a spur under Cain's saddle," explained Andrew. "And when MacFane sat on him—"

"Where is he?" she demanded.

"He has retired to his chamber," said Duncan. "Gavin took him three pitchers of wine, and then MacFane ordered him to get out. Alpin suggested he might have some medicine that would help, but Malcolm refused him permission to enter. When Alpin tried to go in, MacFane smashed one of the pitchers against the door. That was over two hours ago." He hesitated. "He is unable to straighten his back, Ariella."

Ariella turned and ran toward the castle.

"Touch that door again and I'll kill you."

Ariella cautiously opened the door to find Malcolm lying curled on the bed, two empty pitchers abandoned on the floor beside him. He grabbed one as she entered, preparing to hurl it at her. On seeing who she was, he dropped it.

"Go away," he mumbled thickly.

"No."

She closed the door behind her and deposited her basket on the table.

His lids were heavy, his blue eyes clouded with alcohol and pain. "Then bring me more wine," he commanded. "Now."

"I think you're drunk enough, MacFane. I know you're in pain, but getting sotted is hardly the answer."

He laughed, a bitter, jeering sound. "What the Christ would any of you know about pain?"

"I haven't experienced as much of it as you have," she conceded, unpacking the jars from her basket, "but I know something about alleviating it."

"Dear God," he murmured helplessly, "she's going to make me take another bath."

"I doubt at this moment you could get yourself off that bed and into a tub," she said, moving toward him. "Do you think you've broken anything?"

"I think I've broken *everything*."

"Let me see."

His expression grew menacing. "Don't touch me."

"You know, I remember saying the same thing to you when I had that arrow in my arm."

"That was different," Malcolm assured her.

"How?"

"I will kill you."

"So you keep saying."

She laid her hands with infinite gentleness on his injured right arm and began to feel her way slowly along the bone. Despite his threats, he did not attempt to hurt her. Once she reached his hand, she carefully moved each of his fingers, watching to see if he grimaced. Then she examined his left arm.

"Well, you have a few bones still intact," she announced. "Let me ease you onto your back so I can try your legs."

"My legs aren't broken."

"Are you sure?"

"I walked in here on my own, for Christ's sake."

"So the injury is mostly to your back?"

He attempted to nod but was stopped by the flash of pain down his spine.

Realizing he couldn't move, Ariella went to the other side of the bed. She began to lift his shirt, and saw his body stiffen.

"I will be gentle, MacFane," she promised. "Try to relax."

"I can't bloody well relax. I can't straighten my goddamn back." His voice was rough, but she could hear the despair in it.

"I know," said Ariella softly. "But I cannot help you if you will not let me see exactly where your injury is."

She eased down his plaid so the whole of his scarred back was exposed to her. Then she gently laid her fingers against the base of his spine. He flinched, indicating the pain there was great.

"It's all right," she told him, her voice low and soothing. "I won't hurt you."

He exhaled the breath he was holding.

Ariella gingerly proceeded with her examination, moving her fingers up the massive wall of his back, rib by rib. The muscles were locked in spasm, making his body feel as if it were carved of stone. Each time she touched a hard knot of pain, he flinched or inhaled sharply, indicating where the worst areas were. She was gentle but thorough, feeling her way up each segment of his spine, along his shoulders, then down both sides of his rib cage.

"I think you've cracked at least two ribs," she told him as she finished. "The muscles in your back are badly bruised, and as a result they have contracted, which is why it hurts so much when you try to straighten yourself. The bones in your spine feel as if they are not aligned properly, which means they are pinching you, and that is also causing a great deal of pain."

"Wonderful," he remarked tautly. "Now that you've finished torturing me, bring me more wine."

"You must learn other ways of dealing with your pain," she told him, easing down his shirt. "A warrior cannot get blinding drunk every time he doesn't feel well."

"I'm no longer a warrior," Malcolm reminded her bitterly. "So I can do whatever the hell I like."

"Not while you are here, you can't," she countered. "My clan believes you are the great Black Wolf, laird of the Clan MacFane. It is most unseemly for you to drink and throw things at those who are trying to help you." She went to the door. "Try to rest. I'll be back in a few minutes."

"Are you all right?" demanded Duncan as she went into the corridor.

"Of course I'm all right."

"How is he?" asked Andrew.

"He is in a great deal of pain," she said quietly. "His back was bad before, but this fall has made it much worse."

"Will he get better?" demanded Gavin.

His expression was harsh, betraying the depth of his concern. In that moment Ariella realized just how devoted Gavin was to Malcolm. MacFane had once been his laird, and loyalty had been expected of him. But when Malcolm had been stripped of his position and banished from his clan, Gavin had gone with him, to live an isolated existence in a miserable hut. Whatever offense Malcolm had committed, it had not been enough to sever the bonds of their friendship.

"He will get better, Gavin," she assured him. "But I need your help. Please go in there and build a fire so the chamber is warm. I don't think he will throw anything at you. Duncan, please fetch two swine's bladders filled with a mixture of warm water and oil. Also, bring a pitcher of fresh, cool water for drinking. He has consumed more than enough wine for one day. Andrew, tell Alpin I require a jar of the ointment he makes for relaxing muscles and easing pain. Bring it to me in a pot, so I can heat it over the fire. I will also need some long strips of linen to bind around him when I have finished."

"Are you going to bleed him?" asked Gavin. "The MacFane healer always bled him when the pain got bad."

"Did it help?" asked Ariella curiously.

He shrugged his shoulders. "After a few days the pain would generally ease. I don't know if it was because of the bleeding or not."

"My mother didn't believe in bloodletting, so I am not trained in it. If you aren't certain that it helped, I won't try it. Come," she said, opening the door, "let us get the room warm."

Within a short while a blazing fire burned in the hearth, and Duncan and Andrew had returned with everything she had asked for.

"Drink this," Ariella ordered, handing MacFane a goblet. "All of it."

With great effort Malcolm raised himself onto his arm and accepted the cup. "What is it?"

"Water mixed with a powder that will help ease the pain. Because you have consumed so much wine, it may also make you sleepy."

Malcolm awkwardly tilted his head and swallowed it. "How long before it works?" he demanded as she took the goblet from him.

"Not long," she promised. "I need to take off your shirt. Do you think you can sit up a little?"

Humiliated by his helplessness, he forced himself to a hunched sitting position. Ariella quickly stripped off his shirt, then helped ease him against the mattress.

"I am going to begin by rubbing this ointment into your back," she told him, fetching the pot from the fire.

"You may stay on your side for now, but eventually you will be relaxed enough to lie on your stomach."

"I doubt that."

She could not blame him for his skepticism. She rolled up the sleeves of her gown and spread some of the heated ointment over her palms. Then she gently laid her hands against his back and began to massage him. Her touch was light at first, giving his body time to accept her ministrations. Gradually his flinching and sharp intakes of breath lessened, telling her she could increase the pressure. She moved across his back slowly, gently, swirling her fingers and palms over the taut muscles with languid persistence, feeling the warmth of the ointment as it penetrated his skin and brought relief to his aching flesh. She worked in silence, listening to the sound of his breathing, using it as a guide to tell her where the pain was great and where she was having an effect. She kept his body slick, making it easier for her to slip across the bronzed shimmer of his skin, feeling his powerful form rise and fall beneath her soothing touch. After a long while he finally sighed and shifted his position, straightening his spine.

"Turn onto your stomach, MacFane," she instructed quietly.

He did not argue but simply did as she told him. Ariella suspected the powder she had given him had taken effect.

Now that he was on his stomach, it was far easier for her to massage him. She focused on the valley of his back for a while, and when she was finished, she placed one of the warm swine bladders on it, so the muscles could absorb the heat. Then she moved up, gently kneading the solid layers of spasm on each side of his spine. Little by little the hardness beneath her fingers began to yield. Her touch grew firmer, delved deeper, encouraging the muscles to release their grip. When her hands began to ache, she retrieved the other swine bladder, which she had kept warm before the fire, and gently placed it on his upper back.

MacFane's eyes were closed and he was breathing deeply, his head resting against his arm. Wanting him to be as comfortable as possible, Ariella removed his boots, examining his injured leg as she did so. He had told her it had shattered when his horse collapsed on it. She ran her hands up the muscled calf, bent it slightly at the knee, then continued her journey along his thigh. The bone seemed straight enough, and from what she could tell, he had not lost any length. But she knew a bad break could plague a person with pain for the rest of his life. The leg was stiff, so she rubbed some ointment into her palms and began to massage it. After watching him limp this past month, she wondered if there was anything that could be done to ease the ache and strengthen the muscles. Perhaps with exercise—

"I didn't fall."

She looked up at him, surprised that he was still awake. "Pardon?"

"I didn't fall," he repeated thickly. "Someone put a spur under my saddle."

"I know." She continued to massage his leg.

He nodded with satisfaction and closed his eyes again. "I'm not in the habit of falling off my goddamn horse." The words were slurred, but she could hear the anger in them.

She thought of him thundering into her camp wielding his sword in both hands. No, MacFane was not in the habit of falling off his horse. Someone was trying to drive him away. The arrow hadn't worked, so a spur had been placed under his saddle, apparently in the hopes that the fall would not only injure him physically, but humiliate him in front of the entire clan.

"I think it was Niall," he mumbled.

She paused. "Why do you say that?"

"He has never tried to hide his contempt for me." He

lifted his lids and regarded her a moment, his blue eyes suddenly intense. "And I've seen the way he looks at you." His expression was dark, as if the matter angered him. Then he sighed and closed his eyes once more.

Ariella considered this. Niall had shared her loathing of MacFane when he had failed to answer her father's missive. She had even encouraged his fury when her clan had been attacked and MacFane had failed to come. She could understand his expressing his contempt, but could Niall actually be trying to drive MacFane away? To do so would not be in the best interests of the clan. Was it possible his rage was that great?

Deeply disturbed by the possibility, she removed the cooling swine bladders from MacFane's back. He shifted onto his side, his head still resting on the hard pillow of his arm, his dark-brown hair spilling loosely over his massive shoulder. Deciding she would bind his ribs with the linen strips tomorrow, she drew a blanket over him, then stayed there a moment, studying him.

He exuded an extraordinary aura of power and vulnerability as he lay there, injured and drugged, yet somehow still formidable. How cruelly ironic, that after fighting so many battles as the great Black Wolf, his greatest enemy now was his own body. Perhaps she had asked too much of him by bringing him here to train her people. From early morning to late evening he labored—training, planning, overseeing the fortifications to the castle. His demanding days would exhaust a man at the peak of his physical abilities, never mind one for whom it was an effort to cross a room or mount the stairs. And now someone was determined to make him leave, even if it meant injuring him in the process. It was wrong to expect he should remain under such circumstances, even if he had promised to remain until they found a new laird. She must send him away as soon as he was fit to ride, before he was injured even worse that he had been today. In his current state he could do nothing more to help them. It was now up to her to find a warrior who had an army and who could wield the sword.

Yet as she stood beside him watching the even rise and fall of his chest, she could not help but wonder what would happen to MacFane when he left. He had no family or clan who would joyously celebrate his return. Instead he would go back to the dank, filthy hut he shared with Gavin, where his days were nothing but long, empty hours filled with pain, drink, and bitterness. Although this fact had never bothered her before, suddenly she found the idea abhorrent. However MacFane had failed his people, did he really deserve to be condemned to such a miserable existence?

His brow was creased, indicating he still struggled with his pain. He moaned slightly and buried his face in his arm, as if trying to escape his discomfort. A dark lock of hair slipped across the clenched line of his jaw. Without thinking, Ariella leaned over and gently brushed the hair off his face, her fingers grazing the sandy surface of his cheek. MacFane's hand instantly clamped around her wrist, binding her to him with bruising force.

He opened his eyes and glared at her, his gaze menacing as he fought to clear the mists of alcohol and herbs. When he realized who she was, his grip eased, but he did not release her. Instead he pulled her down, until she hovered barely a breath away from him.

"I will not leave you, Ariella," he whispered roughly, "until I know you are safe."

Ariella stared at him, her heart beating rapidly, wondering how he could have known what she was thinking. "You cannot stay, MacFane," she countered. "Whoever wants you gone will not stop until you are dead."

Malcolm released her wrist and waited for her to move away from him. When she did not, he hesitantly laid his fingers against her cheek. "I'm already dead," he murmured, fascinated by the softness of her skin. "I have been for a long time."

They stayed like that a moment, staring at each other. And then, overcome with weariness, Malcolm sighed and drifted into sleep, his hand still pressed against the silk of Ariella's cheek.

CHAPTER 9

Laughter floated through the still evening air, merrily blending with the strains of harp and bagpipes.

"Sounds like they're havin' a fine time," drawled Tavis, scratching at his filthy scalp. "They seem to have recovered, all right."

Gregor sniffed the air. "I smell roastin' meat." He spat heavily onto the ground. "I say we attack now, while there's still plenty of food."

"Aye," agreed Murdoch. "No point waitin' till it's all gone."

"Patience, gentlemen."

Their leader stood with his feet braced apart and his hands lightly clasped behind his back, calmly surveying the MacKendrick castle. "Many an attack has been lost by overzealous men who followed their appetites, instead of waiting for the right moment."

"With these MacKendricks, there's no need to wait," sneered Gregor. "We just go in and take what we want, same as last time."

"They have no defenses, and they sure as hell don't know how to fight," added Murdoch. "We might as well get in there, eat a decent meal, and find a lass to keep us warm tonight." He started to move toward his horse.

"Wait."

The command was given softly, but Murdoch obeyed.

"I agree they will be easy to overcome," said Roderic, turning away from the castle. "But they have been training and fortifying their castle, which might make the task a little more troublesome."

"You said they've been training under a drunken cripple," sneered Tavis. "What could he have possibly shown that group of jugglers?"

"Probably nothing," agreed Roderic. "Still, a new gate was being forged, and they are building the parapet higher."

"But it isn't finished," pointed out Murdoch dismissively. "We can easily get over the curtain wall."

"Once we're in, they'll be too scared to put up a fight," snorted Gregor. "We'll grab MacKendrick's daughter, make her give us the sword, and that'll be the end of it."

"And the beginning," murmured Roderic, turning to look at the brightly lit castle once more.

Fury burned deep in the pit of his stomach as he studied the ghostly silhouette of the unfinished tower. The deceiving little bitch thought she had tricked him. First she had carved open his cheek, forever marring his once perfect face. And then, just as he had found a way to force her to give him the sword, she had foiled him by setting the tower afire. He remembered his shock when he had seen flames leaping out the windows and licking at the dry wood of her prison. In that moment he had believed the powerful MacKendrick sword would never be his.

But she hadn't died.

To make this unexpected revelation even more interesting, Malcolm was here. Roderic could not imagine what had induced his former commander and laird to think he could be of any help to these people. The great Black Wolf was nothing more than a pitiful, mangled animal, who survived the emptiness of his days by drinking himself into a stupor. The MacKendricks were deluding themselves if they thought Malcolm had anything to offer them. He briefly considered the possibility that Ariella had given MacFane the sword, then quickly dismissed it. According to his contact, she did not believe he was the next laird. Given her penchant for physical and moral perfection, this was not surprising. If there was one thing Roderic had learned during the weeks she had so carefully nursed him, it was that Ariella was convinced the next laird would be perfect.

The scarred, lame, drunken Black Wolf hardly fit that description.

He lifted his hand to his cheek and absently stroked the ugly, thick line she had left there. For a while he had nearly had her convinced that he was the man she sought. Then she had gone to that babbling old fool who claimed to see the future, and he had told her he was not. Although disappointed, Ariella was resigned to Alpin's opinion. Apparently the responsibility she felt toward her people outweighed her own personal preferences.

That was when Roderic had realized he would have to take firmer control of the matter.

"The MacKendricks will be no harder to overcome

this time than last," he assured his men. "Once I have the girl, I will make her see how extremely perilous it will be for her people if she does not give me the sword. But we will wait until they have eaten and drunk their fill just the same. Then we will attack, when their minds are clouded and their bodies clumsy."

"But the food will be gone," protested Gregor sulkily.

"The castle will be ours," pointed out Roderic. "We will have them make more."

Moderately appeased by this thought, his men joined the other warriors to inform them of his plan.

Roderic returned his gaze to the golden shafts of light spilling from the windows of the castle. Soon the sword would be his. Once he was certain its powers were transferred to him, he would initiate his new wife to her duties in his bed.

And then he would cut her face, so she would understand the price of inciting her new laird's fury.

The great hall was swirling with color and merriment as the MacKendricks joined hands and danced in a huge circle around the room. The men were dressed in their best shirts and plaids, the women in their finest gowns, which they hadn't worn since the day MacFane had arrived. The tables were laden with platters of roasted meat and fresh fish, great rounds of dark bread, thick wedges of cheese, and sweet tarts garnished with plump berries. All this was being washed down with endless pitchers of ale and wine, and the result could be seen in the sparkling eyes and flushed cheeks of the dancers. Graham and Ramsay were playing their bagpipes with particular enthusiasm from the wooden gallery above, while Bryce and Hugh kept stopping to take a hearty draft of ale before attempting an even more astounding juggling feat.

"That Gavin is the most vexing man," complained Elizabeth, adjusting the neckline of her gown for what seemed to Ariella the hundredth time. "There he is sitting at that table with Angus, Dugald, and my father, *talking*, when he should be up dancing with everyone else."

"Why don't you go over and ask him to dance with you?" asked Ariella.

Her expression brightened. "Do you think I should?"

"It would be terribly forward," said Agnes, clearly uncomfortable with the idea.

"Gavin is a guest here," pointed out Ariella. "He is probably reluctant to invite a woman to dance, for fear she might think he is courting her. But if *you* ask him to dance, no one will mistake his intentions. He will accept to be polite, especially if you ask in front of your father."

"You're right!" said Elizabeth, evidently not troubled by the fact that he might be an unwilling partner. Shifting her neckline marginally lower, she abandoned her friends and made her way across the room.

Gavin watched over the rim of his cup as Elizabeth strode purposefully toward him.

"Gavin MacFane, are you planning to sit in that chair all night, or will you get up and dance with me?" she demanded.

Her father looked at her in surprise. "Have you taken leave of your senses, lass? That's no proper way to talk to a man."

"Gavin is too shy to ask me to dance, Papa," she explained, "so I'm doing the asking for him."

"Young lassies today have such spirit," commented Angus, shaking his head.

Gordon stared at Gavin in bewilderment. "Is this true?"

"Is what true?" asked Gavin.

"That a warrior like you is too shy to ask my daughter to dance?"

"Of course not."

"There, you see?" said Gordon to his daughter. "He's not too shy."

"Well, then, why doesn't he?" persisted Elizabeth, casting Gavin a challenging look.

Gordon frowned, considering. "Are you saying my daughter isn't pleasing enough for you?"

"No," Gavin assured him. "Your daughter is beautiful."

Elizabeth's expression softened. "Really?"

"But that isn't the issue," he added firmly.

"Ah, you're married, then," concluded Dugald.

"No."

"Spoken for?" asked Angus.

"No."

"Not much of a dancer?" suggested Gordon.

"No."

"Well, what is it, then?" asked Dugald.

They were all staring at him, expecting some kind of explanation. "I'm too old for her," he finally muttered.

Angus looked at him blankly. "You're what?"

"Too old." Suddenly he was feeling foolish.

"Did the lad say he was too old?" demanded Dugald, looking incredulous.

"Of course not," scoffed Angus. "He said he was too cold."

"Go on then, Gavin," said Gordon, slapping him heartily on the back. "We MacKendricks are not in the habit of forcing a man to marry a lass just for dancing with her. And if I know my Elizabeth, she's not likely to leave until you say yes."

Gavin looked up at Elizabeth, whose pretty mouth was curved in a triumphant smile. "Very well," he conceded, rising from the table. "Elizabeth, would you honor me with a dance?"

"Why, I'd be pleased to, Gavin," she returned sweetly. "If you think a man of your advanced years will be able to keep up with me."

Ariella watched as Gavin led Elizabeth to the center of the hall. He swept into a low bow, then grasped her hand and proceeded to lead her through a lively dance that Elizabeth had some trouble following. She was eager to learn, however, and by the end of it they both looked as if they might collapse from breathlessness and laughter.

Ariella smiled.

Just a few months ago she had danced with her father in this very room. Laird MacKendrick had been a handsome, accomplished man, skilled at poetry, hunting, and playing the bagpipes. His wisdom and compassion had made him a respected chief, and all the MacKendricks had loved him. Although her clan had been shattered by his death, and the deaths of all the others who had fallen that day, tonight she could detect no trace of sadness in the room. Except in her. She found herself missing her father's comforting presence, and the safe feeling she had known every time he had wrapped his burly arms around her and tickled her cheek with his graying beard as he'd kissed her good night. The burden of her clan's welfare was also weighing heavily on her shoulders this evening. Despite their recent progress, Ariella knew they could never repel an attack for long. MacFane had said so himself.

"Is MacFane coming down?" asked Duncan as he, Andrew, and Niall joined her and Agnes.

"I don't know," she replied. "He is much better than he was three days ago, but I doubt he will feel like joining us. The medication I have been giving him for the pain makes him tired."

"Careful he doesn't grow too fond of it," remarked Niall dryly. "He might find that your powders work faster than all the wine he consumes."

Anger flared within her. "Why do you dislike him so?"

His expression hardened. "You know why, Ariella.

He failed us. Your father and many others died because he couldn't be bothered coming here. My God, you could have been killed. And then he finally arrives, but without his army. He is clearly not the next MacKendrick, yet you permit him to stay here, sleep in your father's chamber, and order us about as if he were." He shook his head in disgust. "His very presence is a dishonor to your father's memory."

Ariella searched Niall's eyes as he spoke. It was obvious he had nothing but contempt for MacFane. Was his loathing great enough that he was trying to drive the man away?

"It hurts me to hear you speak so," she told him quietly, "when you know I would never do anything to dishonor—"

"MacFane is here," interrupted Andrew.

Ariella lifted her gaze to see MacFane at the top of the staircase. He stood tall as he surveyed the room, betraying no evidence of his injury of three days earlier. He wore a new pleated shirt, which was elegantly stitched about the neck and wrists in a pattern of fine gold thread. His green-and-black plaid was neatly belted about his waist, then swept over his shoulder and secured with his battered old brooch. As he looked down at the celebrating MacKendricks, his muscled legs braced wide and his expression cool, he seemed every inch the powerful, commanding Black Wolf, a man of enormous strength and fortitude.

Then he began to stiffly descend the stairs, shattering the illusion.

"He is much better," commented Agnes, sounding surprised.

"Yes," murmured Ariella. She firmly reminded herself that three days ago he had been unable to straighten his back. "He is."

Malcolm struggled to keep his gait even as he crossed the floor, painfully aware of everyone's eyes upon him. This was the first time the clan had seen him since he had been thrown off his horse, and he was anxious to appear strong and fit. In truth, he was feeling much better. Ariella's gentle, persistent treatments of massage, heat, stretching—and a surprising manipulation of his spine that had caused a painless cracking sound—had alleviated his suffering considerably. She had given him detailed instructions about gently stretching and exercising his back, arm, and leg, and he had tried doing so for the first time that day. Although he had been initially reluctant to attend the evening's celebration, the sound of laughter and music filtering through the stone walls of his chamber had been irresistibly inviting. Now that he was up and dressed, he felt remarkably well.

Especially as he approached Ariella.

Her slender form was garbed in a long-sleeved sapphire gown of soft wool, which accentuated her smooth curves. Over this she had arranged a length of beautifully woven scarlet-and-blue plaid, which was fastened to her shoulder by a jeweled pin, and gathered at the waist by a finely wrought silver chain. Her hair rippled across her shoulders in brown and copper waves, like earth and fire, thought Malcolm, watching the golden waver of torchlight playing over it. Once again he was astonished she had been able to conceal her extraordinary beauty from him for so long. Were he to tell the tale to anyone who caught a glimpse of her, that person would have to wonder if he had been completely blind, or perpetually drunk.

"Good evening, milady," he said, giving her a small bow. "Agnes," he added, turning to her and bowing again.

Ariella nodded, surprised by his courtly manner. MacFane seemed to be feeling unusually well, yet the clarity of his blue eyes told her he had not been drinking.

"It is good to see you are better, MacFane," said Duncan.

"Thank you."

"Incredible that a few days ago you could barely stand," remarked Niall. "Do you think your recovery will last?" His tone was flagrantly skeptical.

Malcolm calmly regarded the hostile young man. "I am moved by your concern, Niall. Fortunately, I received the finest care. I am confident that should my back ail me again, Ariella will come to me with her warm oils and soothing touch."

Niall's face darkened with fury.

So it was true, Malcolm mused. Niall was in love with Ariella. Malcolm glanced at her, suddenly concerned that she harbored tender feelings for this handsome man.

It was difficult to tell, given that she was now glaring at them both.

"Forgive me, milady," he said, seeking to soothe her ire. He did not know if it was the occasion, or the fact that he really was feeling well this evening, but he was experiencing an unfamiliar desire to be elegant in his manner. Unfortunately, his memory of how to behave so was fragmented. "I fear I should ask you to dance," he began, "but my condition will not permit it. May I escort you to your table instead?" he asked, offering her his arm.

Ariella looked at him in bewilderment. She had not known MacFane was capable of such graceful manners. Certainly he had made no effort to use them since they had met. But he had not always lived like an animal in the mean hut where she had found him, she realized. He had been raised in a castle as the only son of Laird MacFane, groomed from birth to assume his rightful position as the next chief. The MacFanes were a large clan, known for their wealth as well as for their army. Perhaps there had been a time when Malcolm had enjoyed feasting with his clan. Maybe there had even been a time when he had been able to dance.

Moved by the thought, she reached out and laid her hand on his arm. "Thank you, milord. I find myself weary from standing for so long."

They walked slowly to accommodate his leg, although Ariella thought his limp was barely noticeable this evening. He escorted her to the laird's table, where the council was seated, pulled out her chair for her, then took his place beside her. This was the first time they had sat so, and Ariella found herself strangely overwhelmed by his enormous size. It was as if the table had instantly grown smaller, and she was forced to move to the edge of her chair so she didn't feel crowded by Malcolm's powerful presence.

"Why are you squirming around like that?" asked Angus. "Is there something wrong with your chair?"

"I'm not squirming," Ariella retorted.

"You're looking fit this evening, MacFane," remarked Gordon. "That shirt that Ewen's wife made suits you well."

"Thank you."

Ariella turned her attention to the shirt, which accentuated the enormous breadth of his chest and was handsomely detailed with gold thread. "Annie made you that shirt?"

"It was a gift," Malcolm explained. "A gesture of thanks for settling a matter between her husband and a neighbor."

"The problem with the dog?"

He looked at her in surprise. "You heard about it?"

"This is a small clan. No one can do anything without everyone's knowing."

"I will try to bear that in mind," Malcolm remarked, reaching for the pitcher in the center of the table. "Would you care for some wine?"

She nodded. He filled her goblet, hesitated, then placed the pitcher back.

"Aren't you having any?" asked Ariella in surprise.

"I find tonight I have no desire for it." He removed his dirk from his belt and began to serve some meat onto the trencher they shared.

"So you are really feeling well, then?"

"Yes." He regarded her steadily. "Thanks to you."

His eyes were clear of the mists of alcohol and pain, yet they were as unfathomable as the deepest of lochs. She felt strangely unnerved as she returned his gaze, as if she were seeing a part of him that until now he had kept hidden, or perhaps had himself forgotten existed. This was another aspect of the man once known as the Black Wolf. It was now clear that not only had he been a great warrior, he was also a man who was at ease in polite society. Moreover, he had been a man capable of exercising restraint.

It pained her to think how far he had fallen.

"It will be good to have you back training us tomorrow," remarked Angus cheerfully.

"Angus and I have tried our best to help Gavin in your absence, but he never seemed to hear us. I think the lad is a bit deaf," confided Dugald.

"Really?" said Malcolm. "How odd I never noticed."

A bellowing voice suddenly sliced through the music and laughter.

"*Attack! We're under attack!*"

"It's Roderic!" announced young Colin breathlessly, standing at the hall's entrance. "He and his men are climbing the wall."

Silent shock pulsed through the air.

And then the room exploded with noise.

Chairs and tables were overturned as everyone ran in different directions, screaming and shouting. Some women raced to find their children, crashing into men who bellowed orders that no one was following, while others stood frozen, immobilized by fear.

It was the most appalling display of panic Malcolm had ever witnessed.

"*Quiet!*" he roared, banging his fist upon the table. "*All of you, stop!*"

Incredibly, the MacKendricks stopped.

"We will begin our repulse of this attack by remaining calm," he informed them, rising to his feet. "Colin, how many men does Roderic have with him?"

"I'm not certain," he stammered. "I think about forty."

"And how many men and women do you see in this room?"

He looked at MacFane in confusion. "There are about two hundred fifty, but—"

"So we outnumber this sorry band of misfits and thieves by more than six to one," observed Malcolm. He swept his gaze calmly over the MacKendricks. "This is a splendid opportunity for you to finally practice your training on a real opponent. Only this time you will not be afraid of hurting them. Is that clear?"

The MacKendricks nodded, their faces pale.

"Gavin and Duncan, take your men up to the battlements and keep those men from climbing the wall," he ordered rapidly. "Andrew, you and your men position yourselves above the gate, in case they decide to ram it. Elizabeth and Agnes, lead the women to the towers and shoot anything that moves. Helen, hide the children and the elders downstairs in the secret passage we have been excavating. Take a bow with you, and shoot whoever tries to come through the entrance. The rest of you, fetch your weapons and shields and assume your assigned positions within the courtyard and the castle, in case they manage to breach the wall. *Move!*"

Still shaken, but considerably calmer now that someone was in command, the MacKendricks surged out of the hall to defend their castle.

Ariella knocked over her chair in her haste to follow them.

"Where are you going?" demanded Malcolm.

"I must make sure Catherine is safe, then change into Rob before I go up to the wall head," she explained quickly.

"He already knows you're alive, Ariella. That is why he has returned."

She shook her head. "You can't be certain of that."

"Even if he doesn't know, there is a traitor in your clan who will tell him," he pointed out. "Fetch Catherine and join Helen and the children in the secret passage. You will stay there until I come for you."

"I cannot stay there," she protested. "I must help my clan fight."

"Listen to me," he ordered, moving toward her. "For whatever reason, I believe it is you Roderic wants. Therefore, you make us vulnerable. No one here will continue to fight if you are captured and threatened with harm. You *must* stay out of this, Ariella."

It was impossible, what he was asking of her. She could never stand by while her people were in danger. "I cannot."

Anger flooded through him. "You will do as I say," he snapped impatiently, "if I have to goddamn well drag you downstairs and lock you in there myself!"

"You don't understand, MacFane," she whispered, hugging herself tightly. "He will kill them, one by one, until I come out."

Her voice was trembling, betraying her fear. Malcolm felt his resolve weaken, so completely did he understand her feelings. She loved her people and would rather die fighting to protect them than hide in a dark corner while they fought for her. But he could not permit it. If Roderic found her, it was the end.

And he could not command this battle unless he knew she was safe.

"I will not let Roderic murder your people the way he did before," he vowed adamantly. "Do you hear? If anyone dies, it will be as they fight to defend themselves, not as they stand helpless before him. But in order to direct our defense, I must know you are safe. I cannot risk that you will be killed or captured." He reached out and grasped her chin, forcing her to look at him. "Do you understand?"

"Yes," she admitted reluctantly. "I understand."

Her beautiful face was pale but calm. Yet he could see fear clouding her wide gray eyes. In that moment he felt an overwhelming desire to draw her close, to wrap her in his arms and soothe her with gentle words.

"All will be well, Ariella," he promised, knowing it was foolish to make such an impossible assurance.

She searched his eyes, desperate with the need to believe him. And there, beneath the cool facade of confidence, she saw a flicker of uncertainty. "You don't believe that, MacFane," she challenged fiercely, freeing herself from his grasp.

He grabbed her shoulders and pulled her close. "There is one thing I do know, Ariella. Roderic will not harm you," he swore, his voice low and harsh, "because I will kill him first."

His hold on her was painful, and fury burned hot in his gaze. She was about to jerk away from him when he suddenly released her. Anger still lined his face, but there was something else in his expression she didn't understand. His eyes shadowed with regret, he reached out and trailed his fingers with aching gentleness against her cheek.

"Go downstairs, Ariella," he commanded quietly. "I have a battle to fight."

He turned and climbed the stairs, slowed only marginally by his limp. Ariella watched him until he disappeared, uncertain what to do.

Then the first shouts of battle erupted, and she rushed up the stairs to fetch Catherine.

"Take that, ye fat, hairy swine!" shouted Ramsay as he and Duncan heaved an enormous stone over the parapet.

They watched cautiously through the crenelle as the stone found its mark, slamming into the huge warrior who had nearly reached the top of his ladder. Raising his arms to shield himself from the heavy missile, he instantly lost his balance and toppled backward, taking the ladder and all the men below with him.

"Got him!" exclaimed Duncan triumphantly.

"Actually, we got four," Ramsay corrected, slapping him on the back. "Look, two of the bastards are up and running away."

"They nearly have the battering ram in position," shouted Gavin to the men above the gate. "Is the water ready?"

"Yes!" yelled Andrew as Graham dumped one final steaming bucket into the heavy cauldron.

"Wait," ordered Gavin, watching as Roderic's men ran forward. "Wait—wait—*now!*"

Andrew and his men heaved the hot cauldron onto its side, showering the attackers below with scalding water.

Roars of shock and pain filled the air as the warriors dropped their timber and hastily retreated from the gate.

"Excellent!" praised Gavin. "Keep that other cauldron ready!"

"They're climbing up the back!" shouted Malcolm as he emerged from the castle, sword in his hand. "Groups one and two, get back there and keep them from climbing up!"

Those MacKendricks from the first two training

sessions instantly abandoned their positions and ran along the wall walk to defend the other side.

"Spread out on this side!" commanded Malcolm. "Fill in the gaps!"

"Gavin, would you please step to your right?" called Elizabeth, carefully aiming her bow and arrow at him.

Gavin instantly moved to the right. The arrow whipped by him and struck a warrior who was about to run him through with his sword.

Gavin stared at the man, dumbfounded. Then he raised his eyes to Elizabeth.

"Thank you," he said, impressed by both her skill and her calm.

"Please be more careful." Her voice was taut.

Gavin smiled. "I'll try, Elizabeth."

"Archers, aim for that group down there with the ladder!" ordered Malcolm.

The women in the towers and along the battlements immediately directed their aim at the new attackers starting to climb the ladder. A thick flurry of arrows sailed through the air, striking several of the men and sending the rest scurrying away.

"Excellent shot!" praised Malcolm.

"MacFane, we can't hold them off back here!" shouted Gordon, engaging in swordplay with a huge, burly man who had made it over the low parapet.

"A few more of you go to the back!" ordered Malcolm, moving along the wall head to help. "Archers as well—but only men!"

"Take that, you murdering dog!" grunted Gordon, thrusting his sword into his attacker's belly.

The man's eyes grew round with shock. "Jesus," he gasped, "you MacKendricks were supposed to be easy to kill."

"Quite a surprise for you, isn't it?" snorted Gordon, watching as his would-be murderer collapsed.

"Niall!" thundered Malcolm. "Behind you!"

Niall spun around and swung his sword, deftly hacking into the warrior's shoulder so that he was forced to drop his weapon. "If you want to live," Niall growled, the tip of his sword at the man's throat, "sit down over there and don't move."

Gripping his bleeding shoulder, the man scurried into the corner.

"Thank you, MacFane!" called Niall, but Malcolm was shouting orders to another group and didn't hear him.

Ariella hurried along the corridor to the stairs leading to the battlements. As she passed MacFane's chamber, she noticed a shadowy figure climbing through the window. Pressing herself against the wall, she pulled an arrow from her quiver and set it against the string of her bow. She then took careful aim at the warrior, only to see he had now been joined by another. She bit her lip. It was possible to shoot one, but she would never have time to get a second arrow into position before the other man attacked her. Deciding it was better to kill one than neither, she drew her arrow back.

Suddenly an enormous net fell from the ceiling, snaring both men in a tangled web.

"*Aha!*" shouted Angus, emerging from a corner and waving his ancient sword at the struggling intruders. "Thought you'd sneak in and murder us, did you, you scoundrels?"

"Angus?"

"Oh, hello, Ariella," he said cheerfully. "No need to shoot, I've got these lads under control."

Dugald appeared from the shadows of the opposite corner. "We're guarding MacFane's chamber," he announced, dragging his old sword behind him.

"But how—"

"MacFane knew his window was particularly enticing, its being large and relatively close to the ground," explained Angus. "He asked us to attend to the net the lads strung up yesterday."

"We take turns cutting it down," added Dugald. "Then Bryce and Hugh come and take the prisoners downstairs and lock them in the storeroom. We've already captured six men."

"That's wonderful." It was clear Angus and Dugald were enjoying themselves immensely, and they certainly didn't appear to be in much danger from operating their trap. Ariella shook her head, amazed that MacFane had actually found something useful for the two elders to do.

"You bloody old fools will regret this when we get out of here," snarled one of the warriors.

"Is that so?" asked Angus, chuckling. "Well, laddie, it seems to me you will have far more to regret when the Black Wolf decides to deal with you. He eats young pups like you for breakfast!" he threatened grandly.

"The Black Wolf is nothing but a drunken cripple," sneered the other warrior. "Thrown out by his own clan for letting the women and children be slain while he was drunk—"

"By God, I'll not stand by and listen to such filthy lies," roared Dugald, struggling to lift his heavy sword. "Take it back, or I'll cut your evil tongue out!"

"What's going on here?" demanded Bryce from the door.

"This slimy toad was insulting MacFane," he declared furiously.

Bryce's expression grew hard. "Let's see how much you have to say after you've been locked in a dungeon for a few years," he stated ominously.

Both warriors paled. Despite the fact that Ariella knew Bryce's threat was empty, she could not help but take satisfaction from their fear.

"I'm going to join the others," she said. "Please be careful."

"Don't you worry about us, lass," returned Angus.

"Dugald and I have been fighting since—" He paused and scratched his white head. "Have we ever fought before, Dugald?"

Dugald leaned on his sword for support, considering. "There was that time we fought over Bessie when we were lads," he reflected. "Does that count?"

"Aye, it does," Angus decided. "Especially since I won."

"I don't know why you think that," Dugald challenged, "as I'm the one who married her—"

Ariella smiled and continued on her way.

The wall head was crowded with men and women rushing back and forth as they fought to keep Roderic's men from climbing the wall. If a warrior did manage to scale it, he was shocked to find the MacKendricks waiting with a sword, an arrow, or a well-placed shove that sent him flying backward into empty space. Ariella quickly searched the darkness for MacFane. She found him at the back of the curtain wall, fighting off an enormous man who managed to make him appear almost an ordinary size. MacFane fought ruthlessly, his fury obscuring all hint of his injuries, but his opponent was strong and quick, and ably deflected his blows. Ariella took aim with her bow, but the men were moving too quickly for her to be sure she wouldn't hit MacFane. Through the corner of her eye she saw Gavin rushing toward them to help.

Suddenly a tall fair-haired man climbed over the parapet and grabbed him.

"Drop your weapon, brave Gavin," Roderic ordered, lifting his sword to his throat.

Gavin tossed his weapon down. "You spineless bastard."

"Gavin!" screamed Elizabeth, her eyes round with terror.

Roderic looked at her in surprise. "Why, Elizabeth,

don't tell me you've come to care for this aging warrior. What a pity." He positioned Gavin in front of him, using the man as a shield. "Enough, Gregor!" he called to the warrior fighting MacFane. "He's mine now."

The huge man smiled, revealing a rotting collection of brown teeth, and lowered his sword.

Malcolm fought to control the rage churning within him as he turned to regard his former warrior.

"Hello, Malcolm," said Roderic. "I must say, you look better than I expected. Still, haven't you learned yet that you are incapable of protecting anyone?"

"What do you want, Roderic?" he demanded, his voice deceptively mild.

"Why, nothing more than what every man wants," returned Roderic, shrugging. "A castle to call his own. A few people to see to his needs. And a beautiful woman to warm his bed." His gaze shifted to Ariella. "Good evening, my dear. You are as lovely as ever. I don't even mind that you've cut your hair."

Ariella kept her arrow trained on Roderic, but she had no hope of hitting him as long as he held Gavin.

"Give up, Roderic," Malcolm commanded. "Your forces have been reduced by half, between those who are wounded and those who have been captured. As for the MacKendricks, they have barely begun to fight. You have no hope of capturing this castle."

"Perhaps not," he acknowledged. "At least not this evening. Do put down your bow, my dear," he said to Ariella, "or I will be forced to cut poor Gavin's throat."

Ariella hesitated, then dropped her weapon.

Roderic smiled. "Very good. And now there is a personal matter I wish to settle with your crippled leader. I advise you to tell them not to interfere, Malcolm, or Gregor will cut off poor Gavin's head." He shoved Gavin at the burly warrior, who placed the edge of his blade against his neck.

"No!" gasped Ariella, horrified.

Malcolm slowly raised his sword. "No one is to interfere," he commanded harshly.

Roderic smiled. "Excellent. Now, my friend," he said, lifting his weapon, "Let's see what kind of opponent you are."

Terror surged through her as Ariella watched the two warriors charge each other. Both fought with savage determination, the steel of their blades ringing loudly as each struggled to gain the advantage. Roderic was younger and his body more fit, but Malcolm was driven by a rage Ariella had never seen before. His great broadsword sliced and thrusted, slashing a silvery arc through the black air as he met Roderic blow for blow. He wielded his sword with both arms, and it was clear by his grunts that the battle was an effort for him. Ariella began to fear Roderic would simply toy with him until he tired, then close in for the kill. But Malcolm continued to fight with skill and determination, slowly driving Roderic backward toward the parapet.

"So," began Roderic, still matching Malcolm's movements, "it seems she didn't give it to you."

Refusing to be distracted, Malcolm ignored the comment. The next thing he knew, Roderic had spun about and leaped onto the wall.

"That is enough for tonight, I think," he announced, holding his sword menacingly in front of him. "Off you go, Gregor."

The huge man instantly released Gavin, heaved himself over the parapet, and climbed down a ladder.

"Farewell, sweet Ariella." Roderic shoved his sword into his belt, then grabbed hold of a rope that had been tossed over the merlon and jumped.

The MacKendricks ran to the edge of the parapet. Roderic fell about ten feet, then quickly climbed down and mounted his horse.

"Retreat!" he ordered, wheeling his mount about.

Anxious to comply, his men instantly abandoned their efforts and ran to find their horses.

The MacKendricks broke into a thunderous cheer.

"We did it!" shouted Duncan, slapping Andrew on the back.

"By God, we did indeed!" agreed Gordon. He went to hug his daughter, but she had thrown down her bow and was racing toward Gavin.

"Are you all right?" Elizabeth demanded.

Gavin looked at her in surprise. Tears were welling in her enormous blue eyes, and her lower lip was trembling. "I'm fine, Elizabeth," he assured her.

She stood there staring at him, her face pale. It seemed she needed something more from him, but Gavin wasn't certain what it was.

"I'm fine," he repeated.

Elizabeth nodded and slowly turned away. Then suddenly she let out a little cry, ran back to him, and began to sob noisily against his chest.

Gavin hesitated, uncertain what to do. Finally he sighed and closed his arms around her. "Hush, now," he said, gently stroking her hair. "We're safe now. Everything is going to be all right, Elizabeth."

Malcolm watched in grim silence as Roderic and his men rode away. Uneasy by how willingly his former warrior had abandoned his attack, he turned to look at Ariella. The fear in her eyes told him she too was certain he would return.

"Here's to MacFane!" roared Ramsay, lifting his sword high. "Without whom we never could have defeated those cowardly swine!"

An ecstatic cheer filled the air, followed by the resonant chanting of Malcolm's name.

"MacFane! MacFane! MacFane!"

A group of men surged forward. Before Malcolm could protest, they lifted him high on their shoulders.

"A cheer for the Black Wolf!"

The clan shouted and cheered wildly. Overwhelmed by their idolatry, Malcolm ordered them to put him down, but he could not make himself heard above the noise.

"Let's raise a cup to the Black Wolf, and the magnificent success he has led us to on this wonderful night!" yelled Dugald.

"MacFane! MacFane! MacFane!"

Ariella watched as her people joyfully swarmed around Malcolm. They carried him to the castle doorway, then let him down and swept him inside. Their cries of elation continued as they descended the stairs, herding him to the great hall, where they would celebrate his abilities as a great warrior.

Despite her relief that they had won, she found she could not join them.

Instead she remained standing alone on the battlements, numbly wondering when Roderic would return.

A scattering of stars flecked the velvet cape of deep night.

The castle had finally fallen quiet, after long hours of jubilant revelry. Ariella rose from the bench and leaned against the low parapet, drawing comfort from the rough coolness of the stone against her fingers. This was where the addition to the parapet had not yet been completed, rendering the wall head vulnerable. It was also where one could still sit upon a bench and contemplate the magnificent view of the lands surrounding her castle. Great, dark stands of forest spread thickly before her, sleeping. To the west was the loch, shimmering charcoal beneath a pearly ribbon of moonlight, its deep, cold water home to countless fish, and perhaps even a kelpie or two. And then there were the mountains. They were what she loved most, those glorious peaks rising in magnificent waves, powerful, mysterious, enclosing them in a vast mist-shrouded wall that for years had kept them isolated from the rest of the world.

Until now.

How sweetly, foolishly naive they had been. Her clan had been asleep for a hundred years, hidden amidst these heather-scented mountains, going about their lives. They had known almost nothing of the outside world. Of course, they had heard stories from the odd traveler who stumbled upon them, and from Alpin, who told them of the legends, the leaders, and the wars. And of the great heroes like the Black Wolf. But it had all seemed very far away, part of another place that had nothing to do with them. The MacKendricks had had their own great lairds, and the comfort of knowing that it was not their way to participate in thievery or brutality. All they wanted was to learn to better appreciate the beauty around them, and, if possible, to add something to it. This was why they had built a short parapet of intricate stonework that wouldn't block the view. What they had not understood was that someday someone might come and want to take all of that away from them. That someone would feel they had the right to steal what they had created, to rule them by force, and to wield the power of the ancient sword without being chosen.

This, of course, was what Roderic really wanted—not Ariella, despite his lust for her. Roderic coveted her castle and her lands, and the slavery of her people. Most of all he craved the ability to defeat any opponent in battle. This was the power he believed the sword would give him, though no one actually knew if the legend of the sword's power was true.

And this was why he would return.

She heard a sound, soft as a whisper of breath. Turning abruptly, she found Malcolm standing behind her, his face veiled by the night shadows. She had the feeling he had been there for some time.

"I didn't want to disturb you," he said quietly.

She nodded. "I thought everyone was asleep."

"Everyone is," he replied, moving to stand beside her. "They were excited about their victory, and anxious to celebrate with much ale and wine. If I thought Roderic might be back tonight, I would have ordered them to exercise more restraint."

Her smile was faint, but Malcolm noticed it. "Why is that amusing?"

"It is the idea of your believing someone else is drinking too much."

He tilted his head, acknowledging the irony. Then he placed his hands on the low wall and stared in silence at the magnificent landscape surrounding them. "It is beautiful here," he murmured, wondering why he had never noticed before.

Ariella regarded him in surprise. She had not thought MacFane capable of appreciating anything simply for its beauty. He was a warrior and seemed to evaluate everything only in terms of its military advantage. Was there really a side to him that understood the glory of a perfect night sky casting shadows on the world below?

"Thank you for protecting it."

He shook his head. "Your clan protected it," he corrected. "I merely showed them how."

"You led us to victory," Ariella persisted. "When we first realized we were under attack, everyone panicked. You calmed us all and made us believe we could repel Roderic and his men."

He was silent for a moment, considering. Had he really led the MacKendricks to victory? It was tempting to think so, especially after the outpouring of adulation that had followed Roderic's retreat. For one sweet, brief moment, as they had lifted him onto their shoulders and cheered him, he had almost remembered what it was to be the Black Wolf. He had suddenly felt strong, able, fearless—and needed. But now, in the lonely clarity of late night, he found his battered body aching and his mind longing for the hazy respite of drink.

Hardly the traits of a great warrior.

"Roderic did not expect the resistance he met, which is why he was easy to overcome," Malcolm pointed out. "Next time he will be more cunning in his strategy." He paused a moment, then quietly added, "And more brutal."

Ariella gripped the wall as she absorbed this, trying to take strength from its solid structure beneath her hands. "Perhaps he will not return," she suggested, knowing even as she spoke the words that the hope was a feeble one.

Malcolm turned to face her. "He will, Ariella. Roderic was once a MacFane. I trained him as one of my warriors."

"You trained him?" she murmured, aghast.

He nodded. "Even then he lusted for power. He tried to overthrow me, and I banished him. It seems he is still searching for a clan to rule. He was surprised by your clan's show of strength, but he will come back. What I want to know is, what did he mean when he said you didn't give something to me?"

She looked away. "I don't know."

Her face was lit by a pale cast of moonlight, etching every perfect feature against the darkness. Although her expression was calm, he had the distinct feeling that she did know and didn't want to tell him. He regarded her intently, contemplating the elegant rise of her cheeks, the long sweep of her lashes, the determined shape of her chin. Her auburn hair was rippling slightly in the evening breeze, grazing the softness of her cheek. She was, in that moment, overwhelmingly beautiful. Because beneath that delicate loveliness was a woman of immense courage and strength. A gently bred laird's daughter who would hack off her hair, spread filth on her skin and dress as a lad, if that's what it took to protect her people. A woman who dared fight rather than surrender, regardless of the risks to herself. As she leaned against the moon-washed stone of the parapet and gazed at the forest and mountains beyond, he suddenly understood why Roderic must return.

Had he thought himself even remotely worthy, he too would have fought for her.

Appalled, her shoved the thought aside. His days of being with women were finished, he reminded himself harshly. They had died on that blood-drenched battlefield, when he had been reduced to this crippled, drunken shell. Whatever fragment of spirit or pride that might have survived intact had been eradicated the night he drunkenly led his warriors from his castle, leaving the women and children hopelessly vulnerable to Roderic's barbarism. The innocent deaths that weighed on his soul were too many to be counted, too heavy to be borne. His actions were unforgivable. No woman could ever want a man who had failed his people so hideously.

Especially not a woman with the exalted ideals of Ariella MacKendrick.

"We must find a laird with a well trained army for you," he announced suddenly. "I cannot stay here much longer."

Panic flashed through her. "Why?"

What could he tell her? That it was becoming too difficult, staying in this place where he didn't belong, watching the people slowly grow to respect him? A place where he was forced to rise each morning and prove himself day after day, regardless of his pain or how much he had drunk the night before? A place where he was filled with purpose and felt almost needed? A place where she tormented him every moment with her beauty and her strength, showing him what he could never hope to have?

It was better he leave soon, before leaving became unbearable.

"I said I would stay until you are safe, and I will," he assured her. "But you have a traitor within your clan who sent word to Roderic that you are alive. Now that he has seen you himself, he will not wait long to strike again. Your people have become stronger, but they are not strong enough to defeat a warrior like Roderic. You need a powerful laird with an army, and alliances to fortify you if that isn't enough."

What he was saying was true, she realized. What she could not understand was why the thought of MacFane leaving made her feel so alone. She had always known he would stay only for a short while. Three months. That was what they had agreed to. The sword must be bestowed before Roderic returned, or her people were in grave danger. Once she had chosen the new laird, there was no reason for MacFane to stay. After all, he didn't belong here. He didn't belong anywhere. She would pay him his gold, and that would be that.

She wrapped her arms around herself, suddenly cold.

"Tomorrow I will speak to Alpin. He may be able to help me find the man who is to lead my people."

"A man who is exceptionally strong, relentlessly brave, and driven by his innate sense of honor," reflected Malcolm, repeating the qualities she had described to him. *All the things you believed I once was,* he added silently.

She nodded.

"Those are fine attributes for a laird," he acknowledged, wondering if he had ever come close to meeting those requirements. "But what about you, Ariella? What do you seek in the man who will be your husband? The man you will share your life with, create children with, and grow old with?"

"I have not considered my own desires," she replied,

gazing into the darkness. "They are irrelevant. All that matters is his ability to lead and protect my people."

She said it dismissively, but Malcolm was not convinced she believed it. Her arms were wrapped tightly around herself. He knew her well enough to realize she did that only when she was afraid.

Or when she was contemplating something painful.

"No, Ariella," he said, moving closer to her. "That is not all that matters. The man who will be your husband must be brave and honorable, just as you described." He reached out to brush his fingers against the silk of her cheek, knowing as he did that he had no right to do so. "And he must be respectful of you," he continued softly, "And he must vow to treat you with the gentlest of care."

Ariella stared at him, unable to move. His hand was warm against her cheek, warm and strong and powerful. How was it that the hand of a warrior, a hand that had brought death to countless men in battle, could brush her skin with such reverent tenderness? MacFane's blue eyes were burning into her, and the lines of his face were carved into deep grooves as he stroked her cheek and jaw. She sensed a battle raged within him, a battle he was not accustomed to fighting. His expression was taut with regret and desire, and her heart quickened as she realized she had seen this look before. She knew she should pull away when he gently grasped her chin and tilted it upward. Knew she should protest as he lowered his head. Knew she must say stop as his lips pressed warm and firm against hers.

Stop, MacFane.

She wrapped her arms around his neck and leaned into the solid wall of his chest, kissing him with a desperation she had never felt before and couldn't begin to understand.

Please stop.

He could not hear her. That was why he moaned into her mouth, sharing her desperation as her lips parted and he tasted her deeply.

Please, I beg you, we must stop, she pleaded, clinging to him as if she thought he could somehow protect her, could save her from the threat of Roderic, and her unknown husband, and the terrible, lonely burden of holding the future of her clan within her palm. *We cannot do this,* she added fervently, holding fast to him as his hands began to stroke her hair, her shoulders, her back, touching her with hungry, painful need, as if he had longed for this moment and knew it might soon be torn away. *I must give myself only to the next Laird MacKendrick.* Why wouldn't he listen? she wondered, threading her fingers into the dark fall of his hair, pressing herself closer to his heat, his power, his touch, feeling strangely safe as his arms held her tight against him, safer than she had ever been in her life.

Hot desire surged through Malcolm as he kissed Ariella, tasting the sweet coolness of her mouth, inhaling the sun-washed scent of her, feeling the slim curves of her small form beneath the softness of her sapphire gown. It was impossible, what was happening, he understood that, but somehow he could not bring himself to end it. She was kissing him with a desperation that seemed to match his own, moaning into his mouth as she clung to him and crushed herself against him, filling him with a longing more powerful than any he had ever experienced. It was madness, it was hopelessness, it was wrong, it was all these things and more, yet he could no sooner have pulled away from her than he could have plucked the moon from the sky. And so he stroked the narrow length of her back, the slender curve of her waist, the lush flare of her hips, pulling her closer, closer, learning every detail of her, memorizing her so that when he returned to his dreary, barren life, he would have this moment to remember. He wanted her with a hunger that was shocking, wanted to strip her gown from her and lay her against the smooth stone of the floor and take her beneath the silvery blackness of the sky, with the mountains and the loch and everything she loved so dearly surrounding them. But he could never be satisfied with just one night. To have one night, and know he could never touch her again, would be far more tortuous than never to have her at all. And she could not give him more than that, he realized bleakly. Regardless of how sweetly she was clinging to him.

Summoning every vestige of his strength, he reached up and gently broke her embrace.

"Forgive me, Ariella," he said, his voice a rough whisper. He didn't know if he was asking forgiveness for wanting her, or for not being the warrior she needed. For not being the Black Wolf.

Her senses reeling, Ariella gazed up at him. His expression was harsh, but she knew it was not anger that lined his face. In that moment she suddenly remembered who she was, and where her responsibilities lay. Appalled by her behavior, she took a step back, as if distance might douse the flames raging between them.

"I—I must go," she stammered, suddenly anxious to get away, to break free from his overwhelming aura, which was flooding her with need. She had always thought of him as battered and weak, not just physically, but spiritually, a man who had been destroyed by the trials of his life. But as he stood before her, his tall, muscular form chiseled in shadows and moonlight, regarding her with barely leashed desire, he seemed whole and strong and dangerously powerful. An illusion, she reminded herself desperately. But this time she could not quite convince herself.

"Good night, Ariella." His voice was quiet, yet it was a command nonetheless.

She turned from him and walked away, her shoulders straight, her carriage dignified. *He is not the one,* she told herself fiercely. *Regardless of tonight, he is not the one.*

It was this painful, irrefutable truth that forced her to keep walking, instead of turning back and hurling herself into the warm shelter of his arms.

CHAPTER 10

Her father was calling her.

The sound was faint, as if he were far away, but there was no mistaking the low, gentle timbre of his voice. He called to her with warmth, and even a hint of amusement, as he used to when she was a little girl and had stayed out playing in the woods too long. No matter how late she was, she never feared he would be angry with her. On hearing that sweetly gruff voice, she would gather her skirts in her grubby fists and run as fast as she could toward the castle. Heaving with breathlessness, she would stretch out her arms so Laird MacKendrick could lift her high into the air, spinning her round and round until the world became a vortex of color and light. Her delighted squeals melded with his deep chuckles, causing everyone around them to pause and smile. Finally he would set her down, and she would dizzily stagger a step or two before collapsing onto the sun-warmed grass, watching the sky twirl over her while her father laughed.

Ariella.

She snuggled deeper into the softness of her pillow, remembering.

Ariella, my love, open your eyes.

Her heart pounding, she sat bolt upright.

It took her a moment to accept that there was no one in the room. Voices drifted through the window from the courtyard below, but none were her father's. Feeling chilled, she lay back down and drew the blankets up to her chin. She listened a moment, as if she actually believed she might hear his rich, lusty voice once more. But there were only the normal muffled stirrings of the castle seeping through the thick stone walls.

He is dead, she reminded herself numbly. Killed by Roderic's sword as he tried to protect his daughter and his clan. An honorable, courageous death.

That left a gash in her heart so deep, she sometimes felt she could not endure it another moment.

Surely that was why she had acted so inconceivably last night with MacFane. Seeing Roderic had awakened the hideous, bloodstained memories of the death of her father, of Douglas and Myles, and of all the others who had fallen beneath his ugly avarice. The moment Roderic pressed his sword to Gavin's throat and challenged Mac-Fane, she had been terrified her clan was finished. Malcolm could not possibly defeat such a fit, highly trained warrior in swordplay. And he hadn't. True, he had managed to meet him blow for blow, despite his physical limitations. But if Roderic had not decided to stop, he would have eventually worn Malcolm down.

And then he would have killed him.

It was the fact that MacFane had nearly died for her

people that had sent her into his arms, she decided. She had been overcome with fear and relief, and she had allowed these feelings to cloud her judgment. A ripple of heat pulsed through her as she recalled his enormous body wrapped around her, hard and unyielding as stone, sheltering her from Roderic, and her memories, and even the terrible weight of her responsibilities. His touch had been restless, hungry, the touch of a man who is consumed with need. And she had returned his caresses wholly, pressing herself against him as she kissed him, enjoying the feel of his broad chest and thickly muscled legs against her own small form. Safe and free. That was how MacFane had made her feel last night.

But she was neither safe nor free. She was bound from birth with a heavy responsibility to her people, and they would not be safe until the rightful laird was found. MacFane had said so himself. The sooner she gave this warrior the sword, the sooner they would be secure and MacFane could leave. Which was what he wanted.

After what had happened between them last night, it was best he left soon.

She threw back the covers and began to dress. It was essential her people begin immediately to prepare themselves for another attack by Roderic. They had managed to drive him away last night, but only because he had not expected any opposition. Malcolm was right when he'd said that next time Roderic would be more cunning in his methods. He was not likely to strike for a while, because he had lost some of his men to capture and injury. But his comment to Malcolm clearly indicated he was worried Ariella would bestow the sword before he could steal it. He would not wait long to return. She must find the next MacKendrick before then.

She hurried downstairs and went outside to find her clan already hard at work. Men were hauling the heavy stones that had been thrown over the parapet back up to the battlements, while the women were busy collecting arrows and evaluating them for damage. Gavin was giving directions to several men who were adding bricks to the lowest section of the parapet, while Bryce and Hugh were examining the gate for weaknesses. No one was training, except for a small group practicing swordplay in a corner. As usual, Angus and Dugald watched these proceedings from their elevated platform, calling out loud suggestions no one gave any notice to.

Malcolm was nowhere to be seen.

"Good morning, Ariella," called Angus, waving. " 'Twas a fine battle we fought last night, was it not?"

"It was," she agreed. "We should be proud."

"That net MacFane designed worked splendidly," added Dugald. "We captured seven men last night. That ought to make Roderic think twice about attacking MacKendricks!"

"What happened to the men taken prisoner?" she asked.

"They're locked in one of the storerooms," replied Angus. "It's a pity we don't have a real dungeon to put them in, but MacFane said the storeroom would do fine."

She gazed around the courtyard, searching for Malcolm. After what had happened between them the night before, she was uneasy about facing him. "Where is Mac-Fane this morning? Has he not risen yet?"

"Why, he's gone, lass," said Dugald.

A cold, hollow feeling swept over her. "Gone?"

"Aye," said Angus. "He left early this morning, taking Duncan and Ramsay with him."

"He's paying visits to the clans around us, to discuss the possibility of alliances," explained Dugald. "He left Gavin in charge of training and fortifying the castle and said he would return within two weeks. Did he not mention it to you?" he asked, frowning.

He had, she realized. Last night he had spoken again of the need to make alliances. And to find a laird with a powerful army, who could protect them.

"I—I didn't know he would be leaving so soon," she stammered.

"The sooner we have our laird in place, the better," commented Angus. "The sword must be given to him before that scoundrel Roderic returns." He regarded her intently. "Have you still no idea who he is, lass?"

She shook her head.

"Seems to me MacFane could do it," said Dugald. "I didn't think so at first, but since he has been here, the lad has proved himself a fine leader. All we need is for his great army to join him, and no one would dare strike us again." He cast her a hopeful look.

"MacFane is not the one."

She sensed their disappointment as she said it. It was clear that during the past few weeks her people had slowly grown to admire him. Of course, they were aware of his injuries, and he had not been able to keep his addiction to drink a secret for long. These things no longer seemed to bother them. But her people didn't see him as he really was. They didn't know he was no longer MacFane. That he had been cast out of his clan for some terrible crime, stripped of his title and his name, and relieved of the right to command the warriors he had trained and led so bravely as the Black Wolf. That when she had found him, he'd been living as a wild man, drunk, filthy, and unshaven. And that he had come here unwillingly, drawn only by greed.

Had they known, they would have understood such a man could not possibly be the next MacKendrick.

"Come in, Ariella."

She swung the heavy door open, not at all surprised that Alpin had known it was she. Ivor flapped his giant wings and made a great hooting noise, showing his displeasure at being disturbed. Ariella ignored him as she made her way through the gloom toward Alpin, who was bent over a table, absorbed in the task of sprinkling a silvery dust into a bowl. He chanted something softly and waved his hands, his great white eyebrows furrowed in concentration.

Suddenly there was an enormous flash of light, so brilliant, she had to squeeze her eyes shut. When she opened them, all she saw was a screen of smoke.

Alpin had disappeared.

There was a loud cough as his gnarled hands emerged from the swirling cloud, angrily swatting it away. "It didn't work," he grumbled, stepping out of it.

"What was supposed to happen?"

"I was supposed to turn into a bird. There was a time when I could do it easily. But there hasn't been a need these past forty years or so, and I fear I am sadly out of practice." He sighed. "One must keep these things up, or one loses them altogether."

"You can try again tomorrow," she suggested.

"Perhaps," he allowed, not sounding enthusiastic. "These days I find I tire from the more complicated spells." He gripped his staff and shuffled over to the hearth, where he began to pour a milky liquid into a small pan frothing with yellow foam. "So," he murmured after a moment, "he has left us."

"Yes. For a time."

"And you are afraid."

"Of what?"

"Of your feelings for him."

"I have no feelings for MacFane," she quickly assured him.

He raised a skeptical brow.

"We have a—a friendship," she conceded reluctantly. "Nothing more."

"I see."

Ariella watched him in silence as he reached into a jar marked "Dried Spiders," withdrew a generous handful of the shrunken creatures, and crumbled them into the pot. A musty odor wafted through the room.

"I was wondering," she began after a moment, "if you have had any more visions about the next laird."

"Some. But they have not been clear. It is more a sense of the man, and what he is like, rather than a vision of who he actually is."

"What is he like?"

"You already know, Ariella," he reminded her. "We have spoken many times of the man who will wield the MacKendrick sword. You had to be taught so you would know what to look for."

"I need to hear it again," she said softly. "Please."

Alpin thoughtfully continued to stir his pot. "He has an indomitable strength," he finally began. "Of body, mind, and spirit."

An image of Malcolm's battered, weakened body came to mind. That, and his inability to control his need for drink.

"What else?"

"He lives his life with honor and courage," Alpin added. "He has a deep, inherent desire to help those who cannot help themselves."

Again she thought of Malcolm, who had not wanted to come here until she had bribed him with gold and promised it would be for no more than three months.

"Anything more?"

"People respect him because he is a great leader. And he has done much to earn that respect."

Malcolm had once been a great leader, she allowed. But then he had done something so horrendous, he had been driven from his clan.

Thrown out by his own clan for letting the women and children be slain while he was drunk—

"Is that true?" she demanded abruptly.

Alpin looked at her in confusion. "Is what true?"

It was a lie. It had to be. Even so, she needed to be sure.

"Last night one of Roderic's men said MacFane was

banished from his clan because the women and children were slain while he was drunk." She hesitated, not certain she wanted to hear his answer. "Is that true?"

He regarded her steadily, his black eyes betraying no hint of emotion. "Aye, Ariella. It is true."

She wrapped her arms around herself, a vain attempt to shield herself from this hideous information. From the moment he had failed to appear when Roderic attacked, failed even to answer her father's missives, Ariella had known the Black Wolf was not the one. But Alpin had told her she must find him, and so she had. They had gone first to the MacFane castle, where the new laird, Harold, told them Malcolm had been banished for his crimes. But he had not shared with them what those crimes were.

Had she known, she never would have brought him here.

"You are wrong, Ariella," Alpin said, his voice low. "You were right to bring him here."

She swallowed thickly, struggling to absorb this terrible knowledge about Malcolm. "MacFane has helped us learn to defend ourselves, and for that I am grateful," she admitted. "But now he must leave. The clan is becoming too fond of him. They don't know of his awful past, or the fact that he is no longer laird of his people. They are unable to see him for what he really is."

"Are they?"

"Yes." She went to the door, then stopped.

"MacFane is convinced that Roderic will return."

Alpin said nothing, evidently engrossed in stirring the foamy mixture growing in his pot.

"Will he, Alpin?"

A long moment passed.

"Aye, Ariella," he said finally. "Roderic will return. And when he does, he will not be so easily defeated. His anger is great, and he will seek to punish us for humiliating him."

A shiver of fear went through her. "Then I *must* find the wielder of the sword. It is vital I do so before he returns."

"You mean Roderic?"

"No," she replied, opening the door. "MacFane."

Somewhere, a woman was weeping.

Ariella moved slowly through the thick white mist, brushing her fingers through its cool veil, trying to find her. The woman's sobs were long and tormented, the cries of someone whose heart has been torn in two. Ariella could feel her pain as surely as if it were her own, for the sound reminded her of her own cries when she had lain beside her murdered father and hysterically begged him to come back to her. The filmy gauze around her thickened, making it impossible to see. She closed her eyes and let the weeping be her guide. On and on, through the damp shroud of feathery softness, closer and closer to the pitiful grief pouring from this woman's heart. Finally, sensing she had found what she had been seeking, Ariella opened her eyes.

The curtain of white had parted, revealing a beautiful young woman with red-and-gold hair, kneeling beside a gravely injured black wolf. The animal's flesh was torn wide in many places, his breathing was rapid and shallow, and flecks of pink foam bubbled from his mouth. The woman held his head in her lap and gently stroked him as she wept, touching him as tenderly as she would a lover. The wolf endured her ministrations for a moment. Then suddenly his lips curled into a snarl and he clamped his jaws on her hand. Pain streaked across her ashen face, but she did not cry out. Instead she silently waited for the enraged animal to release her. Once he did, Ariella expected her to run away from the beast, who was obviously crazed by his suffering. Instead the girl raised her bloodied hand and began to stroke him again, soothing him with soft words, and still weeping. After a moment a stream of scarlet began to trickle from her neck, seeping down her chest and into the fabric of her gown. At first she didn't seem to notice, but as her gown became drenched, she weakened. She lifted her gaze, and Ariella was horrified to see her throat had been cut. Finally she sank to the floor, one hand still resting protectively on the snarling wolf.

A warrior appeared, a furious, powerful-looking man with hair the same red-gold as the girl. He roared in horror at the sight of her, lifeless and soaked in blood. Enraged beyond measure, he picked up the wolf as if it weighed nothing and hurled it into the air, far from the body of the woman. Then he knelt and lifted the girl into his arms, cradling her against his massive chest. He turned to leave, permitting Ariella a glimpse of this mighty warrior who had arrived too late.

It was Harold, laird of the MacFanes.

Ariella. Wake up.

She sat up, breathing hard, and searched the darkness. There was no one there. Unnerved, she rose from her bed, draped a blanket around her shoulders, and went to sit before the dying embers of the fire. She drew her knees up to her chest and wrapped her arms around them, feeling small and alone as she contemplated her dream.

It was clear the black wolf she had seen was a gravely injured Malcolm. But who was the beautiful woman weeping openly over him? And why had he turned on her so viciously? It seemed Harold blamed the wolf for her death, which was why he violently threw him into the air. Perhaps that represented Malcolm's banishment from his clan. Was the flame-haired girl one of the many who had died the night Malcolm had been drunk and failed to protect his people? How many women and children had died that night? she wondered. Fifty? A hundred? Two hundred? She shivered, unable to imagine such a horrendous tragedy. The guilt of such a terrible, unforgivable blunder must have been agonizing.

She stayed like that a long time, huddled before the hearth, contemplating her dream. And during those long, quiet hours, as she reflected on the horrific slaughter that had befallen his clan, a realization began to take hold. It was hazy and uncertain at first, but the more she considered it, the clearer and more obvious it became. Finally, as morning light began to creep across the cool stone floor, she accepted the meaning of her dream.

Harold, laird of the MacFanes, the man who had stripped Malcolm of his position and cast him from his people, was destined to be the next MacKendrick.

CHAPTER 11

Malcolm shifted uncomfortably in his saddle, trying to ease the pressure on his throbbing back and leg.

After nearly two weeks of travel, his broken, cursed body was rebelling. Before his injuries he would have thought nothing of riding for ten days or more. But on this journey his back was cramped and stiff as he rose from the damp ground each morning, and during the long hours in the saddle his suffering increased. He had forced himself to stretch his back, arm, and leg several times a day, and perform the exercises Ariella had suggested to him. He wasn't certain, but he thought his arm and leg might be getting slightly stronger. Still, when he lay against his cool bed of grass at night, he felt bruised and exhausted. Because Ariella was not there with her warm oils and gentle, healing touch, he sought relief in the wine and ale they were given each time they visited a clan. He tried to drink just enough to dull the pain, as he wanted a clear head for his negotiations. Although this required an enormous amount of self-control, it pleased him to discover he was capable of knowing when he had had enough. On his return to the MacKendrick castle, he would find a plain, married woman to give him regular massages, and he would continue his exercises. Perhaps, in time, he could learn to manage his pain without the need of drink.

The MacKendrick castle loomed through a silvery veil of mist, its pink-and-cream stonework glistening in the soft light of early morning. A flame of anticipation lit within him, causing him to urge Cain faster. It surprised him that he was so anxious to return.

He had never thought of himself as a man who required comfortable surroundings. After all, he had lived most of his adult life as a warrior, traveling and existing outdoors for months at a time. When Harold banished him, Gavin had built a tiny hut for them to live in. Although Gavin had often talked about expanding it and making decent furniture, Malcolm had ordered him not to. The rough, cramped structure served them well enough as a shelter, and because he was drunk most of the time, he had seen no need for more rooms or fine furnishings. But these past weeks he had been living in an elegant castle, surrounded by exquisite tapestries, intricately carved ceilings, and handsome furniture. Every night on this journey he found himself missing the comfort of his bed, when only a short while ago he had been satisfied to lie on a lumpy straw pallet. He had also longed for the fine meals the MacKendricks served, and the wonderful music performed each night as they laughed and dined, even if he had heard it only from his chamber.

Above all, he had longed for Ariella.

He did not know what had possessed him to kiss her the way he had. At first he told himself it was merely the relief of having defeated Roderic, which had awakened a long-forgotten sensation of triumph and achievement, even though he knew the victory was fleeting. The velvet darkness of the night sky also had its effect, as well as the magnificence of that view he had somehow never noticed before, and the cool summer breeze rippling through the trees below.

Then he would remember Ariella standing alone against the battlements, her auburn hair blowing softly around her as she contemplated the land she loved so dearly. And he would be filled with a desire so intense, he thought he would surely die from it.

He had watched her for a long time, absorbing every glorious detail of her, before she had finally noticed him. She was small and slender, almost delicate in that sapphire woolen gown, yet Malcolm had known he gazed at a woman forged of the strongest steel. Alpin had once told him that Ariella was a fighter, and he was right. Had she been a man, she would have been a formidable warrior. But she was not a man; she was a woman with the heavy burden of finding and marrying the next laird of her clan, whoever he might be. For the sake of her clan, she would lie naked beside a man she barely knew, regardless of whether she desired him or not, and permit him to touch her intimately and plant his seed deep inside her. For the sake of her clan, she would honor and respect this man, at least before others, always deferring to his judgment because he was the one titled laird. For the sake of her clan, she would bear him children and try to give him sons, so the lineage to the ancient founder of the MacKendricks could be preserved. For the sake of the clan, she would put her own dreams and desires aside, just as she had when she'd accepted her father's decision that she marry the Black Wolf, a man she had never even met.

If there was one lesson Ariella had learned far better than he, it was the bittersweet, unyielding lesson of duty to one's clan.

Duncan rode up beside him and gazed contentedly at the valley below. "It is beautiful from here, is it not?"

Malcolm halted his horse and studied the view of the castle rising on its emerald slope, with the blue-black surface of the loch sparkling below it. None of the gloomy, forbidding fortresses of the surrounding clans compared to the graceful lines of the MacKendrick stronghold. Its architecture was a testament to balance and symmetry, an elegant arrangement of rounded towers and perfectly measured crenellations, with many arched windows and newly chiseled archers' slits inviting light through the intricate stonework. It had not been built to keep people out, he reflected, but to invite them in, so they might enjoy its comfort and beauty. And by striving for comeliness, by building out of joy and pride rather than fear, the MacKendricks had created a structure that was not only pleasing, but far more civilized than the great, dark bastions of those who lived in constant fear of attack.

Why had he not been able to appreciate its beauty before?

"I didn't think Roderic would be able to return for at least two weeks," he reflected, noting there was no sign of either him or his warriors. "We relieved him of many of his men. He must either wait until his wounded heal, or try to attract others to his band. Now that he knows the MacKendricks are prepared to fight back, he will have to plan a better offensive."

"But this time we have allies ready to come to our aid," said Ramsay. "Roderic will never be able to defeat the armies of the Campbells and the MacGregors, or the others who have agreed to help us should we need them."

"True," Malcolm conceded. "But these allies are some four hours' ride away, which means they will be of help only if we can hold an attacking army off for at least eight to nine hours. The MacKendricks still need an army of their own."

Why don't you just send for your army, MacFane? wondered Ramsay. "Surely even a small number of warriors trained by the Black Wolf would be more than enough protection."

Malcolm found himself moved by the compliment. Moved and saddened, because the mighty army he had led for so many years was no longer his.

And worse, every one of his warriors despised him.

"My army is engaged elsewhere," he lied, repeating the explanation Duncan had given the clan when Malcolm had first arrived. "Come, let us hurry back," he continued, changing the subject. "I find myself yearning for a long, hot bath."

Duncan raised a brow, as if he thought he might be joking. Then he laughed.

"Why is that amusing?" Malcolm demanded.

"No reason," he replied with a shrug. "I was just remembering when we brought you here." He urged his mount forward and galloped toward the castle.

Malcolm wasn't sure, but he thought Duncan was still laughing.

"They're back!"

"Come quickly!"

"MacFane has returned!"

Ariella's stomach lurched as she heard the excited cries of her people. She had planned to wed Harold before Malcolm's return. But the real Laird MacFane was not able to come immediately, as she had requested. He had sent a message back to her saying he accepted her terms of marriage and would come in about a week. Which meant he would arrive anytime now, possibly even today. She shivered, fearing Malcolm's reaction when he learned of her hastily planned marriage to a man he could only despise. She was also worried about the reaction of her people, who did not yet know of their new chief.

"He's back!" shrieked Catherine happily, racing through the great hall, where Ariella, Elizabeth, and Agnes were cleaning. "MacFane is back!"

"Catherine, don't run," scolded Agnes, putting her broom aside to follow her.

Elizabeth stopped arranging the fresh rushes they had scattered on the floor. "It's a good sign, his coming back so soon," she declared. "It means the journey was a success."

"Perhaps," allowed Ariella, fighting the dread unfurling in her stomach.

"Hurry now, lasses, have you not heard our MacFane has returned?" demanded Angus as he shuffled eagerly toward the door.

"I saw him through my window, and he looks as fit as ever," added Dugald. "A fine warrior returning home." He glanced surreptitiously at Ariella.

Ariella shook her head, wondering at their thinly disguised attempts to promote MacFane to her. She knew the council still hoped she would choose Malcolm as their next laird. But they did not know him as she did, and she could not bring herself to inform them of his terrible past. To do so would crush their illusions and humiliate Malcolm beyond endurance. Despite his hideous failure as laird of the MacFanes, he had brought hope, confidence, and pride to her people.

He did not deserve to be repaid by having her expose the dark truth.

Malcolm was surprised by the MacKendricks' enthusiastic welcome. As he, Duncan, and Ramsay rode by, everyone ran up the hill behind them, then burst into the courtyard, smiling and laughing and asking excited questions about how the men had fared in securing alliances. The moment was warm and enjoyable, reminiscent of when he would return to his own clan in the years before he had become laird.

"What news, MacFane?" demanded Gordon eagerly.

"Did it go well?" asked Gavin.

Angus waved to him from across the yard. "Welcome back, laddie. Did you secure an alliance with another clan?"

"Not just one," he replied, gazing around at the clan. "There are four clans who have signed an agreement to come to our aid if needed. The MacGregors, the Campbells, the Grants, and the Frasers."

Everyone cheered.

"That's wonderful!" burst out Helen. "Now we can all feel safe!"

"Safer," qualified Malcolm. "We still need to—"

"MacFane! MacFane!"

Little Catherine was running toward him, her slim legs bare against her flapping gown, her chestnut hair floating behind her. She raised her arms high so Malcolm could lift her and seat her on Cain in front of him.

She regarded MacFane happily a moment, delighted to be in what seemed to her an enormous place of honor. Then her little face scrunched with disapproval. "You were gone a long time," she said, poking him in the chest.

"Not so long," he replied, though it pleased him she had thought so. He brushed a wayward lock of hair off her forehead. "Only twelve days."

"More like twelve years," countered Catherine petulantly. "I tried to get Ariella and Agnes to teach me to ride, but they said they didn't have time for it. They wanted me to practice my sewing instead." She rolled her eyes, then leaned in close to whisper, "I much prefer riding to sewing."

"I don't blame you," admitted Malcolm. "But I think perhaps you can find time to do both."

"I made you something," she announced, suddenly remembering. She reached into her sleeve and withdrew a folded piece of paper. "Here."

Malcolm carefully opened the sheet. On it was a clumsy drawing of a very large warrior on a disproportionately small horse, riding beside a small girl on her own small horse. Beneath the image, in a childish scrawl, was the title *The Black Wolf and Me*.

"Do you like it?"

"It is wonderful," he murmured honestly.

"I think I made you a little too big for Cain," she admitted, "but that's how you seem to me."

"I will always treasure it," he said, folding it and tucking it under his belt. "Thank you."

She smiled, and he was strangely content.

"It's good you're finally back," said Thomas. "That dog of Ewen's has been digging in my garden again, and I've been waiting to hear what you have to say on the matter."

"I told you I would replace any ruined vegetables," growled Ewen. "You shouldn't bother MacFane with such trifling matters."

"It's no bother," Malcolm reassured them.

"What do you think of the parapet?" asked Bryce. "Gavin here has had us working night and day, but it looks splendid, don't you think?"

Malcolm noticed Ariella standing in front of the entrance to the hall, watching as her clan greeted him. She was dressed in a plain dress of dove gray, but the simplicity of her gown could not begin to disguise her beauty. Her eyes met his. Then she quickly averted her gaze, as if she could not bear to look at him.

"MacFane? What do you think?" demanded Gavin.

Malcolm glanced distractedly up at the parapet. "It looks fine."

He returned his attention to Ariella, only to find her gone.

"We hauled all the rocks back up to the wall head and stored another fifty," reported Hugh.

"And we've been making hundreds of arrows," added Graham. "So we are well stocked if Roderic decides to return."

"Very good," he murmured, suddenly uneasy. Why had Ariella not remained in the courtyard with her clan? Was it possible the memory of what had happened between them made her unable to tolerate his presence?

"You must be tired, MacFane," said Gavin. "Perhaps you would like to rest before you tell the council of your journey."

"Why should a great strapping lad like that be tired?" demanded Angus. "Why, when I was his age, I went on great journeys for months at a time and never felt tired."

"I don't know what you're talking about," remarked Dugald, shaking his head, "as you never had cause to go anywhere."

"I will meet with the council now," announced Malcolm. "Then I will make a tour of the castle, and you can all show me what has been done in my absence."

"And then will you give me a riding lesson?" asked Catherine, her eyes huge and pleading.

"Not today." He chucked her gently under the chin when she frowned. "But tomorrow I will."

"Do you promise?"

He glanced back at the castle, still uneasy over Ariella's cool reception. "I promise."

He could not stay here any longer.

She had spent the last two hours desperately trying to convince herself that perhaps it didn't matter if Malcolm were here when Harold arrived. After all, Malcolm understood that her clan was in need of a powerful laird with an army. Despite all he had achieved here, they both knew he could never be that man. But then Ariella thought of her people racing out to welcome him home, dropping everything to be near him, surrounding him with warmth and admiration as they excitedly relayed their problems and accomplishments during his absence. She thought of little Catherine's beaming face as Malcolm had lifted her onto his horse, and his tender expression as he gently swept an unruly lock of hair off her forehead. A turmoil of emotions had enveloped her as she'd witnessed that moment, rendering her unable to meet his gaze.

When he had first arrived, her people had regarded Malcolm with disappointment, suspicion, even flagrant contempt. Yet he had withstood their antagonism and scorn, had even endured their attempts to drive him away, and, drawing upon a patience and determination she had not believed him capable of, Malcolm had managed to earn the friendship and respect of every one of them.

And when Harold arrived, he would destroy it.

It was inevitable that he would do so. Her people would not embrace the stranger she knew was destined to be their rightful laird. Their hard-won loyalty to Malcolm would not permit it. She had planned to wed Harold before Malcolm's return and take time to apprise him of all that Malcolm had done for her people. She had hoped to persuade her new husband to treat Malcolm with fairness and dignity, and to guard the secret of his past, if only out of respect for her. That was impossible now. Harold would arrive at any moment to find there, the man revered and adored by the MacKendricks, responsible for the slaughter of his clan's women and children. The insult of her people's cool reaction to him, combined with Harold's loathing of Malcolm, would almost certainly lead to Harold's exposing the truth about Malcolm's past in appalling detail. And then, after shattering her people's illusions,

Harold would complete Malcolm's degradation by banishing him from her clan. Malcolm would be publicly humiliated and then exiled, as he had been before.

She could not allow that to happen.

"You wished to speak with me?"

She whirled around. Malcolm stood before her, his enormous figure blocking the shaft of sun that had been warming her as she'd stood gazing at her lands from the battlements. His expression was unreadable, but weariness and pain were chiseled deep in his brow. The long days spent in the saddle and nights upon the hard ground had obviously taken their toll on his damaged body. What he needed now was a few days of rest, combined with some hot, relaxing baths and the soothing touch of her massages. Instead she was going to send him away, back to his crude hut and the lonely, barren life he had led before coming here.

Guilt swelled in her throat, so thick she thought she would choke.

"It seems your journey was a success, MacFane," she remarked, trying to sound casual.

Malcolm folded his arms across his chest and leaned against the parapet, adjusting his weight in a vain attempt to relieve the throbbing in his leg. It was clear Ariella was flustered by his presence, but the fact that she was willing to see him alone quelled the unease that had been gnawing at him throughout his meeting with the council. She looked utterly delightful as she stood facing him, her sunlit hair dancing in fiery strands over her shoulders, and her wide gray eyes regarding him with grave intensity. Desire heated his blood. He longed to take her in his arms and crush his mouth to hers, to feel the silk of her cheek caress the roughness of his jaw, to pull her soft form against him and hold her tight, as he had that glorious night they defeated Roderic.

Instead he remained where he was, achingly aware that she could never be his.

"Our negotiations went well," he replied. "We have secured alliances with four clans who have agreed to come to our aid if needed."

Our aid.

"That is good news," said Ariella, startled and unnerved by the fact that he was including himself when referring to her clan. She inhaled deeply, reminded herself of her purpose, and quickly concluded, "That means you can leave now."

So that was what was troubling her, Malcolm realized, wondering why he had not recognized it immediately. His last words to Ariella had been in this very place, he recalled, resisting the urge to smile. And he had told her he could not stay much longer. Obviously she was worried that because he had secured alliances for her clan, he was going to abandon her, even though she had not yet found the perfect man to fulfill her expectations of a laird. But he had just spent twelve endless days away from her. The idea of leaving her now was inconceivable. Nor could he imagine deserting her people, who had welcomed him back with the same exhilaration and affection he had enjoyed a lifetime ago when returning home from battle.

"Lay your fears to rest, Ariella," he said, moved by her concern. "I am not going anywhere."

Panic swept through her. "But you must!"

He raised a quizzical brow.

"What I mean is—you have already done so much for us," she amended, affecting a calmer tone. "You have accomplished far more than I expected—but we both agreed it would be only for a short while. Now that my people have learned to defend themselves and you have secured these alliances, I am sure you are anxious to collect your payment—which will be handsome," she assured him brightly, "and return home."

Exasperation pricked his patience. Exasperation

coupled with disbelief. Was she saying she did not want him to stay?

"Your clan is still a long way from being able to defend itself," he pointed out. "They have mastered only the most rudimentary level of training, and I am convinced they can do much better. The fortifications of the castle and wall are also far from complete, and I must ensure that they are properly executed. I will not leave until I am satisfied the MacKendricks can adequately defend themselves from even the most skillful—and brutal—attacks."

Desperation rose within her. Harold would arrive at any moment. Why didn't Malcolm just agree to take his payment and go?

"You cannot stay, MacFane."

Malcolm regarded her curiously. "Why not?"

She hesitated. The fact that she was about to marry the man who had seized everything from him would injure Malcolm past bearing. If she was to protect him, he must leave without learning his cousin would once again reap what had initially been his destiny.

"You must realize by your welcome today that the clan has become exceptionally fond of you," she began, grasping for an explanation less painful than the truth.

Malcolm frowned. "What of it?"

"I am concerned that they are growing too attached to you, MacFane," she confessed. That part, at least, was true. "Their loyalty to you will make it difficult for them to welcome their new laird when he arrives."

"Have you found your laird, Ariella?" he asked, his voice deceptively casual.

His gaze was so intense, she feared he could see the truth. "No," she lied, shaking her head. "I have not. But when I do—"

"When you do," interrupted Malcolm, profoundly relieved, "it will be *his* goddamn problem whether or not he can command the respect and the loyalty of your people. God forbid he might actually have to earn it," he mocked, "as I did. Regardless, I fail to see why I should leave because your people have finally started to like me."

"I hired you, MacFane," Ariella protested. "It is up to me to decide when it is time for you to go. And I believe it is best for my clan that you leave now."

"Thank you for making your feelings clear on the subject," he drawled. "But I fear you have underestimated my commitment to your people, Ariella."

"Your commitment to my people has been fulfilled—"

He closed the distance between them and firmly grasped her chin with his hand, forcing her to look up at him. "Listen well, Ariella," he ordered. "I will *not* compromise the safety of this clan by leaving before the fortifications are complete and the people sufficiently trained, just because you fear this spectacular warrior you haven't found yet might object to my presence, or because you think your people have grown overly attached to me." His expression was resolute and his grip almost painful as he finished, "Is that clear?"

Ariella jerked herself free from his hold and glared at him in helpless frustration.

"Good. Now, if you will excuse me, I have much work to do."

She watched in silence as he slowly limped toward the stairs.

He could not stay here, she reminded herself miserably, abhorring the thought of what she was about to do.

However he might hate her, she would not allow him to be destroyed once again by Harold.

"You must help me in this," pleaded Ariella.

"Maybe MacFane will understand," Elizabeth argued desperately. "Maybe he won't mind you marrying Harold, and he and Gavin will decide to stay."

"He cannot stay," Ariella insisted. "Even if he wanted

to, which he wouldn't, Harold would never permit his presence here. Harold is the one who punished him by taking his title and banishing him from his clan. How could Harold be laird of the MacFanes and the Mac-Kendricks, and accept Malcolm's living here?" She shook her head. "It is impossible."

Tears began to well in Elizabeth's eyes. "But why can't Gavin stay?"

"Gavin would never abandon Malcolm. Their friendship is too deep. And even though he followed him willingly into exile, he must not be here when Harold arrives. It is possible Harold holds him partly responsible for what happened. I do not want to rouse our laird's anger." She laid a comforting hand on Elizabeth's arm. "I'm sorry."

Elizabeth swallowed thickly. "I never believed Mac-Fane was the one. None of us did, from the day you brought him here. But somehow, during these past weeks—"

"Nothing has changed," Ariella interrupted. "He is still the same crippled, drunken man he was before. Harold MacFane is the rightful guardian of the Mac-Kendrick sword, and as soon as I marry him, he and his army will keep us safe from Roderic. But the clan has become dangerously fond of MacFane. I believe their loyalty to him will make them resist my choice. Since Harold will arrive any moment, we must send Malcolm away immediately. I will not have the clan face their new laird with divided loyalties. Nor will I subject Malcolm to the humiliation of watching Harold lay claim to that which he has helped build and protect these past months. After all he has done for us, he does not deserve to be repaid so cruelly."

"But to drug Gavin—"

"Gavin will not go willingly if he discovers MacFane is being abducted," pointed our Ariella. "He must also be drugged so he cannot interfere with our plan. You are close enough to him that you can gain access to his wine, make certain he drinks it, then let Andrew and Duncan know when he is asleep. By the time the clan rises tomorrow, MacFane and Gavin will be gone, and our new laird will be on his way."

"But what if MacFane tries to come back?"

"He will not return."

"How do you know?"

"Rage will keep him from coming back," Ariella murmured, glancing out the window.

Outside she could see Malcolm slowly walking toward the gate, his uneven stride betraying his exhaustion. At least a dozen MacKendricks crowded around him as they excitedly described the work accomplished during his absence. Little Catherine was pulling impatiently on his hand in an attempt to gain his attention. Malcolm stopped, looked toward where she was pointing, then ruffled his fingers affectionately through her hair.

When had they developed such a close friendship? Ariella wondered. And how would her little sister react tomorrow when Ariella told her MacFane had left during the night?

"Rage will keep him from returning," she repeated, her voice aching. "And the knowledge that if he returns, Harold will expose the hideous truth of his past to those who have come to care for him."

Malcolm wearily closed the door to his chamber. Now that he was finally alone, he permitted himself to limp openly across the room, unconcerned that anyone would see him. Gavin had left a pitcher of wine and a goblet on the desk, but no food. Malcolm sighed. He was far too tired to dine in the great hall tonight and had hoped there would be a meal and a hot bath awaiting him. Finding neither, he eased himself into a chair and poured himself a cup of wine, deciding to rest a moment before he called someone to arrange for them. He leaned back, winced at the pain that streaked up his spine, then took a hearty swallow from his cup, contemplating his return.

Gavin had managed things well in his absence, as he had known he would. The parapet was almost finished, the gate was completed, and the MacKendricks had replenished the storage of weapons and stones to hurl from the battlements. The next stage was to build out from the base of the curtain wall, to make it more difficult for sappers and miners to chisel at the masonry or burrow beneath it. After that a ditch should be dug and flooded with water, which would further impede attackers who tried to breach the wall. Tomorrow he would organize work parties to begin construction on the wall base, and also to build a timber gallery that would project from the wall head, with openings in the flooring from which missiles could be dropped. Eventually the MacKendrick castle could be virtually impenetrable, he reflected. As long as they had ample water and food and continued to train, it might be possible for them to hold off an attacking army until help arrived from one of their neighboring clans—unless the people who lived in the cottages on the hillside were attacked first, forcing the men to leave the castle and fight in the open. For an attack like that, they would require the leadership of a seasoned warrior, and the power of a highly trained army.

As he had once commanded.

He took a deep swallow of wine. How good it had felt to return today to the excited questions and reports of the MacKendricks, who seemed to have genuinely missed him. He remembered the first day he came here, how elated everyone had been at the arrival of the Black Wolf, with their banners, pipers, poems, and speeches. Then they had watched him limp clumsily onto that platform and learned he had not brought an army with him. Their shocked disappointment as they stared at him had stripped away what little had remained of his mangled pride. Yet today they excitedly crowded around, anxious to hear of his journey and tell him of their accomplishments during his absence. They welcomed him back with the fondness and reverence due a returning laird, even though they were fully acquainted with his physical liabilities and still had not seen any indication of his supposed army.

Was it possible the MacKendricks no longer cared about these things?

The answer was irrelevant, he reminded himself harshly. They did not know the truth and, therefore, did not see him as he really was. Only he knew how monumentally he had failed his clan. If the MacKendricks learned of the innocent blood staining his hands, they would send him away in horror. Not even Ariella would permit him to remain, despite the help he had given her clan.

He shifted uneasily in his chair, reflecting on her incomprehensible assertion that it was time for him to leave. It was hardly the welcome he had imagined she would give him. But then, what had he expected? That she would run into his arms and press desperate, hungry kisses against his mouth? That she would fill his ear with sweet words of adoration, telling him how she had longed for his return, the same way he had longed for her?

He was a fool, he realized bitterly. What happened between them that night on the wall head had been a temporary madness, nothing more. Ariella's responsibility was to wed the next laird of her people, and he was not that man. He had no right to dally with her. He was here to help make the MacKendricks as secure as possible, and to repel any further attacks by Roderic. Once the new MacKendrick was settled here, and he felt certain Ariella was safe, he and Gavin would leave. He would have to, or risk going completely mad from watching Ariella endure the touch of another man.

The thought filled him with helpless rage.

A soft rap on the door released him from his thoughts.

"Enter."

"Your pardon, MacFane," said Elizabeth, entering the room. "Ariella asked me to give you this note."

Malcolm was careful to minimize his stiffness as he rose from his chair. "Thank you."

Elizabeth gave him the message, then hesitated.

"Is there something else?"

"No," she quickly assured him. "That's all."

He waited, but she did not leave. "Are you sure there isn't something else?" he prodded.

"There is something I wanted to say," she reluctantly confessed. "I wanted you to know that you and Gavin have done a wonderful job of training us and—we're all grateful."

"Thank you, Elizabeth," he said, moved by her unexpected declaration. "That means a great deal to me."

Her eyes were sparkling with tears, and her lower lip began to tremble. Malcolm wondered if she was always this emotional.

"Good-bye, MacFane," she whispered.

"Good night, Elizabeth." He found himself almost smiling as the door closed. He wondered if Gavin had any notion that this girl who was so clearly attracted to him had such tender feelings. He would mention it to him, he decided as he unfolded Ariella's note, just to be certain Gavin was careful in his treatment of her.

MacFane,
It is urgent I see you. Please come to my chamber.
Ariella

Malcolm frowned. Why would Ariella send him a note rather than simply come to his room? Was she ill?

He jerked the door open and started down the hall, moving as quickly as his injured leg would permit.

Ariella carefully measured the sleeping powder into the cup, contemplated Malcolm's unusual size, then added another full dose.

It was vital he remain in a deep sleep for many hours, so he would not waken as they moved him. When he finally did emerge from the thick haze of the drug, he would be far from her lands. She set his cup on the table, where a meal of roasted deer, fresh salmon, cheese, and oatcakes had been laid for two, and glanced nervously around the room. The fire was burning brightly, and candles flickered everywhere, bathing her chamber in honeyed light. Although she anticipated that Malcolm would drink his wine as soon as he arrived, the possibility that he might not forced her to create a reason for him to linger awhile. She had instructed Elizabeth to slip into his room and remove the tray of food Gavin had set there for him. When MacFane came to Ariella's room, he would be enticed by the aroma of the food, which would make him want to stay and dine with her. She was not certain how quickly the powder would act on a man of his considerable stature, but she was confident he would be asleep long before the meal was finished. She prayed Elizabeth had equal success in administering the powder to Gavin.

She was startled by a heavy pounding on the door. Before she had a chance to speak, the door was thrown open and Malcolm entered.

"Are you ill?" he demanded brusquely.

Ariella looked at him in confusion. "No. Why?"

His gaze raked over her, assessing, not convinced of her reply. Finally deciding she appeared fit enough, the lines in his brow eased.

"I thought you might be ill," he confessed, suddenly feeling foolish.

"I am well, MacFane," she assured him. "I asked you here because I regretted the way our meeting ended today. I hope we can put the incident behind us."

Malcolm regarded her skeptically, unable to decide if she was sincere or if this was some kind of game.

Sensing his wariness, Ariella busied herself by pouring wine into his goblet, watching as the powder swirled in the crimson liquid. Then she slowly filled her own cup, giving his mixture time to dissolve.

"Will you have wine?" she asked, offering it to him.

"Thank you."

She raised her own cup. "To the success of your negotiations."

She smiled as he took a sip.

"I thought you might join me in a meal and tell me of your meetings with the other clans," she continued, gesturing to the table.

The spicy-sweet fragrance of the roasted meat wafted toward him, making him acutely aware of his hunger.

"Thank you," he said, wondering at her unexpected graciousness.

He waited for her to be seated, then placed his cup before his setting and sat down opposite her.

"So, MacFane," began Ariella as she served him from the platter of salmon, "tell me of these alliances you have arranged for us."

"The first clan we visited were the Campbells, who inhabit extensive lands to the southwest. Although they knew of your clan, they were not interested in coming to your assistance once they realized how small you are. The fact that you lack an army makes you unable to offer them a similar commitment."

"I thought that would be a problem," she mused.

"That is why I had an alternate proposal for them to consider."

"To purchase their services?"

"Not exactly," he replied. "Before we left, I instructed

Duncan and Ramsay to collect examples of the Mac-Kendricks' finest efforts in weaving, tapestry, wood carving, and silver work, and sketches of some of the masonry that has been done here. When I presented these to Campbell, he was considerably impressed. He had never seen such intricate work and could quickly appreciate its rarity and value."

His compliment made her smile. "My people take great pride in their crafts."

"The MacKendricks take great pride in whatever they do," Malcolm observed. "Once they decided they would learn to defend themselves, and I found the right methods to teach them, they pursued their training without reservation."

"It comes from years of disciplined study. When the children are very young, they begin their lessons in crafts, music, tumbling, and writing. After a few years their favorite activities become apparent, and these are the ones they are encouraged to pursue. What begins as a game becomes a study, then a passion, and ultimately a lifelong source of pleasure."

Malcolm took a swallow of wine, reflecting on the lessons of his own boyhood. His father had encouraged his only son to drag a wooden sword behind him from the time he could walk. Later, wrestling was encouraged, and Laird MacFane had been unsympathetic to his complaints of cuts and bruises. Riding was introduced when he was four, and he was quickly playing games wherein he had to spear a stuffed sack swinging from a rope as he galloped past it. Archery had followed, then wielding an ax and learning to throw a dirk with deadly accuracy. As he grew older, the games became more complicated, with several men hiding and trying to attack him at once. His body had grown strong and fit, and he soon began to enjoy the challenge of instigating or repelling an assault. When he was nineteen, his father had bestowed upon Gavin the honor of watching over the future laird. That had been shortly after Gavin's wife drowned herself, following the death of their infant son. Gavin accepted his new position with solemn devotion and taught him everything he knew of military strategy. Over the years Malcolm had been grateful for his relentless training. It had enabled him to become a great warrior, and to lead an army that had been the envy of many a leader. A source of pride, certainly.

But a source of pleasure?

"Are we to pay the Campbells for their protection with our crafts?" asked Ariella.

"In part," he replied. "But paying for protection does not necessarily guarantee it. I wanted to make sure there was a commitment there, an obligation that went beyond merely buying their aid when we needed it."

She looked at him, startled. Once again he was including himself when referring to her clan.

"To foster that commitment and develop closer ties, I suggested that some Campbells might like to stay here for a few months and receive training in the subject of their choice. That way they could enhance their own skills, then go back and teach those lessons to others."

"But it takes years to master the art of weaving, or playing the bagpipes," protested Ariella. "These things cannot be taught in a month or two."

"Exactly. Which means this exchange would be ongoing. People would come, stay for a while, and then go home so others could take their place. We could even establish a special summer program for children, wherein they could learn tumbling and juggling."

Understanding crept over her. "With Campbells visiting and building friendships, the clan will have more reason to come to our aid if we are attacked, because they have a duty to defend their people who are staying here."

Malcolm nodded. "Groups of MacKendricks would also be invited to spend time at the Campbell lands if they chose. The men could train with their army, while their women could make new acquaintances and share ideas about maintaining households."

"Why can't the women train with the army as well?" she demanded.

He resisted the urge to smile. "I think perhaps the Campbells are not quite ready for such an unconventional proposal, but you are welcome to put it to them if you wish."

Excitement grew within her as she considered the benefits of MacFane's idea. By nurturing ties with other clans, they could all discover more about each other. And the friendships that would result would be rooted in peace and learning, not in the ugliness of aggression. It was a splendid plan. "Did Laird Campbell agree to this arrangement?"

"Yes," he replied. "As did the Grants, the Frasers, and the MacGregors. I wanted to gain the approval of both you and the council, however, before inviting them to send the first visitors."

"What did the council say?"

"Angus and Dugald were somewhat reluctant at first," he admitted, "which I anticipated. Your clan has lived in isolation for many years, and it is difficult for them to imagine strangers coming to stay here. But Gordon is not so resistant to change, and he quickly saw the benefits of such an arrangement."

"As do I," said Ariella. "It will be good for my people to make new friends, and share ideas and skills with them."

"Excellent. Tomorrow we will send two messengers to visit the clans and confirm the arrangement."

We.

She dropped her gaze to her food.

He could not stay here, she reminded herself. It was impossible. She was doing this to spare him, not to hurt him. It was not her fault he was not the one. The respon-

sibility for that turn of fate belonged to him. Only Mac-
Fane could be held accountable for what had happened
to his clan that night. And for what he had allowed himself to become afterward.

His sun-bronzed hand was draped casually around
the stem of his goblet, which was almost full. She felt a
stab of alarm. A man of his size must drink the entire
potion, or the powder might not take effect.

"Come, MacFane, you aren't drinking," she noted,
raising the pitcher. "Finish that and I will fill your cup
again."

He gave her a curious look. "It is unlike you, Ariella,
to encourage me to drink."

"I'm not encouraging you," she protested. "I only
thought you might enjoy a little more." She set the
pitcher down.

It seemed he had insulted her, though he didn't
understand how. He took a small sip of his wine, just to
appear accommodating. In truth, he was feeling somewhat tired and had no desire to drink anymore. Obviously his journey had exhausted him more than he
realized, which was giving the alcohol greater power over
his body.

"While I was visiting the Frasers, I heard an amusing
story about your clan," he began, seeking to ease the tension that had arisen between them. "Some nonsensical
legend about a sword."

Ariella's heart quickened. "Really?" she said, attempting to sound only mildly interested.

"Apparently the Frasers have long told a tale about
an ancient sword that once belonged to your clan's
founder," he explained. "They seem to think you still
have this sword, and that it has some kind of magic
power."

"My clan was founded over four hundred years ago,
MacFane," she said, feigning amusement. "As old and
rusted as some of our swords were when you first came, I

doubt any of them are quite that ancient." She managed a small laugh.

Malcolm smiled. "I told them I had never heard of this sword, but they seemed absolutely convinced of its existence," he continued. "Which made me wonder if Roderic has heard this tale, and that is why he is so determined to have control of your people. Perhaps he believes he can force you to give him this sword."

"I cannot say whether or not he heard the story," lied Ariella indifferently. "He never mentioned it to me. I think it is clear he wants to be laird because he owns nothing, leads no one except those foul-smelling swine, and has nowhere else to go."

"You are forgetting something."

"What?"

"He wants you."

He was staring at her intently, his blue eyes shadowed with an emotion she could not identify. Anger, perhaps—making her wonder if he suspected her imminent betrayal of him, if that was why he tarried so long over his drugged wine. Or desire—that smoky, barely leashed hunger that had made him reach out to her before, to hold her and touch her until she was drowning in heat and need. It was frightening to have him look at her so, as if he were stripping away the layers of her lies and defenses, trying to see what lay beneath. She wanted him to stop, yet she could not pull her gaze from his, for fear her inability to meet his scrutiny would be even more revealing.

"I told you before," she began, her voice strangely hollow, "he wants me only because he believes marriage to me will solidify his position as laird."

Was she really so innocent that she believed that? wondered Malcolm. Had she no perception of the unbearable desire she could ignite in a man? He had seen the vile, predaceous way Roderic had leered at her that night on the wall head. And Malcolm had been overcome with rage that someone should dare look upon her so—as if she were something to be conquered—something magnificently strong and rare that Roderic knew would fight him, but that he would eventually be able to break. Not with violence against her, though he would try that, would even find a demented, evil pleasure in it. But with the threat of violence against her people. That was Ariella's greatest weakness, and Roderic knew it. One hand lifted to Elizabeth, or Agnes, or Helen—one sword pressed against the throat of Duncan, or Andrew, or poor old Angus—and Ariella would be on her knees, pleading for mercy and vowing to do whatever Roderic wanted.

He would not allow that to happen.

"These alliances are useful only if we are able to hold off an attack for at least four hours," he remarked. "We still need an army, especially if the cottages on the hill are attacked and we are forced to fight in the open."

We.

She could not bear it, listening to him as he planned for the defense of her people. She could not bear the knowledge that tomorrow he would be far away, forced to leave against his will. And that when he finally wakened and realized what she had done, he would be consumed with hatred.

Against her.

He rose from the table, suddenly restless. "I must write to each of the four clans, asking if they are willing to hire out ten of their warriors. The messengers can take these missives first thing tomorrow. With forty welltrained men we should be able to oppose Roderic's forces for at least as long as it takes for help to arrive." He moved toward the door.

Panic gripped her. He was leaving without having drunk his wine.

"Wait!"

Malcolm stopped. "Is there something else you wished to discuss with me?"

"You haven't finished your meal, MacFane," she said, attempting to sound blithe.

"Forgive me. I am tired, and if I am to complete these missives tonight, I must begin now."

"At least finish your wine," she persisted, gesturing to his goblet. "It may help you sleep better."

"I have had enough."

She watched him in desperation as he limped toward the door. Andrew and Duncan could never overpower him if he wasn't weakened with the sleeping powder. But it was essential he leave tonight, before Harold arrived.

"You must leave us, MacFane," she blurted out, nearly frantic.

He turned to look at her, one dark brow raised. "Why are you suddenly so anxious for me to go, Ariella?" he demanded softly.

"You were hired to train my people, and you have done so," she explained uneasily. "We can take care of whatever negotiations must be carried out between the clans."

Malcolm studied her a moment. She was struggling to appear calm, but her slender fingers clenched the stem of her goblet, betraying her anxiety. Not only did she want him to leave, he realized, she was actually terrified he might refuse. But why? What would suddenly make her so desperate for him to go, when her clan was still in danger?

Understanding crashed over him in a frigid wave.

"So," he drawled, "you have decided on your new laird."

She looked at him in surprise. Her first thought was to deny it, but the fury twisting his face made her think better of it.

"But this is a cause for celebration, is it not?" he demanded acridly. "Ariella MacKendrick has finally found the perfect man to lead her people. A magnificent warrior with a powerful army, who encompasses all of her sacred ideals. Come, now, do not keep me in suspense. Who is this valiant fellow?"

"You do not know him," she replied tautly.

He considered this a moment, wondering if he should believe her. "Well, I can't say that surprises me," he remarked, his tone sneering. "I don't believe I ever met anyone as saintly and gallant as the man you have been seeking. No matter. I look forward to meeting him when he arrives." He moved to the table, lifted his goblet in a mocking toast, then took a bitter swallow.

"You will not meet him, MacFane."

"Why not?"

"Because I do not wish you to."

"I see." His eyes narrowed. "So after all that I have done here, I am dismissed, is that it?"

"I don't know why you are acting as if some grave injustice were being done to you," she retorted angrily. "You never wanted to come here. My father asked for your help, but you refused. Then I went to you and pleaded for your help, and you refused again. When you finally came, it was out of greed, MacFane, not because you wanted to help us."

Everything she said was true. But hearing her say it only intensified his fury.

"Regardless of my reasons, I am here now. The great Black Wolf, at your service, milady," he drawled, giving her a stiff, taunting bow. "Deeply flawed, crippled, with a shattered past and a hollow future. Of course I'm not fit to be this heroic laird you and Alpine have long fantasized about for your people. I'm not so young or strong, and God knows my life has been far from pure. But I am here, Ariella. Do you understand what I'm saying? *I am here!*"

"You're too late!" she flared. "It could have been you, Malcolm. It *should* have been you. If you had only pulled yourself out of your drunken, self-pitying stupor and come, not because you *knew* you could help, but because you believed you *might* have been able to help, maybe then it would have been different. Because that would have been the action of a man of courage. That," she finished, her voice steeped in scorn, "would have been the deed of a true warrior."

"By God, *I was a true warrior!*" he roared. Overwhelmed with fury, he lifted the pitcher of wine and shattered it against the wall. Then he stalked toward her, uncertain of what he was about to do.

She jumped out of her chair, knocking it over in her desperation to evade him. But rage flowed hot and fast in his veins, and Malcolm would not let her escape. Her scathing contempt was more than he could bear. He grabbed her by her small shoulders and heaved her against the wall. Then he braced his hands on either side of her, imprisoning her with the shelter of his battered body.

Anger burned in her silvery eyes, and her chest heaved with breathlessness, barely grazing the fabric of his plaid. This was the woman who might have been his wife. The woman he wanted with a hunger so appalling, a need so crushing, he thought he might shatter from the force of it. And as she stared at him, her cheeks flushed with outrage, her eyes snapping fire, he wanted her to want him, just a fraction of how much he wanted her. He would never be good enough, or strong enough, or pure enough to assume the sacred role of her laird and husband. Perhaps three years ago, before he began this hellish descent into the pathetic shell he had become, he might have fulfilled some of her expectations. But all that remained of the mighty Black Wolf was the crippled failure of a man before her. In that moment he hated her with a passion that was staggering. He hated her for bringing him here and showing him what might once have been his, but now could never be. Perhaps this was God's way of further punishing him, he reflected bitterly, by tormenting him with the knowledge that he had lost more than he had realized that ghastly night he'd led his army away from his castle. That was why He had sent Ariella MacKendrick to him. God wanted her to pull him from the mire of his self-destruction, to bring him to a place where he was given purpose and respect, only to have it wrenched away and be cast back into the lonely, hopeless pit of his life. It was more than he could bear, to be tortured so relentlessly. It filled him with a rage he could not control, and a despair he would never overcome. Not that he did not deserve to be punished so cruelly—oh, no, he was well aware of the justice of the thing. It was only that in this agonizing moment, with this glorious woman who might have been his trapped between his arms, he wanted the suffering to stop.

"I'm sorry, Ariella," he said, his voice rough with anger and regret. "I failed you when you needed me. I was not the warrior you sought. And I did come for the money. But there is something you should know," he murmured, removing his hand from the cool stone wall to brush his fingers against her heated cheek.

Ariella regarded him in confusion, trapped by the pain deeply etched across the hard lines of his face.

"What is that, MacFane?" she managed, her voice barely a whisper.

"I stayed for you."

With that raw confession he lowered his head and captured her lips with his. He kissed her with urgent, brutal desperation, wanting her to the point of madness, and knowing there would be nothing beyond this single, stolen moment. Her mouth was warm and wine sweet, her cheek a silken veil against his rough jaw, and he wanted to remember these things, wanted them forever burned into his mind so when he lay alone each night in the years to come, he would be able to recall the velvet caress of Ariella's lips and cheek against his. She did not fight him, perhaps because she was too startled, but in a moment she would regain her senses and shove him away, and he would never touch her again. The inevitability of this flooded him with anguish, as did the knowledge that she belonged to another, that what might once have been his could never be. An unbearable sense of loss gripped him, squeezing his chest so tight, he felt he couldn't breathe, did not dare even to try, for fear his breath would escape him in a sob. He tasted her deeply, passionately, knowing time was his enemy, that any moment this fragile bond would be broken, and wanting to mark her with his kiss, so when she lay beside the man she had chosen, and endured his touch, she might remember what it was like to be wanted beyond all reason.

Ariella was falling into a dizzying swirl of heat and light and need. It was impossible, what was happening, she understood that, but she did not seem able to gain control of her reeling senses enough to make Malcolm stop. His desire was overwhelming; it pulled her toward him like a powerful wave drawing sand into the ocean. There was fury in his kiss, fury and pain and a terrible desperation, as if he were trying to make her belong to him, while at the same time knowing he could not possibly succeed. It was this that kept her from shoving him away, this burning hunger, this appalling torment, which rendered her unable to do anything except stand against the wall and endure his kiss. And then he began to pull away, and she was overcome with loss, as if all the light in the world had suddenly been extinguished. It made no sense—she should have been relieved it was over, and instead she felt abandoned and empty, a hollow fragment of what she had been a moment ago. *He is not the one*, she reminded herself desperately as the air grew cold around her. But knowing this did not comfort her, did not ease the pain tearing through her heart. Unable to bear it, she let out a cry of despair and reached out to him, drawing him back so she could wrap her arms around his neck and press her trembling lips to his.

Malcolm froze, unable to believe she really wanted this, unable to trust himself to his own reeling emotions. And then he moaned and ground his mouth against hers, tasting her deeply as his hands roamed hungrily over her shoulders, down her back, across her hips, pulling her close so she was pressed against the hard length of him, holding her safe within the shelter of his arms. This was all he needed to make his life whole once more, he realized as he kissed her. If God would only let him have Ariella, he could bear anything.

It was wrong, Ariella thought desperately as she felt him grasping at the soft wool of her gown, quickly easing it up her body and over her head, leaving her only in her chemise. It was a sin, she added as they moved toward the bed, her fumbling blindly with the brooch tacking his plaid to his shoulders. She unfastened his belt and yanked impatiently at the endless length of plaid swathed around his waist, causing it to fall in a ripple of green and black around his thickly muscled calves. His eyes held hers as he removed his shirt, their color the steely blue of a loch just before a storm. Finally he stood naked before her, his scarred, sun-bronzed body washed in the amber light of the fire. In that moment he was neither weak nor crippled. Instead his powerful presence filled the chamber, making her feel warm and safe. This man was not the next laird, and giving herself to him was not her destiny. But in this frozen, breathless moment she ceased to care, which told her she had either gone mad, or had simply broken beneath the relentless weight of duty to her clan. After all their struggle and pain, and for all the sacrifice and suffering yet to come, she and Malcolm deserved to have this moment.

Just this once.

Malcolm bent his head and took her lips in his, pulling her trembling form against him so she could be warmed by his heat. It had been well over four years since he had lain with a woman, and he felt as clumsy and nervous as a lad. Before his injuries there had been countless pretty girls willing to warm the bed of the great Black Wolf, thinking it an honor of sorts, or believing they would then forever be under his protection. He had enjoyed the attention, and had indulged in the soft company of more women than he could count. Once he was betrothed to Marrian, however, he elected not to shame her by lying with another, though no one would have thought less of him if he had. But the desire surging through him was unlike anything he had ever known. It made him feel strong and powerful and whole, it washed him clean of both his past and his future, so that there was only this moment, and Ariella, and the incredible, impossible realization that she wanted him. She seemed small and delicate as she clung to his shoulders, clad only in the thin fabric of her chemise, but he knew this frailness was illusory. The woman he lowered onto the mattress was stronger and more courageous than most men he had known. He had watched her smash her foot into a thief's face when she thought she was about to die, because it was not Ariella's way to succumb without a fight. He had seen her dress as a lad and train with men more than twice her size, always rising when she was knocked down, always striving to do better, because she believed that only through improving her own skills could she protect her people. She had swallowed her fury and sought out the Black Wolf because she had been told she must, and then she had hired him to help her people, even though she blamed him for their suffering. Ariella MacKendrick was a fighter, yes, but she was more than that, he realized as he swept his hands reverently over her.

Within Ariella's small, slim body beat the heart of a warrior.

Ariella kissed Malcolm deeply as her fingers trailed over the warm steel of his massive shoulders, his muscled chest, the rippled plane of his back. She knew his body intimately, she was well acquainted with every jagged scar and pain-drenched muscle, yet she felt as if she were discovering him for the first time. Tonight he did not flinch with pain as she caressed him, but instead seemed to sigh into her hands, as if he hungered for her touch. He was solid and powerful beneath her palms, pulsing with heat and life and desire, and she wanted him with an intensity that was frightening. Each time her hands surged over the hard, sinewy curves, she longed to know him even more, to explore the areas of him that until now had been forbidden, to memorize every detail. She felt small as she lay against him, small yet wonderfully safe, as if nothing could possibly harm her while she was wrapped in Malcolm's arms. But she was also restless with a need she did not understand, a hunger to be touched more, kissed more, to have his heat envelop her, until there was nothing except her and Malcolm and the wall of fire raging around them.

Malcolm tore his mouth from Ariella's lips to kiss her cheek, her chin, the ivory silk of her throat. He touched her through the thin fabric of her chemise as he inhaled the heather-sweet scent of her, driven mad by the barrier, which he knew he could rip open with one firm pull. Instead he laid his hand against her slim ankle and began to edge the garment up, heavily aroused by the softness of her calf, the smooth bend of her knee, the creamy length of her thigh. He nuzzled her chemise off her shoulder and trailed hungry kisses over her, peeling the fabric away as he tasted her, until finally the lush swell of her breast was rising and falling beneath his lips. He flicked his tongue over the coral tip, then took her in his mouth and gently sucked, causing her to inhale with startled pleasure. Her hands threaded into his hair, holding him there, offering herself, so he lingered over the velvety peak, bathing it with hot caresses, until finally he pulled away to give equal attention to her other breast. As he took her into his mouth again, his fingers moved up the soft passage of her inner thighs and gently entered the satin-slick heat of her. She gasped, and he moved up to kiss her mouth once more, tasting her deeply as his fingers caressed the sleek wet petals. She was gloriously hot, and he took his time with her, caressing her slowly, then faster, exploring her reverently, then hungrily, until finally she was raising herself to him and moaning against his mouth.

Ariella was on fire, and with every stroke and kiss the flames burned hotter. She clung to Malcolm with breathless desperation, her hands roaming frantically over the hard breadth of his back, wanting more of him, wanting to feel his heat meld with hers until they were one. *He is not the one,* she reminded herself hopelessly as he rained kisses against her throat, her breasts, the warm flat of her stomach, easing her chemise down until finally he stripped it off and cast it onto the floor. Then he was hovering over the downy softness between her thighs, his breath blowing warm against her. Suddenly uncertain, she tried to roll away, but he clamped his hands around her wrists and held her fast while his tongue flicked inside. She gasped in surprise, but he did not give her time to resist, for his tongue was inside her again, tasting her in quick, feathery strokes. Pleasure washed through her, like warm honey pouring through her veins, and she released the breath she was holding and sank deeper into the softness of the mattress, surrendering to his unbearably glorious caresses. His kiss grew more languid, he tasted every intricate fold of her, lightly, delicately, until a soft moan escaped her throat and she began to writhe against him. He released her wrists to ease one finger inside her, then two, and began to thrust them gently, in exquisite cadence with the stroke of his tongue. Her body became taut and restless, her fingers threaded into the dark fall of his hair, then immediately abandoned him to grip the sheets as her breath escaped her lips in shallow gasps. Just when she thought she couldn't bear it a moment longer, that she would surely die from the sensations surging through her, Malcolm raised himself over her, covering her with his strength and heat.

A hollow, lonely ache had blossomed inside her, making her feel empty. *This is the man who might have been my husband,* she thought, feeling an agonizing sense of loss. She wrapped her arms around his neck and raised her hips until she felt the velvet tip of him pressing against her. The lines of his face were carved in deep grooves as he studied her, sharing her desolation. Then he was filling her, stretching her, banishing her emptiness. He withdrew and then entered her again, slowly, gently, giving her time to accept him. His blue eyes were smoldering as he stared down at her, desire mingled with a terrible sadness, a grief so intense she wanted to weep, for him, for her, for the intolerable cruelty of a life that had cheated them both of what might have been. He paused, his body half joined to hers, and raised his hand to caress her cheek with aching gentleness.

"Ariella," he murmured, his voice rough. Then he lowered his lips to hers and finished in a ragged whisper, "My love."

A flash of pain streaked through her as he joined her body to his, a melding of flesh and blood and soul. She gasped into his mouth, clinging tightly to him. He did not move, except to stroke her cheek as he whis-

pered soft, soothing words into her ear. Tears welled in
her eyes, not because of the pain, but because in that
moment her heart tore in two, and she did not think
she could bear it. Malcolm continued to whisper to her
as he pressed kisses against her damp eyes, her cheeks,
her throat, soothing her with his low, patient voice,
revealing a gentle empathy she had not known he was
capable of. She wished he was oblivious to her suffering, that he would simply satisfy himself and be
done with it. Instead he continued to hold her, and kiss
her, and comfort her, until she thought she would die
from the agony of it. Tomorrow he would be gone, and
she would be forced to marry another and lie in his
arms and try not to remember this glorious, heart-
breaking moment. She inhaled a deep, ragged breath,
fighting for control, fighting to stop the tears that were
leaking in hot streams down the sides of her face. Her
distress caused him to grind his mouth against hers
with savage possessiveness, and a ripple of heat coursed
through her once again. He began to pulse gently
within her, stirring the flames of passion. She ran her
hands across his straining shoulders, the gentle slope of
his spine, the firm curve of his hips, touching him
everywhere as she kissed him with frantic, hopeless
need, trying to eradicate all thought of the past, and the
future, and anything beyond this fire-washed moment.
A new sensation began to bloom within her, one of
heat and hunger and longing; it mingled with her sadness and made her kiss him harder as she lifted herself
to him, wanting more of him, wanting him to be a part
of her, wanting to lose herself completely to the storm
raging between them. His hand slipped down and he
began to stroke her, until pleasure was flowing hot and
fast through every fiber of her body, until she grew taut
with a desire that obliterated everything except the
hard warmth of Malcolm stretched over her, filling her,
enveloping her, flooding her with need. She wrapped

her arms around him and held fast, her breath a series of tiny, fragile whimpers as she rose higher and higher, thinking she could not bear it another moment yet still wanting more, feeling him become a part of her with every rapid thrust and stroke and kiss, until finally she no longer knew where her flesh ended and his began. And then, just when she thought she was about to die from the unbearable pleasure raging through her, she began to shatter, like a star bursting in the night sky, illuminating the world around her in silvery shards of light. She cried out his name, a cry of joy and wonder, and clung to him, feeling whole and safe, knowing nothing could harm her as long as she remained in Malcolm's arms.

Her body gripped him with liquid velvet, stripping away the final fragments of his self-control. Malcolm crushed his mouth against hers as he drove himself deep inside her, feeling her cries echo in the back of his throat, drinking in the sweetness of her pleasure as he thrust into her again and again, losing himself completely to the incredible magnificence of her. Her ecstasy made him feel strong and alive; it washed away the dark years of bitterness and pain with a clear, cooling wave, unveiling the man he had once been. Deeper and deeper he buried himself, losing himself in Ariella's strength, her courage, her resilience, feeling himself become a part of her, and wanting to stay like this forever. Finally he could bear no more. He wrenched his mouth from hers to call out her name, a husky plea and a solemn oath, because in that brilliant, wondrous moment as he filled her with heat and need, he knew with piercing clarity that he would never let her go.

The chamber fell silent except for the hoarse rasp of their breathing and the occasional snap of the fire. They lay twined together, still one, unwilling to speak for fear it would snap the silken bonds that held them together. Ariella clung to Malcolm with hopeless despair, feeling his heart beating firmly against her breast as she fought the tears welling in her eyes. She had never imagined it would be like this. Nothing in her life had prepared her for anything so glorious, or so painful. She no longer wanted to be Ariella MacKendrick, guardian of the Mac-Kendrick sword. She wished she had been of ordinary birth, with the right to select whomever she liked as her husband. Maybe then she could have overlooked Malcolm's failings and weaknesses. But she was a woman with a solemn duty to her people, and her feelings were of no consequence. She inhaled a ragged breath, feeling lost and empty, when but an instant ago she had been flooded with joy.

Malcolm raised his head from the fragrant silk of her hair to study her. He frowned at the tears leaking from her eyes, then lifted his hand to capture them with his fingers. She turned away, unable to bear his scrutiny.

"You think I am unfit to be laird of your people," he murmured as he grasped her chin, forcing her to look at him. "But I swear to you, Ariella, I will not let harm come to them. Do you understand?"

His eyes were burning with intensity, his expression grave, and she did not doubt the solemnity of his vow. But she knew he lacked the ability to uphold it. It was that irrefutable fact, combined with the knowledge of his own clan's slaughter, that caused her to close her eyes, unable to meet his gaze.

"You cannot stay, Malcolm," she whispered painfully. "You are not the one."

Anger swept through him, dousing the fire of passion that had raged but a moment earlier. "By God, you do wear my patience thin with all this talk about 'the one,' " he snapped, rolling off her. He stalked naked over to the table, limping slightly, and snatched up his goblet. "There is no perfect man, Ariella," he informed her harshly. "Any man who is worth a damn has taken risks in life, which means he has made mistakes. Sometimes those mistakes leave terrible scars. But the advantage of making even the ghastliest mistake is that you learn from it. Provided, of course," he qualified in a flagrantly cynical voice, "you are unlucky enough to survive." He tilted his head back and drained his cup.

"My father never made mistakes," countered Ariella, clutching the covers to her breast. "He was always honorable and courageous. He never failed his people the way you did." It was a cruel, cutting declaration, but in this moment she needed to say it. Perhaps because she needed to remind herself of his failings.

Outrage clenched his face. *"Your father never faced the challenges I faced!"* he roared, enraged by her simplistic, infuriatingly sanctimonious reasoning. "He *never* went to war, *never* led an army, *never* even left these isolated, sheltered lands to help another. The one time he was attacked, his clan was so pathetically ill prepared, many were killed, including himself, and very nearly his daughter. Is this what you hold up to me as an example of brilliant leadership?" he demanded scathingly.

"In the end he couldn't protect us," Ariella admitted, wounded by his contemptuous condemnation of her father. "Because he was not a warrior. The next laird of the MacKendricks must be a great warrior *and* a great leader."

He regarded her with bitter rancor. "And you believe I am neither." The statement rolled slowly off his tongue, which was strangely thick and clumsy.

"Maybe once," she allowed, struggling to keep her voice even. "Not anymore."

His pain was staggering. She could see it in the harsh lines of his face, in the wounded depths of his eyes. She never intended to hurt him like this. But she had no choice now. He must understand that despite what had happened between them, he could never persuade her to accept him as laird of her people. And more, she needed to be certain he would not return. That when he emerged from the thick fog of sleep he was rapidly drifting toward, he would hate her with a virulence that would keep him away forever.

The thought of it was unbearable.

Malcolm blinked, trying to clear his vision. Weariness was seeping through him, making him want nothing but to crawl back into bed and take Ariella in his arms and hold her tight against him while he slept. A few hours of sleep, in which he could forget about his past, and his future, and just accept the glory of her, soft and warm against him. Tomorrow he would make her see how wrong she was. Not about his failures, for they were chiseled into the hard rock of time, and there was nothing he could do to change them. But somehow he would convince her there was more to him than the self-pitying, weak-willed, broken warrior she had discovered the day she came to find the great Black Wolf. He was not the warrior he had once been, and he was man enough to admit he never would be again. But it took more than physical strength to make a great laird. It took wisdom, and courage, and honor, and even the harsh, unforgiving lessons of experience. All these he believed he had. And though he had never wanted the awesome burden of leading a clan again, he was willing to make that sacrifice.

For her.

"I am tired," he mumbled, wondering at the effort the words cost him, at the extraordinary will necessary just to move his stiff, aching body toward the bed. "We will talk more of this tomorrow."

She slowly shook her head.

Malcolm stared at her, puzzled by the tears streaming down her face, flowing so fast they dripped off her cheeks and dampened the sheet she clutched to her breast. Why was she weeping so? he wondered, struggling to concentrate. What had made her so unhappy? He frowned, trying to clear the mists swirling through his head. Sleep was surging over him in a heavy, warm wave, robbing him of his ability to think, or speak, or even recall what they had been discussing. But he never fell asleep like this, he realized, taking another uneasy step toward the bed. Ariella was crying openly now, her small shoulders heaving, her misery rising from her throat in shallow, choking gasps. What was the matter with her?

"My God," he murmured thickly as understanding pierced the haze, "what have you done to me?"

Her expression was stricken, but that could not temper his fury. Gavin. He must find Gavin.

He turned toward the door. One step, then another.

Suddenly he was falling into a vortex of darkness, aware of nothing but his rage, and the muffled sound of Ariella's weeping.

CHAPTER 12

Wisps of lavender mist caressed the rose-and-cream stonework of the castle, veiling it in a shroud of cool vapor. It gave the fortress a mythical quality, as if it had suddenly appeared on the emerald crest of the hill and could at any moment vanish. The neat white cottages dotting the hillside heightened this illusion, each chimney exhaling a thin plume of smoke, casting a soft haze into the early-morning light.

Soon, reflected Roderic, his belly tightening with anticipation, *all this will be mine.*

Nearly two weeks had passed since the night the MacKendricks had repelled his attack. At first it had been inconceivable, that these infantile artisans had learned so much of warfare in such a short period of time, they could hold off his rough, seasoned warriors. But the moment he saw Malcolm standing on the wall head, his incredulity hardened into bitter outrage. The fallen Black Wolf, that pathetic cripple who was supposed to be drinking himself to death somewhere on the king's lands, had somehow found his way to the MacKendricks. Even more astounding, his former laird had not appeared to be the slightest bit drunk, or even in much pain, when he had confronted him. At first Roderic had feared this was the power of the sword at work, that Ariella had foolishly given it to Malcolm and it had effected his miraculous recovery. But a few moments of swordplay revealed she had not. Although Malcolm was still a formidable opponent, the sword he carried granted him no special abilities. His right arm was weak, forcing him to wield his weapon with both arms, and though he walked relatively well, his injured leg was a hindrance during the sharp, quick moves of combat. A few minutes of intense conflict, and he would be weakened to the point where he could be easily dispatched.

The problem, Roderic realized as he pensively stroked the thick scar marking his cheek, was that there were now so many others willing and able to fight.

A dozen of his men had been killed or wounded that night, and another ten captured, which left him with a rather paltry band of only about twenty able warriors. Given the castle's new fortifications and the MacKendricks' obvious eagerness to demonstrate their battle skills, a direct attack was now out of the question. The only way to gain possession of the MacKendrick sword was to capture Ariella and force her to give it to him. With the sword in hand and Ariella as his hostage, no one would dare oppose him when he killed Malcolm and took control of the castle. He would finally have a fortress and lands of his own, and lairdship over a clan whose uncommon industry would make him wealthy beyond imagination. More important, he would have the power of this sword, which would enable him to conquer countless other clans, extending his rule throughout the Highlands.

As for Ariella, she would be severely punished for making a fool of him twice. He smiled.

It was time to make the little bitch understand that her new laird's patience had come to an end.

"And that is why he had to go home," finished Ariella, gently brushing a lock of hair off Catherine's forehead.

Her little sister regarded her with wide, despondent eyes. "But he didn't even say good-bye."

"It was very late, and he had to leave right away." She tried to stifle her guilt as she added, "He asked me to tell you he was sorry, and to explain that his own clan needed him."

"But we need him too," countered Catherine. "He was supposed to give me a riding lesson today. He *promised*." Her lower lip began to quiver.

"Our new laird is on his way this very minute, and he is coming with his great army, so we don't need Mac-Fane anymore," soothed Ariella. "And when Harold arrives, we will have a huge party, with lots of music and dancing, and you can stay up as late as you like. Would you like that?"

She shook her head in misery. "I had another embroidery to give MacFane, and now he'll never see it." Her words were choked with tears.

"We can send it to him," soothed Ariella, wrapping her arms around the child. Even as she said it, she knew she wouldn't. She could not justify ordering someone on a week-long journey to deliver a scrap of cloth that was certain only to intensify Malcolm's rage.

And when the sleeping powder had finally worn off that morning, his rage must have been awesome.

"Did Gavin leave as well?" Catherine demanded, rubbing his eyes with her fists.

Elizabeth kept her gaze locked on the plaid she was weaving. "Yes," she replied quietly. "Gavin had to go with him."

Her face was pale and frozen, as if she were struggling to control the despair roiling within her. Ariella found herself wondering just how deep Elizabeth's and Gavin's affection for each other had been. She had never asked her friend about it, but she had not thought their relationship went beyond a harmless flirtation. The bleakness carved into Elizabeth's profile suggested that something far more meaningful had been destroyed by her betrayal. Was it possible, she wondered guiltily, that Gavin and Elizabeth had actually come to love each other?

Whatever their relationship had been, it could not possibly have matched the intensity of what had passed between her and Malcolm last night.

Heat flooded her cheeks as she recalled the weight and strength of his warm body stretched over her, pressing her deeper into the mattress as he filled her with need. How was it that he could have been so powerful and yet so vulnerable, so angry, yet so unbearably tender? She had seen him through drunkenness and apathy, through agonizing pain and humiliation, and, finally, in a moment of tremendous pride and victory. She thought she knew him better than anyone did, save Gavin. Yet last night she realized she hadn't known Malcolm MacFane at all. Everything about him had suddenly seemed new and strange, as if the fallen warrior she had dragged home had gradually been transforming, and last night the final layers of his old character had finally been stripped away.

I stayed for you, he had told her, his eyes burning with desire. And she knew he spoke the truth, that no amount of money could have enticed him to endure the disdain with which he had been treated when he'd first come, the humiliation of exposing his weaknesses for others to ridicule, and the incredible frustration of trying to train those who did not respect him and did not want to be trained. *I stayed for you*, even when he believed he could never train her clan, even when he was shot at with arrows, and purposely thrown from his horse injuring him so badly he could barely stand. All these things he had endured, when he could have simply demanded his payment and left, abandoning her to the threats facing her people.

For her.

And she had thanked him by drugging him, having him bound and gagged, then secretly spirited away from the castle he had worked so hard to secure, and from the people whose respect he had finally earned.

All night she had tried to convince herself she was doing the right thing. Over and over she had told herself this as she wrestled him into his shirt and plaid, the assurance growing more frantic as she watched Duncan and Andrew bind him, roll him into a blanket, then hoist him and disappear down the hidden staircase leading from her tower room. And then, when her chamber was empty and she could hear the sound of horses' hooves thundering through the gate, she had wondered why the room suddenly seemed so large, and cold, and lifeless. She had thrown more wood onto the fire and climbed beneath the cool, rumpled blankets on her bed, but nothing could ease the chill that racked her body. It was as if all of her heat had poured into Malcolm, and now he had taken it with him. She had to betray him, she'd reminded herself desperately. She was trying to protect him, and her people, and even Harold, from the horrible scene that would ensue if Malcolm were here when the real Laird MacFane arrived. She had to spare Malcolm the unbearable cruelty of having his true past revealed to those who had come to trust and admire him.

Most of all, she had to protect herself from the agony

of his hate burning into her as she welcomed her husband and laird.

"Are you saying that MacFane and Gavin won't be coming back?" asked Agnes in astonishment.

Ariella shook her head.

"And Duncan and Andrew went with him?"

"MacFane asked Duncan and Andrew to ride with him, because he wanted to introduce them to the MacLeans to the east, where he thought Duncan could conduct negotiations for an alliance," she lied. "They should be back in a week or so."

She had ordered them to stay with MacFane until he was delivered back to his hut, which was a three days' ride. Then they were to thank him for his services and pay him an amount many times greater than what they had originally agreed upon. Nothing would ever assuage his anger, but perhaps he could buy some land and build himself a fine home. Maybe he could try to make a better life for himself.

The thought seemed unlikely.

"And when is Harold coming?" asked Agnes, evidently concerned by the fact that they had no leader.

"He will arrive anytime now," Ariella replied vacantly. "Perhaps even today."

The three woman worked in silence a moment.

"Come, Catherine," Agnes said suddenly, putting aside her embroidery. "Let us get a large basket and collect some flowers to place in the great hall so when our new laird arrives, it will be beautiful."

"I don't want to pick flowers for him," protested Catherine.

"Then we'll go down to the loch and look for kelpies," she suggested. She rose and held out her hand. "Maybe we will find some pretty stones to add to your collection."

Catherine cast her a doubtful look.

"Go on, Catherine," prodded Ariella gently. "It is

time you went outside and got some fresh air. And if you bring me back a really lovely stone, tonight I will tell you a story about the naughty fairy who caused all kinds of mischief in a little girl's house, and the girl's parents kept thinking she was responsible."

Catherine ground her fists into her eyes again and sighed. "All right." She moved toward Agnes with obvious reluctance.

"That's a good girl," said Agnes. "We'll be back before supper."

She cast Ariella a smile, then grasped Catherine's hand and led her away.

Rage boiled in the pit of Malcolm's stomach, so intense, it nearly eclipsed the pain gripping his back and leg in a brutal spasm.

Now that his mind was finally free of whatever foul substance Ariella had given him, he could feel both his fury and his suffering with gnawing clarity. The result was dangerously overwhelming. If not for the fact that his hands were firmly bound behind his back, he felt certain he would cheerfully kill both Andrew and Duncan for their participation in his abduction.

He tried to content himself with thoughts of what he would do if he ever saw Ariella again.

She had planned it all along, he realized, astounded by his own stupidity. While he had been forging alliances with other clans and doing his damnedest to make sure she was safe, she had been busily arranging her marriage and plotting a way to be rid of him. Now he understood her worried expression in the courtyard on the day he had returned. He had foolishly thought she was charmingly embarrassed by what had passed between them that night on the wall head. Instead she had been racked with worry as she'd watched her clan greet him with all the honor and affection normally bestowed upon a returning laird. In that moment she must have realized how much her people had grown to respect him. Perhaps she had even sensed that he enjoyed their attention, that after all the years of guilt and anger and isolation, he finally felt capable and needed again.

That was when she knew she could not permit him to stay, he reflected darkly.

She had tried ordering him to leave. But after their meeting on the battlements, she realized he was not about to be dismissed like some cowering servant. He had worked long and hard to train her people and to make her castle virtually impregnable. And given what he had to work with, he had been bloody successful. Initially he had agreed to help her because of the gold she had offered. But the minute he had seen the challenges he faced, his compensation became irrelevant. He had stayed because he had been tormented by the idea of Ariella killing herself while waiting for the great Black Wolf. He had seen her statue and had been so moved by her innocence and her beauty, and so appalled by the magnitude of his failure, that he had vowed he would not forsake his tender bride in death. That, of course, was before he realized his helpless intended was actually the filthy, insolent lad named Rob.

A bitter laugh erupted from his chest.

"I'm glad one of us finds something amusing in this," muttered Gavin. "By God, Duncan, after all we did for your people, one would think we deserved better than to be bound and led away like common criminals."

"You are bound so you will not escape," explained Duncan, his tone apologetic. "It is not meant as an insult."

"Insult or not, this rope is wearing my flesh raw, and my back and arms are aching," growled Malcolm. "Do you intend to keep us bound like this for the entire journey?"

"Yes."

"Just where the hell is it that you think we would

go?" he demanded impatiently. "Can you honestly believe I have any interest in returning to your clan after this?"

"Ariella knew you would refuse to leave when she asked," Andrew replied. "You must not be there when our new laird arrives. By the time we have reached your home, it will take you three days to return. The new Mac-Kendrick will have come by then."

"What the hell does it matter if I'm there when he arrives or not?" snapped Malcolm.

"Ariella doesn't want you there. I assume you know the reason why, MacFane," said Duncan, casting him a condemning look.

So they knew he had shared her bed. Malcolm wondered if he had been sprawled naked on the floor of her chamber when they'd arrived.

Christ.

"Rest assured, I wouldn't return to your precious little mistress if you begged me to," he muttered tautly. "The thought of being drugged again, and carried away like a trussed deer, holds little appeal. Release us, and we will be on our way."

"My orders are to deliver you to your home, Mac-Fane," Duncan countered. "That is what I intend to do."

They rode in silence awhile. With every mile the rough rope binding Malcolm's wrists bit deeper into his flesh, and the pain in his body intensified. Finally, seeking some way to distract himself from his mounting discomfort, he asked, "Who is the man Ariella has chosen to be your laird?"

Duncan hesitated. "We cannot tell you."

Gavin frowned. "Why not?"

He shrugged his shoulders, but his expression was uneasy. "Ariella asked us not to."

"Do I know him?" demanded Malcolm.

Duncan remained silent.

"It isn't Niall, is it?" he growled, outraged by the idea.

He had long known of Niall's attraction to Ariella. The man's eyes were lit with longing every time he looked at her. And Niall had never made a secret of his contempt for Malcolm. That was why Malcolm had originally believed Niall had shot at him and placed the spur under his saddle. Later, he was no longer certain. Niall had fought bravely during the attack on the castle, and one of Roderic's men had nearly killed him. If Niall was Roderic's ally, why would he have tried to thwart the assault?

Of course, it was possible that the attacks on him had had nothing to do with Roderic. It could be that Niall had simply been trying to drive him away, at first because he hated the Black Wolf and feared Malcolm might learn Ariella was still alive, and later because he sensed Malcolm's attraction to her.

"Niall has no army," pointed out Gavin. "I doubt he is the one."

Of course not, realized Malcolm. Ariella's first duty was to her clan, and she was well aware that at this moment her clan needed a force of trained warriors.

"Perhaps it is one of the chiefs from the neighboring clans," he speculated, freshly infuriated by the possibility. He quickly reflected on the lairds he had met who were in need of a wife. "It isn't old Fraser, is it?" he sputtered. Laird Fraser led a substantial army of some five hundred warriors, which could easily keep the MacKendricks secure. But the man was well past seventy, with a pasty, shriveled frame, a stingy thatch of yellowed hair, and a dark cave of a mouth that was almost entirely void of teeth. The thought of him touching Ariella made Malcolm sick.

"Don't be absurd," retorted Duncan. "Laird Fraser is far too old to be the MacKendrick."

Of course. Ariella expected the next laird to be perfect, or as near to perfect as she could find. *It could have been you,* she had told him, her voice trembling with anger. *It should have been you.* Had he ever been the man she once thought he was? He had been trapped in this wretched body for so long, carrying the unbearable weight of so many innocent souls upon his back, it was hard to remember a time when he had been young and strong and whole. A time when he had faced the world with the brazen confidence of youth, a clear conscience, and the strength of righteousness planted deep within his soul.

A time when he had been known as the fearless warrior, the Black Wolf.

Weariness swept over him in a debilitating wave, heightening his pain as it blunted the edge of his anger. Ariella was right. He was not fit to be laird of the Mac-Kendricks, and more, he did not want that monumental responsibility. Last night he had thought it was a challenge he could rise to, however imperfectly. He had at least been willing to try. But trying was not enough. And failing was unthinkable. Somehow, during the months he had spent with Ariella and her people, he had gradually deluded himself into believing he was almost a warrior again, or at least a leader of men. And last night, for one brief, shimmering moment, he had forgotten what he had become. Forgotten that he was not longer fit to hold the lives of innocent people in his care.

His anguish was almost more than he could bear.

Ariella could marry whomever she goddamn liked, and she and her clan could either rise or fall to the dangers that awaited them. It was not his problem anymore. His life had been infinitely simpler before he met her, and it would be again.

He focused on the ropes binding his wrists, searching for the knot. It was beyond the reach of his fingers. Another tactic would have to be used to free himself from this intolerably humiliating situation. If he was to go home, it would be by his own choice, not because he had been dragged there against his will.

"I have to stop," he announced, using the easing pressure of his legs to halt Cain.

"Why?" demanded Duncan.

"Why do you think?" he retorted.

Duncan regarded him suspiciously a moment. "Very well," he relented. "We will rest awhile here. But don't get any thoughts of trying to escape, MacFane."

"I had not planned on anything grander than relieving myself," Malcolm drawled. "Unfortunately, with my hands tied behind my back, I cannot get down without assistance."

Duncan dismounted and helped him to the ground. Malcolm looked at him expectantly.

"Well?"

"I'm afraid I will have need of my hands," Malcolm told him, "unless you are offering to lift my plaid."

"Just don't try anything, MacFane," Duncan warned, removing his dirk from his belt. "Turn around."

Malcolm obliged him. Once the ropes were cut from his wrists, he slowly stretched his aching arms, bending and flexing them until the blood was flowing and the muscles were responsive. His weakened right arm was stiff, but it had not fared as poorly as he had expected.

"Feel better?" asked Duncan, sympathetic to his discomfort.

Malcolm spun around and crashed his left fist into Duncan's jaw. Duncan's head snapped back and he went flying to the ground, where he lay perfectly still.

"Much better," Malcolm assured him. "Andrew, kindly remove Gavin's ropes and give him back his weapons," he commanded as he limped over to Duncan's horse and retrieved his sword and dirk.

"I—I can't do that, MacFane," stammered Andrew, reaching for his sword.

Malcolm calmly strapped his sword to his waist. "Don't be ridiculous, Andrew. I may be older and stiffer, but there isn't one move you could make that I haven't taught you myself. Besides," he finished, shoving his dirk into its sheath, "do you honestly think I believe you would actually hurt either of us?"

Andrew regarded him helplessly a moment, uncertain what to do.

Then he slowly dismounted and went to untie Gavin.

Malcolm carelessly opened one of Duncan's bulging leather bags, searching for food for their journey home. He frowned in confusion at the gold and jewels gleaming in the large sack. He opened another bag, and then two more. All four were crammed with riches.

"What the hell is this?"

"Your payment, MacFane," Andrew replied. "For training us to fight, and for fortifying the castle."

Gavin joined Malcolm, who was staring in disbelief at the fortune before him.

"My God."

"We never agreed to a sum such as this," Malcolm protested, wondering what game they were playing with him.

"Ariella expressly ordered that you were to be handsomely paid," Andrew explained. "She wanted you to know how grateful she—we are."

Malcolm reached into one of the bags and scooped up a handful of the glittering jewels. He raised his palm toward the sun, fascinated by the play of warm light on the stones. There was enough there to support him and Gavin lavishly for the rest of their lives. They could purchase an enormous tract of land, build a magnificent home, and surround themselves with the finest furniture and artwork, horses and servants. By God, he could have anything he wanted with this, he realized numbly.

Except Ariella.

"Take it back," he snarled, throwing the stones into the bag.

Both Andrew and Gavin looked at him in astonishment. "What?"

"I don't want it," Malcolm snapped, limping toward his horse. "All Gavin and I require is a small quantity of food, and whatever ale or wine you brought."

Andrew could not believe he meant it. "But——"

"Tell your mistress the Black Wolf does not accept payment for his assistance," Malcolm commanded as he heaved himself into his saddle. His expression was savage as he finished, "Especially from those who betray him."

Andrew looked at him incredulously. "But the night you agreed to come——"

"Food and ale, Andrew," Malcolm interrupted. "That is all." The fury in his gaze warned him not to argue further.

Shaking his head in bewilderment, Andrew went to his horse and unpacked the requested items.

"Duncan will waken in a few moments," Malcolm said, glancing at his outstretched body. "When he does, both of you go home. You need have no fear of my disrupting your mistress's wedding, though I'm sure it will be a splendid event," he drawled. "I will not be returning to the MacKendrick lands. Ever."

He wheeled his horse about.

It was better this way, he told himself harshly. Once again, he was responsible for no one other than himself. He could rise late, drink himself into a blinding stupor, and not worry about anything beyond whether there was enough wine to get him through the night.

The emptiness tearing through him was excruciating.

"What do you mean, he's gone?" demanded Angus blankly.

"She doesn't mean forever," Dugald assured him. "She just means he's gone for a ride, don't you, lass?"

"No," replied Ariella. "I mean he and Gavin have gone home. For good. Didn't Gordon announce it to the clan?"

"Aye, he did," admitted Angus. "But no one believed him."

"Why would the lad leave so suddenly?" wondered Dugald. "It's most unlike him."

"He received an urgent message during the night that he was needed by his clan," lied Ariella, glancing nervously at Alpin. He regarded her calmly, his expression betraying nothing. "He had to leave immediately. But we have nothing to fear," she assured them, her tone falsely bright. "The next MacKendrick is on his way."

"You have selected the one to wield the sword, without conferring with us?" sputtered Angus, incredulous.

"I thought it best not to tell you of my decision until his arrival was imminent," she explained. "Because you were both growing so fond of MacFane."

"Who is it, then?" asked Dugald, somewhat hurt.

"Harold MacFane, Malcolm's cousin," Ariella replied. "He is the one destined to wield the MacKendrick sword."

Angus frowned. "MacFane's cousin?"

"That makes no sense, lass," Dugald told her, shaking his head. "Better we should be led by MacFane himself, who is laird of a great clan and a strong army. No point in settling for his cousin."

"No point at all," agreed Angus. "We'll just explain it to Harold when he comes. I'm sure he will understand." The two men nodded with satisfaction, pleased the matter was settled.

Ariella glanced anxiously at Alpin, wondering if the time had come to tell the elders the truth about Malcolm's past.

"It is your decision," he told her. "But if you don't tell them, Harold will. Who do you think will be kinder in their explanation?"

He was right, she realized. The moment Harold learned that Malcolm had been here, he would reveal the horrible slaughter of the MacKendrick women and children to her clan. He would tell them Malcolm had been stripped of his position as laird, and banished from his own lands, forbidden to return or even to use his clan name.

Her people would feel deceived, by both her and Malcolm.

"There is something I must tell you." She took a deep breath before grimly stating, "Malcolm MacFane is not who he appears to be."

"I should say not," agreed Angus. "Why, when I first laid eyes on the lad, I never dreamed a man in his condition could do the things he did for us."

"Appearances are deceiving," commented Dugald. "Some people look at us and see two old men, instead of the warriors we are."

"MacFane knew better," said Angus approvingly.

"Aye, he did," reflected Dugald.

"I am not referring to his physical weaknesses," qualified Ariella, surprised the elders were so accepting of them. Did they not understand the requirements of wielding the sword? The necessity of finding a laird with superb strength and stamina? "I am referring to his past—"

"And a more honorable career you will never find," interrupted Angus, his wrinkled face beaming with pride. "Why, the feats of the Black Wolf are legendary." He frowned at Dugald. "I don't recall hearing any legendary stories about this Harold fellow, do you?"

"Not one. But I'm sure he must have done something utterly magnificent for Ariella to consider him." He regarded her expectantly. "What did he do, lass?"

"I—I don't know," she stammered. Her gaze fell upon Alpin, pleading for help.

Alpin closed his eyes and drew his snowy brows together, searching for a vision of Harold. A low incantation rumbled in his throat, which grew louder and louder, filling the vast cavern of the great hall. His arms opened wide, spreading his silver-and-black cloak like giant wings, and his frail body began to tremble. Finally he opened his eyes.

"He didn't do anything," he announced with a shrug.

"Nothing?" said Angus.

"Surely he must have done something," protested Dugald. "Why else would the lass have chosen him?"

"He is a strong and fair man," declared Ariella, grasping for something. "He will make a fine laird."

Angus regarded her dubiously. "How do you know?"

"I met him once," she said. "And I saw him in a dream."

The two council members exchanged doubtful glances.

"He will make a fine laird," she repeated.

"So would MacFane," pointed out Angus.

"MacFane is not the one," she stated firmly. "He will never wield the sword, and he will never be a MacKendrick."

Disappointment washed across their faces. They knew they could not argue with her, that the decision was hers alone. But it was clear they did not care for her choice, despite the fact that they had not met Harold. The only way to make them understand was to tell them about Malcolm's past. Yet she could not bring herself to do it. To shatter his image so completely, after the long months he had spent winning her clan's friendship and respect, was unthinkable.

She was not convinced they would believe her anyway.

The sun was painting soft ribbons of melon and gold across the gray edge of the sky. Ariella stared out the window of her chamber, watching for Catherine and Agnes to emerge from the woods, or perhaps to appear on the grassy banks surrounding the loch, carrying their basket of treasures. The day was in its final veil of light, and Ariella had expected them back long ago. She knew Catherine was profoundly distressed by Malcolm's sudden departure, and she wanted to spend the evening with her, helping her cope with her grief. During his time there Malcolm had forged a close bond with her little sister, and Catherine was deeply hurt by the fact that he had abandoned her so unexpectedly. Seeing no sign of her or Agnes, she turned from the window and gazed restlessly about her chamber, wondering how to occupy herself as she awaited their return.

A folded paper caught her eye, peeking out from beneath the plaid draping her bed. Curious, she knelt down and opened it. It was one of Catherine's drawings, depicting a very large warrior on a horse that was far too small to carry him, and a little girl on an even tinier horse. Scrawled in childish lettering along the bottom were the words, *The Black Wolf and Me.* The drawing must have fallen from Malcolm last night, she realized, as she'd unfastened his belt to free him from his plaid.

How was it that Catherine had come to care so much for this broken warrior? she wondered, studying the disproportionate figures. Ariella recalled the day she had brought Malcolm there, and how her clan had stared at him in shock, unable to believe he was the powerful Black Wolf they had so long awaited. Only Catherine had been undaunted as he'd awkwardly dismounted and limped onto the platform. In a gesture of pure, unconditional acceptance, she had reached up and taken his enormous scarred hand in hers. From the very beginning Catherine had been able to see beyond his damaged body, the harsh glares, the angry, impatient responses. It had taken Ariella far longer to realize there was another man trapped beneath that crippled, bitter exterior. A man who had somehow taken charge of the impossible challenges that lay before him. When she first found him, he had seemed incapable of wresting control of his own life. Yet he had come here, however reluctantly, and inspired her people to learn to defend themselves. He had shown them it was not size and might that counted most in battle, but skill, courage, and the conviction that winning was possible.

Catherine had understood his inner strength long before the rest of them.

The pounding of booted feet wrenched her from her thoughts. "Ariella!"

The door crashed open and Niall regarded her grimly, his chest heaving with exertion, a missive crumpled in his fist. Gordon, Helen, Elizabeth, and Ramsay were assembled behind him, their expressions grave.

"What is it?" she demanded. "Has Harold sent a messenger to say he is delayed?"

Niall shook his head. "It is Roderic," he stated tautly. "He has returned."

She had known this moment would come. Alpin had seen it. But she had clung to the hope that he would not return before Harold's arrival.

"We must prepare for battle," she said, affecting the brusque, authoritative manner she had seen Malcolm project when they'd been attacked before. "We repelled his assault once, and we can do so again. All we need do is hold him off until Harold arrives with his army."

No one moved. "He has Catherine," Niall said roughly.

Terror crashed over her, robbing her of breath and strength, and even the ability to comprehend fully what he was saying. "Catherine?" she repeated, her voice a wisp of sound against the pounding in her ears.

"He must have taken her while she and Agnes were out walking," said Elizabeth, wringing her hands together. "Agnes is missing as well."

It was impossible, what they were telling her. They were mistaken. Ariella opened her mouth to tell them so, but Niall held the wrinkled missive out to her, a hideous, indisputable confirmation. Her fingers trembling, she took the sheet in her hands.

> *My dearest Ariella,*
>
> *Rest assured, I am not in the habit of taking children hostage, unless circumstances force me to do so. Unfortunately, you and your clan have resisted me twice, and I will not be made a fool of again. You will come to me, alone, bringing only the MacKendrick sword with you. You will then perform whatever ceremony is necessary to grant me its full powers, and invest me as laird of your clan. Once I am convinced these powers are mine, we will return to your castle, where your people will relinquish their weapons and swear fealty to me.*
>
> *Agnes tells me no one has ever actually seen this sword, as your father foolishly chose not to make use of it. I am not an unreasonable man, and I realize you may need time to retrieve the weapon from its hiding place. You have until first light tomorrow.*
>
> *If you have not appeared in the woods by then, or if you come with others, I will cut little Catherine's throat.*
>
> *Roderic*

The room began to spin. She had lived this moment before, when Roderic had promised he would slaughter her clansmen one by one, until she gave him what he wanted. And so she had orchestrated her own death, robbing him of the single tool he needed to gain possession of the sword. But he would not be fooled again. Even if she did actually kill herself, he would murder Catherine anyway, and Agnes as well, just to assuage his fury.

She dropped the letter to the floor, revolted by the fact that Roderic had laid his hands upon it. More of her clan had crowded behind Niall, silently spilling into her chamber to regard her with wide, solemn eyes.

The decision she faced was impossible. It could be moments or days before Harold arrived. Even if he came before first light tomorrow, Roderic would butcher Catherine as his army approached. The only way she might save her sister and Agnes was to give Roderic the sword and order her clan to accept him as laird. But by doing so, she was betraying her people.

And condemning them to death and destruction, which would be the sword's retribution for her choosing the wrong man.

CHAPTER 13

Malcolm tilted his head back and swallowed deeply. He longed to drain the wineskin of its contents and start on another, but he forced himself to exercise some restraint. He and Gavin still had two more days of travel ahead, and tomorrow night his back, leg, and arm would be yearning even more strongly for the numbing effects of alcohol. He also needed to stay somewhat sober, as in a few hours it would be his turn to watch over their camp.

They had adopted an unhurried pace since leaving Duncan and Andrew. Although Malcolm told himself he was glad to be rid of Ariella and her clan, the prospect of returning to long, empty days in that dark, miserable hut filled him with crushing despair. There was no need to rush toward the pathetic ending of his existence. Better to be out here, lying by a warm fire with a cool wash of charcoal sky over his head and the hard pressure of the earth against his aching flesh. There was a simple, harsh clarity to being in the woods, a melding of space and darkness and discomfort, intensifying his awareness of himself and his surroundings.

"Someone is coming," he announced suddenly, casting aside the wineskin in favor of his sword. He strained to listen. "Twenty riders at least. They must have seen the fire."

Gavin quickly retrieved his bow and quiver of arrows. "I'll watch you from over here," he said, slipping into the darkness of the trees.

The pounding of hooves grew louder, until the ground began to shiver. Finally the first group of riders emerged through the woods, their faces lit by the orange glow of the fire.

Malcolm stared at the three men in astonishment. "Robert? Alex? and Edward? What in the name of God are you doing here?"

"MacFane!" gasped Robert, who led the small party.

"By God, we had not thought to find you here," added Edward.

Malcolm wasn't sure, but he could detect no malice in either their tone or their expressions. Evidently his former warriors were too startled to reflect their true feelings toward him.

"There is only one MacFane," stated a cold voice through the shadows.

The warriors instantly parted for a tall, bearded man astride a powerful gray charger. His shoulder-length hair was the color of firelight, the same color Marrian's had been. He wore a neatly belted plaid of brown and purple, a crudely sewn shirt, and a darkly oiled leather jerkin. On his shoulder gleamed a brooch of finely wrought gold with a massive ruby at its center. It was a brooch

Malcolm knew well, for it had once belonged to his father, before it had been briefly passed to him.

The bitterness that shot through him was staggering.

"Good evening, Harold." His voice was calm, giving no hint of the hostility roiling within him. Even as he struggled to control it, he knew the feeling was unjustified. Harold had done what he had to do when he'd banished Malcolm from the clan. Had the situation been reversed, Malcolm would have done the same.

Or worse.

If Harold was surprised to see him, he hid it well. His gaze swept coolly over Malcolm, taking in every detail of his appearance. "You look well, Malcolm," he finally observed. "I had heard reports describing you as filthy and unshaven, and living as a drunken hermit. Obviously these stories were exaggerated."

It was impossible to tell from the flatness of his tone whether this revelation pleased or irritated him.

"I am faring well enough."

"What brings you to these woods?"

Malcolm's eyes narrowed. "I was not aware that I am under obligation to inform you of my movements."

"You are not," Harold assured him. "As long as you never set foot upon MacFane lands, you are free to travel wherever you like. I ask the question as one traveler to another. You need not tell me if you do not wish to."

His comment made Malcolm feel slightly churlish. Why was he reacting this way? he wondered in disgust. It had been a simple question, nothing more.

"I had some business with one of the clans near here. It is now completed, and Gavin and I are on our way home."

Gavin stepped out from the cover of the trees. "Hello, Harold." He purposely neglected to use the title Harold had appropriated from Malcolm.

Harold barely tilted his head. "Gavin."

"What brings you here with so many men?" asked

Malcolm, watching as several dozen warriors halted their horses in the darkness behind him. "Are you on your way to fight a battle?"

"Nothing quite so exhilarating. I am on my way to meet my future bride." His weary countenance suggested his pending nuptials were more an unwelcome necessity than a cause for celebration.

"Then congratulations are in order," Malcolm managed tautly.

He tried to think of several reasons why Harold could not possibly fulfill Ariella's expectations for her clan's laird. Nothing beyond his own hostility came to mind. His cousin was young, fit, and strong. He was a consummate warrior who had fought alongside Malcolm in countless battles. Harold was also now laird of the mighty Clan MacFane, and he led what had once been the finest army in all of Scotland.

The army Malcolm had raised and trained.

"Who is the fair bride?" asked Gavin.

Harold shrugged his shoulders indifferently. "A girl from the MacKendrick clan. Whether she is fair or not, I cannot say. I have never seen her."

So. It was not enough that she had ordered him abducted to be rid of him. Now she was offering everything he had labored so hard to protect to the man who had already seized Malcolm's very life. Her betrayal was so overwhelming, he barely trusted himself to speak.

"How was this arranged?" he asked, somehow managing to keep his tone even.

"Early this summer three MacKendricks came to me, saying they were looking for the Black Wolf," Harold explained. "Two men, and a filthy lad of about twelve. Like the messengers who had come before them, they were adamant about seeing you, even when I explained you were no longer chief of the MacFanes. Finally I told them where you were. Did they ever find you?" he asked curiously.

Of course. Duncan and Andrew had told Gavin they had first gone to Harold. Which meant Ariella had at least seen his cousin before deciding on him. He nodded. "They did."

"The MacKendricks live within a ring of mountains some distance from here," Harold continued, obviously assuming that nothing had come of their visit. "It seems they have spent their entire existence in virtual isolation and know little about defending themselves. The daughter of the last laird is proposing a match, in the hopes that my army will be able to keep her clan secure."

It is my army, thought Malcolm harshly. And of course it would keep the MacKendricks bloody secure. He wanted to laugh at the irony of it. Ariella would have the Black Wolf's warriors guarding her, after all.

With neither the embarrassment nor the inconvenience of the fallen Black Wolf.

"And what do you get out of this arrangement, Harold?" His voice was deceptively mild.

"The girl claims her people are unusually skilled in artistry and craftsmanship," Harold replied. "The gifts she sent as examples of their work were impressive. As it is time for me to marry anyway, the match is a splendid opportunity to expand my lands and resources."

Naturally, he would look at it that way. Not as a chance to help a clan in need, but merely as an extension of his power. A pragmatic, logical approach.

"This clan is several days' journey from yours," Malcolm pointed out. "How will you manage your duties as laird of the MacFanes if you are living so far from them?"

"I have no intention of staying there," Harold assured him. "Once I have seen for myself that these MacKendricks are capable of producing such goods, I will marry the girl and return home. Her clan will become a sept of the MacFanes, taking our name. I will leave thirty or so men there to protect the holding and run its affairs. Many of my warriors have actually volunteered to live there, as there are so few MacFane women left."

His expression remained bland, but there was no mistaking the condemnation in his tone. *Because of me,* thought Malcolm. *There are hardly any women left because I let them be slaughtered. Including Marrian.*

"I would have thought you'd want more of a marriage than that, Harold," observed Gavin dryly. "Do you intend to visit your wife only often enough to get her with child?"

"I don't intend to visit her at all," he replied. "She will live with me."

"She agreed to leave her clan?" said Malcolm, astounded that Ariella would consent to such a condition.

"Not yet," Harold admitted. "But the issue is not negotiable. I have long been without female company, and I am not looking for a wife who lives so far away. If she will not leave, there is no match."

It would be agonizing for her, Malcolm realized. Leaving her home would be like ripping a piece of her heart out and leaving it behind. But she would do it if she believed it was best for her clan. She would sacrifice anything to ensure her people were safe.

Including herself.

It was not his affair, he reminded himself bitterly. She had been desperate to be rid of him, and now she was. She could bloody well marry Harold and give him all that Malcolm had worked night and day to strengthen and protect. Clearly she believed his cousin was far worthier than he to lead her people. And then she would be forced to leave. She would learn the cruel lesson of having everything you've ever known and loved taken from you in a single blow. And Harold, goddamn him, would have everything. He would be laird of the powerful Clan MacFane, and the tiny, isolated, eccentric Clan MacKendrick. Most of all, he would have Ariella.

Leaving Malcolm with nothing.

Twice now he had lost his world to Harold—not because of his cousin's hunger for power, but because of his own pathetic inability to hold fast to what was rightfully his. Long before his clan and title had been taken from him, he had believed he no longer deserved to be laird. Because of the wretched condition of his body, his inability to survive a day sober, his rage and self-pity—because of all these things and so many others, it made him sick to think of it. And yet, except for Roderic and a few malcontented soldiers, his people had never challenged his right to lead them. They believed, however naively, that he would overcome his physical and spiritual challenges.

Instead, he had succumbed to them.

This was why Ariella had believed he was unfit to lead her people. She condemned him for the failures of his past, as he had for so many years—for being a drunk, for letting his people die, for losing his lairdship and his army. Most of all, she blamed him for not coming when her clan had needed him. *That would have been the deed of a true warrior.* And maybe she was right. When he'd been the Black Wolf, he would have done anything to help another, regardless of the forces against him.

He wanted to be that man again.

"It is late," observed Harold suddenly. "I must take my leave of you."

"You are going on?"

Harold nodded. "Since the night is fair, I have decided to ride through it. If this map is accurate, we should arrive at the MacKendrick castle long before morning."

Malcolm's mind raced, trying to think of some way to stop him. It was vital he reach Ariella first. How he would convince her that he, with all his flaws and failures, was a better choice for laird, he had no idea.

"I wouldn't ride on, if I were you," he warned.

Harold regarded him curiously.

"Why not?"

"The terrain around here is heavily mountainous, and it is easy to get lost," Malcolm replied. "The slightest deviation from your route, and you will be days trekking through the mountains, trying to find your way back. Better to wait until first light and be certain of your bearings."

Harold stroked his beard, considering. Finally he shook his head. "I have led my men on difficult routes before. We will find this place."

"Then there is the storm," Gavin quickly added.

Harold frowned. "What storm?"

"There is a violent storm coming," Malcolm lied.

Harold's expression was skeptical. "How do you know?"

"We heard it from an ancient seer we passed today." He controlled his urge to smile at Harold's sudden interest; his cousin, unlike Malcolm, had long believed in the visions of seers. "Beyond these woods you will be exposed for many miles, with no chance of finding cover. If you make camp here, your men can cut branches and make comfortable shelters."

"Nothing worse than an army of wet, cold warriors trapped in a storm," remarked Gavin, shaking his head. "Puts them in the foulest of moods."

"The seer said the storm would be over by early morning," added Malcolm reassuringly. "You could start out at first light and greet your betrothed dry and rested."

He watched as his cousin weighed the benefits of stopping and waiting for the storm to pass. That would give him and Gavin time to get back to the MacKendrick lands long before Harold and his army arrived.

"The thought of riding through a storm holds little appeal," Harold finally confessed. "And although the night seems calm, I cannot disregard the vision of a seer. Robert," he said, turning to the warrior beside him, "order the men to make camp. We will rest here until morning."

Ariella drew her cloak tighter around her shoulders as she slowly guided her horse through the feathery black columns of trees. Her heart was pounding hard against her chest, and her jaw was clenched. Her people had pleaded with her not to venture into the woods, but she had been adamant. She could not bear the thought of her little sister spending the night alone with a group of savage warriors. Of course Agnes was with her, but the poor girl was so meek, it might well be Catherine who was doing the comforting. Because Roderic had threatened to kill Catherine if Ariella appeared with an escort, she had forbidden anyone to follow her. Despite her fear for her sister, she had not brought the sword. She was going to try to stall Roderic until Harold arrived with his army, which might be as early as tomorrow. Once he came, she prayed Roderic would realize he was hopelessly outmatched, and release her, Catherine, and Agnes.

If not, he would kill them.

Niall and Gordon had vehemently opposed her plan. They had wanted to send out a heavy force of men to ring in Roderic's camp and then attack. Ariella had pointed out that any weakening of the forces in the castle left the women and children vulnerable, which might be exactly what Roderic was hoping for. Also, while Malcolm had taught her people much about defending a castle, she did not believe they were any match for Roderic's brutal warriors. It was better that her clan remain safely behind the castle walls until Harold arrived.

A faint rustling jerked her from her thoughts. Squinting through the darkness, she saw a shadowy figure emerge from behind a tree, his bow and arrow aimed at her chest.

"Move and you're dead."

A pale glimmer of moonlight threaded through the

trees and lit the man's face. Ariella instantly recognized him as the one called Gregor, who had fought Malcolm the night her castle had been attacked.

"I am Ariella MacKendrick," she informed him evenly, her hand casually slipping to the dirk concealed in the folds of her cloak. "Kill me, and your master will never get the sword. Then it is you who will be dead."

His brow arched in surprise. Ariella could not tell which confounded him more—her threat, or the fact that she had dared to make one.

"You will come with me," he finally growled.

He roughly grabbed her horse's bridle and glanced around, searching the darkness to see if anyone had accompanied her. Satisfied she was alone, he began to lead her through the woods. He wove his way deep into the trees, taking her back and forth, perhaps thinking to confuse her. If so, it was a futile effort. Ariella had grown up in this dense growth, and there was no pat of it she did not know.

After a while the scent of smoke began to filter through the air. Her amply built escort led her closer to the aroma, until the orange glow of flames spilled thinly into the shadows. As the light grew brighter, more than a dozen filthy, rough-looking warriors emerged from their hiding places behind trees and rocks. They leaned on their bows and swords and stared at her with dark, menacing desire. A few of them licked their lips, as if anticipating a taste of her.

Ariella glared at them, suppressing her fear with hatred.

"What sweet have you brought us, Gregor?" asked a tall, scrawny warrior with greasy brown hair. He reached out and grabbed Ariella's leg.

Gregor smashed his massive fist into her admirer's gaunt face, sending him flying backward with a yelp.

"Touch her again, Tavis, and I'll kill you," he

promised. His gaze raked over the other men, whose leers had deteriorated into expressions of uncertainty. "She belongs to Roderic."

"Roderic already has a woman," complained a heavyset man with a dark, matted beard.

"And now he has two," snapped Gregor. "Where is he?"

"Over there," said another, pointing with his sword. His mouth split into a smile, revealing a jagged row of rotting teeth. "With the plain one."

He meant Agnes, Ariella realized, fervently praying that Roderic had not harmed her.

She dismounted and followed Gregor through the camp. It seemed there were only about twenty warriors near, but she knew there were others hiding in the woods, watching for intruders. Many of the men lay listlessly beside sputtering fires, their arms or legs bandaged in tattered, grimy rags. Ariella wondered if their injuries were a result of the attack on her clan. However they had gotten them, it was clear Roderic knew he could not breach her castle with such a shrunken, dilapidated force.

That was why he had forced her to come to him instead.

They found Roderic sitting before a fire, contemplating the flames. He looked up in surprise as she and Gregor approached, and then he smiled. The light cast a warm glow across his handsome features, but Ariella could find nothing even remotely attractive in his appearance. The idea that she had once been captivated by the solid structure of his body, the pleasing contours of his face, and that fall of golden hair, of which he was so vain, made her stomach tighten with fury. How could she have thought, even for a moment, that this barbarian was the one to wield the sword? She focused her gaze on the thick, corded slash across his cheek and experienced a grim satisfaction.

Soon you will have a cut so deep, nothing will stop your foul life from draining into the ground.

"Good evening, Ariella," he said pleasantly, rising as if to meet a welcome guest. "I must confess, I had not thought to see you quite so soon." His gaze swept over her; then he frowned. "Where is the sword?"

"Where is Catherine?" she demanded evenly.

"Ah, ever the concerned Ariella," he drawled, apparently more amused than irritated. "Your compassion was what first drew you to me, was it not? I was the handsome, gravely wounded stranger, and you the enchanting fair maiden eager to take me home and nurse me."

"I am not accustomed to leaving people to die," Ariella returned. "Unlike you."

"I am a warrior," he reminded her. "Leaving people to die is my business."

"You are a murderer and a common thief," Ariella corrected acidly. "Killing in battle is not the same as murdering innocent people in their homes."

"It was most unfortunate, that business with your father," he remarked, shaking his head. "You know," he continued blandly, "I would not have killed him had he given me a choice."

Only by incredible force of will did she manage to keep from spitting in his face. That, and the realization that if she roused his fury too much, Catherine and Agnes would be made to suffer.

As her people had been punished when she had cut his cheek.

"Of course you meant to kill him, Roderic," she returned tersely. "He was trying to protect me. You would have killed anyone who stood in your way."

He considered a moment, then shrugged. "I find myself weary of those who tell me what I cannot have," he admitted. "I wanted you and the sword, and saw no reason why I shouldn't have them. I'm young, strong, and a superb warrior. I would have made a great laird."

He moved toward her, his green eyes flickering in the firelight. "Even you, Ariella," he murmured, reaching out to stroke her cheek, "once found me desirable." He bent his head until his lips barely grazed the skin of her ear. "Remember?"

She jerked away, revolted by his touch, his vanity, by everything about him. "I didn't know what you were then," she snapped. "I didn't understand what evil dwelled within you."

"You wound me," he said, mockingly placing his hand on his chest. "But no matter. Tonight my spirits are high, and I find your insults amusing. In the months to come, however, I will take pleasure in teaching you to curb your tongue." He grasped her chin firmly between his fingers as his expression hardened. "Now, where is the sword?"

She raised her chin. "You still haven't told me where Catherine and Agnes are."

He blinked, as if he did not know whom she was speaking of. Then he tilted his head back and laughed, releasing his hold. "You are still worried about Agnes?"

Uneasiness rippled through her. "What have you done to her?"

"Nothing," he replied, trying to control his amusement. "Nothing she didn't want."

Her unease bloomed into panic. "By God almighty, Roderic, if you've touched her—"

"Bring Agnes to me," he ordered Gregor, cutting her off.

Ariella watched as Gregor lumbered heavily across the camp. A tent had been erected in a small clearing some distance away, and a guard stood watch in front of it. The man stepped aside as Gregor approached, permitting him to open the flap a crack and call Agnes's name. After a moment the fabric doorway parted, and Agnes emerged. Her carriage was straight and her gait even as she walked toward them. She appeared neither surprised by the sight of her mistress, nor afraid of the prospect of facing Roderic.

"Agnes," said Ariella anxiously, "are you all right?"

"I'm fine, Ariella." Her gaze went to Roderic. "Did she give it to you?"

"Not yet. She wanted to make certain you and Catherine were all right first." His mouth curved in amusement.

Apprehension tightened in Ariella. Why were Roderic and Agnes so at ease with each other?

"Catherine is fine," Agnes assured her. "She is asleep in the tent. Give Roderic the sword," she instructed, moving beside him, "and we will all go home."

A harsh realization began to seep over Ariella. At first it was so incomprehensible, she resisted it. She stared at Agnes, vainly trying to rationalize her blithe demeanor and the fact that she chose to stand near her abductor. A wash of firelight spilled across the fabric of her plain grown, which was clinging tightly to the generous curves of her body. A sharp intake of breath caught in Ariella's throat.

In that moment, the small, round swell of Agnes's belly was as undeniable as the terrible truth that it revealed.

Agnes recognized her shock and laid her hand protectively over the child growing within her. "Give Roderic the sword, Ariella," she repeated, almost pleadingly.

"You told him," murmured Ariella, her voice hollow. "You were the one who told him about the sword when he stayed with us."

"Aye, I told him," Agnes admitted.

"Why?" she demanded, still reluctant to accept the girl's betrayal. During the five years Agnes had worked in the castle, she had always seemed caring and reliable. That was why Ariella had entrusted her to look after Catherine when her father had been killed. With Agnes's support Ariella had been able to take on more responsibility in managing the affairs of her clan. How could this meek serving girl be the one who had jeopardized the safety of her clan? "Why would you betray your people like that, Agnes?"

"He loves me," Agnes said simply. "And Roderic will make a good laird. You once thought so yourself."

Ariella shifted her gaze to Roderic.

He tossed her a look of arrogant amusement.

"He doesn't love you, Agnes," Ariella informed her coldly. "He is incapable of loving anyone except himself. He told you that so he could use you. And you were foolish enough to believe him."

"He said he would come back for me, and he did," Agnes argued. "And he has promised me that once he is laird of the MacKendricks, he will marry me."

"He didn't come back for you," Ariella retorted. "He came back for the sword."

"Not just the sword," qualified Roderic. His gaze burned hotly into Ariella. There was no mistaking his meaning.

Ariella resisted the urge to draw her cloak tighter around herself. He would never touch her again, she swore.

She would kill him first.

"Did you try to drive MacFane away?" she demanded, still overwhelmed by Agnes's treachery.

Agnes nodded. "Once I knew you were alive, I wanted to get word to Roderic, so he would come back. But then MacFane came and began to teach us to fight. I was afraid Roderic might be killed if we learned too much from him. Since MacFane didn't seem to like staying with us, I followed him into the woods and shot at him, hoping his anger would make him leave. Unfortunately, I hit you instead." She looked genuinely remorseful as she finished, "I didn't mean to hurt you."

"And the spur?"

"By that time MacFane knew who you really were.

The clan was coming to respect him, and our fighting skills were much improved. I was afraid you might decide to give him the sword, so I put the spur under his saddle. I was sure he wouldn't want to stay after that, especially since the clan could see how weak he was."

"That was your error," said Ariella tautly.

Agnes regarded her uncertainly. "What was?"

"Thinking MacFane is weak."

Roderic snorted. "You are so fond of looking after injured beasts, you can't see them as they really are."

"You are right," Ariella agreed. "The fact that I nursed you is evidence of that."

"MacFane may have taught your people a few tricks about fighting, but the man himself is little more than refuse. He has been since the day Gavin dragged him home in a cart, mangled and useless. And still he was made laird. By what right?" he demanded, his voice thick with contempt. "Because he was Laird MacFane's son? Any fool could see I was a far better choice to lead the MacFanes than he. But when I tried to convince the council of that, they rejected my claim."

"And so you attempted to overthrow Malcolm by force," Ariella supplied. "But you failed. And he banished you."

"I didn't have enough warriors supporting me at the time," he acknowledged, shrugging. "And Malcolm's army was still loyal to him. So I had to suffer the indignity of being driven from my clan with nothing, while Malcolm enjoyed the comfort and privileges of being a laird. But that didn't last long." His mouth twisted with malevolent satisfaction. "Surely you have heard about the unfortunate fate of the MacFane clan?"

Ariella stared at him, aghast. "You killed all those women and children?"

"What women and children?" asked Agnes, frowning.

"The responsibility for their safety lay with Malcolm," said Roderic. "I was merely trying to demonstrate to the MacFanes that they had made a grave blunder in choosing him over me. Unfortunately, after convincing the Sinclairs that they were about to be attacked by the MacFanes, it was difficult to control them. The great Black Wolf, of course, was drunk that night and had no comprehension of the danger he was in. We sent a false message that the MacKays were under attack and needed him to come with his army. Stupidly, he believed it. He ordered his warriors to ride with him to the MacKay lands, leaving his precious castle with virtually no one to guard it."

Horror flooded through her. She had long known Roderic was ruthless. He had unveiled the vile depths of his soul the day he murdered her father and killed her people in his bid to force her to give him the sword. But until this moment she had not truly understood the appalling extent of his depravity.

"You slaughtered the women and children of your own clan." Her voice was heavy with loathing.

"It was not my clan anymore," Roderic pointed out indifferently. "They had banished me."

"Dear God," whispered Agnes, her face ashen. "How could you do such a terrible thing?"

He barely spared her a glance as his hand whipped across her mouth. Agnes cried out and stumbled backward.

"Don't *ever* speak to me that way," he snarled.

She raised her trembling fingers to her lips. The pain shimmering in her eyes froze into fear as she examined the blood on her fingertips.

"Get back in the tent," he commanded brusquely. "I'm sick of looking at you. You are of no further use to me anyway."

Pity lanced Ariella's anger as she saw Agnes stare at her lover in hopeless bewilderment. If not for Agnes's treachery, her sister and her clan would be safe tonight, she reminded herself fiercely. Instead they were in grave danger. Although Roderic might decide to spare their lives in these woods, if she was forced to give him the sword, she and her people faced endless years of misery and torment. And should he choose to use the sword to expand the realm of his power, other clans in the Highlands would fall beneath his brutal rule. All because of this silly girl, who had been so thoroughly duped by the handsome face and silken charms of a monster. Ariella wanted to feel nothing but contempt for her. But she could not forget that she too had once been captivated by Roderic's fine appearance and honeyed words, if only for a short while.

It was this recognition of her own naïveté that caused her to murmur gently, "Go on, then, Agnes. Catherine will be missing you, and the babe within you needs you to rest."

Too shocked to speak, Agnes regarded her despondently. Tears began to spill down her face as she turned and scurried back to her tent, no longer the self-assured young woman she had seemed when she'd first emerged.

"Not an ounce of fire in that one," Roderic observed caustically. He stroked the scar on his cheek as his gaze slithered down her body. "Unlike you."

Ariella glared at him and said nothing.

"Perhaps we should continue this conversation in private," he suggested, gesturing to a tent several yards away. "After you, fair Ariella."

The warriors lying by the fires smirked as she walked past them. Ariella kept her head high and drew her cloak tighter around herself. *He will not touch me,* she reminded herself stonily, feeling the solid form of her dirk graze her thigh. She knew she might be able to stab Roderic once they were inside his tent. But without the presence of Harold's forces surrounding the camp, Roderic's warriors would then murder Catherine in retaliation.

She would have to find another way to freeze the fires of Roderic's lust.

The tent was warmly lit by a pair of candles burning low in an intricate silver candelabra. A favorite of her father's, the piece had graced his table in the great hall since she'd been a child. It sat upon a handsome desk that had been carved by Angus in his youth. Roderic's bed was a pile of finely woven plaids strewn carelessly across the ground, each of which had been lovingly woven by the women of her clan to keep their families warm. Hate seized her in that moment, so overwhelming, her hand nearly reached for her dirk. She inhaled deeply. She was responsible for far more than simple revenge.

Roderic dropped the flap of the tent, enclosing them in the fabric dwelling. "Where is the sword?" he demanded brusquely.

"I don't have it."

His expression hardened. "I am not in the mood for games, Ariella. Give me the sword, or Catherine will be dragged in here and I will slice her throat open before your eyes."

"I have no doubt you would," said Ariella, feigning far greater calm than she felt. "Which is why if I had the sword, I would have given it to you by now."

His expression grew pensive. It was clear he did not know whether or not to believe her. "Where is it?"

"I gave it to Laird MacFane."

"You're lying. Agnes told me both Malcolm and Gavin left last night, and you do not expect them to return."

"I am not speaking of Malcolm," she clarified. "I sent the sword to Harold MacFane, my betrothed, as a token to seal our marriage contract. He is on his way here now, with his great army."

Rage hardened his features.

"But Harold does not know of the sword's powers," she quickly assured him, fearing she had roused his fury too much with her lie. "And the sword will not respond to him. Whoever would wield the sword must complete a trial first, and Harold has not done this."

Roderic eyed her suspiciously. "What sort of trial?"

"I don't know," she admitted. "No one has ever witnessed it, and the trial is different for each who attempts it. Alpin has said it is a test of courage and strength." Both of which Roderic had in abundance, she realized miserably.

"Agnes never mentioned anything about a trial," he countered. "She said you could just give the sword to me."

"Agnes wouldn't know about the trial. My father inherited the sword by right of birth, as did his father, and his father before him. It is only when there is no direct male heir that the duty of choosing a new laird falls to the eldest-born daughter. Once that man is chosen, he must successfully complete this test."

He scowled, irritated with this unexpected delay. "If the sword has no powers, why did you send it to Harold?"

"I sent it to him as a symbol of my troth," she explained. "The sword itself is an object of great beauty. Even without its magic, it is still an exquisite example of artistry and craftsmanship."

"You're trying to trick me. When Harold comes, you will have him perform this trial and come after me, wielding this sword with all its powers."

"Do you think I would risk the life of my sister in such a way?" she demanded impatiently. "The fact that I came here tonight, unarmed and unescorted, is proof I am conceding to your demands. I have left orders that when Harold arrives, he is to give the sword to one of my men, who will bring it into the woods. Your warriors will lead him here, and I will give it to you. Your success or failure during the trial is entirely up to you," she finished. "If you fail, you cannot try again."

"I will not fail," he assured her. His eyes narrowed.

"You should worry more about what will happen to Catherine if you are lying to me."

"I am not lying."

He studied her a moment, contemplating her assertion.

"Well then, sweet Ariella," he said finally, removing his sword, "it seems we have some time together before Harold's arrival." He reached out and pulled her toward him. "I think it is time we finished what we once began."

Ariella did not flinch when he placed his hands on her shoulders. She stood frozen as he opened the silver clasp fastening her cloak about her neck, and barely shivered as the heavy garment slid down her and pooled on the ground. Even when he sank his hand roughly into her hair and forced her head back, she regarded him with deliberate calm. And then, just as he lowered his mouth to hers, she stated in a soft, cold voice, "There is something you should know, Roderic."

"What is it?" he asked, his lips a breath away from hers.

"I cannot bestow the powers of the sword if I am no longer chaste."

He raised his head slightly and studied her. "You're lying," he decided, his mouth curving with amusement. "You tell me this because you despise my touch."

He was right. She fought to control her revulsion as his breath blew hot against her.

This is the man who murdered my father.

"I do despise your touch," she agreed. "But I am not lying."

He smiled and lowered his mouth again. And then he hesitated, suddenly uncertain.

"You are lying," he repeated. "Admit it."

"I am not lying."

His green eyes darkened with annoyance. Releasing his grip on her scalp, he wrapped his hands around her throat and began to squeeze.

Ariella struggled for air. He was allowing her just enough breath to speak, but she did not plead with him to stop. His strong fingers tightened until her throat was completely closed. Flashes of color and light began to burst in her head, and a deafening sound screamed in her ears. She closed her eyes, suddenly afraid he might actually strangle her in his determination to get the answer he wanted.

Abruptly, Roderic released her.

She inhaled a deep, ragged breath before raising her eyes to his. Then she allowed him to see the depths of her loathing. "Rape me now, and the sword will never be yours," she spat.

She watched as his lust for her battled his desire for power. Suddenly he turned away in angry frustration.

"Gregor!" he shouted.

The heavy warrior raised the flap of the tent.

"Put her in the tent with the other two," Roderic commanded stiffly. "Make sure they are under constant guard."

Gregor regarded Ariella in surprise. Ariella returned his gaze with cool disdain. She thought she detected a flicker of admiration in his eyes, but she could not be certain.

"Come with me."

She donned her cloak, then walked past Roderic and followed Gregor into the cool night air. The other warriors looked at her in astonishment, wondering how she had won this reprieve. Hating all of them, Ariella kept her spine straight and her eyes straight ahead.

Each of you will pay for your crimes against my clan, she vowed silently.

She entered the somber glow of the tent to find Agnes huddled on a blanket, weeping openly, and little Catherine by her side, dabbing Agnes's bloodied mouth with the hem of her gown as she tried to console her. Catherine looked up at her with wide, unbelieving eyes.

Then she flew off the ground, wrapped her arms tightly around Ariella's waist, and buried her face in the warm folds of her sister's cloak.

"Ariella," she began in a tiny, quivering voice, "can we please go home now?"

"Not just yet," she murmured, ruffling her fingers through the child's silky hair. "But soon."

Despair gripped her as she made that promise. She had managed to stall Roderic until the arrival of Harold, and she was with her sister, which was what she had wanted. But they were trapped. Her people were no match for the brutality of Roderic's warriors. And even if Harold arrived with his entire army, Roderic still had Catherine as a hostage. Until Ariella gave him the sword, and he had been invested with its powers, her sister was in grave danger. But if she did that, she was condemning her clan, and possibly other clans as well, to decades of intolerable suffering.

Suddenly overwhelmed by the pitiful sound of Agnes's weeping and the desperate clutch of her sister holding fast to her for comfort, she found herself wishing, however illogically, not for Harold, but for Malcolm.

CHAPTER 14

A blaze of fire etched the graceful lines of the castle against the velvet darkness. Torches spat and wavered every few feet along the battlements, creating a magnificent ring of flames, and amber light streamed from the arched windows, turning the intricate stonework to gold. The sight was as welcoming and glorious as any Malcolm had ever witnessed.

His fury deepened.

Instead of mourning his departure, even for one brief night, the MacKendricks had evidently decided that a grand celebration was in order. Of course, he reflected darkly. They were anxiously awaiting the arrival of their brave new laird and wanted to give him a spectacular welcome. They had done no less for Malcolm. On the day he had first come here, Ariella had dragged him into a frenzy of jugglers and poets, tumblers, speakers, and falling banners, not to mention those god-awful pipers. At the time, he had been infuriated at being made the object of such undeserved adulation. He had known that the moment he dismounted, her people would regard him with shock and pity, and wonder why they had gone to so much trouble to welcome a cripple. Yet tonight, as he stared in silence at the brilliant flames painting the MacKendrick castle in ripples of orange and gold, he found himself wishing that the castle burned for him.

As Ariella had last night.

"Obviously they are expecting Harold tonight," remarked Gavin, halting his horse next to Malcolm's. "They want him to see he is gaining something of rare beauty."

"Harold could never appreciate what Ariella is offering," Malcolm remarked scornfully. "The fact that he would force her to leave her home is evidence of that."

"You once would have done the same, Malcolm," Gavin reminded him. "It is not logical for a great chief to spend his time living on a small tract of land hidden amidst the mountains. Harold needs to be with the MacFanes and his army. The MacKendricks and this castle are but additional possessions to him, nothing more."

"As is the wife he is coming to claim."

"You can't expect him to have any feelings for her. He has never met Ariella. At least not as a woman," he qualified, smiling. "Somehow I doubt she mentioned in her letter that she had visited him once as a lad, with bare, grubby legs and filthy, cropped hair."

An image of Rob filled his mind, standing defiantly before him, his slim legs braced apart and his arms folded across his flat chest. Malcolm shook his head, still amazed that Ariella had been able to deceive him for so long.

"Poor Harold might remember her squalid appearance too well," he remarked wryly, "and reject her offer."

He continued to study the castle, wondering how Ariella would react when she learned he had returned. Would she fear his wrath? The thought evoked a perverse smile. It would be good to see her tremble in the face of his fury. It might help ease the pain and weariness he had been battling from the moment her foul drug had cleared his senses. Yes, he would make her fear him, he decided. At least for a short while.

He leaned forward in his saddle, suddenly uneasy. "Listen."

Gavin listened a moment. "I hear nothing."

"Don't you think that is peculiar?"

Gavin regarded him quizzically. "Why?"

"The MacKendricks love music and revelry, whenever there is the least cause for celebration," Malcolm explained. "If they believed Harold was coming tonight, they would have organized a feast for him. Don't you think there would be lots of laughter and music on such an occasion?"

Gavin shrugged. "Perhaps their celebration is finished. Or maybe they didn't want to begin until Harold arrived."

Malcolm contemplated this a moment, then shook his head. "It is not so late that they would be finished," he argued. "And even if they haven't begun, Graham, Ramsay, and the other musicians would be practicing their welcoming piece. On the day we arrived, we could hear them blasting away on those bloody bagpipes for well over a mile before we rode through the gate."

Gavin frowned and looked back at the silent castle. "You're right."

Malcolm urged Cain forward, his eyes searching the darkness. As they rode into the light spilling from the castle, he saw nearly two dozen shadowy figures positioned on the wall head.

"That's odd," he murmured. "They look almost as if they are—"

Two arrows ripped through the air and sank into the ground on either side of him, causing Cain to rear.

"Christ almighty!" he roared, trying to calm his horse.

"Don't move another inch!" warned Angus from the wall head. "Or we'll fill you so full of arrows, your blood will flow like water through a net!"

"I've got one aimed straight at your evil, festering heart," added Dugald menacingly. "One wee move, and you're dead!"

Malcolm looked up incredulously. "Angus? Dugald? What in the name of God do you think you're doing?"

An uncertain silence followed. Then Angus's white head cautiously poked through the battlements, his eyes squinting as he struggled to see through the darkness. "MacFane? Is that you?"

"It is. And Gavin too. What on earth is going on?"

"The lad is back!" shouted Angus jubilantly. "Hear me, everyone, the Black Wolf has returned!"

A relieved cheer rose into the night as those lying in wait on the wall head surged forward to see for themselves. Anxious questions began to fly at him from every direction.

"Did you bring your great army this time?" demanded Gordon.

"Are they hiding in the woods behind you?" asked Bryce.

"We were certain you would turn back," called Helen, waving.

"Alpin said a warrior was coming, and we knew that had to be you," said Ramsay. "Even though Ariella told us it was Harold."

"When Ariella explained you had to leave," added Graham, "we couldn't believe she meant for good."

It was wonderful to be welcomed back so. But the

warmth flooding Malcolm's chest was tempered with a stab of unease.

Something had happened in his absence.

"Open the gate," he commanded.

He rode forward as the heavy wooden gate swung open, and the new portcullis was quickly raised. Once he and Gavin were in the courtyard, the portcullis dropped and the gate slammed shut. Young Colin came running forward to take hold of Cain.

"Welcome back, MacFane," the boy said eagerly.

"Thank you, Colin." He grunted in pain as he dismounted, then angrily dismissed the sensation. "Cain needs extra care this evening. He has traveled far today."

"Yes, milord." His face flushed with solemn pride, he took Gavin's horse, then turned and led the two enormous chargers toward the stable.

Moving as swiftly as his stiff leg would allow, Malcolm entered the great hall, where much of the clan had assembled. His gaze swept over the torchlit room and a sea of anxious faces. Duncan and Andrew, he noted, had returned, and were regarding him with grave concern. Elizabeth stood in a far corner, her face pale and frightened.

Ariella was nowhere to be seen.

"Where is Ariella?" he demanded.

There was a moment of troubled silence before Niall grimly stated, "Roderic has her."

Dread gripped him, so overwhelming he could barely draw a breath. "What do you mean?" he managed, his voice low.

"Roderic and his men captured Agnes and Catherine earlier today," explained Duncan, his expression reflecting his relief that Malcolm had returned. "He sent Ariella a message demanding the MacKendrick sword in exchange for their release. He wants it by first light, or he will slit Catherine's throat. Ariella was so terrified he would hurt Catherine, she went to Roderic tonight, without the sword. She is hoping to delay him until Harold MacFane arrives with his army."

Malcolm accepted a wrinkled leaf of paper from him and swiftly scanned the message. "Christ almighty," he swore furiously. "Does Roderic actually believe this idiocy about a magic sword?"

The clan exchanged uneasy glances.

Malcolm looked at them in exasperation. "Don't tell me your people truly believe you have a sword with magical powers."

"Well, now," began Angus hesitantly, "it just so happens we do, lad."

"Aye," agreed Dugald. "We've had it now for some four hundred years."

"Four hundred and twelve," Gordon corrected. "According to Alpin, and he would know, of course. That was the year the great MacKendrick slayed a terrible two-headed beast with it."

Malcolm didn't know which astonished him more, the fact that they actually believed this drivel, or that Ariella's life was in peril and he was wasting time standing here listening to it.

"For God's sake, if you have some rusty old relic that you think is magic, just give it to Roderic and be done with it."

"It isn't that simple, MacFane," said Niall. "Only Ariella can bestow the sword with its powers."

"And whoever she gives it to immediately becomes the next MacKendrick," added Andrew. "We shall be forced to follow him."

"That is ridiculous," he growled impatiently. "There is no such thing as a magic sword, and you people can follow whomever you damn well please, not some depraved bastard with an ancient weapon in his hand."

"If Ariella gives the sword to Roderic, he will become the next MacKendrick," said Gordon, his expression dead serious. "It is that simple."

"Which is why it is Ariella's responsibility to guard the sword from one who would harm us," explained Angus. "She must choose the right one."

"That is her solemn birthright," added Dugald, "and her duty."

Malcolm fought to control his anger. Although he didn't believe this nonsense, it was obvious the Mac-Kendricks did. Which meant Ariella probably did too. And someone had obviously convinced Roderic as well.

What the hell was the matter with all of them?

"Suppose what you are telling me is true," he began, trying to sound as if he were at least entertaining the possibility. "With Roderic holding Ariella, Catherine, and Agnes hostage, what choice do you have but to give the sword to him?" His expression was harsh as he finished, "Do you have any idea of the barbarity Roderic is capable of?"

No one answered.

Yes, he realized grimly, searching their anxious expressions. The first time Roderic attacked, he had given the MacKendricks a brief but thorough taste of his cruelty. It had been nothing compared to the heinous slaughter he had inflicted on the MacFanes. But it had been enough to make them understand the gravity of their situation.

"We have no choice here," he informed them. "And even less time. Give me this sword, and I will take it to Roderic now. I will make certain he releases his captives before I actually place it in his hands. If what you say is true, and only Ariella can bestow the sword with its powers to another, it won't matter if he has the weapon alone, will it?"

"But then the sword will be gone," pointed out Andrew.

Then make another one, he thought cynically.

"Once I know Ariella, Catherine, and Agnes are safe, I will get it back for you," he offered instead.

Angus looked uncertain. "How will you do that, lad?"

"With our help, of course," interjected Duncan. "When Ariella, Catherine, and Agnes are free, we can attack Roderic's camp."

"We have already proved our ability to fight them," pointed out Niall. "We must drive them away, so they will never try to attack us again."

Murmurs of agreement rippled through the room.

"No," stated Malcolm firmly.

Duncan gave him an exasperated look. "Why not?"

"Luring men away from their home and loved ones is a favorite strategy of Roderic's," he explained. "I once fell prey to this tactic. Roderic made me believe another clan was under massive attack and needed my army's protection. I led my warriors away, leaving only a small force at my holding." He paused, reluctant to continue. "The devastation to my clan was—unspeakable."

The MacKendricks regarded him sympathetically, not understanding the magnitude of his error.

Or that what had occurred was entirely his fault.

He could no longer lie to them, he realized. Somehow, in that moment, as they stared at him with such unmitigated trust, he wanted them to know the truth. And so he continued in a low, harsh voice. "Over two hundred women and children were slain that night. Young and old. Sick and able. Even women with child were not spared. Roderic and his allies murdered as many as they could—because the great Black Wolf, Laird Mac-Fane, was drunk. And I stupidly, drunkenly, believed the enemy I was facing was elsewhere. For that unforgivable error I was stripped of my lairdship and banished forever from my clan. I am no longer MacFane," he finished roughly, "and I lead no great army. Gavin and I live alone in a crude hut, some three days' journey from here. That is where Ariella found me."

Shocked silence gripped the room.

Malcolm gazed at their appalled faces with rigid calm, betraying none of the pain tearing through him. He had to tell them, he told himself stonily, watching the admiration in their faces vanish. No one spoke, too aghast by his revelation to find words.

I deserve this, he thought savagely, battling the despair shredding his soul. *I never deserved their admiration and respect. They gave it to me under false assumptions, thinking I was still the Black Wolf. They could not see me as I really was.*

Only Ariella could.

It was agonizing, facing their shocked stares. Still, he endured it. Not only had he failed his own clan, he had also lied to the MacKendricks about who and what he was. They had every right to despise him. But regardless of their contempt, he was going after Ariella—with or without her clan's approval, or even this absurd sword they spoke of. Nothing would stop him from bringing her, Catherine, and Agnes home.

Just as nothing would stop him from killing Roderic.

"You make it sound as if this terrible event were your fault," remarked Angus suddenly, cracking the silence.

"It was my fault," Malcolm assured him brusquely. "The welfare of my clan was my responsibility. Had I kept my warriors there, those women and children would be alive today."

"But you acted based on what you knew," argued Dugald. "You believed there were others who desperately needed your help."

"I was drunk," he said in disgust. "I never should have taken so many men with me."

"Perhaps," allowed Gordon. "But if there had been a terrible attack on another clan and you had arrived with too small a force, would you then be responsible for their deaths as well?"

Malcolm looked at him in surprise. Why were they defending him?

"It was a difficult decision, regardless of whether you were drunk or sober," commented Duncan. "Just a moment ago I suggested all the men here go into the woods to find Roderic and his men. If you hadn't been here, that is what we would have done."

"But if we had, and the women and children here were killed, we would not have blamed Duncan," said Ramsay. "The sole responsibility for that tragedy would still belong to Roderic and his men."

Bewilderment rendered him silent. Why could they not see that the attack on his clan had been his fault?

"What is done is in the past," pronounced Angus sagely. "All we can judge you on, MacFane, is your actions while you were with us. And you have never done anything except try to protect us, to the very best of your considerable ability."

"Aye, that's true," said Bryce.

"If it hadn't been for you, Roderic would have captured us the last time he was here," pointed out Niall. "You taught us how to fight back."

"You convinced us we could actually win," added Hugh.

"You made us all feel like warriors," finished Helen. "Even the women."

"Ariella would never have brought you here if she hadn't believed you could help us," pointed out Graham. "Regardless of your past."

He could not believe what they were telling him. They were accepting his failure to protect his clan. And the fact that he had lied to them.

"Getting back to this business with Roderic," said Duncan, as if Malcolm's crime was no longer relevant. "I say we let MacFane take the sword to Roderic immediately, secure Ariella, Catherine, and Agnes's release, and then try to retrieve it. As long as Ariella doesn't give the weapon to Roderic herself, he will not have its powers."

"It's a sound plan," agreed Gordon. "We don't know if Ariella's attempt to stall Roderic will work. And we have no idea when Harold will arrive with his army."

"He will arrive sometime tomorrow," interjected Malcolm, troubled by the fact that he had delayed his cousin's arrival. Harold was traveling with a small army of some fifty highly trained, seasoned warriors. Their presence at that moment would have been invaluable. "Possibly by midday."

Dugald regarded him curiously. "How do you know?"

"Gavin and I encountered him on our journey. When I realized his purpose in coming here, I convinced him to make camp for the night, so I could arrive first."

Gordon frowned. "Why did you do that?"

"So he could speak with Ariella, of course," supplied Angus, smiling. "That's it, isn't it, lad?"

"Where will I find this sword?" demanded Malcolm, ignoring the question.

"You must speak with Alpin," said Dugald. "Only he knows where it is kept."

"Fine. The rest of you, return to your positions immediately," he commanded. "Every inch of the surrounding area is to be watched for the slightest movement. Gavin will assume control while I am gone. Two thirds of you will be on guard, and the other third will sleep. You will alternate every two hours. It is possible Roderic and his men are waiting for us to exhaust ourselves during the night, so we will be tired and inattentive come morning. Don't let that happen."

They nodded. Now that he had assumed control, their expressions were grave but filled with purpose.

"Very well, then. Move."

He watched as the clan quickly dispersed.

Then he headed toward Alpin's chamber so he could retrieve this ridiculous old sword.

•   •   •

The enormous owl flapped its wings and hooted noisily as he threw the heavy door open, protesting his presence. Malcolm scowled at the ill-tempered creature and limped purposefully toward the back of the dimly lit chamber. He found Alpin hunched over a table, calmly chopping up a leathery stack of shriveled bat wings.

"So," murmured Alpin, slowly gathering the debris into a gnarled white hand, "you have returned."

"I have come for the sword, Alpin."

Giving no sign that he had heard him, Alpin began to meticulously measure pinches of the desiccated wings into a bowl.

"Roderic has Ariella, Catherine, and Agnes," Malcolm elaborated, deciding the old man didn't realize his clan was in grave danger.

Alpin sprinkled one more pinch of wings into the bowl, then tossed the excess over his left shoulder.

"I know."

Squinting at the bottles cluttering his table, he eventually selected one marked "Oil of Herring," lifted it toward the candle flame to be sure he was reading the label correctly, then began to add it drop by infuriating drop into the bowl.

"I must have the sword to save them," Malcolm persisted, growing agitated. "The clan says only you know where it is."

"That is true," he agreed.

He put the bottle down and picked out an earthen jar, lifted the lid, and cautiously sniffed it. Satisfied by what he either smelled or did not smell, he withdrew a silver spoon from a pocket deep within his cloak, skimmed it along the surface of the jar, and added a dollop of its brown contents to his mixture. "But it is up to you to find it," he declared cryptically.

Malcolm felt the thin thread of his patience snap. "I

don't have time for this nonsense," he growled, turning to leave.

"You must make time, MacFane," Alpin warned.

Malcolm stopped, inhaled a deep breath, and then demanded in a remarkably level voice, "Can you give it to me, or can't you?"

Alpin shook his head. "I'm afraid I cannot give it to anyone. I can only tell you where you might find it. Whether or not you do is entirely up to you. And Ariella," he added, placing the lid back on the jar.

"Fine. Where *might* I find it?"

"The MacKendrick sword is sheltered in the woods, where it has remained, untouched, for some thirty years. Had Ariella's father kept it by his side," he reflected, shaking his head, "the suffering Roderic inflicted on the clan might never have happened."

"Why didn't he?"

"Neither MacKendrick, nor his father, nor his father before him ever used the sword, except during the ritual in which they were invested with the powers of laird. Because we are a clan of peace, the sword has come to be a solely ceremonial object. Its actual powers have not been tested for well over a hundred years."

"Which means no one has ever witnessed its power," pointed out Malcolm dryly. "I'm amazed no one has thought to question whether it actually has any."

Alpin smiled, untroubled by his cynicism. "The sword is not an object that can easily be taken. You must go into the woods, alone and unarmed, and sleep there tonight. As you sleep, you will dream. Follow the directions of that dream, and you *may* be told where to find the sword. If you find it, you *may* be permitted to take it."

"I haven't time for this bloody nonsense," Malcolm concluded. "Ariella's and Catherine's lives are in danger, and I'm not about to go wandering into the woods unarmed so Roderic can find me sleeping beneath a tree. I will go after them without the goddamn sword." Irritated that he had already wasted so much time, he began to limp toward the door.

"Then they will die."

He stopped.

"The Black Wolf can strike now, guided by his reckless fury, or he can listen to me. One choice will inevitably lead to their death. The other holds at least the possibility of their survival. The decision is yours," Alpin finished mildly, as if it mattered not a whit to him what Malcolm decided.

Malcolm hesitated. He didn't believe in seers or magic swords, he reminded himself angrily. But everyone else there seemed to, including Roderic. If the Mac-Kendricks had some rusty old sword hidden in the woods, he probably should try to get it before facing Roderic. His position would be far stronger if he held something that Roderic desperately wanted.

As things were now, Roderic was in a far more powerful position than he.

"What happens after I dream?" he demanded.

"Your dream will lead you to the place of the sword. Once you are there, you will be required to successfully complete a trial."

Malcolm barely refrained from rolling his eyes. This whole thing was growing more ludicrous by the minute. "What sort of trial?"

"I do not know," admitted Alpin, shrugging. "It is different for each who seeks the powers of the sword."

"I don't seek its powers," Malcolm assured him sardonically. "I want only the weapon itself."

Alpin nodded. "*If* you complete the trial successfully, the sword *may* appear for you, but only if Ariella wills it. If she does, it means she has accepted you as laird of her clan."

A helpless laugh erupted from his chest. "Then I needn't waste my time with this," he decided. "Last night she had me drugged, bound, and spirited away in the dead of night, precisely because she does not believe I am even close to being a fit laird for her clan. Even if I pass the trial, which is highly improbable, given the weaknesses of my body, Ariella will never will the sword to me. She wants to give it to Harold."

Alpin shuffled toward the fire and began to stir a thick, mossy mixture steaming in one of the pots. "Are you certain?" he asked quietly.

The next laird of the MacKendricks must be a great warrior, and a great leader. You are not the one.

"Yes," Malcolm replied, enraged anew by the memory of her contemptuous dismissal of him. "I am."

Alpin considered this a moment. Finally he sighed. "When first she believed she was to wed you, MacFane, Ariella created a childishly heroic image of you in her mind. This was woven in part with my visions, and the tales she had heard from the occasional traveler. You were the mighty Black Wolf, and your feats were legendary. Your failure to appear the moment she needed you most irrevocably shattered that image. Roderic murdered her father and her people, but, unfortunately, she blamed you. I sent her to find you anyway. When she did, she was appalled by what you had become. And in her fury and disappointment she judged you by what you once were, at least according to legend and her fantasies, rather than what you are." His keen black eyes regarded him intently. "And you, Malcolm MacFane, have been guilty of the same distorted vision. Neither of you have learned that we are not condemned by the failures of our past, provided we have not intentionally inflicted suffering. With all the limitations that are sometimes so cruelly thrust upon us, it is what we do today, and tomorrow, that matters."

"Ariella has seen what I am today," Malcolm pointed out. "I'm not the same pathetic drunk she originally dragged here. And she still rejected me."

"Of course she did," Alpin agreed, waving his hand

dismissively. "How can that surprise you? Ariella's foremost duty is to her clan. The requirements of the next laird have been made clear to her since the day of her mother's death. It is not a task to be taken lightly. But the longings of the heart and one's actions are sometimes two very different things. You cannot judge Ariella's true feelings by what she does out of duty to her people."

"I believe Ariella's actions reflect her feelings quite accurately," Malcolm countered, chafing at the memory of the previous night.

"As your actions reflected your feelings when you so heartlessly denied Marrian your tenderness and warmth?"

He stared at him, startled. How could Alpin possibly know about that?

"She loved you," Alpin continued, unperturbed by his confusion. "As much as any young girl loves a handsome, brave warrior who is destined to be laird of his clan and her husband. Naturally she was frightened when you returned so gravely injured. Frightened and confused. But she still loved you. And wanted you. Yet you deliberately pushed her away."

"She didn't want me," Malcolm objected. "She felt pity for me."

"Because no woman could want a man with such a horrendously battered body and spirit?"

He looked away, unmanned by the truth.

"Then tell me, MacFane, how do you explain what happened between you and Ariella last night?"

The memory of her clinging to him stirred his body. Her kisses had been sweet with desire, her touch restless and burning, as if she were trying to capture something she wanted desperately but knew she could not have. Standing before her in that fire-washed chamber, he had felt neither ugly nor pitiful. For one brief, impossible moment he had felt whole and strong, like the man he had once been before that terrible day on the battlefield. Ariella had seen him naked before, had laid her patient, soothing hands on every jagged scar and aching muscle. She, more than anyone, knew the full extent of his injuries and imperfections.

Yet she had wanted him with a passion he had never known.

It meant nothing, he reminded himself bitterly. Wanting him in that heated, stolen moment and thinking he could be laird of her people were two entirely different things. Therefore, pursuing this ancient sword was a waste of time. He could barely bring himself to believe it might actually exist. But if by some remote chance it did, and finding it depended on Ariella's wanting him to lead her clan, then he had no hope of ever doing so.

He should find some rusty old substitute and seek out Roderic now, before more precious time was lost.

"You must try to find the sword, MacFane," Alpin told him sternly, interrupting his thoughts. "No matter how ludicrous or unfeasible this quest seems, you must try."

The old man's eyes were grave, two pools of black glittering against the sagging folds of his decrepit face. An inexplicable chill swept through the room as he held Malcolm with his gaze. In that frozen, hushed moment Malcolm could almost believe that this ancient man had seen a hundred or more years rise and fall across the emerald ring of these mountains. Alpin had no special powers, he reminded himself firmly, and although he couldn't understand how the old man knew so much, Malcolm was damn sure he wasn't a seer. But something in the intensity of that aged black gaze cracked the armor of his cynicism.

If saving Ariella and Catherine meant going after the sword, then he would do so.

But if by first light he did not hold it in his grasp, he

would go after them anyway, and kill Roderic with his bare hands.

The air was sweet with the fragrance of crushed pine needles, damp earth, and the faint breath of heather wafting down the mountains. They were dark, mysterious scents, far different from when they played upon a sun-warmed gust of midday wind. They permeated his senses as he slowly threaded his way deeper into the thick woods, sharpening his awareness. After a while the world began to roar with the uneven sigh of earth shifting beneath his feet, the soft cadence of his breath, the steady pounding of his heart. Never before had he been so acutely conscious of himself and his environment. If Roderic's men were scouting the area, he would sense their presence long before they were near.

Of course, with no weapon other than his exhausted, limping body, he had virtually no chance of surviving an attack.

He was an idiot to have allowed Alpin to convince him to do this. And yet, despite the insistent voice of logic telling him he was wasting time and should turn back, he did not. Instead he warily moved through the black pillars of trees, wondering how much farther it would be before he found a place to lie down and sleep without waking to find his throat carved open. The prospect kept him moving. That, and the fact that with Ariella and Catherine in danger, the last thing on earth he wanted to do was take a nap.

Roderic was clever, he mused, infuriated by his own stupidity. Malcolm had focused his attention on making the castle impenetrable. He had analyzed the structure and demanded the installation of every fortification possible. He had risen at the ungodliest hour every morning, no matter how weary and alcohol sodden he was, to drill endlessly beneath drizzling skies with a preposterous assortment of pipers, tumblers, and poets. And slowly, incredibly, he had transformed them into warriors. Not warriors who would savagely kill and maim in the bloodiest of battles, as his own men had. But brave men and women who were ready and able to defend their homes and loved ones. He had not done it for the lure of gold, though that was what initially had drawn him here. He had done it because he owed an immeasurable debt to Ariella for failing her so miserably. And after learning she lived, he had labored even harder to make the MacKendricks safe, realizing that her very survival endangered her clan. Every weakness of the castle had been exhaustively appraised, the training intensified, and alliances with neighboring clans secured. He thought he had done everything within his power to keep the MacKendricks safe.

What he hadn't foreseen was Roderic resorting to the despicable act of using Catherine to force Ariella to surrender.

He had reached the densest part of the woods, where the trees clustered together and formed a high, feathery arch. A thick mound of moss and ferns grew beneath him, which appeared to be dry. This was as good a place as any, he decided, stiffly lowering his aching frame onto the soft mattress. Leaning back against a tree, he stared into the surrounding shadows, wondering how the hell anyone could expect him to actually fall asleep. Realizing, however, that sleep was a requisite, he folded his arms across his chest, closed his eyes, and ordered himself to relax.

Barely a moment passed before he was aware of being watched. He snapped his eyes open and instinctively reached for his dirk. His fingers grazed only his plaid, and he remembered in frustration that he had no weapons with him.

The ghostly silhouette of a wolf stood a few feet away,

perfectly still. Malcolm kept his gaze locked on the powerful creature as his hands swiftly searched the ground for a heavy stick or stone. There was nothing. The wolf took a step toward him. Malcolm's body tensed, preparing to fight it with his bare hands. Another step, this time more faltering. The animal was limping, Malcolm realized, experiencing a stab of empathy. The wolf studied him a moment, its amber eyes emanating not menace, but wariness and curiosity.

I am losing my mind.

What could possibly make him think this wild creature wasn't about to tear him to pieces? And yet, after another moment of perusal, the wolf lay down, placed its head on his front paws, and let out a long, weary sigh.

It was strange, but now that he no longer felt threatened, the presence of the animal was almost comforting. Malcolm also sighed and closed his eyes, overcome with exhaustion, and inexplicably calmed by the fact that this deadly animal was near, watching over him. He settled back against the tree, still aware of every whisper of sound, and rapidly fell into the warm waters of sleep.

Ariella's screams jerked him awake.

He opened his eyes to see a wooden tower engulfed in flames, exhaling a black cloud of smoke and cinders into the air. He rose from the ground and tried to run, but his legs were leaden and he could barely move. When he finally reached the blazing structure, it began to collapse, showering him with fire. He kicked the door open and went inside, choking on the acrid haze. His eyes were stinging, his flesh almost melting from the scorching heat, but still he limped up the stairs, knowing full well the fire was closing behind him as he did. He would find Ariella and take her out of here, or die in the attempt.

It was that simple.

Three doors faced him on the next floor. Ariella's voice called to him from each. He hesitated barely an instant before heaving himself against the third door. She stood trapped amidst a ring of flames, which were lapping at the hem of her white gown. Malcolm raced toward her, wrapped his arms around her, and pulled her from the inferno. But fire now blocked the doorway, and there was no escape for either of them. He had failed, he realized desperately, sinking with her onto the stone floor.

"Forgive me," he pleaded roughly, brushing a lock of auburn hair off her forehead. Suddenly she began to change; she was no longer Ariella, but Marrian, who lay pale and still in his arms. She reached up and tenderly laid her hand against his cheek, her blue eyes liquid with regret. Then she disappeared, and in her place a thin shoot emerged from what was now the ground. Up and up it grew, until finally an enormous tree with leaves of flame stood before him. A terrible heat radiated from it, and the air was thick with the battle stench of blood and death. From somewhere high in its branches, Ariella was screaming. He let out a roar of rage and began to climb, stiffly, slowly, his treacherous body protesting every movement. The leaves of fire lashed his face and arms and legs, burning his clothes and flesh, filling his lungs with a heat so intense, he did not think he could endure it, but he did, because nothing mattered except that he reach Ariella. Finally he was close enough to grasp her hand, but as he pulled her toward him, the last of his strength drained away. They began to fall through the fiery leaves, and Malcolm knew he had failed once again.

"Forgive me, Ariella," he pleaded, closing his arms around her to cushion her fall, in the vain hope that she might somehow survive.

Ariella stared at him, her gray eyes wide and uncertain. And then suddenly her mouth curved into a gentle smile. "Follow the wolf, Malcolm," she whispered softly, pressing her lips to his. "He will lead you home."

Malcolm shook his head, overwhelmed with despair. "I have no home."

She raised her fingers to caress his cheek. "Follow the wolf." Then she disappeared, leaving him alone.

Malcolm sat upright, breathing deeply.

It was still dark, but the first gray shadows of morning were imminent. The wolf's eyes met his. Then the animal suddenly leaped to its feet. It took a few steps, turned to look at him, then disappeared into the trees.

Malcolm awkwardly rose and began to follow him, his leg taut with pain, his back aching from lying on the cool ground. He thrashed his way through the darkness, breaking through a dense growth of trees and bushes as he struggled to keep up. He had no idea where he was, but somehow that didn't bother him. The wolf moved swiftly despite its limp and was forced to stop occasionally so Malcolm could close the distance between them. They traveled for what seemed a long time, but the woods remained dark, and Malcolm was not sure his perception of time was accurate. On and on they went, until finally the wolf disappeared behind a thick wall of bushes. Breathing heavily, clenching his jaw against the pain, Malcolm separated the dense foliage and stepped through.

The darkness lifted with a sigh to reveal a glittering blue loch nestled below a heather-cloaked mountain. The air was perfectly still, leaving the veils of mist shrouding the purple peak to hang immobile, as if they had been delicately painted against the dove-gray sky. Beside the loch stood a glorious thickly branched tree, with brilliant, wavering leaves of rust, melon, and gold. The wolf stood beside it, staring at him. Malcolm recognized it as the tree from his dream, except that its leaves were not flames now, but only the color of flames, and no desperate screams poured from it. He approached it with caution, aware that its beauty could be deceiving. The wolf waited patiently for him. As he drew nearer, the wolf glanced at the trunk. Malcolm followed its gaze to see a brilliant flash of silver.

Frowning, he moved closer.

A magnificent sword leaned against the hoary bark, its intricately carved hilt studded with enormous sapphires and rubies, its gleaming silver blade radiating an aura that was almost blinding in the soft light. At first Malcolm could do little more than stare, so overwhelmed was he by the weapon's sheer artistry. It was unlike any he had ever seen, and he could not imagine the countless hours of expert, loving craftsmanship that had gone into creating such a splendid piece. He reached out and wrapped his hand firmly around the hilt. It conformed perfectly to his grip, as if it had been forged to fit no palm other than his. Using both arms, he raised the weapon high into the air, then brought it down with a savage slice. The sword was solid and well balanced, yet remarkably light.

It was, without question, the most extraordinary weapon he had ever seen.

The sword may appear for you, but only if Ariella wills it. If she does, it means she has accepted you as laird of her clan.

It was impossible, he thought, staring at it now in disbelief. It was unthinkable. Ariella had made it eminently clear he was not worthy to lead her people. And she was probably right. Yet here he was in this green, silent enclave, with the warm, solid hilt of the MacKendrick sword planted firmly in his grasp.

Follow the wolf, she had told him. *The wolf will lead you home.*

He glanced over at the wolf. The animal calmly returned his scrutiny. Then it suddenly turned and disappeared through the emerald wall leading back to the woods, leaving him alone.

Malcolm did not follow. The wolf had brought him here. By doing so, it had shown him where Ariella's troubled heart truly lay.

Until Roderic was dead and Ariella safe in his arms, he had no home.

CHAPTER 15

Ariella closed her fingers around her dirk, enjoying the cool touch of steel against the warmth of her palm.

Gray threads of light filtered through the fabric walls of her prison, heralding the arrival of morning. She held up the weapon and watched it glimmer in the somber shadows.

Soon you will be buried deep in Roderic's chest. Then my father's life will finally be avenged. And the lives of all the others Roderic has taken in his bid to steal that which does not belong to him.

Whatever happened, Roderic would die. His lust for the sword was absolute, and as long as he lived, he would threaten the safety of her people. Ariella could not permit that. It was her duty to keep her clan safe, and to make certain the MacKendrick sword did not fall into the hands of one who would abuse its powers. Harold was on his way, but when he arrived without the sword, Roderic would realize he had been tricked. In that moment his rage would know no limits. He would put a knife to Catherine's throat, until Ariella finally surrendered and gave him what he wanted.

She had no choice but to kill him first.

All through the night she had desperately tried to think of a plan to get Catherine and Agnes away from the camp. Without her sister Roderic lost his power to threaten her. He would not kill Ariella, because she was the only one who could give him the sword, though he would take pleasure in trying to force her to submit to him. She intended to kill him first. Once he was dead, she could expect no mercy from his men. All she had hoped was that Catherine and Agnes might somehow escape. Now that morning was sifting through the dark shadows of her tent, she realized this was impossible. Roderic's warriors completely surrounded the camp and filled the woods. If her sister and Agnes somehow managed to break free, they would quickly be found and dragged back. The thought of little Catherine being hunted down like an animal was too ghastly to contemplate.

If they were to die, they would die together.

Regret tore deep into her throat. Not for the sacrifice of her own life, which was of no significance compared to the protection of the sword and the safety of her people. But for Catherine, who was so young and had already suffered so much. She also felt sorry for Agnes, despite her betrayal of her clan. Agnes was a foolish girl who had been blind to the evil soul of the man she had chosen to love. It was not difficult to understand. Even Ariella had not seen Roderic as he really was until the day he attacked her castle. Given the swell of Agnes's belly, it was clear that by that time she already carried his child. He must have seduced her during the weeks he'd spent convalescing at the castle, while trying to capture Ariella's heart at the same time. Roderic was adept at concealing his vileness behind the shield of his handsome face and practiced charms.

Unlike Malcolm, who never pretended to be anything other than the bitter, broken warrior he was.

It agonized her to think of the wrath that had spilled from him in their final moment together. For the rest of his life he would hate her with a vehemence she could not bear to contemplate. Still, the pain searing his gaze as he had collapsed to the floor convinced her she had had no choice. She could not have faced Harold with Malcolm standing by, despising both of them. And she wanted to shelter both Malcolm and her people from the horrendous truth of his past, even though she could no longer condemn him for it. The blood of those innocent women and children dripped solely from Roderic's murdering hands. Ariella knew Malcolm well enough to realize that, drunk or sober, he would have done anything within his power to save them, had he been able.

Just as she now realized he would have come at her father's request had he believed he'd had anything to offer.

The heavy, sleep-drenched sounds of the camp stirring to life pulled her from her thoughts. An unpleasant litany of groans and belches told her Roderic's men were reluctantly rousing.

Soon it will be over, she thought, calmly caressing the blade of her dirk. *Roderic will be dead. And the sword will be safe.*

The ground began to tremble with the pounding of hooves, and excited cries rang through the camp. Ariella slipped her dirk into her cloak and moved to the entrance of the tent, where she cautiously parted the opening.

Roderic stood in the center of the camp, his thickly muscled arms crossed and his legs braced, listening to the report of three riders. It was clear he had risen early, or perhaps had not slept at all, for his face was freshly shaven and his hair brushed to a golden gleam. He wore an intricately stitched shirt and a precisely arranged plaid that Ariella instantly recognized as the handiwork of her clan. Evidently he wanted to look his finest as he forced her people to kneel before him and swear their undying loyalty.

The only weapon you will receive today is my blade thrust deep into your foul heart, she thought darkly.

Roderic stroked his scar pensively as his men finished their report. His expression was calm, but also perplexed, as if something had happened he had not expected. He gave some orders to his men, which Ariella could not hear. Then he turned and strode toward her tent.

"Agnes! Catherine!" she hissed, retreating from the entrance. "Wake up!"

Catherine sat up and sleepily rubbed her eyes. "What is it?"

"Roderic is coming."

Agnes's tear-streaked face contorted with fear. A purple stain had formed around her mouth where Roderic had struck her, and her lower lip was swollen and crusted with blood.

Ariella gave them both an encouraging smile. "It will be all right," she assured them gently. "Just stay there and don't say anything."

"Good morning, miladies," called Roderic pleasantly, entering the tent. "I trust you slept well?"

Ariella glared at him.

"Excellent," said Roderic, undisturbed by her manner. "I would speak with you a moment, Ariella." He raised the tent flap so she could precede him outside.

She adjusted her cloak around her shoulders and stepped into the cool morning air. Roderic's men were hastily collecting their weapons.

"What is it?" she demanded, feigning far more calm than she felt. "Does Harold come?"

"It seems you have a gallant savior on his way to rescue you, fair Ariella," drawled Roderic. "Your wounded Black Wolf has been spotted riding toward the camp. Alone."

She tossed him a scornful look, wondering what game he played with her. "That is impossible. MacFane has left MacKendrick lands. Forever."

"Impossible or not, he comes," he assured her. "And he is carrying a magnificent sword, the like of which my men have never seen. Which leaves me to wonder if you lied to me about sending the weapon to Harold." He roughly grabbed her hair and jerked her head back, forcing her to look at him. "Did you, my sweet?"

"No."

Her mind raced as she absorbed what he was telling her. MacFane was coming here. Alone. Which meant he was either drunk or mad. Obviously he had returned to her castle and learned of Roderic's demand for the sword. And so it seemed he was bringing a false sword, which he would offer to Roderic under the pretext that it was the weapon he sought. She could think of no other explanation.

The moment Roderic held the weapon in his hands, he would cut Malcolm in two, with or without the sword's powers.

"If you didn't give the sword to Malcolm, how did he get it?" demanded Roderic furiously.

Grasping for a plausible answer, Ariella quickly offered, "*If* it is MacFane who comes, and *if* he has the sword, then he must have stolen it from Harold. There is no other way he could obtain the weapon."

Roderic's green eyes narrowed. "Malcolm is far too weak and drunk to steal anything from Harold." His fingers wrapped around her throat. "I think you lied to me, my sweet, and gave the sword to him."

"Can you honestly believe I would give the sword to MacFane?" she demanded scathingly.

He hesitated, considering. Then he abruptly released her. "Either way, that goddamn sword will be mine," he vowed. "And to celebrate this glorious occasion, my first act with it will be to sever Malcolm's head from his shoulders. That will be a more than fitting retribution for all the misery he has caused me."

"You tried to destroy him, and he cast you out, which was a far more lenient punishment than you deserved," declared Ariella. "So you went back and savagely slaughtered the women and children of his clan. How can you possibly think you are the one who has been wronged?"

"I should have been laird of the MacFanes," he snarled. "Yet that honor went to Malcolm, despite how unfit he was, because the laws of tanistry said he must inherit the position of his father. Any fool could have seen I was a better choice than that drunken cripple."

"Malcolm was a far superior choice, regardless of his weaknesses," Ariella retorted. "To lead a clan requires honor and integrity. It is a responsibility that calls for absolute devotion and unfailing courage, even when you think you cannot possibly bear the burden of it another moment. *You* want to be a laird because you believe forcing people to submit to you will give you power," she observed, her voice dripping contempt. "A true laird would seek the duty because he believed he had something to give, not because he wanted to take."

Roderic crossed his arms and regarded her sardonically. "And you believe Malcolm has these valiant attributes?"

"Malcolm has them and more," she assured him. "Because he knows what it is to suffer. Yet he summons the strength to rise every morning and go on helping others, in spite of that suffering. That," she finished caustically, "is a kind of power and courage you could never understand. It is the difference between thieving, murdering scum like you, and a true warrior like Malcolm MacFane."

"I am flattered, milady, by your faith in me."

Ariella gasped and whirled around.

Malcolm sat tall upon his black charger, regarding them both with deliberate calm. Unlike Roderic, his shirt and plaid were rumpled and worn, his dark hair tangled, and his jaw bore the shadow of some two days' growth. Weariness had chiseled the lines of his face into deep grooves—weariness, and pain, and perhaps even a hint of concern, though Ariella could not imagine he could have cared what happened to her after her unforgivable betrayal of him. And yet, despite his lined face and disheveled attire, despite the jagged scar down his weakened right arm and the pain she knew at that moment was gripping his back and leg, an extraordinary power and confidence emanated from him. His stature was tall, his body taut, his expression deadly calm. His gaze flicked over her in a cursory, almost disinterested appraisal. Then he clamped his attention on Roderic. To all who watched, it seemed the Black Wolf was only vaguely concerned with her well-being. But Ariella had glimpsed a terrible rage smoldering deep within his eyes.

In that moment she almost believed Malcolm's fury alone would enable him to kill Roderic.

"What an unexpected surprise this is!" quipped Roderic, clearly enjoying himself. "Here I was thinking I was going to have to face Harold and his army, which would have probably meant sacrificing poor little Catherine. But you have come instead, and my men assure me you were actually foolish enough to journey alone." He paused and stroked his scar, considering. "You're not drunk, Malcolm, are you?"

"No," replied Malcolm, his voice deceptively soft. "I'm not."

"Excellent! And I see that you have brought the sword."

Ariella glanced at the weapon Malcolm carried at his side, her confusion growing. It was a magnificent piece, with a heavily jeweled hilt and a deadly sharp blade that flashed silver in the soft morning light. Although she had never seen the MacKendrick sword, this weapon was a splendid rendition of what her father had once described to her. Could her people have consulted Alpin and created this copy for Malcolm to bring to Roderic? His own sword was nowhere to be seen. Her heart sank as she realized what Malcolm's purpose must be. He had been naïve enough to come in good faith, thinking simply to exchange the sword for Ariella and Catherine's release.

He did not realize Roderic would never let him leave alive.

"Bring Agnes and Catherine out here," Roderic ordered, glancing at Gregor. "I would hate for them to miss this."

Malcolm calmly watched as Agnes and Catherine emerged from their tent. He was careful to keep his expression bland, even when he saw the ugly bruise staining Agnes's mouth.

"MacFane!" burst out Catherine happily. "You came back!"

"Aye, Catherine," he said. "I came back. Now, return with Agnes to the tent. Ariella will fetch you shortly."

Gregor looked questioningly at Roderic.

"Take them back inside," he ordered, shrugging. "It seems he does not want them to witness his death."

Malcolm waited until the two girls disappeared. "Actually, Roderic, it is the sight of your death I wish to spare them," he informed him dryly. "Although," he reflected, "I think perhaps Agnes will not find your pending demise overly distressing."

Roderic threw back his head and laughed. "By God, Malcolm, you do have the most incredible ability to delude yourself. You have done so ever since that day Gavin dragged you home like a squashed insect, and you allowed yourself to believe you were actually fit to be laird."

Malcolm shook his head. "I knew I wasn't fit to be laird. I accepted the responsibility because it was my duty to do so. And because I believed one day I might be worthy of the honor again."

"Well, you never were," Roderic snapped. "You were pathetically weak and lame, and you couldn't get through more than an hour without drowning yourself in alcohol. You scarcely knew what was going on in your own clan. When I offered to become laird, you should have accepted your condition and stepped aside. Even Ariella could see you're unfit to lead her people," he sneered. "She may have used you for your military knowledge, but she would never give you the sword."

He was right, Ariella realized miserably. She had used Malcolm. Used him, then discarded him when she no longer needed him.

And, impossibly, he had come back for her.

She gazed at him despondently, wanting to plead for forgiveness, but Malcolm kept his gaze firmly locked on Roderic. His carriage was relaxed, and his expression bore an enormity of calm she found disconcerting. How could he not be enraged by Roderic's cutting remarks?

"Once again, Roderic, you seek to take that which you have no right to," Malcolm observed quietly. "It would appear you have learned nothing from your banishment."

"I learned that I deserve more," Roderic corrected him. "And finally I shall have it. I will be laird of the MacKendricks, a clan that, though of no military consequence, has immense potential for making highly profitable goods. With the money, I can create an army greater even than yours was, Malcolm. And with that sword," he continued, his eyes raking hungrily over it, "I will conquer other clans, until I am the most powerful laird in the Highlands."

"So you intend to enslave the MacKendricks and pour the profits from their labor into an army, which you will use to tyrannize others. How noble."

"I'm not interested in being noble."

"And you actually believe a mere sword can bring you all of this?"

Roderic smiled. "Give it to me, and let us find out."

Malcolm moved as if to hand him the weapon, then hesitated. "I will have your word first that once you have the sword, you will not harm Ariella, Catherine, or Agnes."

"You're not in a position to make demands."

"Perhaps not," he acknowledged. "But I have brought you the sword, as you requested. You must honor your end of the bargain."

"Give it to me, or I will bring Catherine back out here and cut her throat," threatened Roderic, smiling. "You know I will, don't you?"

"Yes," Malcolm admitted quietly. "I know you will." He began to raise the sword.

"Not like that," Roderic snarled, quickly pointing his own sword at him. "You will fall before me on your knees and offer it to me, as I was forced to kneel before you the day you banished me from my clan."

Ariella watched as pride battled Malcolm's desire to see her safe. Finally, realizing he had little choice, he relented. Clutching the sword in his left hand, he awkwardly dismounted and began to limp slowly toward Roderic.

His carriage was dignified, but now that he was off his horse, he could no longer conceal his pain and stiffness. His gait was heavy and uneven, and it was obvious he was struggling to move without wincing. Despair welled inside her. Perhaps, with a few days of rest and gentle care, he might have been strong enough to face

Roderic, at least for a brief fight. But Malcolm had been journeying to other clans for nearly two weeks, and had just ridden many grueling hours to return to her lands. The long days in the saddle and nights sleeping on the hard ground had demanded too much of his severely damaged body.

Roderic would slay him with the ease he would a helpless child.

Tears veiled her eyes as Malcolm stopped before Roderic. His expression resigned, he clumsily sank to one knee and held the sword before him. She had brought him to this, she reflected, her heart wrenching. If not for her, he would still be living in his hut with Gavin. He would be bitter, drunk, and lonely, but he would be safe. Instead he was here, about to be slain, because he erroneously believed that by sacrificing his own life, he might save her. What he must not know, she vowed, biting hard upon her trembling lip, was that once she refused Roderic the powers of the sword, she and Catherine would be killed anyway. In this final, unbearable moment, Malcolm deserved to believe, however mistakenly, that he had succeeded in saving them.

"What sweet retribution this is," observed Roderic, his tone thick with contempt. "To think that just over two years ago, it was I who knelt before you. I swore then not to rest until you were destroyed. Your subsequent shame and banishment appeased my desire for vengeance somewhat. But nothing," he continued, raising the point of his sword to the base of Malcolm's throat, "compares to the utter perfection of this moment."

Malcolm regarded him impassively, still offering his magnificent sword.

His face lit with triumph, Roderic reached for it as he drew his own weapon back.

Terror flooded Ariella. Without thinking, she grabbed her dirk and hurled it through the air.

In that same instant Malcolm swept up his sword and slashed a deep groove in Roderic's arm.

A bellow of pain shattered the stillness of the woods. Roderic clamped his hand on the dagger protruding from his left shoulder and jerked it out. Then he stared in bewildered fury at the blood streaming from the gash Malcolm had sliced in his forearm.

"You destroyed me once," said Malcolm, on his feet now with the sword flashing before him. "Did you honestly believe I would permit you to do so again?"

Stunned by this unexpected turn of events, several of Roderic's men moved forward to help their leader.

"Stay back!" Roderic snarled. He grunted as he struggled to raise his sword. Pain shot through his bleeding arm, forcing him to lower it again. He cast Malcolm a look of unmitigated loathing. "Injured or not, I will slay you on my own, Malcolm." Grimacing, he used both arms to raise his weapon.

The two blades met in a silvery crash, sending a puff of sparks into the filmy morning light. Malcolm instantly withdrew and thrust again, and again, but Roderic was a formidable opponent despite his injuries, and he expertly parried his attack. The two warriors began to circle as they fought, filling the air with the scraping and ringing of steel. Malcolm fought with deadly determination, fiercely rejecting his own weariness and pain. In this moment, he would not submit to the pathetic frailty of his body. He would fight Roderic with every shred of his strength and heart and soul, until the bastard lay bathed in his own blood.

Even if Malcolm had to die with him.

He moved clumsily, hindered by his leg, and unable to duck because of the rigidity of his back. He compensated for this by making his blows hard and rapid and sure, hoping to catch Roderic in an instant of weakness. Roderic was younger and far more fit, but the blood pouring from his right arm and the tight grip of his face told Malcolm his suffering was considerable. Like him, Roderic needed both arms to wield his weapon, making them more equally matched. Malcolm met him blow for blow, slicing up and thrusting down, his jaw clenched and his chest heaving as he struggled to open flesh. His right arm began to tire, slowing his movements. Roderic instantly sensed his advantage and made two swift jabs with his sword. Malcolm leaped back, but not quickly enough.

Pain blazed through his left arm where the muscle had been split.

"Give up, Malcolm," taunted Roderic, his sword held before him. "You now have two useless arms instead of one. Surely you must realize this is a battle you cannot win."

Malcolm inhaled, fighting to keep his concentration on the battle instead of on the warm stream leaking down his arm. *It is a minor wound,* he assured himself harshly, refusing to look at it. *It is nothing.*

"There is something you are forgetting, Roderic," he observed, his voice low and cold.

Roderic raised his brow with skeptical amusement. "And what is that?"

"I have the sword." Malcolm's mouth curved into a smile.

A flash of uncertainty shadowed Roderic's features, which he quickly suppressed. "You may have the weapon," he allowed dismissively, "but not its powers. The weapon alone will not help you."

But you don't know that for certain, reflected Malcolm, watching a glimmer of anxiety twist the smugness of Roderic's features. Seeking to take advantage of it, he summoned the dregs of his waning strength and raised the sword menacingly before him.

Suddenly a brilliant shaft of sunlight hit the jewel-encrusted hilt. An inexplicable heat began to radiate into Malcolm's palms, as if the sword were somehow absorbing the light and energy of the sun. The heat penetrated his flesh and surged up his arms, soothing the weary, severed muscles and banishing the pain. And then it was flooding his entire body, like liquid fire racing through skin and muscle and bone, eradicating all sensation of weakness and suffering. In one glorious moment he felt powerful and whole, like the great warrior he had once been. The sensation could not be real, he realized blankly. It was some trick of his mind that caused him to feel so impossibly fit and well. Illusion or not, he straightened his back with fluid ease, then dared to adjust his weight until his injured leg supported him more fully. Roderic stared at him in confusion, as if he too could see that a change had overtaken him. Seizing the moment, Malcolm drew back his sword and raced forward, somehow trusting he would neither stumble nor fall.

Roderic crashed his blade defensively against Malcolm's, then groaned with effort as he fought to throw him off. But a terrible, deadly determination burned in Malcolm. Summoning an awesome strength he had lost years ago, and not giving a damn whether it was real or imagined, he swiftly drew his sword back, then drove it with every fragment of his being into Roderic.

Roderic's green eyes widened with surprise. He glanced down in horror at the jeweled hilt protruding from his gut, each magnificent stone still glimmering in the sun. Blood began to pour from him in a scarlet stream, soaking his shirt and his finely woven plaid.

"Christ, Malcolm," he managed, his voice a rasp of sound against the stunned silence. "How the hell did you do that?"

Malcolm tightened his grip on the sword and pulled it out. A gush of crimson spurted after it.

"You had to die, Roderic. There could be no other way."

Roderic stared at him blankly, clutching his belly. Blood pulsed over his hands and dripped down his front, then spattered onto the earth by his feet. Rapidly weakening, he sank to his knees. He gazed longingly at the sword in Malcolm's hand. Then his eyes fell hard upon Ariella.

"It should have been me," he said, his voice caught somewhere between an accusation and a whimper. He opened his mouth to say something more, but all that came out was a helpless, gurgling sigh. He cast her a final look of fury.

And then fell forward in a lifeless heap.

Ariella stared at his body in disbelief, as if she thought he might suddenly rise and threaten her again. Blood began to seep into the ground, forming an ugly, dark stain around him. She hesitantly raised her eyes to Malcolm.

His attention was fixed on something behind her. Ariella turned to see Gregor advancing toward them, his deadly ax raised.

"So, MacFane," he growled as Roderic's other warriors formed a wall around them. "Now it is your turn to die."

"Perhaps," allowed Malcolm, not appearing overly concerned. "As splendid a weapon as this is," he reflected, indicating his sword, "I doubt I could kill all of you by myself."

"You can't," agreed Tavis, smirking. "But don't worry. After you're dead, I'll take good care of your pretty sword."

Gregor scowled. "Why should the sword go to you? You're not our leader."

"And neither are you," interjected Murdoch. "Now that Roderic is gone, I am in command. And I hereby lay claim to both the sword *and* the lass." He cast a yellow, leering smile at Ariella.

"I don't see why Murdoch gets to be the bloody leader," grumbled a warrior from behind Malcolm.

"Neither do I," added another disgruntled voice.

"We should choose a new leader."

"And whoever we choose gets to kill MacFane."

Murmurs of agreement rippled through their ranks.

"I hate to interrupt such an important discussion," sighed Malcolm apologetically, "but I feel compelled to point something out to you."

"What?" snapped Gregor, clearly irritated that he might not have the pleasure of killing him.

"If any of you move so much as one step, not one of you will leave these woods alive."

Gregor regarded him blankly. Then he threw back his head and roared with laughter. "That's a bold threat for just one warrior," he remarked appreciatively.

"It would be," agreed a pleasant voice, "were he just one warrior."

Her heart pounding, Ariella pulled her gaze from Malcolm to search the surrounding woods.

Gavin emerged from the thick curtain of trees beyond the clearing of the camp, mounted on his horse.

Gregor snorted. "So it's both of you we have to disembowel, is it? Well, I think we can manage that without too much trouble—"

His bravado faded as Duncan, Andrew, Niall, Ramsay, and Graham appeared. They were followed by others, until finally some thirty mounted and armed men of the MacKendrick clan had formed an impregnable ring around Roderic's warriors.

"By God, if it's a battle you want, MacFane, it's a battle you'll get," roared Tavis, raising his sword.

"A somewhat rash decision, I think, given the impossibility of your situation," remarked Malcolm. "Rashness is not the mark of a good leader," he pointed out, addressing the rest of Roderic's men.

"These MacKendricks barely outnumber us," scoffed Gregor. "And though they fought us off at their castle, they know nothing of the savagery of open battle." He raised his ax. "We will slaughter them like trapped deer."

Malcolm swept his gaze over the MacKendricks and frowned. "Are you certain you have counted accurately?"

Gregor, Tavis, and Murdoch regarded the ring of men around them with smug satisfaction.

Malcolm tilted his head slightly, indicating that they should look behind them.

Bewildered, Ariella followed his gaze.

Scores of warriors had silently moved into an endless line that threaded between the trees. Many were mounted, others were on foot, but all wielded a shimmering array of swords, axes, spears, bows, and shields. The plaids arranged around their waists were of different colors, indicating they came from not one, but several different clans. These were the clans with whom Malcolm had forged alliances, Ariella realized. He must have sent riders out before coming here, bearing the urgent message that the MacKendricks were in danger.

And, incredibly, these warriors had come.

"Throw down your weapons and raise your hands to your heads," commanded Malcolm. "Or I will order these men to attack and not stop until every last one of you lies scattered in pieces upon the ground."

Gregor, Tavis, and Murdoch regarded each other uncertainly.

And then they reluctantly tossed their weapons onto the ground. The rest of their men instantly followed, many of them bumping elbows in their haste to raise their hands.

"Excellent," praised Malcolm. "Move forward and take them prisoner," he ordered, gesturing for the neighboring clans to come forth. "They will be tried as a group for their crimes, and then divided amongst you to serve their sentences. I don't want any of them lingering here."

The circle of warriors closed around them and began to herd them away.

"Where are Catherine and Agnes?" demanded Niall, riding forward.

"Here!" cried Catherine, scrambling out from the tent, with Agnes hesitantly following. Catherine grabbed her skirts in her fists and raced toward Malcolm. On seeing Roderic's body, she froze.

"Come here, Catherine," ordered Malcolm, wishing she had not witnessed the ghastly sight.

"Is he dead?" she demanded.

"Yes."

She studied Roderic a moment longer, then raised her eyes to Malcolm. "Did you kill him?"

He nodded.

"I knew you would," she said, her tone approving. "He was a very bad man." Her eyes widened. "You're hurt!"

Malcolm barely glanced at his wounded left arm. Blood was streaming down his hand and dripping off his fingers. "It looks far worse than it is," he assured her. He was not entirely sure that was true, but he was encouraged by the fact that he felt little pain. "Once we are home, I will clean it and you will see it is nothing."

"You must have a bandage for it now," argued Catherine, stooping to tear a piece off the hem of her gown. She awkwardly wrapped the grimy length of fabric around him. "There," she said with satisfaction. "Much better."

"Thank you." He brushed a lock of hair off her face. "Now, go back to the castle with Agnes and the men. Ariella and I will be along shortly."

"I—I don't think Ariella wants me to escort Catherine back, my lord," stammered Agnes. She glanced nervously at Ariella.

Malcolm frowned. "Why not?"

"Agnes is thinking I would like to take Catherine back myself," interjected Ariella quickly. "But Catherine is tired, and I cannot leave right away. Therefore I am entrusting you to see that she is safely escorted home, Agnes." She gave her a meaningful look.

Agnes stared at her in surprise. And then a solemn dignity seemed to restore her spirit, visibly lifting her from her shame. "As you wish, milady," she said quietly. "She will be safe with me."

Catherine cast a pleading look at Malcolm. "Can't I stay here with you?"

Leaning on his sword, he bent down until he was almost her height. "I am embarrassed to confess I have misplaced the drawing you gave me the other day," he admitted softly. "If you go home now, you may have time to make another one before I return. Would you do that for me?"

Catherine smiled. "Of course." She gave him a quick, hard hug, then picked up her ragged skirts and ran toward Agnes.

Roderic's band and the warriors from the neighboring clans were gone, but the ground shuddered as an army of some fifty mounted warriors began to appear through the trees. Their horses were splendidly draped in cloth of scarlet and gold, and the MacFane crest was emblazoned on the heavy shields the men carried. A tall red-haired man was leading the impressive force. Harold raised his hand, signaling for his men to halt, then regarded Malcolm.

"The storm of which you spoke never happened."

Malcolm shrugged his shoulders. "You know I have never put any faith in the visions of seers, Harold. If I did, I would have expected ours to have forewarned me about Roderic's attack."

Harold frowned at the blood-soaked body on the ground. "Is that Roderic?"

"Yes," said Malcolm, gesturing for Bryce and Ramsay to take the body away.

Harold looked at Malcolm in surprise. "Did you kill him?"

"Yes."

A flash of respect, and perhaps even relief, crossed his handsome, weary features. For the first time Malcolm caught a glimpse of the heavy burden Harold had been forced to carry since he'd assumed lairdship of his clan. It had not been a position he had sought, or even wanted. He had accepted it out of duty, after the blackest chapter of the clan's history, in which his own adored sister had been slaughtered and he had been forced to banish his dear cousin and friend.

Malcolm had never acknowledged just how arduous that responsibility had been.

Harold's gaze fell upon Ariella. "Is this Ariella MacKendrick?" He directed the question to Malcolm, as if he believed Ariella incapable of speaking for herself.

Malcolm nodded.

Harold studied her a long moment before quietly asking, "Will she be my wife, Malcolm?"

"No," he replied, his voice hard. He did not bother even to glance at her as he finished. "She is already wed."

Ariella knew she must object to his lie. She had formally offered herself to Harold. It was her duty to honor that contract. And yet she said nothing. She stood there and numbly stared at Malcolm, transfixed by the incredible power and authority emanating from him.

Harold regarded Ariella intently, perhaps giving her the opportunity to dispute Malcolm's claim. "My congratulations, milady," he offered finally, his tone void of either bitterness or rancor. "I wish you many years of happiness."

"You have traveled a long way, Laird MacFane," observed Duncan, addressing Harold. "We invite you to stay with us a few days, to eat and rest. A feast is being prepared for tonight, which I'm sure your men will enjoy."

"You will find the MacKendricks are not lacking in

unmarried, feminine company," added Gavin, sympathizing with Harold's disappointment in not obtaining a bride. "And many of them have a taste for adventure. Your men may find a wife or two among them. Just stay away from the fair-haired one called Elizabeth," he warned, shifting his gaze to Gordon. "She is already spoken for." His intentions made clear, he turned his horse and galloped toward the castle, leaving Harold and his warriors to follow.

"The rest of you return to the castle," commanded Malcolm. "Roderic's men must be guarded, and preparations should be made to feed and entertain all those who came to our aid today."

"Aye, MacKendrick," said Gordon, dismounting from his horse. His sword positioned before him, he lowered himself onto one knee and bowed his head in a gesture of loyalty. "It shall be as you wish."

Malcolm looked at him in surprise. "Rise, Gordon," he protested. "You know I am not MacKendrick—"

He stopped, overwhelmed by the sight before him. All the MacKendrick warriors were dismounting and falling to their knees, their heads respectfully lowered.

"*Hail MacKendrick,*" they said, their voices a solemn pledge in the stillness of the cool morning air. "*Hail our brave laird, wielder of the sword.*"

He stared at them in silence, too moved to speak. And then he looked away, fighting to affect the hard, emotionless mien he had once known so well, yet in this moment was unable to summon.

By the time he turned back, the MacKendricks had mounted their horses and were disappearing through the thick tapestry of trees.

Ariella stared at Malcolm in shock. Her perception of him was suddenly so clear, she could barely look upon him without fear of being blinded by the brilliant aura that seemed to radiate from both him and the magnificent sword flashing at his side. He stood tall and powerful before her, one arm roughly bandaged and dripping blood, his weight shifting slightly to favor his injured leg. His physical weaknesses remained, she realized, for it was not within the sword's powers to cure the frailties of the body. And yet, even with these limitations he was without exception the strongest, bravest, most honorable man she had ever known.

He was the next MacKendrick.

"I was wrong," she whispered, the words small and ragged. She swallowed, struggling to maintain her composure as she tried to make him understand. "I thought the warrior who would bear the sword must be perfect in body and spirit. Alpin spoke of indomitable strength, and I could see only your weaknesses. But he meant a strength of integrity and soul, not of body. He also spoke of honor and courage. I could not forget how you refused to come when my father wrote you. But he was referring to the courage needed to overcome one's fears and failures, and to stand and fight again. I didn't understand," she admitted, appalled by the narrow, childish simplicity of her vision. "I thought the next laird of my clan must be flawless, as I believed my own father to be. Of course he wasn't." Her voice began to break as she conceded, "He was just a man, and men make mistakes. You once told me that, but I couldn't accept it."

She brushed helplessly at the tears leaking from her eyes, wanting to be dignified in her apology, and failing miserably. "To accept it meant I would have to blame my father for the horror Roderic inflicted on my people. My father allowed us to be weak, and did not have the wisdom to keep the sword at his side, because he did not believe in war. And so he and others of my clan were killed. But I couldn't bear to blame him for that," she choked, losing her battle against the hot streams running down her cheeks. Unable to face him, she bowed her head and finished in a tiny, rough whisper, "And so I blamed you."

She sank to her knees, drowning in shame as she steeled herself for the lash of his rage.

Malcolm moved toward her and, using the sword for support, stiffly eased himself onto his knee. Then he grasped her chin and raised her head, forcing her to look at him.

"Can you not feel it, Ariella?" he murmured, his tone achingly gentle.

She inhaled a shuddering breath and regarded him uncertainly.

He released her chin to graze his knuckles across the silvery trail of tears wetting her cheek. "I was dying," he stated gruffly. "And I didn't give a damn, because I knew I would rather be dead than endure one more hour of pain, and guilt, and failure. It was so much easier not to feel," he confessed, "and not to be responsible for anyone. But then you came along." He traced his fingers reverently along the contour of her jaw. "So filled with life and burning with hatred. And suddenly I couldn't escape who I was. With all your anger and contempt, you roused a fragment of the warrior buried deep within this battered body. And once you had roused him, you refused to let him succumb to his weaknesses again. You wrenched me from a hopeless existence and brought me to a place where I could be of use. By doing so, you helped me to heal. Not my body," he qualified, "which is damaged beyond repair, but my soul—until I could conquer my fears and was ready to accept the enormous responsibility of leading a people once again."

"But then I sent you away," she protested miserably. "You had changed, yet I still could not see beyond your weaknesses."

"You would not permit yourself to believe I was fit to be laird of your clan. At least not openly. But sometimes," he reflected quietly, "one's deepest feelings are revealed only through the purest actions of the heart."

Ariella followed his gaze to the sword lying on the ground beside them. And suddenly she understood. Anger and the tight fetters of duty had kept her from admitting that Malcolm was the rightful bearer of the sword.

Except in her heart.

"I love you more than life, Ariella," he murmured, his voice rough with emotion. "And if you will permit me, I will lead your clan to the best of my abilities, and proudly bear the name MacKendrick as my own. I will wield this sword with honor, justice, and compassion, and I will gladly lay down my life for any member of the MacKendrick clan. All this I will do, and more, despite my many weaknesses and failings." He gently kissed the palm of her hand, then pressed it hard to his chest. "For you."

His heart beat strong and sure against the coolness of her palm. Joy flooded through her, eradicating her anguish and guilt. She threw her arms around him and crushed her lips to his, tasting him deeply, desperately, wanting to drink in his power and his tenderness, and in turn, to share with him the love she could no longer deny. She began to hungrily touch his back, his shoulders, his chest, needing the steely warmth of his flesh against hers. Her fingers inadvertently caressed his wounded arm, and he inhaled sharply.

"Does it hurt badly?" she asked, concerned.

"It is a scratch," Malcolm told her dismissively. "I had forgotten about it." He drew her close and began to nuzzle the silky skin of her neck.

"We should go back to the castle so I can tend to it," Ariella whispered, threading her fingers into the dark fall of his hair.

"We should," he agreed, unfastening the clasp of her

cloak. "But it is very crowded there." The garment slid to the ground, unveiling the soft contours of her gown.

"No doubt the clan is arranging a grand welcome for you," she predicted. She sighed with pleasure as his hand closed over her breast. "Graham and Ramsay are probably practicing their bagpipes as we speak. And Angus and Dugald are sure to want to recite their poetry."

Malcolm buried his face against her throat and groaned.

"I think we should rest first, don't you?" she suggested, her voice taut and breathless. She rose and began to lead him out of the clearing, threading her way deeper into the green-and-gold light of the forest.

They came upon a bed of ferns growing lush beneath a quivering canopy of trees. Sunlight played in lemony ripples upon this sweet-scented mattress, over which Ariella carelessly tossed her cloak. Then she turned, pressed her body to his, and kissed him. She did not tremble as he removed her gown, for the sun was warm upon her skin, and the muscled heat of his naked flesh soon burned against her. She clung to Malcolm as he lowered her onto the cloak and stretched over her, sharing his strength, his desire, his joy, kissing her and stroking her and tasting her until she was filled with liquid heat and aware of nothing but her need to be with him, always.

"Ariella," he whispered hoarsely.

She opened her eyes to find him studying her, his blue eyes burning with such intensity, she felt exposed to the depths of her soul. She raised her fingers to trace the grim line of his lips, then laid her hand against the roughness of his shadowed cheek.

"I love you, MacFane." She drew her brows together, considering. "Or shall I call you MacKendrick now?"

"There is no need for such formality between us," he assured her, lowering his mouth to kiss her eyes and nose. A trace of a smile curved his mouth as he finished, " 'My lord' will do." He buried himself deep inside her, making them one.

She gasped, whether with outrage or pleasure he could not be certain. He laughed and kissed her tenderly, feeling gloriously strong and whole as they pulsed together beneath the flickering ribbons of light.

ABOUT THE AUTHOR

KARYN MONK has been writing since she was a girl. In university she discovered a love for history. After several years working in the highly charged world of advertising, she turned to writing historical romance. She is married to a wonderfully romantic husband, Philip, whom she allows to believe is the model for her heroes.

Bestselling Historical Women's Fiction

✴ AMANDA QUICK ✴

____28354-5 SEDUCTION . . . $6.50/$8.99 Canada

____28932-2 SCANDAL . . . . $6.50/$8.99

____28594-7 SURRENDER . . . . $6.50/$8.99

____29325-7 RENDEZVOUS . . . . $6.50/$8.99

____29315-X RECKLESS . . . . $6.50/$8.99

____29316-8 RAVISHED . . . . $6.50/$8.99

____29317-6 DANGEROUS . . . . $6.50/$8.99

____56506-0 DECEPTION . . . . $6.50/$8.99

____56153-7 DESIRE . . . . $6.50/$8.99

____56940-6 MISTRESS . . . . $6.50/$8.99

____57159-1 MYSTIQUE . . . . $6.50/$7.99

____57190-7 MISCHIEF . . . . $6.50/$8.99

____10076-9 AFFAIR . . . . $23.95/$29.95

✴ IRIS JOHANSEN ✴

____29871-2 LAST BRIDGE HOME . . $5.50/$7.50

____29604-3 THE GOLDEN

BARBARIAN . . . . $5.99/$7.99

____29244-7 REAP THE WIND . . . . . $5.99/$7.50

____29032-0 STORM WINDS . . . . $5.99/$7.99

Ask for these books at your local bookstore or use this page to order.

Please send me the books I have checked above. I am enclosing $____ (add $2.50 to cover postage and handling). Send check or money order, no cash or C.O.D.'s, please.

Name _____

Address _____

City/State/Zip _____

Send order to: Bantam Books, Dept. FN 16, 2451 S. Wolf Rd., Des Plaines, IL 60018
Allow four to six weeks for delivery.
Prices and availability subject to change without notice.   FN 16 5/97

Bestselling Historical Women's Fiction

❧ IRIS JOHANSEN ❧

____28855-5 THE WIND DANCER ...$5.99/$6.99

____29968-9 THE TIGER PRINCE ...$5.99/$6.99

____29944-1 THE MAGNIFICENT
ROGUE ....$5.99/$6.99

____29945-X BELOVED SCOUNDREL .$5.99/$6.99

____29946-8 MIDNIGHT WARRIOR ..$5.99/$6.99

____29947-6 DARK RIDER ....$5.99/$7.99

____56990-2 LION'S BRIDE ....$5.99/$7.99

____56991-0 THE UGLY DUCKLING...$5.99/$7.99

____09715-6 LONG AFTER
MIDNIGHT........$22.95/$29.95

❧ TERESA MEDEIROS ❧

____29407-5 HEATHER AND VELVET .$5.99/$7.50

____29409-1 ONCE AN ANGEL .....$5.99/$7.99

____29408-3 A WHISPER OF ROSES .$5.99/$7.99

____56332-7 THIEF OF HEARTS .....$5.50/$6.99

____56333-5 FAIREST OF THEM ALL .$5.99/$7.50

____56334-3 BREATH OF MAGIC ....$5.99/$7.99

____57623-2 SHADOWS AND LACE ...$5.99/$7.99

- -

Ask for these books at your local bookstore or use this page to order.

Please send me the books I have checked above. I am enclosing $____ (add $2.50 to cover postage and handling). Send check or money order, no cash or C.O.D.'s, please.

Name _____

Address _____

City/State/Zip _____

Send order to: Bantam Books, Dept. FN 16, 2451 S. Wolf Rd., Des Plaines, IL 60018
Allow four to six weeks for delivery.
Prices and availability subject to change without notice.   FN 16 5/97

Don't miss any of these breathtaking
historical romances by

Elizabeth Elliott

Betrothed ___57566-X $5.50/$7.50 Can.

"An exciting find for romance readers everywhere!"
—Amanda Quick, *New York Times* bestselling author

Scoundrel ___56911-2 $5.50/$7.50 Can.

"Sparkling, fast-paced...Elliott has crafted an exciting
story filled with dramatic tension and sexual fireworks."
—*Publishers Weekly*

The Warlord ___56910-4 $5.50/$6.99 Can.

"Elizabeth Elliott...weaves a wondrous
love story guaranteed to please."
—*Romantic Times*